"You're still as beautiful as ever."

"Flatterer," she said.

"No. I have no need to flatter you."

She laughed and pulled him down on top of her as she lay back on the bed. They kissed and clung to one another, and it was as though she had been lost in a maze for years but had finally stumbled out of it. His lips felt *right*; his arms felt *right*; he felt *right*. So long, so long had she missed him. She wanted to cry aloud how she had wanted him for so many years, and that she had missed him, but she did not. Instead, she returned his kisses with all the ardor of her heart . . .

KATHRYN ATWOOD

MY LADY ROGUE

A JOVE BOOK

MY LADY ROGUE

A Jove Book / published by arrangement with
the author

PRINTING HISTORY
Jove edition/September 1986

ISBN: 0-515-08670-3

Jove Books are published by The Berkley Publishing Group,
200 Madison Avenue, New York, N.Y. 10016. The words
"A JOVE BOOK" and the "J" with sunburst are trademarks
belonging to Jove Publications, Inc.

PRINTED IN THE UNITED STATES OF AMERICA

For
Fred and Lucy,
without whom this book
would have been finished much faster,
but who can always make me smile, no matter what

ACT ONE

February 1804

One

"Hand me my hairbrush, won't you, darling?" Ariel de Juliers Greystone asked languorously as she shifted on the vanity bench. With that slight movement, her loosely belted dressing robe opened, then slipped downward, revealing her smooth and exceedingly bare shoulders and back. The robe whispered softly to the carpeted floor, where it lay, a pool of peach silk.

John Haversham stared at the fallen garment, then at the length of her white back. Flushing to the roots of his hair, he sprang up from the daybed on which he'd been lounging, to comply with her request.

She watched in the large mirror as her flustered fiancé sought to obey her wish. "No, no, not the tortoiseshell one, dear. The silver one next to the bed." She pointed with long fingers toward a table. Her hands were graceful, and the delicate nails well tended. They were the hands of a noblewoman, and if there were some in society who thought Ariel Greystone could not be considered a member of the nobility, it could not be denied she was of gentle birth.

"Yes, that's it." She lifted the corners of her small mouth as she accepted the brush from him. His fingers jerked as she swept her hand against his. "Thank you, John," she murmured huskily.

She lowered her thick black lashes over her green eyes,

knowing fully the effect this would have upon him. Her large eyes tilted in an almost oriental way, and certainly they were one of the most startling features in her very remarkable face. At times she possessed a most guileless expression in those wide verdant depths, while at other times her gaze was far less than innocent. They were proud, bold eyes that never hesitated to meet any man's or woman's directly. Her face was oval, blessed with high cheekbones that enhanced the foreignness of her appearance, and her skin, soft and supple, was tinted a delicate ivory. Her chin was slightly pointed and on anyone else might have indicated a somewhat obstinate nature. Her full lips were naturally red. It was said by men who knew her that she possessed a mouth made to be kissed, something she used to her advantage when kisses were called for. Her frame was slender, too, as her hands indicated; her small bosom was high and firm, her waist narrow, her hips slim. It was almost a child's body—but with a woman's face and a woman's desires.

"Oh, Ariel, I, that is—" Haversham began, his words rushing together. He flushed even more and stopped in confusion.

He was forever blushing, for he had a fair complexion, almost girlish in its delicacy. Most certainly it was a barometer of his feelings, coloring from the lightest pink when he was simply pleased about something to a dark crimson when he was exceedingly embarrassed—or wanted something. As he did now.

She turned her full attention to him.

"Could I—I mean—would you mind . . . if I brushed your hair?" His blue eyes showing his longing, he gazed at her.

Such a simple request. And here she'd thought it would be something much more wicked! Her voice was a sensuous whisper as she answered. "Certainly, John, although first you must take the pins out."

His fingers trembled as he plucked at the jeweled pins. One by one they slid out, but not without some pulling of her hair, which caused her to press her lips together lest she snap at his clumsiness. She shook her head, and her hair cascaded loose, falling in an ebony waterfall to her waist. She could not abide the current fashion of short hair for the names of some of the

styles, *à la victime* and *à la guillotine*, were unhappy reminders
of a fate that had almost been hers.

Haversham ran his unsteady hands down her smooth hair.
He was very close now, and she could feel the warmth of his
body radiating against her shoulders as he pressed himself
against her.

She closed her eyes as he picked up the silver brush and
carefully ran it through the long tresses. He was more gentle
than many lady's maids she'd employed in the past. He's a
good boy, she told herself not for the first time, and realized
she was smiling faintly. A good boy, for although he was the
same age as she, she could not bring herself to think of him as
a man; he seemed so young. To be altogether generous about
the matter, he was not overly bright nor terribly interesting.
Too, his conversation certainly lacked in spirit. Despite all of
this, Haversham had one asset that at present she highly
desired, an asset that had attracted her to him from the first.

He possessed a sizable fortune.

A fortune that she, alas, did not have.

Restraining a slight sigh, she opened her eyes and stared
meditatively in the mirror at her boudoir, one of the larger
rooms in her house.

The unmade bed was an oversized antique dating from
Tudor times, with gauzy curtains hung around it to keep out
errant night drafts—or prying eyes. The carpet was an
heirloom, as well, of Turkish design in blues and greens and
golds. The other furniture—the vanity, the immense wardrobe, the two side tables, the washstand and settee, lounge
and chairs—all had been made many decades before, and if
one cared to examine them closely, as well as the furniture in
the other rooms, one would detect faint signs of a genteel
shabbiness.

A genteel shabbiness that dated from her childhood, and
that was growing tiresome.

She was just six and twenty, already a widow these past few
years, and now employed as an actress. Like her mother, she
had been one since she was twelve. Almost a lifetime ago, she
reflected somewhat ironically.

At present she was in *The Soldier's Daughter*, the Andrew

Cherry play currently running at London's Theatre Royal. There she was well known, though certainly not in the class of someone like Mrs. Siddons—not yet, she told herself firmly —and while her earnings were not paltry, her expenses were even greater, for her mother was ill. She had been so for quite some time, and the doctors' bills were extremely high. There were so many of them, and day after day they piled up until she feared she would drown amidst a sea of duns. Unfortunately, her list of creditors grew with each passing week, and she was tired of their waiting at the theatre for her, tired of their plaguing her for payments.

Tired . . . so very tired. A wave of intense weariness swept across her, momentarily making her dizzy, and she breathed in deeply, forcing herself not to give in to the weakness, to be collected once more. She hoped Haversham hadn't noticed her mood, but the love-struck man was still very much engaged in brushing her hair. The past few years had been a terrible struggle as she sought to achieve some success in the London theatre world—a success that would mean relief from the crushing weight of bills.

But she was fast becoming exhausted with this never-ending struggle, and panicked, for she didn't know what to do. Thus a few months earlier, as she morosely reviewed the stack of bills, she had conceived of a plan that might provide a solution. As distasteful as it was to her, she had decided she must marry for money.

Other women made such alliances, certainly for less cause than she. Was not the continuing health of her mother important? Could she allow her mother to waste away, perhaps die, for lack of care?

No.

After much deliberation, and review of the unattached men of her acquaintance, she had selected a candidate: John Haversham.

He had fit the bill for several reasons. He was young, and handsome in face and figure, with his slightly curling blond locks and disarming blue eyes and slender body. Too, he was always a gentleman. While he might not be the most ideal husband, for he was somewhat dull, he did possess a quality that appealed greatly to her. He was exceedingly easygoing, and so enamored of her profession that she knew he would not interfere with her way of life; nor would he seek to control her in her any manner.

How very unlike certain other men, she thought suddenly, drawing her brows together in a frown at the resurgence of an unpleasant memory of some five years ago.

At that moment Hally, her personal maid, burst into the room. The girl obviously was upset, for she kept wringing her hands and in her haste had forgotten to knock first, or even to bob a curtsy.

"There's a gentleman in the next room come to see you, madame," the girl said hurriedly. "He's very anxious"—here she glanced back over her shoulder at the door—"I really tried to keep him out, Mrs. Greystone!" She stepped fully into the room and slammed the squeaking door.

Too surprised to chastise her maid or even to remember to slip the robe around her shoulders, Ariel started to speak, but before she could do so, the door flung open with a clatter, and into her boudoir strode a man.

The crown of the intruder's head nearly grazed the doorframe under which he instinctively ducked. He wore a tightly cut coat of black cloth with military-style brass buttons, and a faultlessly white shirt with a muslin cravat. His narrow hips and muscular thighs were encased in buff-colored nankeen and his gleaming black boots came to his knees. His unfashionably long hair, brushing his broad shoulders, was dressed in a somewhat unruly style she suspected resulted from carelessness rather than deliberate design. It was a shade of brown charitably termed maple. In its depths were several strands of glittering gray. A black patch covered his left eye; the other eye was a cold gray, the gray of a winter's morning mist, and gave his angular face with its high-planed cheekbones and thin lips a harsh expression.

Although she had not seen the man for some years, she recognized at once his proud and arrogant form.

It was Lord Christopher Drake—the man whom she'd almost married five years ago. The man whom she most hated in all the world.

Two

In that second he entered the boudoir, the locked gates of her mind were wrested open against her will, and the memories came flooding through, bringing with them all the pain and anger of that period.

Five years ago, despite a stormy courtship of some considerable length, they had at last decided it would be prudent to set a date for their wedding.

When the day of the eagerly awaited nuptials was no more than thirty-six hours away, she had, without warning to anyone—particularly to her astounded bridegroom-to-be and her bewildered mother—broken off the engagement.

Trembling with anger and sadness, and dreading what she must do, she had sat at her desk to write a note to Drake, explaining her reasons. Even now, she could still recall the wording.

"My lord Drake,

"I must confess that almost too late my eyes have been opened, and I see now that it would be folly for us both to marry. I know now you are not the man destined as my husband. You have betrayed my trust in you, my lord. You have lied to me; you have wronged me by—"

Wronged me. A chill went through her as she remembered the scene that was frozen into her memory.

Drake had been acting strangely during the previous week. He had been very quiet while they were together, and several times she had caught him looking at her oddly. When she asked him what was wrong, he had merely shaken his head. Then while attending a party in the country, she had noticed he had been absent for some time. After an hour, she had gone in search of him.

And Ariel had found Drake. She saw him leaving the summerhouse with a woman. But it wasn't just any woman. It was her closest friend, the friend she most trusted. Her friend; her fiancé. Together. Her closest friend—coming out of the summerhouse together. Ordinarily she would have thought nothing of it, but she remembered his odd behavior. And too, her friend's face was flushed, and Drake had his arm linked through hers, and they were talking in a low, intimate tone. She heard her name mentioned, and then they laughed.

The color draining from her face, Ariel stepped back, concealing herself behind a tree. It was all too obvious what had been going on . . . what they had been doing this time and who knew how many other times. So obvious, so painfully clear to anyone who used the eyes in her head. Yet she hadn't seen until she could no longer ignore the terrible truth. Anger, humiliation, and a deep hurt assailed her until every part of her body throbbed with pain. She pressed her fingertips against her burning forehead, and closed her eyes, and tried to weep for her loss, but the tears would not come. Too late, she thought sadly. Only it wasn't too late. She could do something about it, and she would. She returned to the party, left without a word to anyone, and once at home, she sat down to write a letter to him.

It must end. No matter that she loved—had loved—him with all her heart. No matter, for she knew the terrible truth now.

"You have greatly wronged me by your vile actions, by your—"

She stopped writing, dropped the quill pen, and covered her face with her hands. Sobs racked her body, and the tears dampened her cheeks. Finally, when the sobs were controlled, she scanned the meager lines, then crumpled up the letter and tossed it away.

Without explanation, she sent back his ring, adamantly refused to see him when he called upon her and her mother later in the day, and secluded herself in her rooms, allowing no one to enter. The following night she went to the theatre, dully performed in the current play—one whose name she could not now remember—and then came home to lay awake at night, wondering if she had done the right thing.

After a week, the visits and notes stopped, and she knew it was all over between them. Her friend tried to visit; she refused to see her.

Life resumed: bleaker, lonelier, certainly far less stormy than before. Less interesting, too. She performed in one play after another, and although she scanned the various audiences for some glimpse of him, she did not see him again. In time the heaviness in her heart seemed to recede, and once more she accepted invitations. She and her mother, Etoile, never discussed the dissolution of the engagement. Etoile had asked, but Ariel indicated quite plainly that she did not wish it brought up. She waited dully for the announcement of the marriage of Drake to her friend, but none came, and she realized bitterly that he had betrayed her friend as well.

Within a short time after that terrible period in her life, she met, was wooed by, and married Lt. Anthony Greystone of His Majesty's Royal Navy.

When they had been wed for not quite a year, Anthony reported for sea duty. In what she considered one of the most ironic and bitter turns of chance, it came to pass that Anthony served upon the same ship as Drake. She had never told Anthony of her prior engagement, and he, in his frequent letters to her, never mentioned Drake other than to say his fellow officer seemed cool toward him.

Soon after leaving England, Anthony Greystone was killed in the fierce naval battle of Copenhagen in April 1801. In that same battle, Drake was injured when a musket ball shattered his left eye. That was the last she had heard of him.

Indeed, this was the first time she had seen him since they . . . she . . . had broken off the engagement, the first time she had seen him with the black patch across the empty socket.

She stared at it unabashedly, thinking it gave him rather a sinister look, one that complemented his stern manner. Immediately she chided herself for her foolishness.

If he noticed her gaze, he gave no indication. In fact, he barely acknowledged her presence. Instead, he escorted the astonished Haversham to the door, then pushed Hally from the room, whereupon he locked the door and slipped the key into a pocket.

Astonished, she could only stare at his adacity.

Fierce sounds thundered from the other room as Haversham pounded on the door and demanded to be let in at once.

"Ariel, my dear, can you talk? What is that beast doing to you? Ariel! Answer me!" His voice grew more and more frantic. He sounded as though he feared for her very life. What did he expect Drake to do? What did *she* expect him to do?

Drake did not answer, but remained where he stood, gazing at her.

She knew she had to reassure Haversham, or at least stop the incessant noise. "I'm all right, John," she called. "Don't worry, please. I'll be fine." Her voice was low, but apparently Haversham heard her, for he stopped shouting. Was she all right? she wondered. The pounding on the door had ceased, but not in her head, and she closed her eyes momentarily. "I'll talk to you later, John. This evening at the theatre."

"Very well." His voice sounded mulish. She heard nothing from the other room, then the sound of retreating footsteps followed by the slamming of an outer door. The maid, crying softly, remained a few minutes more, entreating her mistress to unlock the door and let her in, then sighed deeply and left.

In the sudden silence Ariel recovered her composure and glared at the intruder, and when she spoke, her voice was filled with barely contained fury.

"I see you haven't changed, my lord. You have always— and continue to—act presumptuously, as though I were some horse or dog owned by you; and I must confess it is one of the attributes I most heartily despise in you."

He seemed not at all ruffled by her passionate outburst, which further irked her. "Indeed? I believe that is how you see the situation, although no one else does."

"At least," she responded tartly, "I see with two eyes."

He did not respond to her stinging barb, but simply strode across the room, snagged the rung of a chair with his booted toe, and pulled it to him. He sat with much elegance and glanced down idly at the peach robe still on the carpet.

Growing red faced at her state of dishabille, she hastily

picked up the robe and slipped it around her shoulders. He glanced at the crumpled bedcovers.

Her flush darkened. "It's not what you're thinking!" she exclaimed hotly, then silently cursed herself for speaking. She didn't give a fig for what he thought.

Acutely uncomfortable in his presence, and in the lengthening silence, she turned back to the mirror and began brushing her hair. The minutes passed, and still he did not speak. Finally, she could stand it no longer. She slapped the brush down.

"What do you want?" she demanded. "What is the reason for this rude intrusion?"

The corners of his thin mouth lifted into what could almost be called a smile; the expression did not reach his single good eye.

Even now, after all that had happened to both of them, she still thought him the most handsome man she'd ever seen. There were lines on his face that hadn't been there when they'd been affianced, but she was sure he could still turn a woman's head. As he had done so many years ago—almost a lifetime, it seemed—when she was much younger and far more innocent.

Steepling his long fingers, he continued to watch her with that disconcerting gaze. Her eyes dropped to her lap. At length he stirred and spoke.

"The reason I have come is this: I wish to enlist your aid, Mrs. Greystone."

Three

Containing her surprise, Ariel raised an eyebrow, hoping it would convey her skepticism. "I doubt that most sincerely, my lord. You never needed me nor my aid—not five years ago, and, I am most sure, not now."

"We must—for the moment—put the past behind us," he replied.

At that moment she realized he was serious about asking for her help. But, she reflected bitterly, he had always been serious, to the point of seeming solemn, even harsh. That still did not mean he really needed her—or her aid, she corrected.

"Go on," she said, her voice harsh. Her fingers tightened on her robe, bringing it more snugly around her.

"I represent the government; more specifically, Prime Minister Addington."

The government? The prime minister? What was all this? She felt confused by his unusual revelation.

"What is this nonsense? Explain at once, my lord, for I really don't have the time to dawdle and listen to old tales."

He did not smile, nor had she really expected him to. He settled back into the chair, crossed his legs, and seemed to lose himself in contemplation. With an effort, he roused himself, and when he spoke it was in a musing tone.

"After the Copenhagen battle in '01, I was pulled from military duty for many months while my injuries slowly healed. When I was once more restored to health, I was transferred to a government post in England where I reported directly to Prime Minister Addington. Then in March 1802, after the Peace of Amiens with the French was signed, a new branch of the government was formed, one based on an idea formulated by Pitt when he was in office—one which operated completely in secret. This new branch reported only to the prime minister, and was headed by me.''

She made an impatient gesture with her hand. The silk of the robe whispered as she shifted, and she was acutely aware that she wore nothing underneath it. "I really don't see what all of this has to do with me."

"Ah, but you see, there is a connection."

"Well, please explain it." She knew her tone sounded waspish.

"I don't know how much you know about politics, Mrs. Greystone, although if I remember correctly, you never had much interest in the matter, deeming it a most boring subject, fit only for the likes of me."

She glared at him.

Once more he shifted, his gaze never leaving her face. "The situation is this: Mr. Addington is deeply concerned about Napoleon Bonaparte's plans—as are all loyal English subjects." If that was meant as a slur against her patriotism, she would choose to ignore it—for now.

He continued. "If Napoleon were content simply to rebuild France after the terrible chaos and devastation of the Revolution and the wars of the past decade, I think no one would deter him from that very admirable task. I am sure all nations would applaud his actions. Unfortunately, he is not satisfied to do that, and has set his sights beyond the boundaries of France."

Napoleon, he went on to explain, had sought to be more than a military leader. He had gone to Paris, ended the Directory, and had become a virtual dictator. Two years before, in 1802, he had had himself declared first consul of France with the right to appoint his successor, and with each year that passed he had acquired more power, all of it centralized in himself.

To France he had brought reform, as well as a secret police, censorship, and the arrest of political enemies. But, too, he had brought prosperity, stability, and he was France's most popular man.

Now, though, France, better fed, more comfortable, and safer than at any time in the past decade, looked hungrily beyond its own boundaries. It looked to its traditional enemy.

England.

She frowned. "I still—" she began.

"Hear me out." On his feet now, he crossed to the fireplace. There he examined a Sèvres vase on the mantelpiece, then turned back to her. "You were born in France six and twenty years ago of an aristocratic English father and a well-born French mother. After your father died, your mother fled the Terror of the Guillotine with her fourteen-year-old daughter and came to this country."

"I hardly think a résumé of my life is necessary."

He continued as if he hadn't heard. "While you have English blood in your veins, and have lived here for almost half your life, you still feel some ties with the land of your birth. Quite natural, I would think."

"Thank you," she said sarcastically.

"You are also a loyal English subject. Of that I am certain."

She did not respond, for she didn't understand where this conversation was leading, although she had a strange tingling in the pit of her stomach, a tingling suggesting she would not be pleased with what he had to say.

"You are beautiful." She acknowledged the compliment with a slight bow of her head. "You are an actress. Napoleon believes theatre is the glory of France and has thus eagerly sponsored the revival of the Comédie-Française."

The tingling had become an aching dread. Wishing her mouth were not so dry, she cleared her throat. "Well?"

"Those are my reasons," he said.

"Your reasons?" she echoed.

"Yes, for asking you to work for me."

"Work? As what? I don't understand what you are saying, my lord. Why would you wish an actress to work for you?"

His gesture was sharp, impatient. "I thought I had made it abundantly clear, Mrs. Greystone. I want you to be a spy!"

Four

❧

"A spy!" She stared incredulously at him. "I can't have heard right, my lord. This is rather farfetched, even for you. A spy! What an absurd notion!" She laughed, although she did not feel amused. "I am an actress—nothing more, nothing less, as you once so kindly pointed out."

He did not seem at all disturbed. " 'Tis true you are but an actress, yet there are many qualities which recommend you. As I stated before, Napoleon has a passion for the theatre —and you are an actress, and a well-known one. You are clever"—here he gave a mock bow in her direction—"and you still maintain relations in that country. You speak the language as a native, and could move into the first consul's circle with singular ease. And too, I know that you need money. I will pay handsomely," he added.

For the span of several heartbeats she said nothing; then: "Get out. Get out at once, my lord!"

He bowed low. "I will wait to hear from you."

She grabbed her hairbrush and threw it. He ducked the missile easily and, chuckling at her display of temper, unlocked the door and left, closing it softly behind him.

She glared. Thank God he was gone and out of her life— again.

Or was he?

She stared into the mirror as she pondered Drake's incredible offer.

He wanted to hire her as a spy—or so he claimed. A spy who would work in France against Napoleon Bonaparte. For the English government. And he would have her believe he headed some secret branch of the government that reported exclusively to the prime minister. How utterly preposterous!

"Indeed," she murmured aloud, her lips curving slightly. Did he think she was so utterly naïve as to believe such a tale? Once, perhaps, once long ago when they'd been affianced, but she was no longer so innocent, so trusting. No longer.

And yet . . . what if he was telling the truth? What if he really was the head of such a secret group within the government?

It couldn't be, she told herself firmly. She thrust back a long curl trailing over her shoulder and nodded to herself. It couldn't be the truth because Drake didn't speak the truth. He said only what he thought might sway others. Oh yes, she knew that well. He had a silver tongue.

'Twas simply an absurdity, nothing more, nothing less.

She could sit no longer. She decided not to call Hally to assist her, for the girl would be filled with a hundred questions, none of which she wanted to answer now. Rising, she let the robe fall off her shoulders and went to the satinwood armoire. The doors open, she gazed unseeing at the numerous gowns hanging there, and her thoughts strayed.

Spying. She knew virtually nothing of it—except that she could be imprisoned or killed if she were caught.

Imprisoned or killed. 'Twas a fine future he wished for her, a fine end to her life. She frowned. Why had he thought of her after all these years? Surely there were others who fit the qualifications as well as she? And yet how many did she know who knew French as she did, who knew people there, who . . . Enough. Perhaps there were none, none except her. It was she upon whom they depended, to whom the prime minister himself looked—

She caught herself at once. Oh no, she wouldn't permit herself to indulge in such theatrical notions. Such imaginings were fine for the stage, but quite another thing when there were no props, no audience, and a very real threat of danger.

He had come to her, she told herself as she pressed her lips together, because he assumed he could still have his way with her, and that she would accede as she had done before.

No longer, though.

She pulled out a white muslin gown with short puffed sleeves and decided to wear the green velvet sash and the green slippers. She draped the gown across the bed and sat once more at the dressing table. She ran a hand through the tangle of her long locks.

Yet it was an intriguing offer, especially if he paid handsomely. But then again, no money was worth the danger.

Yet she thought of that maddening half smile playing on his thin lips and could not be sure.

Prime Minister Henry Addington, former Speaker of the House of Commons, had negotiated the Peace of Amiens in March 1802, had abolished income tax, and had severely reduced government expenditures, resulting in the hampered effectiveness of the British army. He sincerely did not believe Napoleon Bonaparte posed as much of a threat as everyone else seemed to believe, despite the fact that Britain and France had been at war since May 1803.

Drake's job was to convince him otherwise: that Napoleon presented a very real threat, and that the French leader seemed single-mindedly determined to invade England.

It was true that Drake had lied to Ariel when he told her Addington was concerned about Napoleon's plans. The truth was, he himself was concerned, as was William Pitt the Younger, who had resigned in 1801 as prime minister, and others in the government as well.

Addington remained adamant despite all the evidence to the contrary provided by Drake.

Before Pitt left office he had created the secret department Drake now headed, but he had not had the opportunity to see its work. Addington did in early 1802, after much convincing that just such a department was necessary. He claimed it was totally in opposition to the Peace of Amiens, but Drake and Pitt did all they could to argue forcefully that the English intelligence system should not be laid to rest while the two countries were at peace. When war broke out, Addington informed Drake that it was fortunate the intelligence system was still intact. Drake prudently said nothing.

Drake's spies had proved effective in following Napoleon's activities, and more than ever Drake was convinced the French leader was determined to invade England.

If only he could now persuade Addington of it. He was sitting opposite Addington's desk, and had been for the past hour. He restrained a deep sigh, and idly fingered the patch covering his left eye socket. When he was tired, or angry—and he was both—it ached. If he had been alone, he would simply have removed the patch and rubbed the puckered skin there, but he could not. He pushed the ache from his thoughts. Shifting position, he spoke again.

"As you can see from Hendricks's latest dispatch, sir, Moreau and Pichegru were arrested." Both men were French generals who, along with Georges Cadoudal, a royalist who had lived in England until the year before, had tried to seize Bonaparte in an ambush in mid-January. The attempt had failed, and in February the conspiracy had been uncovered.

Addington nodded reflectively. "Yes, yes, but they *were* plotting against Bonaparte's life. It is to be expected they would be arrested."

"Yes, sir, but the point is, I believe Bonaparte is going to seize this opportunity and round up his political opponents. When he does so, he will be able to implement plans for the invasion."

"Ah, the invasion again." Addington sat back and rubbed the bridge of his nose. He stared at the other man. "Always the invasion."

"They tried in '03."

"Rumors."

Drake pressed his lips together. The '03 incident was more than rumor: The French fleet had been on the verge of invasion, when abruptly, it had been called off. He had the papers to prove it. "I think, sir, it was more than rumor, as was documented at the time by—"

"Yes, yes, yes," the other man cut in impatiently.

Drake suspected little would be gained by today's session, and he was not pleased. Addington was clearly out of patience with him, a circumstance that happened more and more frequently of late. He must proceed with some care, then.

"Enough of this for now, Drake. Tell me about the other matter." Addington settled back in his chair. "How goes the recruitment?"

"I approached her today, sir." Drake was not convinced that "approach" was an accurate term for the earlier confrontation.

"And?"

Drake's lips twitched as he remembered how she had thrown her hairbrush at him. "She is slightly reluctant at present; I do not think she is fully convinced I am serious."

The prime minister frowned and shook his head. "I am not so certain about this. If she's going to prove to be unworkable . . ."

"No, sir, she won't. Simply allow me more time to . . . persuade her. I am sure I will have her convinced soon."

"I hope so, for your sake."

Drake said nothing.

"That's all for now, Drake. Keep me informed, won't you?" Addington had already dismissed him as he reached for a sheaf of papers on his desk.

As Drake left the building, he reviewed the fruitless conversation with the prime minister. He had spoken confidently of his ability to convince Ariel to work for him, but now he had to admit to himself that he was not sure. Of course, he had expected her to react angrily to his appearance and his offer, but how long that anger would last he didn't know. She had already been angry at him for five years.

Five years. Could it really have been so long? Yes, he thought, and sometimes it felt even longer. He paused, touching the patch.

What had she thought of that? he wondered. She hadn't seen him since Copenhagen; much had happened, and he had changed. She had, too. She had grown even more beautiful than when he'd last seen her, if that was possible. And more spirited.

A rusty chuckle escaped his throat. *That* seemed almost impossible.

He had been totally unprepared for the fullness of her

beauty, unprepared to see her sitting naked, her robe at her feet. Although he had not shown it, in those short minutes he had taken in every detail of her, the lustrous cascade of hair, the flashing green eyes, the slight tilt of those high breasts, the rich curve of thighs, the hidden promise beyond. He closed his good eye and remembered the sweet silkiness of her hair, the warm softness of her arms, the honeyed kisses, the musky scent of their love.

He swallowed dryly, then abruptly shook himself. He must recall where he was. In the present, not the past, and what was done was done. Had been done for five years now, and he could not forget it. Ariel had not.

He started walking again, ruthlessly driving the memories from his mind. He had other matters to concentrate upon this busy day. He was scheduled to meet with Pitt to discuss the French crisis, and the "recruitment," as Addington termed it.

First, though, he had a very important obligation.

Five

Ariel sat at her writing desk and penned a note of apology to John Haversham. She offered no explanation of Drake's untoward behavior, nor did she identify him. That would not be so difficult to do, after all. What other man in London was as tall and imposing and wore a patch upon his left eye? Still, even if Haversham discovered Drake's name, he did not know what had happened five years ago.

She frowned suddenly at the note. Even if Haversham did dig into her past, what did it matter? Other women changed their minds and ended engagements. She shrugged and dusted the paper, then lightly blew away the grains of sand. After she had put a wafer upon it, she rang for Hally to have the note delivered at once.

Later, she bathed. She sighed, settling back against the enamel tub, and let the heat erase the tensions of the day. She closed her eyes, and her mind leaped hours ahead to this evening's performance.

She must think about the play, or her mind would drift to Drake and his offer, and she did not want it to do that. He had already ruined her day as it was.

When she finished her soak, she wrapped herself in the bath sheet Hally had left out and went in to apply talcum and perfume. Her fingers skimmed the tops of the various bottles. Most of the expensive perfumes had been presents from ad-

mirers, as had many other lovely objects in her home. She
frowned, recalling what Drake would have said about that
practice.

But, of course, she did not care what Drake thought or said.

She pushed his image out of her mind once more and called
for Hally. She had changed her mind and no longer wanted to
wear the white muslin. Today it seemed too young and innocent, something she didn't feel. Instead, she dressed in a
muslin with a maroon velvet tunic over it. She sat impatiently
while her hair was dressed in a Grecian style, with the hair
drawn to the back of the head and tied in a bunch of curls.
When the last curl was barely in place, she leaped to her feet,
overturning her chair and startling poor Hally who gave a
frightened squeak.

"Get a hold of yourself at once, Hally, before you have an
agitation of the nerves and the doctor prescribes some dread-
ful-tasting yellow powder."

"Yes, ma'm." The girl ducked her head, bobbed a curtsy
and handed a beaded reticule to her, and bobbed another
curtsy.

Ariel was on the verge of saying something about unnecessary curtsies but decided it would only upset Hally. She
picked up a Paisley shawl in pink and brown tones and started
from the room.

"One moment, ma'm," Hally called.

"Yes?" Ariel knew her tone was impatient.

"You almost forgot this, ma'm." She ran across the room
to hand a wrapped package to her mistress.

Her mother's present. She had almost left it behind and
would have been most displeased to discover that oversight
once she arrived.

Downstairs, she sent word to Wawles, her coachman, to
bring the carriage around front. He did so almost at once, and
when Hally had helped her into her pelisse, she went outside.

As the carriage rolled through the bustling streets of London, she prided herself that she had not once seriously considered Drake's incredible offer since he had left. Well, not
quite. . . .

Stirring impatiently, she pushed back the curtain and saw a
gentleman astride a large chestnut. Once they were parallel to

the coach, she recognized him as the earl who had come to see her perform last week. He had brought her a large bouquet of flowers, as she recalled. The earl touched his fingers to the brim of his beaver hat, but before she could speak, the coach rounded a corner, and she could no longer see him.

She little doubted she would see him again. At least she hoped so. Rumor had it he was quite rich, as well as unattached, and certainly he was handsome, even more so than John Haversham. Perhaps, she mused, she should consider the earl rather than Haversham.

The coach rattled to a stop. She glanced out the window, surprised to see they had already reached her mother's town house.

Wawles helped her out, then went to stand by the head horse as she quickly climbed up the five steps to the front door. A brisk wind had sprung up, and she was eager to get inside.

She knocked once, and the door was opened at once by Nooks, a man who served her mother in many capacities.

"Good afternoon, Nooks." She handed him her pelisse and gloves and settled the shawl about her shoulders as she walked into the small marbled entry hall.

"Good day to you, Miss Ariel." He spoke in a habitually low voice that had traces of a northern accent. Her mother had inherited Nooks from her late husband, and there had never been a servant more devoted than he. He was tall, over six feet in stocking feet, and broad across his shoulders. His arms were sinewy with muscle, and his legs had the circumference of small trees. His face was pleasant, though the scars across his forehead and cheeks gave him an awe-inspiring expression.

She highly suspected that Nooks, whose beefy hands could be as gentle as any woman's, had spent his early days at sea, and not in any innocent pursuit. But nothing of his life before he came to work for the de Julierses was known, for he did not speak of it, and neither his mistress nor her daughter ever pressed him for details. If her father had known any part of the man's past—and she suspected he had—he had kept mum 'pon it.

"How is my mother faring?" she asked as they walked

down the hall. Every day she came to visit, and every day she asked the same question.

Nooks shook his head solemnly. "Not good today, I fear, Miss Ariel. She's been askin' after ye since early. I told her not to fret because ye'd be here right as clockwork."

She nodded, and chewed on her lip to keep the tears from spilling out. Her poor mother. It was so difficult some days to keep a brave face in front of her. Nooks saw her distress and covered her hand with his, swallowing it completely.

Her mother had never been robust, and the early years of her life had been difficult. She had been left an orphan at a young age and had gone onto the French stage when she was just twelve. For the next six years Etoile Marchall had been wooed alternately by actors and managers and admirers, all of whom had been infatuated by the girl's frail beauty and in-nocence, and all of whom had wished to coax her into their beds. They had been unsuccessful in their efforts, and the flir-tations had ended abruptly when she turned eighteen.

One night the young scion of a transplanted English family visited the Royale Theatre to watch Mademoiselle Marchall in a Molière comedy. After the performance, Robert de Juliers came backstage to meet her and was totally enchanted. They began seeing one another, and within two months they were married. In another year they had a daughter, Ariel; a year later a stillborn son. After that, there could be no more chil-dren. With the passing of the years, Etoile's health had grad-ually deteriorated. Body and mind had suffered greatly after Robert's death when Ariel was ten years old.

Ariel could not remember a year that her mother had not weakened with one illness or another. Recently her health had become even more precarious, and Ariel greatly feared for her life.

She drew herself out of her somber reverie and wiped sur-reptitiously at her eyes with a lawn handkerchief provided by Nooks.

"It's a hard time, Miss Ariel, fer ye and her." The servant rubbed his chin. "We do what we can fer her, miss, but ye know the madame." He shook his head ruefully. "She's as stubborn as rain, just like his lordship was."

Ariel's father should have been a nobleman, but when his

family had been cheated of their birthright, they had come to France. Nooks, who knew of this, had always referred to her father as "his lordship."

"Yes, I know, Nooks. She will not consider moving to Italy or Spain, where it is far warmer and her health would be much improved." She knew her mother wouldn't consider the move because of the expense: Ariel could not afford it, a circumstance she deplored with all her heart. "I shall go up and see her now."

He nodded sympathetically. "She's in the Rose Salon, as always. Waitin' for ye." The Rose Salon was her mother's favorite room for it was the sunniest in the otherwise dark house. Nooks seemed on the verge of saying something more to her, then stopped, apparently having changed his mind.

She took the package Hally had reminded her to bring along and quickly ascended the carpeted stairs. She passed down the gloomy corridor, paused outside a painted door, and knocked softly.

"Entre, ma chérie," called a voice from the other side of the door.

Ariel pushed open the door and looked into the room, named for its gilt and rose pink decoration. Sunlight glinted through tall windows set in one wall.

"Good morning, *maman*."

"Afternoon, you mean!" pronounced the frail woman reclining on the rose velvet settee. "Come in here at once and sit by me." She patted a cushion.

Ariel obediently followed her parent's dictate; she crossed over to the settee and was about to hug her small-boned mother when she heard the door close. Someone coughed discreetly behind her. Frowning, she whirled around.

"You!" she exclaimed.

"Indeed," murmured Christopher Drake.

Six

◁◦❂◦▷

"Why are you here disturbing my mother?" Ariel demanded harshly.

"Oh, but most assuredly he is not disturbing me," Etoile de Juliers protested softly in her heavily accented English. "Kit —er, Lord Drake," she amended quickly when she saw the thunderous expression on her daughter's face at her use of the old nickname, "has been so kind as to pay me a visit and has brought me a tin of chocolates." She indicated a large foil-wrapped box on the mahogany table next to her. "Would you care for one, *ma chérie*?"

"No," Ariel replied shortly. "Thank you, Mother." Suspiciously she eyed Drake, who had crossed the salon to stand impassively by the fireplace, one arm draped along the mantel-piece. He had been staring into the fire, but was now watching her, listening to the interplay between mother and daughter.

Why was he here? she wondered. Why now, of all times? She asked him outright.

"I have been seeing your mother for some time."

"For some time!" she echoed. The room momentarily blackened as dizziness seized her. She almost sank down upon the settee but then braced herself. She would show him no weakness. Completely astonished and hurt, although not understanding why, she looked first to her mother, then to

Drake for confirmation. "How long has this misalliance been going on, *maman*?"

Etoile laughed. "Ariel, you know it is hardly that."

"How long?" she demanded, aware of her rude tone. It didn't matter—not after what she had just learned.

"For some time," Drake answered finally. He flicked an imaginary speck from the sleeve of his wine-colored coat. Although she thought he looked quite dashing in maroon coat and breeches with the tall black boots, she also wished him in Hades. "Now, while it is acknowledged the former bride-to-be and I stopped speaking, it did not follow, however, that I might not wish to continue my acquaintance with my mother-in-law. My almost mother-in-law," he amended.

"I see." Ariel's lips were pressed together, completely drained of color.

"Ariel, don't be angry," her mother pleaded. "Kit has been so good to me."

"Kit" again! Her mother knew she hated that nickname. She had not hated it when she had bestowed it upon her fiancé. Her dislike of the name had come after the end of their engagement.

"I think it best," said Drake, his concerned gaze fixed on Etoile, "that I leave now that your daughter has arrived."

"So soon?" Etoile's voice sounded disappointed. It was obvious she wished her handsome caller to linger.

"So soon," he agreed. "You know I will call upon you again, Etoile." He picked up his hat from a side table, nodded to Ariel, kissed Etoile's hand, and departed.

It was clear now what Nooks had wanted to say below—he had wanted to warn her that Drake was with her mother. Why had he changed his mind? Because he'd been paid by Drake to say nothing? She could little doubt it.

As the door closed, Etoile sighed theatrically, while Ariel found she was once more glaring at a door through which Drake had left. It was happening too often.

"Come, *ma chérie*, do not be in such a taking," her mother said jovially. "You know Kit means no harm. He only comes to lighten the loneliness of an old sick woman."

"You aren't old, *maman*."

"I am sick," Etoile pointed out.

Ariel could not leave the subject alone.

"Why was he here, *maman*?" She sat now beside her mother and took the other woman's small hands in her own. They were cool, and trembled slightly. "What did he want?"

"Just to visit, *ma chérie*. That is all." Etoile's eyes, thought, would not meet her daughter's.

"Just to visit?" Ariel shook her head. "That I doubt. We both know Drake always has a reason for what he does."

"This time," the older woman said softly, "I think you are wrong. He has come simply to keep me company. Is that not sweet?"

Ariel, who suspected her mother was not telling the complete truth, could scarcely accept "sweet" as being one of Drake's admirable traits, and so she did not answer, but rather turned to look fully at her mother for the first time since she'd arrived.

She thought there were more lines from pain and worry on her mother's face. Her brown eyes were shadowed. All that suffering—it was too much for one tiny woman. Yet, despite all that had happened, there was little gray in her mother's black hair, and for all the sorrow in her face, her appearance was really quite youthful. Indeed, the two women could almost have passed as sisters. Etoile's frame was trim, for while she no longer led an active life, she rarely ate more than three bites of anything—much to the silent despair of Ariel, who greatly feared her mother would waste away.

"How are you feeling today, *maman*?" she asked. "I was so . . . flustered . . . I forgot to inquire. Pray forgive me."

Etoile airily waved a slender hand, one of the same slender hands Ariel had inherited. "I am no worse, nor no better, *ma chérie*. I awoke very early, feeling better than I had in days, and so, not wishing to disturb anyone, I decided to rise—"

"You didn't! You know you should wait for Nooks or Lizzy."

"I know, I know," she said, sounding only slightly remorseful, "but I felt so refreshed I thought I could get out of bed alone. I did not wish to be a bother. Alas," she said with a slight shake of her head, "I could not do it." She sighed.

"Found her on the floor, I did!" said a new voice from behind Ariel.

"What!" Ariel glanced from her mother to the plump woman who had just entered quietly. "What are you saying, Lizzy?"

"Yer mom fell flat on the floor, she did, but Nooks was there in a nonce's eye and got her up—without any damage to herself, I might add. No thanks to her silly notions." At this last the servant cast a severe eye on Etoile, who ducked her head guiltily.

"Oh, *maman*, must I worry now about this?"

"No," she replied in an almost childlike voice. "I won't do it again."

"Until the next time," Ariel said dryly.

"Until the next time," Lizzy echoed, sighing gustily. "Sorry to interrupt, ma'm, but I've come to give you your afternoon medicine."

Etoile made an unladylike face. "Must you?" She gazed at her maid and her daughter, then threw up her hands in defeat. "Do it, if you insist."

Ariel sat quietly while her mother took the various drafts prescribed by Dr. Liggott. Finally, Lizzy left and mother and daughter were alone in the salon.

"Oh, I almost forgot! This is for you, *maman*." She extended the package to her mother.

"Oh!" Etoile was delighted. "So many presents today! Whatever is the occasion! It cannot be my birthday, can it?" Her fingers plucked at the paper, ripping it in her haste, and at length she withdrew a slim volume sheathed in dark maroon leather.

"Molière," she whispered, clasping the book to her chest. "My favorite." She glanced at her daughter, her dark eyes shining with tears. "Thank you, *ma chérie*, thank you so much."

Ariel smiled at her mother's obvious pleasure. "You are welcome, *maman*. I found the book at my booksellers a few days ago and knew at once I must have it for you. I think you will enjoy it."

Etoile fingered the gilt lettering on the spine and lovingly caressed the morocco cover, but cast a worried look at her daughter. "It must have been very expensive, *ma chérie*. You know you cannot afford such frivolities. Perhaps you should take it back." She held the book out.

Ariel ignored the gesture. "I had some money put away for such things. You must not fret." Etoile relaxed and began carefully thumbing through the book. Its purchase meant future scrimping for Ariel, but she had been unable resist when she saw the book. Molière was her mother's favorite playwright, and too, there was a sentimental value to the book. Included in its contents was the play at which her father and mother had met.

"Thank you again, *ma chérie*." Etoile had found the play and was openly crying.

Ariel patted her hand, then, after a moment, spoke. "I must go now, *maman*. I will see you again tomorrow."

"Oh, so soon," Etoile sighed, and nodded her head. "Do well."

"Thank you." She kissed her mother's soft cheek and left, her spirits low. This day had not been good from the start; she could only hope the performance would go more smoothly.

Once in her coach, she reviewed the visit with her mother. So, she had discovered Drake spying upon her, somehow coercing her mother. For what? To help persuade her daughter into helping him? Etoile had acted quite unwell today, no doubt strained from Drake's presence. Perhaps when she reached the theatre she should send a note around to Dr. Liggott. Of course, Nooks and Lizzy had doubtless done that when they'd discovered her on the floor earlier, but sending the note would help alleviate some of her worry. She sighed, and wished the night were already over.

It took too little time to reach the theatre, and once arrived, she gazed at the building. The Theatre Royal—although nearly everyone referred to it as Drury Lane, which was actually the street on one side. It had been built by Thomas Killigrew under a direct charter from Charles II, and there, on May 7, 1663, it had opened. In 1672 it had burned and was rebuilt, and in 1791 it was decided to build a new theatre because the original was in such bad repair. In 1746, George II, while attending a play, had heard of the defeat of Prince Charles Edward at Culloden Moor, and in 1800 there had been an at-

tempted assassination of King George III by an old soldier.
The theatre reached its peak under Garrick's management in
the mid-1700s, and there Mrs. Pritchard, Kitty Clive, Mrs.
Sarah Siddons, John Philip Kemble, Mrs. Jordan had all
acted. Gradually its glory had waned, and it was now not as
respectable as it had once been; Covent Garden Theatre was
now the respectable theatre in town.

But still she stayed. She had been there for many years, and
knew that she would have to start looking for a new theatre
company before long. Until then, Drury Lane was her home,
she told herself. She braced herself for the performance that
evening.

"Mrs. Greystone!"
"Ariel, my darling!"
"Come here, my love!"
The masculine shouts, all rather good-natured, followed her
as she left the stage to head back to the green room. There,
and only there, she mused somewhat wryly, would she meet
her adoring public, for unlike other actresses, she did not prefer to wait for her admirers to surge upon the stage after a performance.

Her adoring public. A public consisting of men, aristocratic
and common alike, who seemed to have one intention: to
bribe their way into her heart and thus her bed. A bed she had
kept remarkably solitary, considering the persistence of her
admirers, considering her profession, considering she did not
like living alone.

Reaching the door of the green room, she was barred from
entering it by a man's arm nonchalantly thrust out in front of
her.

Irritated, she glanced up from the bouquets of flowers she
held in her arms. "Oh, Stanton, it's you."

The dandyishly dressed man with the tousled blond hair,
very much à la mode, grinned down at her from his great
height. "Of course, Mrs. Greystone, it is I. Whom were you
expecting?"

She smiled coolly at him. "Why, no one, of course." She
spoke lightly, but her words were untrue. She *had* been expecting someone, someone named Christopher Drake. Even dur-

ing the performance, her usually steady concentration had been broken once or twice as she looked out across the well-lit auditorium, searching the boxes. But she had not seen him anywhere. She had been filled with disappointment.

As she made her slow progress backstage, she'd hoped she might glimpse him in the crowds of well-wishers. Again her search had been fruitless.

"Get out of here, Carlyle," said a rough male voice, "and leave the lady alone."

She blinked in surprise as she recognized Philip Denton, another of her admirers, glaring with ill-concealed dislike at Stanton Carlyle. The latter was quite unaffected by the other's bullying tone.

"Oh, it's the puppy," he drawled, and smiled condescendingly at the younger man while he looked at him through his quizzing glass.

"Puppy, is it!" thundered Denton. "I'll show you who's a puppy! I'll—"

"Please, gentlemen!" Ariel interrupted, fearful one hothead would call the other out. "Please, let me pass—I wish to go to my dressing room."

"Allow me to escort you," Denton suggested, offering her his arm.

"No, no, no. Pray allow me," Carlyle said at the same moment.

"I fear, gentlemen," she said, glancing down at the bouquets, "I am prevented from taking either of your arms." She did not like to play favorites between these men, for they were not as genial as Haversham.

"Damn," said Denton, before he could answer, "there's Haversham."

Across the greenroom, Haversham waved, and she nodded. Obviously he had received her note. He made his way slowly through the press of people and bent to give her a kiss. The three men, Denton and Carlyle still arguing, trailed after her and were joined by others. Ariel managed to make some progress in the direction of her dressing room, and when she finally reached the door, she turned.

"Now, gentlemen, I must bid you *adieu*," she said in her sweetest tone.

"Oh come, Mrs. Greystone," pleaded Denton, hurt evident on his youthful face, "just let us in this one time."

"Surely you'll need . . . expert help with all those hooks and buttons," suggested Carlyle, a lewd expression slipping across his face.

"I have a tirewoman for *that*," she responded lightly.

"Ariel, love," Lord Rothwell cajoled, "let us in and we'll not look. We promise!"

Haversham wasn't speaking, and in fact he was looking surly. She knew she must do something quickly.

"Oh, come now," she said. "I don't trust the lot of you, and neither do you!" There was laughter. "Here." She thrust the great mass of flowers into Denton's and Carlyle's arms, darted past the amorously reaching hands of Rothwell, and slipped into the dressing room to lean against the closed door. As an added precaution, she turned the key in the lock and took it out. That should keep them for a while, she told herself triumphantly.

Slowly she let her breath out and tried to relax. As she crossed the room, she passed the large oriental dressing screen and noted that several unfamiliar vases sat on the table next to it. Arranged in them were red roses, their blooms unusually large considering it was still February and roses were not due for many months. Their sweet perfume filled the room.

She eased into the chair at the dressing table, leaned back, and looked at the flowers. Hothouse flowers, no doubt, and exceedingly expensive by any account. No doubt another admirer. She shook her head as if to dismiss the thought and pushed back the straggling hair that had come loose.

For a brief moment she stared at herself in the mirror, but the glaring light made her look more tired than she really was. Her stage makeup was already smearing. She did not, she suspected, look like the toast of the stage—this stage, or any other, for that matter. She felt bedraggled.

Quickly she removed the makeup with a cloth and felt better with her skin cleaned. She closed her eyes and rested her chin on the heels of her hands. Outside in the green room, she could hear the rumble of voices, and once someone knocked imperiously on her door. She ignored the summons, and after a moment the person left.

She thought about the play tonight. It had not been her most successful performance, for she had worried about her mother's health the entire time. She was glad Etoile had not seen her perform. And while she had not done well, she knew none of the men waiting for her were particularly concerned about her dramatic—or comedic—interpretation of her role. She doubted many in the audience had even noticed anything was amiss.

She sighed, tried to push all her worries away, but they wouldn't leave.

A slight scuffling sound came from the direction of the screen in the corner.

Opening her eyes, she stared into the mirror.

Someone had stepped from behind the screen.

A man.

It couldn't be . . . not after . . . no . . . but it was.

Him.

Again.

Lord Christopher Drake smiled.

Seven

❧❦❧

"You again!" Ariel could not believe he stood before her once again—the third time in a day, when it had been years since she'd last seen him. Despite her astonishment, she recovered quickly. "Leave me alone, my lord," she demanded. "You have been dogging my steps and plaguing me all day."

He continued to look at her.

"Get out now, or I shall call for the manager."

"You'll have to get to the door first," he said with a thin smile on his lips.

Perplexed, and feeling a little defeated, she ignored what she considered a threat. "What do you want? Why are you following me?"

"Have you considered my offer?" He crossed the room in three powerful strides and sat down beside her, taking her hand in his.

Ariel trembled at his touch, for she *had* loved him greatly five years ago. Even after they had parted, she had not stopped loving him.

After that severance she had been lost, foundering in some alien world of conflicting emotions, and eventually she had sought comfort and company. She had found both in the likable person of Lt. Anthony Greystone, a longtime admirer. So it was she found herself marrying him, a few short months after he had asked her for her hand, a few short months since

36

she had terminated her previous engagement.

Greystone was closer to her age than was Drake, who was some ten years her senior. He was classically handsome, and quite amiable, and life with him, as brief as it was, was totally peaceful—a state she found exceedingly dull.

When her husband left for his tour of naval duty, she returned to the stage.

It was there on the stage that she learned of his death. She did not collapse, as those around her had expected, but rather she continued her performance, and when it was over she took no bows but went straight to her dressing room and cried . . . cried for her lost husband, who had been, after all, a good and kind man; cried for her lost fiancé; cried for herself.

As the years passed after Anthony's death, she often thought of Drake and from time to time idly wondered what their life together would have been like. Knowing he would not want to see her again, she had not sought him out.

Now, to confuse her totally, he had swept back into her life—just as handsome, just as intriguing, just as infuriating, and with him he brought an offer of money as well as adventure. He knew too well how difficult it would be for her to refuse such an alluring combination.

Still, he held her hand and stroked her. She shivered, aware that her breathing had become hoarse. She bit down on her lip and abruptly pulled away. She rose and went behind the ornate screen and began unfastening the hooks on her costume.

He did not ask her again, and she thought for a few minutes before she answered.

"Perhaps, my lord, if you were to take me to dinner tonight, we might find an opportunity to discuss the matter." She pushed the bodice of her dress away and let it drop to the floor. She let the skirt drop as well. Usually she took more care, thinking of her poor overworked helping woman, but tonight she was distressed, and her mind was on other matters.

There was not a moment of hesitation. "Dinner it is, Mrs. Greystone. You'll find I have no complaints 'pon that head."

She finished changing, slipped quickly into her own dress, and came around to face him.

She smiled expansively. "An expensive meal, my lord, a

very expensive one is what will do."

They went to a private club. Situated in one of London's
older and still-prosperous sections, it catered to the aristocracy. One did not enter the club unless one were a member of
the peerage or were being escorted by one who was.

Once inside the door, Ariel paused to survey the room. It
was not overly large, nor too small—just the proper size for
intimate meals. The floor was carpeted with oriental rugs, and
on the walls white candles glittered in gold sconces. Overhead
the crystal chandeliers threw rainbows of color across the
diners and their tables. Red velvet curtains separated the tables
in the corners from those scattered about the room, and
everywhere the wood was very dark and highly polished. She
was pleased at finding herself here in this most exclusive of
places.

She saw that Drake was smiling, no doubt suspecting what
was on her mind. It was one of his more infuriating abilities-
—he had always seemed to know what was uppermost in her
mind. And he had never hesitated to inform her of such.

The maître d', impeccably attired in black, swept up to them
and bowed low. "This way, my lord," he said, the trace of a
foreign accent in his voice. "Your usual table awaits."

"Not tonight, Edwin. Is there a private room available?"

The man's eyes flicked briefly to Ariel, and she knew what
he thought. "But of course, my lord. Come this way, please."

As they walked through the room, Ariel grew aware of the
quizzing looks directed toward her. She had been recognized
by many dining there, and she was causing quite a stir, for actresses were not considered highly respectable. She saw several
diners nudge their neighbors and whisper.

She smiled smugly. Let them whisper; for she had as much
right to be here as they. If her paternal great-grandfather, the
marquis, had not been cheated of his birthright and driven
from his own homeland, she would have been dining here,
too.

If Drake was aware of the scandalized looks, he paid no attention.

Edwin escorted them into a secluded room. It was far
smaller than the outside room, but just as expensively fur-

nished, with a heavy table and two solid chairs in the center. The table was covered with a white lace cloth, the edges of which were trimmed with tiny crystal pendants. A simple arrangement of flowers was the only centerpiece. Oil paintings of the hunt adorned one wall; against another were shelves on which sat Chinese vases. A third wall was concealed by a curtain, and she wondered what was behind that.

Drake ordered wine for them, as well as several appetizers. When they were alone, he leaned back in his chair and gazed at her.

"Are you suitably impressed?" he asked, amused.

She lifted an eyebrow. "By you? Never."

"Ah, that always seemed the fatal fault that lay between us."

"Many things lay between us," she whispered.

"Oh yes," he replied, his voice now maddeningly sensuous, "many things." The flickering light from the candle painted deep caverns in his face, and his one eye gleamed almost feverishly.

Acutely uncomfortable, she flushed as she recalled the times they had made love, those afternoons of complete abandonment, and she fervently hoped he could not see her blush. He had not been her first lover, but he had been the only man who could bring her such intense pleasure, pleasure that had not been forgotten, even after five years. She fanned herself, aware that the heat from her face had spread throughout her body. She hoped the wine would come soon; she needed it to calm her.

She rose suddenly and went to the wall with the drape across it and whisked the velvet back. Behind it she saw an alcove—with a bed large enough for two.

"Very convenient," she remarked dryly as she returned to the table.

"It has its uses."

The wine arrived shortly afterward, and they sipped it in silence. It was very fine, she thought, not with surprise, for he had never been a man to spare expense.

The red wine was followed by oysters, clams, mussels, and crabmeat. They spoke very little. All at once she had become almost shy with him, and she concentrated on the various *apéritifs*. They were followed by *potage aux fines herbes* and *pot-au-feu*. She had never tasted such rich soups, and she savored each spoonful. After the soups came breast of veal, ham with a honey glaze, braised beef tenderloin, veal cutlets, roast capon, and squab. With each dish came more wine. Freshly baked bread accompanied the main courses, as well as mushrooms sauteed in wine and potatoes in a dill sauce. A bowl of fresh fruit and French and Dutch cheeses rounded out the meal.

She could not believe all the food that had passed before them—or that they had eaten it all. She was aware, too, that she had drunk much more wine than she usually did. She felt light-headed at present but hoped that would soon pass away.

When they finished dining, Drake pressed the linen napkin to his lips, sat back, and looked at her. "Do you approve now?"

"Yes, very much so, Drake. The chef must be French."

"Yes."

Before they could speak further, after-dinner cordials were brought, and they enjoyed the drinks in silence. She lingered over hers, wishing the pleasant interlude would last, but sometime during her second cordial, he made a sharp gesture and she suspected that the pleasant mood was about to end.

When she had set the glass down, he spoke.

"I do not know how I can convince you I am serious about this, Mrs. Greystone. You must believe I am." His expression was earnest; she did not trust it. He had been so in the past, and nothing good had come of it.

She said nothing, but rather took another sip of the liqueur that reminded her of the fragrance of plum blossoms.

"I said I would pay you quite well."

She waited.

"Come now, you can't earn much as an actress. What would it come to? Some seventeen or twenty pounds weekly?" His voice was sharp.

"Hardly!" She felt insulted. "I earn far more than that, and while I am not the highest-paid member of the company, I have so far managed to earn my way quite comfortably, thank you!"

"So far."

"So far! And will continue to do so." She tossed her head, and remembered too late that he had always teased her about the gesture, which he said reminded him of the wild mares of France.

He did not even seem to notice. "Your mother is very concerned about the accumulating bills."

"My mother worries about everything, as you will remember."

"But mostly about you."

"You sound concerned," she said.

"I am."

She resisted the urge to laugh.

" 'Tis true, Mrs. Greystone. I am concerned about you, and your mother. That is why I am willing to pay you . . . let us say a sum of twenty thousand pounds."

She stared blankly at him. Twenty thousand. Pounds? Surely this was some sort of a joke . . . a hideous one, at that.

"You don't believe me."

"No, I don't," she said bluntly. "Would you?"

"Frankly, no, though it is the truth." He paused. "I will pay that sum for your services."

"Why, my lord? Why me? Why that amount?" She frowned across at him and watched the shadows play across his face in the candlelight. The patch over his eye was black as night, and yet it seemed to her as though there were an eye in the empty socket and that it was boring into her.

"I have given you my reasons for selecting you over other actresses."

"Does this job mean so much to you?"

He inclined his head. "It does."

She looked away as she considered. He had come to her three times in one day. He had spent a large amount upon this meal. He had risked her scorn. All to ask for her help.

"I don't know," she replied honestly. "I need time to think. After all, you sprang this upon me only this morning, and I haven't had sufficient time to consider your proposal."

"Don't take too long, my dear."

"I won't," she replied with some asperity. There he went again, pushing her. Much of the good feelings she had cultivated in the past few hours lifted, to be replaced with sour ones. Too, she wished he would not call her "my dear." It brought back too many memories, all of them pleasant.

"How long?"

"How long what?"

"How long before I have your answer?"

"I don't know. Don't plague me so!"

"Ah," he said, shaking his head again, "there I go again."

"I do not find you amusing in the least," she replied icily.

"Perhaps you find those such as Haversham or Denton more amusing?"

She remembered the dark glances directed by those gentlemen at Drake when they had left for dinner. "Why do you care if I find them amusing or not?" she asked.

"I don't."

She pressed her lips together to keep the angry retort back. She glanced away, then said in a cool voice, "Perhaps we should leave now."

"I think so. Our business is finished for the evening."

Business! she thought peevishly as he pulled back her chair and helped her to her feet. That was all he cared about—business with her. That was all the evening had meant to him.

Yet, a more reasonable part of her pointed out, what else should it have been?

Nothing, she said irritably, and did not realize she'd spoken aloud until he asked, "I beg your pardon?"

She shook her head as she felt her face burning, and she resolved to be more careful with him in the future. If there were a future, she corrected. Which she sincerely doubted.

On the return trip they spoke not a word. The journey seemed to take far longer than it should have. She would not have been surprised in the least to learn he had arranged with his driver to take the long way home.

Why would he do that? she asked herself.

He would do it because . . . because . . . Her mind grasped at reasons, failed to come up with one of substance. He would do it because he felt like it, she concluded, and because he knew it would irritate her. He always knew how to do that.

At that moment he announced they had arrived.

"At last," she murmured.

He simply chuckled.

On the front step he paused and studied her in the moonlight.

"I urge you to think quickly, Mrs. Greystone." He bent and gave her cheek a swift kiss; then he climbed into his coach and it pulled away.

She stared after him. He had kissed her. True, it was on the cheek . . . but . . . he had kissed her. After all those terrible years, after all that had transpired between them. A kiss.

Pleasure mingled with suspicion. She put one gloved hand to her cheek, as though she could still feel the imprint of his warm lips.

Nonsense, she thought a moment later, and shook herself. She let herself in and was met by Coates, her butler, who bowed and took her pelisse and gloves.

"Good evening, madame. Was it a successful performance tonight?" The elderly butler greeted her each night during the season with this same question.

"Yes, Coates, it was. I went to dinner afterward. With Lord Drake."

The tilt of his head indicated his displeasure at this news.

Not everyone was totally enchanted with him, as he so boldly assumed, she thought with some malicious pleasure. She bid Coates a good night and headed directly for the stairs.

As she paused on the third step, her hand resting on the polished banister, she could not help but wish Drake's kiss had not been on the cheek, but rather on her lips.

She shook herself at such nonsense, and went up to bed to dream dreams filled with the image of a one-eyed man.

Eight

❦

The following afternoon Ariel received a note.

It read: *What is your decision?*

She angrily crumpled the paper, tossed it away, and thought no more of it.

The day after, a second note came, its contents the same. Again she threw it away.

The third day, she received not a note, but a visitor.

She was just preparing to leave to visit her mother, when Drake was shown into the salon.

"To what do I owe this dubious pleasure?" she asked dryly.

"I'll come directly to the point, Mrs. Greystone," he said. "Have you made up your mind?"

Astonished, she stared up at him. "I've scarcely had time!"

"Three days," he pointed out ungraciously. He strode to the windows, where when she looked to him, the light shone in her eyes.

"That's not long enough, my lord, as you well know. There is so much to consider." She took a turn around the salon. "If I agreed, and if something should happen to me, who would look after my mother? Who would pay her bills? You know she is incapable of working."

"That would be taken care of."

"By you?" she asked, her tone incredulous.

"Yes."

She stared out another window. Snow had painted the streets white. Ice had formed on the outside of the window, and she reached out to trace the delicate patterns.

"Leave me alone," she said finally. "Stop haunting me. Allow me to have time to myself, and I'll make my decision."

"When?" he pressed.

"When I'm good and ready!" she snapped.

He went to the door. "I'll be waiting to hear from you, Mrs. Greystone. Good day." He bowed, polite now, and left quietly.

She pressed her fingertips against her eyes, feeling a headache starting. He wanted too much too soon.

She left the window and settled before the fire, staring moodily at the flames. The flickering colors blurred before her, and she could feel her eyelids drooping. She sighed softly and fell asleep.

It was a sleep disturbed by strange dreams. *He* was there. She was in a maze, and everywhere she turned he was waiting, watching, with that single cold gray eye staring at her accusingly. Down one avenue she found her mother reclining on a couch, staring accusingly at her. She retraced her steps, and found another branch of the maze that led to the stage, and as she ran out onto it, the entire audience stood as one, and pointed to her, and shouted as one, "Traitor." She cried aloud, and fled, and was once more running through the maze, stumbling down dark, twisting paths, lost and frightened, until at the end of one lane she saw her husband. Crying with relief, she ran toward him, but as she grew closer, her steps faltered, for this was not the Anthony she recalled. His youth and handsomeness were gone, had rotted away to bone and decaying flesh, and maggots crawled through his empty eye sockets. He loomed before her and whispered, "Traitor," his breath the fetid air of the grave. She screamed and woke.

Embers glowed in the grate. No candles had been lit, and the room was completely dark, as dark, she thought, as the maze. She shivered, recalling her horrible dream.

Traitor. Everyone in her dream had called her such. Would she be one if she refused the job? Why should she accept it, other than for the money . . . and the adventure? What was she to gain by it?

She was scared. She didn't want to leave her safe and comfortable job. She liked the company, and if Drury Lane was having problems and did not have the fine reputation it had in the previous century, certainly it was still respectable. Why should she trade it for something so uncertain? Why? Because he asked.

Sighing, she rose heavily to her feet and resolved to think of it no more. It was too late to go to her mother's, so she would have to go directly to the theatre. Perhaps there she would have refuge from the phantoms of her dream.

Despite what Ariel believed, Drake did not enjoy pressuring her. He had to do it: Addington pressured Drake, Drake pressured Ariel, and eventually, he knew, she would give in. Or would she? he asked himself.

He stretched out his legs as he reclined in the comfortable chair before the fire and reached out to the side table to grasp the crystal glass and sip the wine Pollock, his manservant, had brought to him a short time before. The wine tasted sweet and unleashed bittersweet memories.

Their courtship. It had lasted two years before she had ended it. Two years, and in that time he thought he had come to know her well, but he hadn't.

His many memories were all too vivid. He remembered the winter afternoons, the light dull and gray, that they had spent in her rooms, long cold hours made fleeting and warm by their love. Crisp mornings when he had awakened with her by his side, and he had rolled over to gaze down at her as she slept, almost like a child, her long curling lashes caressing her cheeks, her lips so pink, her breath soft and warm. He had kissed her gently awake, and she had opened her glorious green eyes and smiled up at him, glad to see him, glad to have him with her. He remembered her soft touch, her pliable mouth, her—

He brought his fist down on the table with a crash that sloshed the wine out of its goblet. Angrily he snatched the glass up and tossed the remaining wine down his throat. He threw the glass at the fireplace and watched impassively as it shattered into a thousand glittering shards.

Shattered like his life. All those memories were of before he

had been so horribly injured. He had believed his world had
ended when she had, quite without explanation, ended their
engagement, but he saw now that was not so, that really it had
not all been for the best. For she could not have loved him
with his one eye. She was too beautiful and loved perfection
too well, and his had been marred. Now he was hideous, a
scarred demon whom no woman had loved since. Oh, to be
sure, he'd had any number of whores since that time, but they
were paid to love, and in the night all cats are gray. Not so in
the morning.

He had to convince her. Somehow. He had to make her see
she was the only one who could help him, the only one who
could get close to Napoleon Bonaparte.

He loved his country, almost as much as he had loved, still
loved, Ariel. One was a lost cause, the other wasn't, and he
would not see his country invaded by others. So he sought his
lost love's help, and risked incurring even more of her wrath.
Because he had no choice, because he trusted no one else.

He reached for his glass, remembered where it lay, and felt
sheepish. His temper was the demon, not his face, and usually
the demon slumbered; but on occasion, it stirred. He rose to
his feet. He would have to make the demon sleep, for he didn't
wish it to drive her away.

Not for a second time.

"You're late, Mrs. Greystone." The manager of Drury
Lane tapped an impatient foot and consulted a pocket watch
dangling from a gold chain.

She stared at Richard Brinsley Sheridan. He was a well-
known dramatist, his most famous play being *The School for
Scandal*. A member of Parliament, he was a leader of the
Whig party and had succeeded David Garrick as manager of
the theatre at the age of twenty-five. His partner had been
Kemble, the actor, a brother of actress Sarah Siddons, but the
two men had quarreled over the percentage of their holdings in
the theatre, and Kemble had left two years earlier. Now
Sheridan managed the theatre alone, and he was not successful, for while he was an intelligent, personable man, he
had no head for finances.

She admired his work and he admired her acting, and while

they were not close, they always found much to discuss. He
had never been this sharp before, and she was astonished.

She arched an eyebrow. "I beg your pardon?"

His voice was curt. "I said you are late."

What did he mean? "By only a few minutes, Mr.
Sheridan," she replied, somewhat confused by his accusation.
"I was delayed today."

He shook his head. "That isn't good enough, Mrs.
Greystone. By a few minutes or an hour, it's all bad in the
theatre, as you should know by now. Do not permit it to happen again." And with that he stalked away.

She stared after him. He had never chided her for tardiness
before, not even when she had been delayed by more than an
hour, and tonight she had been late by only a few minutes.
What had brought this on?

She didn't have time to consider his rudeness, and she
headed straight for the dressing room, where she found a
stranger waiting outside.

"Mrs. Greystone?" he asked.

"Yes," she acknowledged, suddenly wary. He did not seem
like an admirer, although he was not poorly dressed. Perhaps
she was simply on the defensive.

"I have come about an urgent private matter. Could we talk
inside?" A number of the other actors and actresses, as well as
those who worked behind the scenes, had stopped what they
were doing to listen.

"Yes, of course."

She ushered him into the room, firmly closed the door
against the eavesdroppers in the hallway, and turned around
and faced him. She did not ask him to sit.

"What is this about?" she demanded. She was trying very
hard to be polite but found it difficult.

He looked her straight in the eye, and she realized now that
he was a tradesman.

"There is, Mrs. Greystone, the serious matter of a delinquent bill," he replied matter-of-factly. His voice was neither
sympathetic nor accusatory.

She blinked. A delinquent bill. There were so many, she
thought wearily. Which one? She felt a throbbing in her head,

signaling the advent of a headache, and she wished the man would go away.

"Yes?"

"My master has been very lenient."

"Perhaps if you identified yourself," she said waspishly, "I might know more of what you are speaking!" Creditors. Never before had they come here.

He grinned and made a sloppy bow. "Oh, sorry, ma'm. I'm Browne from Granger's Chemist Shoppe."

The chemist her mother used. Or, at least, one of them, but her account there was always the highest.

"Yes, Mr. Browne?" Her voice was more hesitant now.

"As I said, my master's been lenient and he's extended your credit for some time, but I'm afraid the bill must be paid in full now."

"In full!"

He nodded. "Sorry, ma'm, but Mr. Granger says he can't carry you no more. He needs to be paid now."

"I need only a little more time, a few weeks at the most." She wished her voice did not sound so plaintive.

Browne shook his head. "He can't, and that's the end of it, ma'm." A sly look came over his face. "I happen to know you'll be paid at the end of this week, Mrs. Greystone, so you can't plead you don't have it. We need it now."

She stared at him numbly, unable to respond. She became aware of how quiet it had grown outside the room, and she knew the others had overheard. A dull red spread from her neck to suffuse her face, and she tried desperately to cover her embarrassment. Grabbing her reticule, she jerked it open and flung a handful of coins at him, some falling onto the floor in her haste. "Here's your damned money. Now get out of my dressing room."

He counted the silver. "It's half—"

Her voice rose. "I don't care how much it is. You'll get the rest at the end of the week—when I'm paid, as you so reminded me. You won't get another penny before!" In a most unladylike fashion she pushed him from the room and slammed the door against the curious eyes in the hall. When she was alone, she leaned back and felt tears of anger and frustration roll down her cheeks. Her fists were knotted, her lips pressed together so tightly she could taste blood where she had bit them.

How dare they harass her? She always paid, albeit slowly, and surely Mr. Granger should know that. She and her mother had dealt with him for many years now, and he knew they always paid him in full in the end. Always.

She brushed away the tears, stared at herself in the mirror, and shuddered at the sight she presented. She breathed deeply, for she needed to be serene for the play.

It must be almost time for the play to start! She had forgotten about it while the odious Browne was there. She imagined what Sheridan would say if she missed her cue!

Her performance was miserable. Perplexed, Sheridan had stared at her, and the other actors had frowned, and the audience had been restive.

Miserable? Her performance had been perfectly terrible, the worst of her long career.

She rushed backstage to her dressing room without waiting for the usual admirers—how mortifying if none of them showed up. Quickly she changed into her street clothes and went outside to Wawles and the coach.

On the drive back home she hoped some of the tension of the day would ease, but it didn't. Instead, she felt as though she were a tightly coiled spring and looked down to see her gloved hands clenched. Slowly she relaxed them.

At home she went directly to her room, flung off her clothes, and crawled into her nightdress. Safe in her own boudoir, she closed her eyes wearily. Why did she feel so utterly drained? She seemed to have no strength left.

Was she ill? She swept the back of one hand to her forehead, but it felt cool. No illness of the body, but perhaps of the spirit. The day had defeated her; this evening had defeated her.

Morosely she recalled each wretched detail of the play. She had missed three—four?—cues; to her great horror, she had actually forgotten several lines in the first act; and the leading man had stepped on the hem of her skirt and almost pulled it off her body. She'd continued through the play holding on to it with one hand.

Hally had left some wine, and Ariel poured a glass and sipped it as she gazed at the fire. It tasted good, warming her throughout. Finally, she stirred and yawned. She must get to bed. It was probably late by now, and she couldn't sleep the entire morning away. There were things she had to do, after all.

She set the goblet down, crawled into bed, and within minutes was fast asleep. She slept, unburdened by dreams.

Nine

Ariel overslept, and it was early afternoon before she came downstairs to breakfast. Feeling even more tired than the night before, she tried to convince herself she really did have an appetite, and was halfway through eggs and buttered toast when Coates entered the dining room.

Benjamin Coates was a tall, spare man given to lengthy silences. Not unkind, he was simply a man of few words. He had been highly suspicious at first of anyone of a French nature, but she knew he was the most loyal of servants now.

"The morning post, ma'm."

"Thank you, Coates."

He set the salver down on the corner of the table and waited.

"Have my coach brought around in half an hour, please," she asked, not glancing up.

"Very well, ma'm." He continued to stand by the table.

She paused as she put more butter on her toast and glanced up. "Is something amiss, Coates?"

"You have had several . . . male callers already, madame. At nine this morning."

"Callers?" Everyone who knew her well knew she rose late.

He cleared his throat and gave her a meaningful look. "Not gentlemen, if you catch my drift, ma'm."

A feeling of dread began growing inside her, and her fingers tightened on the knife. She carefully set it down. "What did these . . . male callers want, Coates?"

"They said they'd come about some . . . unpaid bills."

More creditors! These, and the one last night—they all wanted their money now. Why?

Her voice was calm. "I see."

His gaze was fixed on some point behind her head. "I informed these men you were not at home, ma'm. However, they insisted upon waiting. When I fetched Mr. Wawles, they were more than readily convinced you were indeed out."

She smiled as she imagined the bulk of the gentle Wawles frightening them away.

"Did they say if they would be back?"

"No, ma'm, they did not, but I thought they looked to be persistent customers, madame. I'd watch my step, if I were you. I fear they might be waiting at the theatre."

"Thank you, Coates. I shall certainly be most careful. Perhaps I'll have Wawles come with me. That should send them packing."

His bony face creased into a rare smile. "That it should, ma'm." He bowed. "I'll call for your coach now." With that, he left the room.

She pushed away her plate. Her eggs and toast were cold, and she had little appetite left. She sifted through the morning correspondence. A frown slowly formed as she stared at the mail.

All bills; not a single letter or invitation.

She had never received so many in one day. Never. Duns, and more duns, and all within the past two days.

Something odd was going on. She glanced up at the clock on the mantel. She was going to be late to her mother's if she didn't hurry. Later she would worry about the bills. Much later.

Again Sheridan accused her of being late. She denied it, knowing she had been on time, and they fought. It was not a good evening. Nor was the next evening. Again he commented on her lateness, even though she had made it a special point to arrive early.

The night after, other things bothered him as well. The

other actresses had been complaining about her, he alleged. They said she was trying to dominate the play and was stealing others' lines. There were other charges, all of which she thought totally nonsensical.

Her temper flared at the unfairness, and she told him in no uncertain terms what she thought of the other actresses.

"Further," she said, and paused to catch her breath, "I think these are the silliest charges I have ever heard—and the most untrue, too. You know that well, too, Mr. Sheridan." She folded her arms, aware that others watched.

Unmoved by her outburst, he said, "Mrs. Greystone, you know I have admired your skill in the past, but I have been made painfully aware that it is suffering greatly. I feared you were unread for this role, but I thought I should give you the chance to prove youself. However, upon reflection, I think the role was—is—too much for you, and I do not think you have sufficiently learned it. There have been complaints about your missing cues, forgetting lines and more, all of which makes it more difficult for the cast to perform. And while a certain amount of this sort of forgetfulness can be excused, I fear this amount cannot."

She felt very light-headed. "I've had other matters on my mind of late."

He frowned and tapped a foot. "I suggest you push 'other matters' from your mind once you step onto my stage. Unless you wish to seek employment elsewhere."

"Have I heard correctly? Are you threatening me?"

"Not at all, Mrs. Greystone. I am simply advising you."

She was left completely speechless. The witnesses to her shame slowly drifted away, and she was soon alone.

That night, after she retreated to her bed after what she thought the absolutely worst performance of her career, she reviewed the past few days. The charges were trumped up. She hadn't arrived late. No one had complained about her beyond the usual petty jealousies. Yes, she had forgotten a few cues and lines, but so had the others, and Sheridan hadn't threatened to fire them.

There was also the matter of the suddenly insistent creditors. Earlier they had reassured her she had plenty of time to pay them.

Something was wrong, very wrong, and she had a feeling that meant . . . meant what? A feeling that somehow this was all quite unnatural, as if someone had begun to agitate Sheridan and the creditors. As if someone were behind it, masterminding it.

Someone like Drake.

She should have known. It was always Drake, always interfering, bossing her around, bothering her, trying to run her life.

Plaguing her.

Well, he would soon learn it was best to leave her alone now. She thought how dismayed—how shattered!—he would look tomorrow when she visited him.

She snuggled below the coverlet and fell asleep, a smile of vengeance curving her lips.

"I thought I would find you here," she announced as she was shown into the room. She dismissed the bewildered servant, took her hands out of her fur muff, and waited.

Drake appeared most unworried by her entrance. "Good afternoon, Mrs. Greystone," he said pleasantly. "Where else would you expect to find me? After all, this is my home."

"That's not what I mean," she said, "and you know it."

He had been reading when she was announced, and now he set the book down on his lap, one finger marking the spot. She strode across the library until she stood a few feet away from him, forcing him to lift his head.

"To what do I owe this dubious pleasure?" he asked, his voice dry. "I sincerely doubt it's a social call." He thought she looked beautiful—she was so angry that her eyes glittered, and he wanted nothing more than to crush her into his arms. Something, he knew, she would fight.

"You are right about this not being a social call. Quite right!"

"Well, then, I am right. Go on." He arched a dark brow.

Her lips tightened to a pale line, and he saw her hands clench. He had seen her angry in the past, and what a veritable hellcat she had been, but never had her anger been so controlled as now. Controlled, he thought ruefully. She was—they both were—older now.

She tossed her head. He loved it when she did that. He found it endearing and spirited. "I have come to inform you that I know what you are doing."

"Oh?" His tone was filled with amusement now. "It would appear that I am reading—or was before I was interrupted."

"No," she said tightly. "You know I don't mean that." Her eyes locked onto his face, and her gaze did not waver. "I know now about the pressure you have been putting on me this past sennight." He said nothing to this all-too-true allegation. "I know you have managed to have my creditors dun me, and that you are somehow coercing—or should I say bribing?—Mr. Sheridan into making my life at the theatre miserable. I know all of this. You cannot hide it any longer!" She crossed her arms. Again he remained silent. "Have you nothing to say?" she demanded.

His shrug was elegant. "Why should I, when you seem to know everything?"

"Ah, then you do not deny it?"

"No."

"Oh." His ready admission of his transgression took the wind from her sails. She wasn't sure how to proceed now. She had been certain he would deny all charges, whereupon she would proceed to lay the facts before him, strip his pride from him like thin strips of skin with her righteous anger, and when he was quivering from her wrath, she would depart without another word. Except that it wasn't going according to her plan.

"Is that all you came to say?"

"No." She made an effort to recover, feeling the anger and frustration of the last few days flooding back. Her voice was steady when she spoke. "No, that is not all I have to say, my lord. I resent very much your high-handedness in 'arranging' my life. I have done quite well without you in the past five years, and will continue to do quite well without you in the future, and I would kindly appreciate no further interference from you."

His voice was calm. She could not, for all that she tried, seem to shake him. "You seem to forget that it was you, not I, who ended the engagement, Mrs. Greystone."

"Our past feelings for one another have no bearing upon this matter!" she said angrily.

"Ah, but I think our past feelings, as you term it, have everything to do with it." He rose, and was so close to her she was forced to step back. He grasped her upper arms before she could elude him. She could not contain herself, and a shudder rippled through her body, but whether it was from dislike or some half-remembered desire, she could not tell.

"Let go of me," she whispered. Her mouth was dry, and she could scarcely speak, but she willed herself to.

Obediently he dropped his hands to his sides.

Her voice was almost a whisper. "Again: I do not like what you have done, and wish you to stop at once." She would not look at him, could not, for she was trembling and could feel flashes of heat, then cold, coursing through her body. Where he had touched her arms, she seemed to burn with a fierce heat.

"I cannot promise."

"Then I cannot say what I will do, only that I will no longer tolerate this treatment from you." Finally she raised her eyes to him. His one gray eye seemed so cold, so remote, so very uncaring, and she wondered that she had ever believed she knew him.

"Very well," he replied coolly.

She turned on her heel and marched across the library, her body still trembling. He did not move. When she reached the door, she looked back, appraising him.

"I am very glad I broke off our engagement, my lord. In the past I have from time to time regretted my actions, but now I know I was right, for I see all too clearly what you are."

"Which is?"

"A monster." With that she slipped out the door, quietly closing it behind her.

Ten

Fire leaped upward in sinuous tongues, flickered, beckoned seductively to her. She cringed, fearing the flames would reach out to embrace and burn her. Higher they jumped, blazing yellow and red and orange, while sparks shot out into the shadows beyond. Fascinated, she watched. Beyond the curtain of fire loomed a dark shape, and she turned to run, but her feet seemed rooted to the earth. She tried to cry out, but could not.

Upward the menacing shadow loomed, billowing higher and higher, a darkness threatening to swallow her. Closer to her it roiled. It surged and ebbed and eddied and grew, and then it spread its dark wings above her and floated downward, maddeningly slow, swallowing her. She felt something hard snake around her, pulling her closer to its maw, and she screamed and screamed, and tried to pull loose, but it would not let go. It melted and became two strong arms holding her close, and she heard a man's breath, saw the outline of a head. He reached down and their lips met.

Overhead, lightning forked through the midnight sky and thunder rumbled, and the earth surged beneath her feet. As she and the man touched, she shivered, feeling the tendrils of a half-forgotten emotion curling in her very core. The tendrils took root, grew, became an ache coursing through her. Her veins flowered with blood that seemed to boil, and her mouth opened under the pressure of his. His tongue, sure and strong, darted in to caress hers, and she moaned as the pleasure swept through her, and she clutched at his bare shoulders, her nails pressing, digging in his fevered flesh, leaving bloodied trails. Their bodies twisted closer, and she could feel the throbbing of him, could feel his heart beating against her chest. They gripped each other harder, until their skin melted and melded.

Around them the flames burned blue, then orange, then white, and they leaped upward to the lightning, and joined with it, and the sound was deafening. Wave after wave of white-red heat beat against her, making her tremble and call out. She closed her eyes and saw the flames as they fanned higher and faster, faster and higher, until all at once she was moaning, crying out in pain and pleasure, clinging to his sweat-slick body, writhing as his hands caressed her breasts, her stomach, the moist triangle. His tongue and fingers were insistent, burning, demanding, and she ached and was inflamed with desire. She stroked his body, running her fingers lightly over the toned muscles, stroking the warmth and hardness of him. Their bodies entwined and became one, they sought all the pleasure they could give, could receive, and the fire consumed them, burning them, but she did not feel it, felt only him, only him, and she opened her eyes, and it was—

Drake.

Sitting bolt upright, she stared blankly around. For a moment she didn't know where she was and was scared. As she awakened, she realized she was in her own bedroom.

The flames and heat, all of it, had been only a dream, a nightmare. She pushed back a damp curl that had fallen over her eyes. Trembling, she touched her arms. The skin was warm and moist, almost as though they had . . . almost as if he . . . No, she insisted, it was only a dream. There was nothing real about it.

Nothing.

And yet, the dream . . . nightmare . . . had been so real, so convincing. Shivering slightly, she wrapped her arms around her raised knees and rocked gently, recalling all too vividly the passion of the dream.

It had been convincing because five years ago she had foolishly lain with him, within the warm circle of his arms, had discovered the mysteries of his body. But that was in the past, was all behind her now.

Or was it?

The past seemed to be coming to the present now. *Plaguing* her, and she could not restrain a smile.

The past . . . so much good and bad. She wrenched her mind away. She wouldn't think about it, or him, or how wonderful it felt to have his arms around her, his lips on hers.

She closed her eyes as she rested her head on her knees. Once more in the darkness of her mind she saw the flames. At last she stirred again and lay down, rolling onto one side. Wearily she bade sleep come. But it would not. For hours she tossed, seeking sleep, and her bed sheets grew hot and crumpled, and still she could not rest. She could not dismiss from her mind the exquisite touch of his fingers as he sought the center of her pleasure.

He awoke in darkness, and the air was warm and musky. His skin was damp, almost feverish, and he drew in a deep breath.

He had had a dream, a dream of love and passion, of a woman.

And the woman had been Ariel.

He laughed shortly and sat up, rubbing his face with one hand.

Not Ariel. Surely not after all these years. It was someone else, someone who looked like her, but who wasn't—

No, it had been she.

He could vividly recall all of it. They had been making love, and there had been flames that burned to the heavens, and lightning that arced overhead, and darkness around them, sheltering them and there had been Ariel.

The softness of her skin, the line of her cheek, the grace of her neck and shoulders. He had caressed her, kissed her lips, her thighs, stroked her until she was aching with pleasure, and she had moaned and writhed and called him by name, and she had pressed her fingers, her nails, into his shoulders, digging, clutching, as they had melded into one and then—

Then it had all gone away.

Just ended.

And he had awakened abruptly, out of breath, hot to the touch, his desire unquenched.

Somewhat unsteadily, he rose and padded across to the fireplace. He poured some wine and sat on the floor and stared into the flames.

It had been so real, the sounds, the caresses, the heat.

So real. He frowned, and tossed down the remainder of the wine and set the glass back on the table. He stood and stretched, and massaged his shoulders. They ached as they had in the dream. He felt something sticky on his fingers, pulled his hand away, and knelt by the fire to see better.

Blood stained his fingertips.

"Suspended?" Her voice was an echo of his. "Why?"

Sheridan studied her for a moment, then glanced away. "I told you why, Mrs. Greystone. You are insubordinate. You flaunt the rules of the company; you do not consider others, or our schedules—"

"Nonsense," she interrupted, her voice cold. "You know as well as I do that those are lies. Christopher Drake has been talking to you—and paying you as well, I've little doubt. I know the theatre has financial problems, and I am sure he has been aiding you—in return for a 'small' favor." She stared at him. "Am I correct, Mr. Sheridan?" She did not wait for his answer; his silence confirmed her suspicions. She drew herself up proudly. "There are other theatres in London, and I am sure I will find someone who can appreciate my abilities." With that she stiffly walked away. He did not call her back.

Outside on Russell Street she stopped and realized how severely she was trembling. From anger. Hurt. And shame.

She had been suspended from the job she loved, that she needed to survive, and it was all *his* fault. It wasn't right that he should come back into her life and interfere this way. It wasn't fair.

Ah, but who ever said— began an inner voice.

No! she thought savagely. I won't listen!

The voice subsided.

It was because of this ridiculous offer. That damned job. Her problems had begun there.

"I've come to enlist your aid," he'd said.

What utter, utter nonsense, and she damned him for show-ing his face to her again.

She pressed her lips together, hunched her shoulders for a moment, then threw them back and walked briskly away from the theatre. At the corner of Russell and Catherine she stopped to look back at it. Drury Lane. Her home for years. No young actress would turn down a job there. Hers would be filled in no time at all, and she wouldn't be able to return.

No matter. Sheridan had suspended her; she had gone one step further by informing him she would go elsewhere. There were other theatres in the city, and she would find another job. She would show him—and Drake!

Covent Garden didn't need young actresses at the present, she was informed.

Nor did the Haymarket.

Nor did the Opera House.

Angry and resentful, she kept on, determined to find work. It was the same tale with Sadler's Wells, the Royal Amphi-theatre, and the Royalty. She would not even consider the Royal Circus on Blackfriars Road.

Not a single London theatre would accept her—not even with her credentials. After nearly three weeks of searching, she was frustrated and angry and defeated and didn't know where to turn. Not to her mother, for Etoile, as much as Ariel loved her, was in league with that devil. Ariel had no friends from the theatre, and none of her admirers were paying calls except for one, John Haversham, and he was more than willing to provide a sympathetic ear and a willing shoulder for her to cry on, if she so desired.

But she did not so desire. Not at present, for she was too angry and wanted only to talk—or rather, to rail against her misfortune.

"Don't be distressed, love," Haversham said when she next saw him. "It's not the end of the world, after all."

"It is for me. Whatever will I do? I suppose I could swallow my pride and wait for Sheridan to lift the suspension." She sighed. If he ever did. For all she knew, he might already have hired someone to replace her.

"Well . . . ," Haversham began.

"Well what?"

"You know you don't have to go back to a theatre."

"I don't understand, John. What are you suggesting? That I quit? And what would I do?" She knew she was being short with him, but she couldn't help it.

His smile faltered for a second. "You don't have to return to the theatre, Ariel—you could leave it." When she did not reply, he continued as though he thought she hadn't understood. "You know, you could stop being an actress." He reached out to stroke her cheek.

The anger and frustration boiled up inside her, and she lashed out at him.

"I have absolutely no intention of ever voluntarily leaving the theatre, John. Especially to become some man's mistress, or wife!"

He stared at her for a moment, his babyish face hurt, and then said he thought perhaps he ought leave now.

Stricken, she watched him bow out of the room, and she wanted to call him back to apologize, but the words stuck in her throat. She didn't move as he rode away.

For a long time she sat, until the light faded from the windows and the room grew dark, sat until Hally crept in to light the candles. Even then Ariel did not stir, and, frightened by her mistress's expression, the maid left hastily.

When a clock somewhere in the house struck eight, Ariel stirred. She looked around, as if noting for the first time where she was, and she rose a little stiffly and went to the window.

Eight. She should have been at the theatre, would have been preparing to go onstage. Before. But not now. She passed a hand across her face. She was tired . . . so very tired of trying to find a job, tired of being told she wasn't right for the role, or that they didn't need actresses, that they didn't need *her*.

So tired, and she missed her work, and she worried about money. She had enough put away so that she could pay her immediate bills for several weeks, but if she were unemployed any longer, her savings would dwindle. Would disappear. How then would she care for her mother?

She pressed her cool fingertips against her burning eyelids and drew in a ragged breath.

She could wait. Maybe something would open in a few days. And maybe it wouldn't. Still the creditors would dun her. Oh yes, she could wait, and nothing would change. She would still have no job.

There was only one alternative.

He had been so clever, had maneuvered her until this was the only avenue left.

She had no choice.

Slowly she turned and left the room. Downstairs, she called for her carriage. The trip was interminable, and when she arrived she wasn't surprised to learn he was in. Pollock left them alone in the library.

Ariel went across to the fireplace and held her hands out to the warmth. She looked at him as he stood so close to her.

"I can't fight any longer. I'm too tired. I'll work for you, my lord. You win."

ACT TWO

March 1804

Eleven

⚜

Ariel's training as a spy began the next afternoon.

They had arranged to meet in the park, ostensibly for a ride. He told her nothing more.

They were to meet at three. It was now half past, and Ariel had still not arrived.

Drake trotted his restless chestnut up and down the lane and scanned the crowds. No sign yet. His mount tossed its head, whinnied, and pranced. He stroked the horse's neck.

Today he had dressed with special care, taking more time than usual. Normally, he cared little for what he wore, much to the despair of Pollock. Had Drake been left to his own devices, he would have worn whatever was most handy in his wardrobe. Today was quite different, though. He wore a chocolate brown riding coat of fine cloth, buckskin breeches, a beaver hat, and hussar boots with tassels. He had even suffered Pollock to tie his cravat, and while it was not in the latest style, it was impeccable.

He swung his riding whip thoughtfully against his boot and frowned. He nodded to several acquaintances, but did not urge his horse forward so that he could talk to them. He had no wish to involve himself in idle conversation. It would make it awkward when Ariel showed.

If she showed, he corrected.

And why shouldn't she? Yesterday, when they had met again, she had seemed willing to cooperate. Perhaps she'd had a change of mind and decided she could do without his offer. And if she had . . . He shrugged, trying to feel nonchalant, but he knew he could not replace her.

He would give her until four o'clock, he decided, and then he would leave the park. If she wished to contact him, she could do so by sending around a note to him. Otherwise, he would not contact her for a day or so.

But he reminded himself that Ariel had always been late, as long as he'd known her. She seemed unable to arrive anywhere on time. The more he thought about it, the angrier he became. She knew he couldn't spare the time to wait on her convenience. She had always known that, and yet she'd persisted in being late.

The tap against his boot became insistent, and he was about to turn his horse around to leave, when he spotted her. She was cantering toward him on a fine gray.

She reined in a few feet from him. "I'm sorry I'm late, my lord. My mother— That is, Nooks came around this morning for me. My mother had a fever all night long, and it had not yet broken this morning. I stayed with her until she was resting more comfortably, and then I hurried to change."

His anger faded as his concern for Etoile took over. "I am sorry to hear this news. You say she is better now?"

Nodding, she brushed a hand across her cheek where a curl had come to rest. He noticed for the first time how exhausted she looked.

"She was sleeping when I left, and was certainly much cooler to my touch, thank God. I just don't know what's to become—" She choked a little and stopped, and looked away, plainly embarrassed. She cleared her throat, then looked back, her emotions under control. "Well, come now, my lord, what are we to do besides ride?"

"I'll tell you in due time. However, we are expected elsewhere."

They wound their way through the clogged streets of London and within an hour reached a house on the fringes of the city. It was enclosed by an immense stone wall, and only its roof could be seen from the road. As they approached the iron gates, a servant swung them open. Once inside, Ariel surveyed the house. Its two brick-and-wood stories were of a rambling design that suggested many architectural styles. Once within the compound, she and Drake were effectively cut off from the city. No sounds drifted in, and it was almost as though they had been swept away to the countryside.

They trotted down a short gravel drive, then stopped just a few feet short of a marble portico, the main entrance to the house. As Drake helped Ariel down, he looked up at her face and was surprised to see her blushing. He was suddenly very aware of his hands around her waist, and when he set her down, his hands felt as if they were on fire.

The door opened at that instant, and a man hailed them as he took the marble steps two at a time. "Drake, good to see you. I didn't think you'd make it this afternoon."

Drake made a slight bow in the other's direction, casting a sidelong glance at Ariel. "We were detained, Sir Broderick."

"Hope it's nothing serious."

"I trust not."

Ariel had been silent throughout this exchange, and now Drake turned toward her. "Broddy, this is Mrs. Greystone; and this is my old friend Sir Broderick Chalmers, an ex-seaman too, but one who has made something more of himself than I."

"Nonsense!" Chalmers exploded into laughter and clapped Drake on the shoulder. "Indeed, he is pulling your leg, madame."

"I suspect so," she said quietly.

"Ah, well, good." He smiled at her and received a quiet smile in return.

Drake watched her look at Chalmers as Sir Broderick bent to kiss her hand in an old-fashioned manner. Chalmers was as tall as he, with a muscular form well set off by his exquisite clothes. His face was rugged, not exactly handsome, but he had a manly quality that endeared him to women. Even now, Drake could not but wonder if Ariel found Chalmers attractive. He pressed his lips together at the unexpected stab of jealousy and told himself it didn't matter if she did. He couldn't have cared less.

Or did he?

It was more than apparent that Chalmers was quite smitten with Ariel. Many men were, Drake reminded himself, for she was a beautiful woman, and there was the allure of her profession, as well.

"Do we have to stand out here all day and freeze in the wind, Broddy, or could we possibly go inside now?" Drake asked. He had intended the query as a good-natured gibe, but it came out brusquely.

Chalmers smiled affably, quite unperturbed by Drake's impatience. "Of course not! My fault completely, and what a fool I am to keep you both out here!" Chalmers slipped Ariel's arm through his. "Now, let me escort you in, Mrs. Greystone."

Drake, following the pair up the stairs, listened as Chalmers recounted the history of his house and family to Ariel. Drake had heard it numerous times and paid little attention to it, for with each telling the tale grew more elaborate.

The floor of the entry hall was inlaid black and white marble, and overhead a four-tiered crystal chandelier gleamed in the afternoon sunlight. They passed through a long hallway, the walls lined with portraits of Chalmerses long since dead, and at least reached a salon of vast proportions. After they settled into brocaded chairs around the marble fireplace, Chalmers rang for tea.

"Are you sure we have time for that, Broddy?" Drake asked, then told himself he was being overly hasty.

"Quite. We'll be getting a late start today, so there isn't much that can be done, anyway. I thought we might just plan our days."

"Excuse me," Ariel said at that moment, looking first to one man, then the other, "but could one of you gentlemen please explain what I am doing here?'

Chalmers stared at his friend. "Good God, Drake, don't tell me you didn't tell her!"

Drake grimaced. "I didn't have time. We were late as it was, and once here I thought—"

Chalmers didn't wait. "My dear young lady, you are here to learn to be a spy!"

She cast a glance at Drake.

"Oh, it's safe here," he said. "Broddy and I have been working together for some years now. He aids in the training."

Chalmers smiled, showing off his dazzling teeth to good effect. "I am one of the surest shots in England, as well as one of her leading swordsmen."

Modest, thought Drake sourly; but underneath his ill-humored mood, he recognized the truth of his friend's words.

"I shall explain," Chalmers continued. "Each day we will discuss with you what we expect you to find. That will include what to listen for, as well as how to recognize it. Also, you will be instructed in the art of shooting a pistol, wielding a dagger, and, I think"—here he looked to Drake for confirmation and received it—"handling a sword."

"A sword!"

"Have you ever used one?"

"Never—except upon the stage, and it was wooden."

He smiled again. "Mine are a good deal heavier than wood, but I think you shall be able to manage quite well. You look quite strong."

She met his gaze calmly. "I am."

A servant entered at that moment. After filled teacups were passed around and the servant had withdrawn, Chalmers said, "Now, to business. We'll talk a little bit longer, and then, Mrs. Greystone, I wish for you to ride out here tomorrow afternoon and your training will begin in earnest."

"Very well."

Drake looked up sharply from his cup. Had he heard an eager note in her voice? He dismissed the thought.

"I'll be here, too, Broddy," he added casually.

Chalmers quickly masked his surprise. "Oh? Good, old man, although I thought you beset with mountains of work and not able to spare any time for this sort of thing."

Drake smiled. "I do have work at the office, but I want to help with Mrs. Greystone's training as well."

"Good, good." Chalmers's voice seemed a little constrained. "Perhaps you should come tomorrow at eleven?" He looked to Ariel for confirmation.

"That would be fine," Drake said. "We'll see you then."

Chalmers escorted them outside. When the two visitors reached the gates, Drake turned around and saw Chalmers was no longer on the portico. The afternoon sunlight had faded while they'd lingered in the house, and now a cold wind blew. Small snowflakes swirled in front of the horses' noses, and their breath puffed in the air. From time to time he gazed at her, confident that she would notice him doing so in the gloom. If she did, she gave no indication. She had been very subdued today, without any fire. Most unusual. Perhaps it was because of her mother.

They did not speak until they reached her house, and there she thanked him.

"Will you be returning to your mother's?" he asked.

"I think so; there is no other place for me to go tonight."

He was not unaware of the barb. He had done what must be done. "Do you wish me to come with you, Mrs. Greystone?"

She shook her head. "No, I'm sorry, but I wish to be alone with her. If you would, call upon her tomorrow, though."

He nodded. "Very well." He took her hand in his and raised it to his lips.

She looked up at him, a wry smile touching her lips. "You are being most gallant, my lord."

"I can be . . . at times."

"At times."

He pulled his brows together in a thoughtful frown. "Mrs. Greystone, if there is anything else amiss that I—"

"No, please," she said quickly, "there is nothing for you to do. I am simply tired from sitting up with my mother. I will be fine after a good night's rest."

"If you insist."

"I do." She pulled her hand away. "I must go in. I'm cold, and must change."

"Ariel." The sound of her name stayed her.

"Yes?"

What would he say to her? he wondered. What could he say? Liquid fire surged through his veins as he gazed at her, as he stared down into her lovely green eyes. He wanted to hold her, wanted to kiss her. Something of what he was thinking must have been conveyed to her, for she took a step backward.

He bent and kissed the top of her head, then watched as she slipped through the open door. He waited until it closed and then spun away to snatch the reins of his horse. He swung up into the saddle, then trotted off without looking back. He missed the slight movement of a curtain at a front window.

Twelve

Ariel aimed the pistol and fired.

"Excellent," Drake called as he crossed the room to check on the mannequin. Her aim had been true, for the ball had gone through the mannequin's chest. "You are a most apt pupil."

"I had very good instruction," she said calmly.

He frowned, not knowing if she meant him or Chalmers, then decided he would accept it as a compliment to him.

Ariel gazed at the still-smoking pistol. It was one of a pair of flintlock pocket pistols made by John Prosser of Charing Cross, and its smaller size made it more adaptable to a woman's hand. She was receiving her instruction in a converted outbuilding at the back of Chalmers's property. Once a stable, it now housed his collection of firearms and swords. It was secluded, and they were safe from prying eyes. For the past sennight, she and her instructors had been concentrating on pistols—how to load them, how to fire them, how to clean them. Later, she would receive instruction on how to handle a dagger. Drake had deemed it unnecessary for her to learn to handle a sword; the likelihood of her having to use one was quite remote. A pistol and dagger were quite another matter. Too, Drake wished to teach her how to defend herself with her hands. Chalmers had been reluctant, but Drake had pointed out that a weapon might not always be at hand for her. He prayed she would never have to put the pistols to use, but she really was an exceptional shot, particularly when he considered that she had never held a pistol before. But then, as he well knew, Ariel did many things capably.

"Back inside now," he said.

She handed the pistol to one of Chalmers's servants, a discreet man who had never spoken to her, and returned to the house, where they found Chalmers in his book-lined study.

"I saw you earlier, my dear," he said as he strode forward to take her hands in his. "You are quite the excellent markswoman."

"Thank you, Sir Broderick."

"Come, come now, Mrs. Greystone, haven't I told you to call me Broddy?"

She shot an amused look at Drake. "Very well, Broddy."

"Ah, here's tea." He smiled as they sat at opposite ends of a green and white striped settee. "I hope you'll both stay to supper. Masters has outdone himself in anticipation of your dining with me."

"I really couldn't—" she began.

"'Please, Mrs. Greystone," Chalmers pleaded, a hurt look in his eyes.

Drake raised his teacup to his lips and wished that it contained something stronger.

"Very well, Broddy."

"Good." He turned to Drake and arched an eyebrow. "And you, old friend?"

Drake smiled. "I'd be more than happy to accept your invitation, Broddy."

The other man's smile faltered momentarily, but then he regained his composure. "Excellent. Fenton," he said to the servant who had waited on them, "please tell Masters that there will be two more for dinner tonight."

"Very good, sir." Fenton left the room.

"I thought you said your cook knew we were staying," Ariel said.

"Ah, not precisely. He was anticipating it, as was I." Once again he smiled, and Drake found himself wishing that his friend would stop acting so ridiculous. He knew Broddy was entirely serious, and that didn't help ease his black mood.

"Well, you look up in the boughs tonight," the other man said. "What's amiss?"

"Nothing. Simply coordinating various matters in my head." His reply had come out curtly, but there was nothing he could do now. "Mrs. Greystone," he said.

"Yes?"

"How is your mother faring?"

"Much better, my lord. And thank you, Sir Broderick—Broddy, I mean—for the basket of fruit. It cheered my mother considerably."

Drake raised an eyebrow. "What's this?"

Chalmers shrugged. " 'Twas nothing."

"It was no such thing, Sir Broderick. Why," she said, her voice growing eager in a manner Drake disliked, "she was thrilled to receive it, and the doctor said it was one of the best things for her."

"Then I shall send others."

"Oh no, you couldn't—"

"But of course I could." He smiled again. "I wish to do whatever I can to help your mother."

Drake brought his cup down with a crash on the saucer and watched as a tiny crack appeared in the plate. "I broke it," he said, his voice tinged with chagrin.

"No matter. Fenton will replace it."

Drake nodded, but then grew aware that Ariel was watching him. No doubt she was embarrassed by his behavior. To be truthful, *he* was.

They chatted a while longer; then Chalmers rose to say he would check on the progress of their dinner. He bowed over Ariel's hand and left.

Once the door had closed, she turned and looked at Drake. "You don't like him."

"Nonsense. He is a friend."

"But still you don't like him."

"Absolute drivel, Mrs. Greystone. Your mind is cluttered with piffle."

Her temper flared. "It is not, as you well know! And I am not imagining this." She stopped, a slow, sly smile forming on her lips. "Are you jealous, my lord? Is that why you have been so grumpy today in his presence?"

"No."

"Ah." She relaxed against the back of the settee and nod-ded to herself. "I thought so."

He rose and went to a window to stare out at the snowy landscape. It was almost dark now, and it would be turning much colder. Perhaps it would even snow. Perhaps they would be forced to spend the night here. Perhaps . . . perhaps nothing. "I think you are making much over nothing."

"Perhaps."

He disliked that superior tone in her voice. He whirled. "And if I am jealous, what of it, might I ask? Remember, it was not my idea to terminate the engagement." She flushed at that. "This may come as a surprise to you, Mrs. Greystone, but it was many years before I overcame my hurt—and my love for you. It did not end on that day, as yours so obviously did. And if some . . . feelings . . . still linger, and if I feel some jealousy—which I most certainly do not!—then I can hardly be raked over the coals for such!"

In the silence of the room there was a dry cough from the other end of the study.

Drake whirled.

Chalmers had entered while Drake was talking. "Masters says dinner will be served in an hour. Would anyone care for drinks?"

"I would," Drake replied shortly.

"A sherry for you, Mrs. Greystone?" Chalmers asked as he smiled at her.

"Yes, thank you. Broddy?"

"Yes?" He paused on his way to the liquor cabinet.

"If you are so insistent upon my calling you Broddy, then I insist that you not be so formal with me." She smiled, dimp-ling, and the look she gave Broderick out of those exotic green eyes cut deeply into Drake. "Please call me Ariel. All my friends do."

"Excellent . . . Ariel."

Drake pressed his lips together. Broderick and Ariel chatted a while longer, while Drake drank his wine and brooded, and before long it was time to go in for dinner. Before Drake could make a move, Chalmers offered to escort her into the dining room, and that left Drake to trail after them.

As he watched Chalmers seat her, he knew he'd made a mistake. He shouldn't have brought Ariel there at all, not even for the instruction. He could have done it completely by himself. But he'd thought he wouldn't have the time, nor the patience if she proved slow, and so he'd gone to Chalmers, who had helped him before. His friend who wasn't helping him in this matter.

"You're not saying much," Chalmers said as they dined. "Aren't you enjoying the meal, Drake?"

"It's fine. Excellent, as usual." In fact, he had not even been aware of what he was eating. He glanced down at his plate. Slices of roast beef had been piled on it, along with creamed potatoes in dill, and winter vegetables. It *was* good. Now he would simply have to concentrate on enjoying it. He watched as Ariel flirted expertly with Broddy. She paid no attention to him. He knew what she was doing, and she was succeeding quite well.

Oh yes, she'd been right. He was jealous, very jealous, of Chalmers for commanding her attention. Jealous because this wasn't the first time it had happened between the two men. There had been a woman once before, years before Ariel, a woman for whom he had cared, and foolishly he had introduced her to Chalmers, and soon she had left him for the other.

It was his fault, too, and not that of his friend. He was too dour, brooded too much, was not adept at turning a compliment. No wonder the women did not flock to him.

But he did not want women flocking to him. He wanted one woman only.

Tonight he wanted her more than anything else. Tonight he did not have her.

After dinner, Chalmers announced that he wouldn't be available next week as he was going out to his country estate to check on various matters that could no longer wait his attention. Drake and Ariel were to continue meeting at his house.

Ariel glanced at Drake but did not say anything. Drake tapped his finger thoughtfully on the arm of his chair and sipped at his wine.

The three chatted a while longer, and finally Drake rose. "I think perhaps I should leave now. I've work to do in the morning."

"So soon?" Chalmers did not seem in the least sorry to see him go.

"Yes, I'm sorry. It was an excellent meal, as usual, Broddy." He went to Ariel. "I will see you in the morning, Mrs. Greystone. At the usual time, I trust," and there was a hint of irony in his voice. He little doubted what would occur between Chalmers and Ariel once he left.

Fenton appeared at that moment and whispered something into his master's ear. Chalmers went quickly to a window and pushed aside a curtain. He looked back over his shoulder and beckoned to Drake.

"I think, dear fellow, that you might be changing your mind, after all."

Drake stared through the glass. Snow fell heavily, and he could see only a few inches beyond the window.

"Fenton says it's terrible outside, and I could not be a good host and permit my guests to venture forth in such a blizzard. You must stay the night."

Drake protested, but the other man would not listen. He instructed Fenton to prepare the guest rooms and said he would be delighted with their company.

"And my dear lady, will you stay? You have not said!" Her host looked expectantly toward her.

"Of course, Broddy. I would be delighted to spend the night here." And with that she smiled at Drake.

A few hours later she made her excuses and went to bed. Both men watched as she rose gracefully and left the room.

"A delightful woman," Chalmers said, stretching his legs out toward the fire.

"In some ways."

"Ah, yes, you two have a history of fighting." He shook his head. "A shame."

"Yes."

"Quite an accomplished actress, I understand, though I have not seen her upon the stage."

"She is good."

Chalmers chuckled. "Drake, what has come over you tonight? I've never seen you so taciturn. Was it something I

said? Have I insulted you in some manner? I beg your pardon
if I have!''

He sighed. "No, Broddy, that's not it.'' He rubbed the skin
under the patch. It ached tonight. Perhaps it was the cold.
" 'Tis nothing of import, so do not concern yourself.''

"Very well.'' Chalmers proceeded to elaborate on Ariel's
accomplishments, and Drake listened and watched the clock.
It amused him to know they both wanted to go upstairs, knock
upon her door, and slip into her room to wish her more than a
good night. Chalmers was an excellent host, and Drake knew
his good breeding would not permit him to leave before his
guest did—unless his guest so directed.

And his guest was quite content to stay put.

Finally, when the clock had chimed three, Drake rose and
stretched. "I'd best be thinking of going to bed now, I suppose. Ariel and I will have training tomorrow.'' He glanced
sharply at the other man.

"Yes, yes.'' Chalmers had suddenly become impatient.
Drake knew why and was in no hurry.

"What do you suggest?''

"Suggest?'' Chalmers frowned, his thoughts obviously elsewhere. "What do you mean?''

"For the training,'' Drake gently reminded him. "What do
you think of the dagger tomorrow? We could concentrate
upon that until you leave.''

"Leave? Oh yes. The dagger will be fine.'' He waved a
vague hand. "We'll settle that on the morrow, Drake, when
we're both wide awake.''

"Ah yes, I think that would be better.'' Drake smiled and
strolled toward the door. Chalmers followed so closely behind
that when Drake stopped, Chalmers almost bumped into him.
"What do you say to another drink, Broddy?''

"Drink? What? No! I mean, it's fine if you want to stay
here and have another one, old man, but I've had enough and
I think I'll call it a day.'' He made a show of yawning. "Tired,
and all that. I'll see you in the morning then.''

They walked up the stairs together and paused on the land-
ing. Chalmers had arranged it so that Ariel's room was to the
left of his and Drake's to the right. He would hear Drake
whenever he left his room.

They headed down the corridor. Neither spoke. Outside Chalmers's door, their host stopped and smiled.

"Good night, Drake."

"Good night, Chalmers."

Drake went on to his room and paused just inside the doorway. As expected, he heard a door open, then footsteps receding down the hall. There was a soft knock down the hallway, and he waited. Nothing happened. He stepped out into the gloomy corridor and saw Chalmers rattling the doorknob. The door seemed to be either locked or barred. Chalmers looked up at that moment and saw Drake.

"Just checking to make sure that Mrs. Greystone is safely tucked away," Chalmers said, his voice nervous. His hand dropped from the doorknob.

"I trust she is?"

"Oh yes, quite. Well, good night again, old man." Chalmers headed into his room.

"Good night again, Broddy." He was smiling as he went into his room and closed the door. He knew Broddy wouldn't try to get into Ariel's room again tonight. It was obvious she wanted no nighttime visitors.

From the bed where she had been safely tucked in for hours, Ariel listened to Drake and Chalmers as they stopped outside her room. She heard two doors close.

She glanced at the dresser she had shoved in front of the door earlier. It was bulky, and would take a great deal of effort for someone to move aside.

She knew Drake would not attempt to enter her room. Broddy, she didn't trust.

Oh, to be sure she had flirted with him, using the wiles she had learned upon the stage. She had enjoyed it, too, knowing it made Drake more jealous. The whole point of this evening's exercise was simply to make Drake incredibly jealous.

She liked Broddy well enough, but not enough to invite him into her room. She intended to keep him out as best she could, even if she had to move all her furniture against the door.

Alerted by a noise, she cocked her head and listened intently. Stealthy footsteps approached her room. There was a pause, and she caught her breath, waiting. Someone tried the doorknob gently. When the door did not swing open, the doorknob was jiggled, then rattled, and an attempt was made to force it open.

Then she heard voices.

"Just checking to make sure that Mrs. Greystone is safely tucked away." Chalmers, outside the door.

"I trust she is?" Drake's voice was faint, as though he were by his room.

"Oh yes, quite. Well, good night again, old man."

"Good night again, Broddy."

She heard both doors close again and smiled. She trusted the matter was settled for the night, and now she could get some sleep.

She reached out to snuff the candle, then lay down. She was tired, for her training was strenuous, made more so by having Drake around, for he watched her constantly. Too, she still worried about her mother.

Finally she closed her eyes, snuggled deep beneath the warm covers, and bade sleep come. But it was a long time visiting her, for her mind was filled with thoughts of Drake, of his kisses, and his embraces, and no matter how she tried to deny them, she could not. She must face the fact that she truly ached, that she wanted him, and that perhaps, just perhaps, she might still be in love with him.

Thirteen

"How am I doing, my lord?" Ariel lowered the embossed dagger and stared across at her instructor, who seemed lost in reverie.

He looked up. "I beg your pardon?"

"I asked how I was doing?"

"Fine, as always, Mrs. Greystone. Your skill with weapons is remarkable."

"For a woman."

"Yes, for a woman, for most—all in my acquaintance, I might add—are not trained in such matters. Not all spies need these skills, it's true. However, it's always best to be prepared for the worst. Are you tired, or would you like to continue?"

"I'd like to continue, please."

He was pleased. She moved back into position, and he lunged for the knife. She whirled, daintily stepped aside, and grabbed him by the neck with one arm. The cool metal blade rested against the skin of his throat for a moment before she released him.

"Good," he said ruefully, "although you must remember that your adversary will be struggling. Still, I think you have the basics. Is there anything else you'd like to review?"

She thought for a moment, then shook her head. "No, not now."

"Then that's enough for today. We should go in to change

for dinner, and later we'll talk about the situation in France.''

Political discussions were part of her training, too. He hoped to acquaint her completely with the politics of the French situation, thereby improving her listening skills once she reached France. He had told her on more than one occasion that sometimes even the most innocent of statements was important.

As they walked back to the house, she was on his left side, and could study the patch without his noticing it. A faint scar trailed out from under the black material. He reached up to rub the area under the patch with his gloved fingers.

"Does it bother you?"

"What?"

"Your . . . eye."

"Sometimes."

His tone was short. Obviously he did not want to talk about it. But she did.

"Are you ever in pain, my lord?"

He turned his head so that he could look at her. "Do you mean from the loss of my eye? Not now, though for the first year or so there was extreme pain."

Her reply was soft. "I am sorry to hear that, my lord."

"Well, that's all in the past, as you so cheerfully remind me."

They did not speak further until they were inside. He said he would meet her later in the study, where they would have wine before they dined.

She was now staying at Chalmers's house during her training because it was more convenient. The day before, Chalmers had left, and now she was alone with Drake. Completely alone.

And she did not mind that at all.

She took special care in dressing for dinner. Afterward, she paused to look at herself in the oval mirror in her room. She wore a silk dress of the palest salmon, with puff sleeves edged in beige lace. A gold ribbon was threaded through her black curls, and around her throat she wore a simple strand of coral. She wore beige silk slippers, and she reached for a shawl, in case it grew cooler that evening.

She smiled at her reflection. The pale orange brought out

the vivid green of her eyes. Eyes, her mother had said many times to her, that were just like those of her paternal great-grandfather, Revel de Juliers, the Englishman cheated of his title. Traveling abroad, he'd been attacked by bandits and left for dead. His memory gone, he had wandered through Europe, then returned to England, drawn to it for some reason. He became a highwayman and met Ariel's great-grand-mother. She, too, rode the high road, and the money she acquired went to keep her estate and to pay off her brother's gambling debts held by Edward, Revel's half brother. When Revel's memory returned, he sought to right the wrong done by Edward. In the end, Theone stole the family's jewels from Edward and saved Revel from hanging. Revel and Theone quickly departed for France, where they were married, and in southern France they purchased an estate and set about to raising a family. They had two children, a boy and a girl, and when the boy grew to manhood he married a Frenchwoman. The son of that union had been Ariel's father.

The tale of Revel and Theone had been told and retold, and Ariel never grew tired of it. How exciting it must have been in those days. What strong and daring people they had been, her great-grandfather and great-grandmother. She sighed. Now her family consisted only of actors, without a trace of excitement in their uncluttered lives.

Except, she corrected, for Drake's proposal. The money to pay the bills was important to her, but so was the excitement, the excitement her great-grandparents had known. She would not be riding the high road, but she would be doing something equally dangerous, and she hoped they would have been proud of her.

She adjusted the shawl around her shoulders and left the room. She found Drake in the study. One booted foot was on the grate, and he was staring intently into the depths of the fire as though his very life depended upon it. He was so caught up in his meditation that he did not hear her.

She cleared her throat quietly and he looked up.

"Ah, Mrs. Greystone, you are looking ravishing as ever." He bowed.

"Thank you, sir."

She sat and took the glass of wine he offered her, then

sipped it and stared thoughtfully at him.

"You still call me Mrs. Greystone, my lord, and not Ariel," she said lightly. "You need not be quite so formal."

"Indeed? You said that the use of your first name was reserved for your friends. Am I one?"

"No."

"Then you shall continue to be Mrs. Greystone."

"Very well, my lord."

Silence grew between them. The log in the fire shifted on the grate and crashed to the hearth. She glanced at him, but he was not looking at her, and that irritated her a little. She straightened her shawl and sighed, and still he did not turn toward her. She wondered what his thoughts were. Were they of her or his business? Knowing him as well as she did, he probably thought only of business.

When Fenton came to announce dinner, they still had not spoken.

They dined quietly, too, with him asking only if she found the food good, and her commenting that she had never had such succulent roast beef. Afterward, they retired to the study once more.

When she thought she could stand the silence no more, she took a sip of her wine and said, "I had a strange dream some weeks ago."

He looked up from the chair by the fire. The light of the flames cast black shadows that played across the planes of his face and made him look most sinister. "Indeed?" His tone was polite.

"Yes. You were in it."

He sat up a little at that. "Oh?"

"I didn't know it was you, at first. It was a dream that was"—she paused, at a loss for words—"quite intimate," she finally concluded, aware that she was blushing. She put her hands up to her burning cheeks.

"Very interesting," he mused. "What night did you have this dream?"

She was surprised by the sharpness of his tone. "The night of the fourteenth."

He frowned. "The night of the fourteenth . . . and mine was . . . No, it couldn't be. 'Tis simply a coincidence," he murmured, but he shook his head slowly, as if not entirely convinced.

She was intrigued now. "What is a coincidence?"

He stood. "I had a dream of a similar nature on precisely the same night."

A chill traced its cold finger down her spine. "The same night?"

He nodded. "I remember flames."

"A wall of them," she said.

"Yes, and—"

"And there was a shadow that seemed to spread its wings." She was talking very fast now.

"Yes, yes, and the flames were shooting upward, and turning blue and orange, and—"

"Burning us . . . with desire," she said, her breath catching a little as his gaze bored into her. She was aware of how warm and close the room had become, and she let the shawl fall. She took a deep breath and gently fanned herself. He was still gazing at her, and his face was shadowed, for he'd turned away from the fireplace. She stood up somewhat unsteadily. She didn't know what to do, and yet she couldn't sit down again. At least not yet. She had to do something. She took a tentative step forward.

"Mrs. Greystone."

"Ariel," she corrected.

He came quickly to her, taking her into his arms. She rested her head against his shoulder. His arms were warm and strong, and she relaxed.

"Ariel," he said, and bent his head down. She raised her face. Their lips met, and she caught her breath sharply. Then her mouth opened under the pressure of his. His tongue slid in, gently exploring. Sighing softly, she slipped her arms around his neck and pressed herself closer, feeling the nearness of him. He reached up with one hand to stroke her hair, and the fleeting touch sent shivers down her spine.

They stood, not speaking, only kissing softly. Finally, she broke away and took an unsteady step backward. She looked up to see him watching her carefully with that one gray eye, but saw no harshness in his face.

"My lord—" she began.

"Kit," he corrected, and, reaching out, took one of her hands in his. He pressed a kiss on it, and his lips seemed to burn her skin.

"Kit." She stopped.

"No words are necessary," and he pulled her into his arms again.

They kissed again, and she lost track of time in the circle of his arms. It was as if they had never been parted, as if they had always been together, sharing their days and nights. His kisses were strong and sweet, and she returned them with a fervor she had forgotten she had ever possessed.

He smiled down at her and ran a fingertip lightly down her cheek, tracing the line of her jaw. "I want you, Ariel," he said huskily. "Here. Tonight. I can't wait."

For answer, she reached up and kissed him on the lips. "I want you, too, Kit. But not here, not in the study."

He nodded just once. "Upstairs."

"Not together, I think."

"You go first. I will come to you later."

She ran lightly up the stairs to her room, where she blew out all the candles except the one on the bedside table and undressed with shaking hands. When she realized what she'd done, she promptly pulled her clothes back on. She wanted him to undress her. She blew out the other candle and settled into a chair by the fire.

She did not have long to wait.

There was a soft knock on the door.

"Come in."

He strode across the room to her and took her into his arms again and held her close. She could hear the fierce pounding of his heart, and knew the beat of hers matched his.

She raised her eyes to him. "Take me to bed, Kit. I want your love again."

"What my lady desires, my lady receives," he said softly, and in one fluid motion picked her up and took her to the bed. Eagerly she reached for him.

Fourteen

❦

In the firelit room she watched as he stood and shrugged out of his coat, letting it slip to the floor. He pulled off his boots, untied his cravat. She sat up then and began to undo the buttons of his shirt. With each button more bare chest was revealed, and as she stroked the curling dark hair, she felt the heat of his skin against her fingertips. He let the shirt slip to the floor, then inched his breeches down. She stared, his body once more new to her. She remembered the times before when they had made love, and yet did not remember, for those years were viewed now as through a haze. His body had changed. He was lean as ever, his shoulders just as wide, his hips just as narrow as she remembered. He was still tanned, as though he spent long hours in the sun, and that she well recalled. But it was the scars on his body that fascinated her. They had not marked his body before, and she could not keep her eyes from them.

He looked down at a crescent-shaped one just above the left hip.

"I almost died after the battle of Copenhagen."

"I didn't know."

His voice was ironic. "How could you?"

"You said it took you a year to heal. . . ."

"For the more obvious wounds to mend, yes, but there were others that stayed far longer and took years to get better."

An ugly puckered scar ran across his flat abdomen for
several inches. She placed her finger against it lightly, and he
sucked in his breath sharply.

"Does it hurt?" she asked, fearing she had harmed him in
some way.

"No, no, it doesn't, but the memory of the pain hasn't gone
away yet, I fear. It aches on some days."

Scars crisscrossed his hardened, muscular legs, his back, his
lower torso. With all this evidence of his suffering, she could
not believe that he had somehow managed to survive. One battle could not have done this, she told herself, and yet what did
she know of war. To her, he looked as though he had been tortured and then left for dead.

"Do I repel you?" he asked. He reached for his breeches.

"What are you doing?" Her gaze broke away and she
looked into his face.

"Dressing," he said curtly.

"Why?"

"I knew I shouldn't have come up. I should have known
what would happen." He was sitting on the bed now, fasten-
ing his breeches and then reaching for his boots.

"Stop it!" she said. He ignored her. She reached out and,
grasping his arm, shook it.

Startled, he turned around to stare at her.

"You don't repel me, Kit. You mustn't think that, for it's
not true. But your body *is* different. I haven't seen it for a long
time and it has changed. You must grant me time to grow accustomed to it." He did not respond, and she wondered if he
had heard her. "Do you understand? I wasn't horrified by
your scars. I was just thinking of the terrible pain you must
have suffered receiving them."

He licked his lips. "You don't want me to leave, then,
Ariel?"

"Leave?" She blinked, confused. "I don't understand what
you're saying."

"Other women have wanted me to leave when they saw my
body."

"No! I cannot believe it." She sat next to him and put her
arms around him. "I want you to stay with me," she whispered into his ear. "I want you to make love to me. Now."

He kissed her, and their lips clung together warmly. She breathed deeply, feeling a contentedness she had not known in too long. After a while, she pulled back gently and smiled up at him.

"You'd best get undressed again."

"I suppose so," he said, his voice marked with humor, and he proceeded to take his breeches off.

When he turned around, she gazed at him, at the taut muscles, strong arms and legs, the jutting manhood that bespoke his passion for her, and wondered that any woman could have rejected him. Guiltily she remembered that she had ended their engagement, but that had been for something totally different. She had never rejected him in bed. Never.

He knelt before her and delicately disrobed her, his hands as gentle as any maid's. His hands lingered as he removed her dress and chemise, brushing her shoulders and hips, and as each layer of clothing was removed, she could feel her skin tingling, her breath catching. Her clothing rustled to the floor.

When she was at last naked, his gaze swept across her, taking in every detail of her petite body, and he smiled. "You're still as beautiful as ever. More so," he said, raising her chin.

"Flatterer," she said.

"No. I have no need to flatter you."

She laughed and pulled him down on top of her as she lay back on the bed. They kissed and clung to one another, and it was as though she had been lost in a maze for years but had finally stumbled out of it. His lips felt *right;* his arms felt *right;* he felt *right.* So long, so long had she missed him. She wanted to cry aloud how she had wanted him for so many years, and that she had missed him, but she did not. Instead, she returned his kisses with all the ardor of her heart.

When he released her she was breathless. She panted for a few minutes and then murmured, "I think we have much catching up to do."

"I agree," he said. "We have been too long absent from one another." He raised himself up on one elbow and stared down at her. His long capable fingers traced her lips, then moved to her earlobe.

She giggled. "Stop it!"

"Still ticklish, eh?" He grinned.

"Kit!"

"Oh no, I can remember times when I begged you to leave my ticklish spots alone and you didn't." With one arm, he held her arms down so that she couldn't move his hand away from her ear.

"That was different!" She burst out laughing again. Her eyes watered, and the tickling, which actually felt very good, reverberated through her entire body, fanning her desire.

"Ah, yes," he said, mock-serious. " 'Twas always different for you." Suddenly he removed his fingers, and his lips were at her ear. His breath was warm and sent a shiver down her back. He nuzzled the lobe; then his tongue flicked out, sketching the delicate shell of her ear. She shuddered with pleasure.

"Kit," she whispered. Her arms were free now, and tightened on his shoulders. Her dark lashes lowered across her eyes as she ran her tongue across her bottom lip. She was so dry, so warm, so hot; it was as if the fire in the grate had grown to a bonfire.

"You're so beautiful, Ariel," he said, pulling her to a sitting position. "So beautiful that I ache when I look at you."

"No," she said, shaking her head against his shoulder. Her hair fanned out, and he caught it, gathering the fullness with both hands at the nape of her neck. He wrapped it around his fist and stroked its silkiness, and for several minutes they did not move. Then slowly she sank back onto the bed and smiled at him. "Come to me," she said.

"As always."

He lay next to her and stroked her face, caressing her cheeks, her chin, her lips. He dropped kisses upon her closed eyelids, kisses as soft as the brush of a butterfly's velvet wing. Her skin tingled, and the back of her neck prickled. As if sensing it, he slipped a hand behind her and massaged her skin.

Her mouth opened under his, and their tongues probed, thrust, withdrew, and their breaths mingled, warm and one. Her breath was coming faster now, and she was growing so hot, so very hot, burning as if from fever, but it was a fever of love. The fever burned through her legs, through her body, into the very core of her brain, burned and burned, and ignited even more fires of passion.

His fingers, so capable, so sure of their path, trailed across her neck, stroking the hollow of her collarbone, lingered on the plane above her small bosom, then moved to cup her breasts. He began to gently knead them, and she murmured her pleasure. His hands flicked across the tautness of her rosy nipples, and they stiffened. She shifted, feeling the delight tightening her lower body. She opened her eyes to see him smiling. Firelight flickered across the left side of his face, leaving the other side in shadow.

"You are a fiend," she accused in an undertone. "An absolute fiend!" His fingers had swept across her flat abdomen, startling her.

"Of course I am," he said. He knelt now alongside her, and his hands coursed across her body, touching here and there, pressing lightly, bringing the level of her pleasure to such an intensity that she didn't think she would be able to tolerate it much longer. When she reached for him, he moved out of her way.

"No," she said.

"Oh yes."

He kissed her breasts, first one, then the other, his lips brushing their firmness. His tongue found one delicate nipple and lapped at it, kissing it, and she twisted her hands in his hair. Pleasure jabbed through her, and the heat was growing until she was sure the room would burst into flames. With one hand he caressed her stomach, slipped to the tops of her satiny thighs, and there his hand lingered, maddeningly still. She shifted, but still his hand did not move, and she quivered from the touch of him upon her.

And then his lips traveled slowly down the length of her body, across her stomach and hipbones, down, down, and . . . stopped before he reached the juncture of her thighs. He rose up and kissed her on the lips, and she savored the taste of him, half-forgotten with the passing of the years.

It was so wonderful to have him here, to be with him, to be loving him, she thought, and she could not believe they had ever been separated, that time had flowed differently for them. It was five years ago, and she was once more facing him for the first time that first afternoon they had made love. Though she had not been a virgin, she had blushed when he undressed her, and had hid her breasts with her hands. He had laughed gently, and pulled her hands away so that he could kiss the palms. And then . . . then she had relaxed.

"Now," he said, his breath so soft against her ear, "now."

Without hesitation she began brushing her hands across his body, feeling the ridges and depressions left by the scars, but feeling also the hardness of his muscles, the strength of his body, the power of it. She ran her hands through the hair on his chest, let them wander down across the flatness of his belly, to the tangle of hair between his legs, and then up once more to grip his shoulders so that she could kiss him. Their mouths opened, and once more their tongues probed gently.

Again his fingers glided down her body, down her legs, then up, maddeningly slow, to the moist tangle of dark hair at the juncture of her firm thighs. She breathed deeply at his feather-soft touch. Her legs opened as she arched her back, and she reached out, cupping his testicles in her hands. He moaned aloud, his eyes half-shut, as she rhythmically stroked the velvet-soft skin and murmured to him. Her fingers slid down the length of the throbbing shaft, and she could feel him shudder with pleasure. She drew her fingers up slowly, her nails just barely tracing the delicate veins, and he gasped as his eyes flew open.

"Ariel, Ariel!" he cried, burying his face against her breasts. He kissed the shadowed area between them, and she laughed, feeling the joy and wonder in her heart. She shifted and her hands gripped his tight buttocks, her fingernails digging into the flesh. He cried out and threw himself upon her. They clung to one another and stroked and caressed, touched and nibbled, bringing each other to a frenzy.

Waves of passion and lust assailed her, thrusting her higher and higher to those dizzying heights, made her tingle and ache, made her burn with an ardor she had never felt. She pressed her face against his shoulder so that she wouldn't cry out. His hands, so strong and capable, so gentle and loving, they were all over her, opening her to incredible pleasure. The room, painted red by the firelight, glowed and whirled around and around, and she was in the center, and all around her was the firelight and the flames and the burning.

She fondled him with one hand, her hand burning with the heat of him, and stroked his back and buttocks with the other.

All the while his fingers provoked her nipples until she thought
they could stand no prouder. They thrust their proud heads
toward the ceiling, and she smiled at him, and he bent to kiss
her. His hands drew across her flat stomach, across her slim
hips, down the white flesh of her thighs, then up, slipping into
her warmth to bring her more pleasure, more heat. All around
them the flames danced brightly in the darkness, and she
reached out to them, and called his name, and felt the hardness that was him pushing, prodding, seeking her. She released
him and wrapped her arms around him. She opened up, welcomed him, and arched her body to meet him as he entered
her.

He sighed and his hold on her tightened. They kissed again,
no longer so gentle, their teeth grating, their tongues exploring. They were locked in their embrace, and together they
thrust, rising and falling back, together, always together, up
and down, and theirs was a rhythm as old as the world itself,
but for them it was as new as their love. And she could feel the
long hardness of him inside her, pushing and thrusting harder
and harder until her world became all bliss and flames and inside her veins ran fire. She bit her lip and cried out, a wild
animal sound that matched his own growls.

Together they twisted and rolled across the dampened
sheets, and she clung to him, and he to her. Then came the
sound of a thousand goblets breaking, and in that second she
smelled the musk of love, and it was intoxicating as any wine,
and the rushing grew, enlarging, increasing, until she saw
nothing except his face and beyond him the dancing flames,
and then she was crying out, her voice mingling hoarsely with
his, and the world exploded into a kaleidoscope of flaming
colors that engulfed them. They rocked together, locked as
one for all time, their sweat-slick bodies adhering. She felt ripple after ripple of pleasure, of joy, and she knew she was
weeping for her face was damp, but she didn't know why, nor
did she care. And down from the heights, like hawks, they
swooped, together, embracing, kissing, and slowly, ever so
slowly, they floated downward, and the passion ebbed, and
the colors spun away, and the flames flickered and died down,
and once more they were on the ground, and they were still
locked together, and the sound of her own heart beat loudly in

her ears. As her breath returned to normal, she opened her eyes.

Drake smiled and bent to kiss her inflamed lips, and she ran her tongue provocatively against his. He shuddered, and his hold on her hair tightened. He was tangled within her hair, and black locks spread across her pillow, across his shoulder, and down his back. He brushed aside a strand that had fallen into her eyes.

She was still panting, still finding it hard to completely catch her breath. They had not yet spoken, and as she gazed up at him, she realized how much she loved him, how much she wanted him, how much she had missed him. Those five years had been agony, only she had been too stupid to realize it. Until now.

"Kit," she said, and kissed his cheek.

"My darling." His fingers stroked the planes of her face, lingered on the delicate lobe of her ear, and she shivered.

They kissed once more and lay comfortably in each other's arms for a while, doing nothing more than listening to the other's breathing, to the other's heartbeat, and then slowly again, without words, he roused her, caressing and fondling her, bringing her quickly to a climax that assailed all her senses. Afterward she lay, damp and sated, in his arms. She had forgotten how good a lover he was. He was the best she had ever known. Only Drake had brought her to the fullness of passion. Only Drake had been able to make her body and mind feel so alive.

After a while they rolled to face each other and began kissing. The intensity of their kisses increased, and their passion blossomed once more, and again they were as one.

Afterward, replete, they both dozed. She was the first to wake, and she gave a long sigh as she watched him sleep beside her. She touched his lips, tracing their long thin line with a finger. Never opening his eyes, he kissed her hand.

"I'm awake," he said softly, and rolled over onto his side to prop his head up with one hand.

"I'm glad." She stretched her arms high over her head. She was so comfortable, so happy, and she wanted this evening never to end. He kissed the skin between her breasts, lapped gently at it. Shivering with delight, she reached over and wrapped her arms around his head, pulling him closer.

His voice was muffled when he spoke. "Are you planning to smother me?"

"Yes," she declared gaily, and, releasing him, inched her way down on the bed until they were face-to-face. She threw her arms around him again, pressing herself against his warmth. "Make love to me again, Kit. I want you so much." Her voice was hoarse with passion, and she quickly drew her tongue across her lips.

He gave her a quizzical look. "Again?"

"Again," she said firmly.

"Ah, I am always willing to oblige my lady." He mocked a growl, nuzzled her shoulder, and rolled over onto her, then sat back.

Smiling up at him, she played with the hair on his chest, ran her fingers down his narrow waist to caress his hips. His mouth came down on hers, and hers opened willingly. His breath was soft and warm, and white fire raced through her body, her legs, igniting desire as it coursed. His hands caressed her breasts, stroking the pink aureoles until her nipples stood taut. She groaned under his passionate ministrations, and he pulled back to smile down at her.

"Devil," she whispered.

"Devil mistress," he rejoined.

"I love you," she said, her eyes never leaving his face. She hadn't meant to say it, but there it was.

He seemed on the verge of saying something, then shook his head. A cloud seemed to pass across his face, but before she could ask him what was wrong, he responded. "I love you, Ariel. I truly do."

Somewhere in the house a clock chimed four.

"It's late," she said, and the world, which had seemed so far away, returned.

"Very," he agreed, and lay down gently beside her.

They said nothing for a long time. As their bodies cooled, he pulled a coverlet over them. Finally, he stirred.

"I should go."

Her grip on him tightened. "Don't."

"The servants—"

"I don't care if they see us."

"This isn't my house," he reminded her.

"Yes, I know." The thought of Chalmers was like a dash of cold water on her. She seemed to sober almost instantly. "If you think you should go . . ."

"I do, Ariel," he said firmly, "although I don't wish to leave, of course. I wish we could spend the rest of the night—morning—whatever—together. But we cannot. We have work to do."

"Work," she repeated, and the thought of that, too, chilled her.

How silly for her to have spent the night this way, to have hidden from the truth, for that was precisely what she had done. She had simply sought refuge from the present and all her problems by escaping into the past—or into this night's re-creation of it. Only, there was no real escape.

Tonight they had been closer than ever before . . . even closer than when they had been engaged. And she liked it. She enjoyed his company, liked to listen to his voice. She liked all of this, and secretly, almost guiltily, she wondered if there might not be a future for them. Through half-closed eyes and the screen of her long lashes, she watched his strong profile, and it seemed as though it glowed with a golden light.

Suddenly, without warning, he pushed back the covers, shattering the idyllic mood, and she was jarred out of her drowsy state. He bent to give her a swift kiss, then rose and began to pull his clothes on. She watched wordlessly, feeling an ache as though he were already gone. When he was completely dressed again, he sat down on the bed and took her hands in his.

"I will see you later. I will come to you tonight, Ariel," he said, his voice intense.

She nodded, afraid to speak.

He bent, pressed his lips firmly against her, and once more she could feel the passion stirring. She fought against it, resisted it, and finally was able to look up at him without trembling.

"Until later, Kit."

He stared down at her a moment and stroked her cheek, then nodded and headed for the door. He turned back, raised a hand to her, then was gone.

Alone once more, she stared into the fireplace. The flames had died down until only embers glowed red. Embers like their love and desire that had been fanned tonight into a conflagration of passion and want, need and love. Flames that had licked at them greedily, flames that had engulfed them.

But an unspoken objection lingered. What if . . . what if he were leading her on like the first time? What if she discovered he was simply using her?

"No!" she cried out loud, flinging her hands against her ears as if she could shut out the unwelcome words. "No, it won't be that way!"

Because she would not allow it. This time, she vowed, this time she would have all of him—or she would have none of him at all.

She told herself she must sleep, certainly she must rest, for it had been an exhausting night. Long after the clock had chimed five, she fell into a slumber unmarked by dreams.

Fifteen

The following night he came to her, and the next evening as well, and every night he spent with her, in her bed, until Chalmers returned to his house.

If Chalmers ever suspected that something had occurred between them, he never let on, and he continued to wage his own, unsuccessful campaign to woo her. In mid-May, a little over two months since she first came to the house, her training was completed.

At that time Drake announced she was ready. Chalmers wasn't so prompt to utter such a pronouncement, saying he thought she might need more practice.

Suspecting the true reason why he demurred, Ariel merely shook her head and said she agreed with Drake. Chalmers was not pleased.

All during her training they had discussed the situation in France, but in late May it changed drastically, for on the eighteenth the French legislature declared Napoleon Bonaparte emperor of France.

Drake said they could no longer delay.

At the end of the month he took her to meet William Pitt, who had replaced Addington as prime minister on the first of the month. Addington had been toppled through his own pacifistic policies. Drake had tried to warn him, but obviously to no avail.

Pitt was charmed by her, and claimed he was a devoted admirer of hers, having seen her in many plays. He offered her his congratulations on her courage and patriotism and wished her the best of luck on her venture. Although she did not say so, she rather thought she would need more than luck on her mission.

Afterward Drake took her to dinner, where they lingered over an exquisitely prepared meal and fine wine and for hours talked of nothing consequential. Later in the evening they returned to his house.

Pollock brought them wine in the library and then discreetly left. The doors leading to the balcony had been left open, and a faint breeze stirred the curtains. The fragrance of freshly blooming flowers drifted in, and she sighed, for it seemed as though winter had left just a short time ago and spring had come too quickly. Soon it would be summer. Summer . . . and where would she be? she asked herself. She took a sip of the wine, savoring its sweetness, and studied Drake.

Tonight, indeed all day long, he had been preoccupied, as though there were things he had to say and he was reluctant to say them.

The night before, she had bid farewell to Chalmers, who had still not given up and had asked to take her to dinner in a few days. She had declined, saying she must get on with her job, and reluctantly he had agreed. But he exacted a promise that when she returned, she would have dinner with him.

Now Drake drummed his fingertips on the tabletop, then rose and strolled to the open doors. She came up behind him and put a hand on his sleeve. He started, not having heard her approach. Outside the night was black, but in the sky, despite the pall of smoke that hung over London, she could see a faint glimmer of stars, and that sight gave her heart. Tonight she would leave her worries behind.

"What is the matter, Kit?"

"Matter?" His thoughts seemed far away.

"You seem so lost tonight. I thought, perhaps, that something was wrong. With you, with me, or with us. I don't know. I can't tell."

He looked down at her. "Nothing is amiss, I assure you, my dear." His face, though, belied his words. He looked out the doors again.

She rested a hand on his shoulder and squeezed sym-

pathetically. Suddenly he turned and swept her into his arms.
Their kisses were swift and frenzied, and they sank to the
floor. He held her tightly, kissing her so hard that she couldn't
breathe. With hands that trembled as if from fear, he began
undressing her. When her last article of clothing had been
removed, he pushed them away impatiently and bent his head
to kiss her breast, his tongue flicking over the rosy nipple. It
stiffened, and she cried out as the fire began kindling within
her once more. Reaching out, she pulled at his coat, managed
to ease it off his shoulders, and then began tugging at his
cravat and shirt.

When his chest was bare, she stroked his warm skin, tugged
playfully at the curling dark hair there, touched his nipples,
and gripped his shoulder. She kissed his chest, ran her fingers
along the band of his breeches.

Tonight there was an aura of sadness and regret about him.
She would not dwell on these thoughts; rather, she would
give herself up to joy. She wanted to think of nothing beyond
the two of them, nothing beyond their pleasure.

He brought his mouth down on hers, even as his fingers
trailed down the swell of her breasts, where they lingered as
they caressed her soft skin. His hand moved across her stomach, down to the dark, warm triangle of her womanhood. She
groaned, and opened eagerly to him. She closed her eyes and
thought how much she loved him, how much she wanted him,
and how she ached when they were not together.

He withdrew from her, began to stroke her body, kissing
and touching her, bringing her quickly to a frenzied height, a
height touched by the flames of passion. He murmured to her,
words she could not understand, but whose meaning she
knew. They kissed, their breaths mingling, and she ached for
him in every part of her body. She guided him, strong and
hard, into her, and she clung to him, her hands gripping his
shoulders. He thrust deeper and deeper, delving into the secret
place of her, becoming one with her, and they both cried out
loudly with pleasure. They were lost in a vortex as wave after
wave of ecstasy washed over them. Back and forth they
rocked, locked in their timeless embrace. Then, all too soon,
the timeless rhythm slowed. She drew in a deep ragged breath
and pushed her damp hair out of her eyes.

She stared around the room, not recognizing it at first, not remembering where she was. She had been so lost in him that she had not seen anything else, had not been aware, and only now could she draw back a little and realize there were two heartbeats, not one.

She gave a shaky laugh, and he stared at her, the gray depths of his eye charged with love. She was so overcome that tears began slipping out of her eyes, running down her cheeks, making her hair even damper.

"What is it, my love?" he asked, alarmed, and tried to brush her tears away with his fingertips.

She shook her head, unable to answer, and clung to him as the sobs welled up out of her soul. Wave after wave assaulted her. His arms tightened around her and held her close as he murmured sweetly to her. She wished the moment would go on forever.

Finally, her crying stilled and she closed her burning eyes. He kissed them gently, his lips cool on her warm flesh. Wordlessly he stroked her long black hair, traced the line of her cheek and jaw, and when she was under control, she looked up at him through eyes still bleary with tears.

"Are you all right, Ariel?" he asked.

She nodded. "I'm fine. I really am," although her voice betrayed her.

"What is the matter, my darling? Why are you crying?" He touched her damp cheek. "Is it something I—" He left it unsaid.

"I . . ." She choked a little, swallowed, went on. "I love you, Kit. I always have, I think. I was just overwhelmed by it for a moment, and saddened over what happened. I'm so sorry." A few tears slipped out of her eyes and he caught them on his fingers. "So sorry about—"

"Hush," he said, putting his hand gently against her mouth. She kissed his hand. "Hush, my dear, let us not speak of it now."

She nodded, and they lay wrapped in each other's arms, lost in their own thoughts. Finally, he stirred, and she knew their wonderful interlude was over. She knew she must return to the real world.

They kissed once more. "We should dress," he said, and he

reached across her for his shirt.

She nodded and sat up, her hair flowing down to create a screen. She did not want him to see the tears that welled up in her eyes once more. She dressed quickly, finishing before he did. She went out on the balcony and leaned against the iron railing. The wind cut coolly through her thin dress and across her bare throat, but it was welcome. She threw back her head and felt a fine mist washing her face.

Clouds had scudded across the sky since they were last out on the balcony, and many of the stars were obscured.

"Perhaps it will rain tonight," he said as he joined her.

"I hope so."

They were silent for a few minutes, watching the night, black and cool, and then he moved away. His voice seemed remote when he spoke.

"We have a few things left to discuss, Ariel."

"I know." Her voice held sadness.

He reached out, took her hand, and squeezed it.

"Come then."

She nodded and reluctantly followed him inside once more. He poured them each another glass of wine. He downed his quickly, filled a second, that he proceeded to sip more slowly.

She settled into a wingback chair covered in a silver and olive brocade, and set her glass on the teak table beside her.

He preferred to stand, leaning against the fireplace, so that he could watch her.

"Our business?" she reminded him.

"Yes." He stared down into his wineglass, sipped at it, then looked back at her. "I am afraid that the hardest part for you, Ariel, is about to begin."

She lifted an eyebrow. "The hardest? I thought that would be in France."

"No, I don't think so. I think this next chore will require your most competent acting."

"Go on."

He stopped, took another sip of wine, and his face looked a little pained when he spoke. "By the way, you will be restored to your job at Drury Lane. I spoke with Sheridan yesterday."

"I see." The anger at losing her job returned. Anger at Sheridan, and yes, at Drake for his interference.

"So you will return to the theatre, and all will go on as it was. Except—'' He swallowed the rest of his wine. ''Except that you must be openly critical of the war effort.''

''Our war effort?''

He nodded. ''Because most people know you are half French, and because of your outspokenness on the subject, it will be assumed that you are on the side of France.''

''I don't understand how this will help.'' The breeze from outside was now too cool, and she wished he would close the doors. She shivered, but suspected it was more from nerves.

''It will help because it will pave your way more easily for acceptance by the French. When a well-known actress such as yourself begins to speak out against the English side of the war, all the newspapers will be quick to write articles about it. This news will find its way across the Channel to France, and soon they will learn that not all is well in England—that is to say, that not everyone supports the government.''

''And then? What will happen? I have this dreadful feeling that doom is about to descend.''

''Almost,'' he said with a half smile. ''You will become outspoken, critical, cynical, and grow all the more notorious. Something most actresses would die to achieve.'' She let that pass. ''And then you will be asked to leave the country.''

''What?'' She was startled by this.

''How else did you think you would get to France?'' he asked, his voice a little ironic. She shook her head. ''You'll be asked to leave. You will depart for France, and there, I am quite sure, they will welcome you with open arms. The rest is up to you.''

''A fine kettle, Kit.''

''Yes, I know. But what else would you have me do? The French would be highly skeptical if you simply left England and appeared there. You would not be permitted into any inner circles as you would be regarded—and rightly so—with much suspicion. This way—if you create a public scene, they will believe more easily that you are a traitor to your country.''

''Traitor,'' she repeated slowly. The word chilled her, and she wished a fire blazed in the fireplace.

''Yes.'' He regarded her for a moment. ''I'm sorry, my dear, but—''

''Please, Kit, no apologies. I know what I have to do, and I

will do it. I am sure you have thought over all possibilities.
There is nothing else I can do, I suppose.''

He shook his head.

There was silence for a few minutes between them; then she
stood. ''Really, I must be going now. I have so much to do.''

She held out her hand, and he swept her into his arms,
pressing kisses against her lips, her eyes, her cheeks. She
closed her eyes and rested her head against him and felt his
strength. If only it would pass into her, she thought, for she
feared she would not be able to do what he wanted, what had
to be done.

Finally, they drew apart, kissed once more, and he escorted
her to her carriage.

Drake watched as the coach pulled away, watched until its
lights were only a faint glimmer in the night, then turned and
went inside.

He returned to the library and sat in the chair she had so
recently vacated. It was still warm, and he touched the brocade.

He was a monster. She had accused him of that once before,
and she was right. He was a monster because of what he did.
He loved her, knew that he had always loved her, and now he
was sending her to France, into a situation from which she
might not escape.

He had no choice. It was his love or his country, and he
could not turn his back on either.

He did it because he had to. But he would do all in his power
to prevent her from being harmed. That much he knew. And if
anyone should hurt her—or kill her—then that man or woman
would not live long.

He shuddered at the thought. He set the glass down and
strode to the open French windows, wishing not for the first
time, that he were in a different line of work.

Sixteen

Ariel managed a hasty sip of wine that burned the back of her throat, took a deep breath, and smiled dazzlingly at the men clustered around her. She was dressed in a green satin that matched her eyes, and emeralds in gold settings glittered at her ears and throat. Earlier she had taken much care in dressing, for she wished to achieve a certain image. She had been successful. She had caught a glimpse of herself in an oval gilt mirror when she entered an hour ago. She had seen high color in her cheeks, eyes that sparkled, and she thought she had never looked so appealing. She was the very image of the willful, headstrong actress with not a single care in the world.

That was her role tonight, but how far from the truth it was, she thought ruefully, fanning herself.

Now, smiling faintly, she glanced around the crowded room. If only her courage would not fail her.

It was one week since she had dined at Drake's house, and that week had seen much activity for her. She had returned to Drury Lane, and no one had said a word to her. Sheridan had simply nodded to her, almost as if she had never been gone at all. Her colleagues had appeared pleased to see her, bewildering her all the more. Before her suspension, Sheridan had claimed they were angry with her. Yet now they were being as nice as possible. None of it made much sense.

She couldn't let it bother her for she had much to do. The

first thing was to begin studying the script for the new play.

Soon the invitations had begun trickling in, and finally she had accepted one to a soirée at Lady Roscoe's. She had let it drop during rehearsal that she would be attending. No doubt that had been passed along. Tonight she would speak out against England for the first time.

Before she left home she'd had several glasses of wine to fortify herself, but they had only made her more nervous. The ride to Lady Roscoe's had seemed all too short, and she had felt anger at Drake for imposing on her this way. But she reminded herself of the much-needed money, and for a while the anger had subsided.

Lady Roscoe's town house in Grosvenor Square was very fashionable, and this was the last party she would be giving before closing the house for the summer. Ariel had never before been invited to the woman's social events, and she knew Drake had arranged the invitation. No doubt he wanted her there because more people would hear her in this setting than anywhere else. Anyone who *was* someone would be here tonight and would hear what she had to say.

When Ariel was ushered into the large mirror-lined salon, there had been a few raised eyebrows. No one would let her forget that she was an actress. Still, her profession scarcely kept the men away, and a handful of them trailed after her wherever she went. She stopped by one group, accepted a glass of champagne offered by a liveried servant, and listened to the conversation. As she had expected, it centered on one thing exclusively.

". . . the French Senate proclaimed him emperor, I've heard! 'Tis the most shocking . . ." A matron in a white dress much too close-fitting for her overendowed form raised her fan and waved it rapidly in front of her face as though she were in momentary danger of fainting.

"It's been rumored that he's already begun to sign his papers with a simple *N*." The speaker, a florid man in his fifties, shook his head. "I don't know what's to become of things now."

"Damned Corsican!" his companion muttered, then sipped his champagne.

". . . bearing the threat, of course, though I don't suppose now that Pitt's in office we'll be sitting back and letting them overrun us, eh?'' said the first male speaker.

She waited until she thought she could unobstrusively join into the conversation, and she was given that opportunity when Lord Rothwell spoke to her.

"And what do you think, Mrs. Greystone?" He beamed at her, and she knew what he was doubtless thinking. Because she was an actress she could not possess a brain in her head, nor ever be worried by a single intelligent thought. That opinion of her intellect had never deterred the gentleman from trying to worm his way into her bed.

She smiled beguilingly at him and watched as his eyes strayed to her low-cut bodice. She had selected a dress that gave her bosom more swell than usual.

"I really don't see what all the fuss is," she said in clear tones. She was accustomed to speaking so that those in the back rows of theatres could hear.

"The fuss?" said the older gentleman, turning to fully appraise her. From the look in his eyes he obviously did not dislike what he found. "I don't understand, my dear." He introduced himself as Edmund Lacey. His companion, a much younger man, was Joseph Galton.

She took another sip of her champagne. "I mean the fuss about Napoleon becoming emperor."

"He did not *become* emperor," Galton corrected her as though he were speaking to a child, "but forced himself upon the French people."

"But I still don't see what everyone is objecting to." She gave him a wide-eyed look. "After all, the French have had so many problems in the past decade. Their nation has been torn asunder, their government destroyed. Would it not be best for them to be unified?"

Lacey chuckled expansively, humoring her, and she disliked it. She did not care to be condescended to, especially by a balding, florid, elderly gentleman who looked as if he wanted nothing more than to put her upon his knee and pinch her and steal a kiss.

"I think you misunderstand the situation, my dear," he said heartily.

"Oh no, not in the least," she replied. "I understand the

situation quite well, for I lived in France for many years."

"Well, that explains it," said Galton.

"Explains what?" she asked. Lifting an eyebrow, she turned her cool green eyes on him.

"Explains your volatile nature."

She laughed. "I assure you, sir, that I am hardly volatile . . . yet."

"Well, come now, Mrs. . . . ." Lacey stopped.

"Mrs. Greystone. Mrs. Ariel Greystone."

"Ah," he said, his face lighting as he recognized the name. "The actress."

"Yes, the actress," she said sweetly. "And you were saying?"

"I was going to ask your opinion."

"I don't believe as others do, for I think Napoleon will be good for the French." She could hear fewer people talking than had been just a few minutes before. She knew her voice carried, knew they were listening now. She pressed on. "There has been too much chaos in the past, and it is time that someone brought some order to the country. I think Napoleon can do just that. I believe he will be the strong hand that guides France to its glory once more." She sipped her champagne. "And yet he faces much adversity, for how can Napoleon heal his country when the English continually bicker with him? This diverts his attention from his goals. He should be left alone so that he can begin his good work. Alas, I do not think our government will permit him to do so."

"But, my dear," protested the matronly woman who had introduced herself as Lady Appleby, "surely Napoleon cannot be the chosen one, and certainly not as emperor of the French! Particularly when it is he who has appointed himself as such. That is hardly correct, and after all, he's almost a peasant! And a Corsican one at that!" She seemed shocked at the notion.

Ariel shrugged, affecting the Gallic gesture. "The Bonapartes are most certainly not peasants, my lady. They trace their lineage back through many centuries—more than can be said for some aristocrats in this country. And I see little difference in what Napoleon has done recently and what kings in other nations have done in times before. Who appointed them? Most of them were granted their sovereignty by the right of succession through their families—an ancestor proved to be the best, the strongest warlord, and thus became the ruler. War and conquest elected that man, not the people he ruled. Napoleon has appointed himself emperor, but he has done it peacefully, without resorting to war.''

There was a rustling among those listening as what she said was repeated to those standing on the fringes. She could feel the heat rising in her face at her audacious words, so she quickly took another sip of her champagne.

"As I understand it," said Galton slowly, eyeing her speculatively, "you're saying that Napoleon has just as much right to sit on the throne as does King George."

"Yes," she said, her gaze level with his.

"Good God!" someone uttered in shocked accents.

"She must be mad!" someone else said.

The reference to King George was not well received by the present company, for it only served to remind them that poor King George's mind was bedeviled from time to time.

Lord Rothwell stared at her, his mouth agape, and Lady Appleby excused herself with a disapproving sniff. Others, though, pressed closer to hear what was being said.

"You're wrong, Mrs. Greystone," Lacey asserted, puffing his chest out until he reminded her of a pigeon. "You really are wrong in your assessment."

"I beg to differ, Mr. Lacey. No king is appointed by divine right, as Louis XIV claimed nearly two hundred years ago, but neither are kings appointed by the citizens of the government, as in America. Rather, royalty is the first and foremost of autocracies, and Napoleon has just as much right to be on his throne as do any of the other leaders of Europe."

A hush had fallen over the salon now, and all eyes were staring in her direction. Many guests were angry; others were shocked.

Lord Rothwell, who had remained silent during her discourse, perhaps because he was stunned by her answers, finally took courage to speak. "Mrs. Greystone, I beg you —please do not say any more."

She looked boldly at him. "And why not, my lord? Is it because you find what I say unpleasant but true?

"Good God, no!" His eyes shifted left, then right. "It's just that . . . others are listening."

"As they should be!" she declared. She smiled lazily at him and saw him catch his breath. Yes, he was most definitely under her spell. At least for the moment. "But, certainly I would hope others here would listen to me."

"Yet the war," someone said.

"Ah, yes, the war. A waste on England's part and one we could well do without, for we don't need the added burden of a useless war devised by the scheming mind of a bellicose politician," she declared.

A well-dressed man whom she had noticed earlier spoke in the silence that followed her words. "I think, madame, that what you are saying borders on treason."

"You are mistaken, sir, for I have said nothing more than the truth, and have offered my opinion when it was asked by these gentlemen." She gestured toward the three men, who now collectively took a step back as if fearing they would be associated with her.

"No, Mrs. Greystone, I believe it is you who are mistaken. Your words are treasonous, and cowardly as well. I think it is time you left."

Her face was burning as though she were flushed, but she gritted her teeth. "Leave?" she asked archly. "Because I have expressed my opinion?"

"An opinion which is highly unpopular, I might add, madame."

"The truth often is. It is an opinion," she continued darkly, "that was much in favor when Mr. Addington was prime minister."

"But he no longer is," the stranger pointed out, "and his opinions are also out of favor since it was shown that his weak position was detrimental to the country and to the war effort."

"Oh? Are you a leaf that dangles from a branch and turns this way and that with every little breeze that blows?" She was growing very angry now, and wondered who this obstinate fellow was. He reminded her rather strongly of Drake.

"Hardly that, madame, but I do know something about politics—something I fear you do not." There was some nervous laughter at this. The man's lips were smiling; his eyes were not.

She took a step toward him, a stringing reply ready, just as Lord Rothwell cleared his throat.

"Er, Ariel," he said. He tugged at her arm, and she slapped his hand away. "Come, my dear, perhaps we should leave. There are other entertainments we can seek."

She glared at him. "If you desire to leave, Jack, you are quite welcome to do so. Only please recall that I did not arrive with you."

"Er, yes, I know, m'dear, but it's simply that I thought, well . . ." He rolled his eyes. "Y'know, my dear, you aren't very popular tonight, what with what you're saying and all. Stands to reason."

"I have never run away from a disagreement," she informed him politely.

"Oh." He ran a wet tongue across his lips, turned, and slunk away into the crowd.

Coward, she thought. She gazed at the stranger, who was waiting for her to act. They were all waiting, waiting for something scandalous to occur.

Out of the corner of one eye she could see Lady Roscoe plowing through the crowd like a ship under full sail. Before their determined hostess could reach her, the man who had not yet introduced himself left the room. She watched as the others around her slowly drifted away, until at last she stood in the center of the room by herself.

She decided not to give Lady Roscoe the satisfaction of tossing her out. She would leave on her own initiative. She faced the other woman just as her hostess hurried up to her slightly out of breath. Ariel extended her hand and smiled.

"Thank you, my lady, for a very enjoyable evening. I'm so glad you invited me."

Lady Roscoe's slightly bulbous eyes gaped at her. This did not seem to be how she had planned to rid herself of Ariel. "Oh, well, of course, that is, I really think, Mrs. Greystone—"

"Indeed, I am quite glad I could make it, and I look forward to attending another soirée," Ariel said loudly, and moved toward the door. The other guests made way for her as though she were diseased. Her flabbergasted hostess did not follow.

At the door Ariel paused. Lord Rothwell would not meet her eyes, and Galton was glaring at her, as was the portly Lacey. She smiled, as brazen a smile as she could muster, and left. As she walked through the entry hall she could hear them talking.

". . . she's French, I've heard, and you know their loyalties."

". . . treasonous . . ."

". . . could be charged, indeed, I am afraid. Sedition would be . . ."

"She's an *actress*, after all, so what can you expect?"

"Still, the very idea that someone like *her* would criticize . . ."

She smiled a bitter smile in the darkness and was glad to be out of there. A cool breeze blew along the street, and she breathed deeply, feeling incredibly shaky now that she was alone. She stared down at her hands. They were trembling, and she held them against her body in an effort to keep them still. It had been very hard for her in there, hard to speak out as she had when faced with the animosity of a roomful of people.

And this was only the first night. What would they think later? Would there be a later? She could not bear to give it much thought. She was just thankful that it was over for now.

Her flushed face cooled, and she started toward her carriage, when suddenly a form loomed out of the bushes. She stopped in alarm, and her hand flew to her necklace.

She heard a low chuckle. "Have no fear, my dear; I am no robber."

"You!"

It was Drake. In the faint light streaming from the windows of Lady Roscoe's town house, she recognized him. He was the last person she'd expected to accost her from the bushes, and any joy she might have had at seeing him was dampened by the manner in which he'd greeted her.

"What are you doing here, Kit?"

"Spying on your progress, as it were."

"Oh." She supposed he should be interested in how his plan

was coming along. "And do you approve?"

"Generally."

"Good."

"And did you approve of my undercover?" he asked.

"Your what?"

"The gentleman you sparred with, the one who did not identify himself."

She blinked in surprise. "He's one of your men? You mean—?"

"Yes, and yes. I put him there to provoke you."

"You are a devil." There was no trace of humor in her voice.

"Yes, I know. But come, Ariel, you must admit that it was successful. He did his job well."

"Yes," she admitted reluctantly. It was Drake's man who had planted the seed that what she spoke was treason. That word would be on the lips of many the next morning. Was that not what they wanted?

Drake bent down to stroke her cheek. "Don't worry, my love. Everything will come to rights in the end—have no fear of that." Suddenly his head came up at a slight angle as though he were listening to something. She heard nothing. "I must go now. Someone is coming. Take care." He kissed her swiftly, then was gone with only a rustle of the bushes to betray where he'd been.

She continued walking toward the parked coaches. She heard footsteps behind her but resisted looking around. When she reached her carriage, she nodded to Wawles, who looked surprised to see her that early. She had only been at the soirée for little over two hours. Surely a record time for her.

Once inside her carriage, she looked out to see Rothwell getting into his.

Coward, she thought not for the first time, her lip curling in derision.

Her coach started up, and she settled back against the seats and wearily closed her eyes. She thought of what had been said earlier. It was fine for Drake to tell her not to worry, for it wasn't his reputation that would be under fire. She passed a hand over her face as she realized that no one had ever told her this would be easy.

The money, she reminded herself, she must think of the money. A fortune for her and her mother. But even the thought of the tantalizing amount was not sufficient to calm her. She sighed heavily and wished she did not have to do this terrible business but knew she had no choice.

Seventeen

❦❦❦

The next two nights Ariel attended parties where once more she was outspoken for the French cause. Again, her reception was hostile, and at the end of each evening she left feeling low in spirits. On the third evening she began to see the results.

She waited in the wings at Drury Lane to go on stage. Twenty minutes before Sheridan had reported that ticket sales were down drastically. The season was not yet over, and not all Londoners had left for the country, so there was no reason for a half-full house.

Or was there? she'd asked herself.

She heard her cue, swept out onto the stage, and was met by silence instead of the usual applause. She sneaked a glance at the audience. There were few smiling faces even though the play was a comedy. And there had been few laughs since the play started.

She walked downstage and paused as a rippling sound came from the audience. She blinked in the light as she recognized the sound.

Hissing.

The sound increased. She was being booed. Never before had such a thing happened. Resolutely she continued, forcing herself to pay no attention to the unruly audience and to completely immerse herself in her role. But they had been waiting for her to walk out onstage.

"There she is, the traitor!"

"Get 'er off the stage!"

"Frenchie!"

"French doxy!"

"Traitor!"

The catcalls grew harsher and more explicit. By now the performance was completely disrupted, and the leading man glared at her, as did the leading lady. Something soft and squishy plopped onto the stage at Ariel's feet.

It was a rotting cabbage, and it was followed by a rain of eggs and other vegetables. The actors sought refuge behind scenery until Sheridan stepped out wih raised hands. The rain of garbage ceased. He said the play would continue and those dissatisfied with the performance would be gladly reimbursed. As he walked offstage he glared at Ariel.

The play continued, and she moved woodenly, reciting with little feeling. She was constantly aware of the restive audience, the rustling and whisperings, the rude comments.

She declined to take a bow, but simply fled backstage to seek the sanctuary of her dressing room. It was deserted. For the first time in her career no one came to congratulate her, to flirt with her, simply to see her. Not even the regulars, Stanton Carlyle or Philip Denton or Lord Rothwell, showed. And Haversham was missing as well.

She was about to leave, when she heard a knock on the door. Sheridan entered, looking like a fox caught sneaking into a henhouse. His eyes raked over her traveling clothes.

"I won't keep you long, Mrs. Greystone." She dreaded what he had to say. "As I said before, attendance was down. Further, many in the audience demanded refunds of their money. I was obligated to return it, though we are not in a financial position to do that."

"Yes?" she asked when he stopped talking.

"I feel—all of us feel—that it might be wise for you, and for the theatre, if you quit. At once," he added.

"Quit?" This time he wasn't speaking of mere suspension as he had before.

"Yes, quit. Completely."

Her disbelief faded, to be replaced by anger. She knew the theatre would do better without her.

"Very well." She brushed by him.

"Mrs. Greystone."

She whirled to face him. "Yes?"

"I'm sorry."

She went out of the room and returned home, where she poured herself a glass of wine. She drank glass after glass, then fell into bed and slept without dreams until Hally roused her late the next morning.

"Ma'm," the girl said, "Mr. Haversham's sent his card around and says he'll be comin' by in an hour."

"An hour!" Ariel sat up quickly, groaned when her head thundered, and gazed groggily at the clock whose face would not come into focus. "What time is it?"

"Nearly noon."

"Oh Lord, I shouldn't have slept so long. Oh, Hally, my head aches." She swung her legs over the side of the bed and paused as wave after wave of nausea washed over her. She closed her eyes momentarily.

"I'll fetch a cold compress, madame, for your head, and perhaps some attar of roses would refresh you," the girl suggested.

"Perhaps," Ariel said, although she felt nothing would revive her now. "An hour, you say? Lay out the white muslin with the blue scarf," she instructed. "No, no. The one with the peach sash, I think. Nothing too bright today, I think. Oh, and the satin slippers as well." She pressed her fingertips against her throbbing forehead and rose unsteadily. She made her way to the dressing table, where she sat abruptly.

She was appalled at the dark smudges under her eyes and the bleakness of her expression. Surely she had not drunk that much last night. No, it was all that had happened yesterday.

And now John Haversham was about to arrive, and here she sat looking like one of the three witches of Endor.

She went to the washstand and splashed water on her face and neck, then toweled herself dry. Hally styled her hair and threaded a peach-colored ribbon through the dark tresses. Finally she stood and submitted to being dressed. She could barely think for her mind was a blank. She did not even have time for breakfast before she had to go to the salon to greet him.

"Good morning, John."

"Ariel." He nodded nervously to her.

"Come sit, John." By now he would have had his arms around her and be pressing kisses upon her lips. Something was definitely wrong today, and her headache increased.

"I-I don't have the time, Ariel. Sorry. I'm riding this afternoon."

He would not look at her, and she grew impatient. "Why have you come then? There must be some reason."

"There is." He swallowed, looked up at her, then down at his boots. "I won't be able to take you to the Emerson fête this Friday." A chill settled over her. "And further . . ." His voice trailed off, then he resolutely began again. "I am afraid, Ariel—Mrs. Greystone—that I cannot continue seeing you. You see," he said hurriedly, as though he feared she would interrupt him, "I could not marry someone who harbors unpatriotic feelings such as you have been expressing. You do understand, don't you?" he asked anxiously.

"Yes, I understand."

"Good!" He actually grinned and came across the room to shake her hand. "I knew you would, Ar— Mrs. Greystone. Well, I must be going now. Can't keep the others waiting." He turned back at the door, and his smile faltered. "I am sorry."

Then he was gone.

She remained standing, too numb to sit, to do anything except think of what he had just said.

Her job, the man she'd planned to marry, all were now gone from her life. Finally, her paralysis faded, and she managed to sit down. She could only wonder if what Drake offered was truly worth the trouble and heartache she was encountering. She was called a traitor, denounced in public, booed offstage, hated and despised by those who did not understand why she did this. She was not sure *she* understood. She had tried to anticipate what would happen, but she had never believed it would be like this.

Never.

What a fool she'd been.

In the balance, did paying her bills matter if her reputation, her life, was destroyed?

*   *   *

"I don't understand," Etoile de Juliers said.

"Trust me, Etoile, when I say there is a good reason for what Ariel is doing." Drake's voice was earnest as he sat on the edge of the chair and watched her. She reclined on a couch and looked ill. Indeed, she looked worse than two days before, when he'd last visited her.

"A good reason," she repeated.

"Yes." He paused. "Etoile, do you trust me?"

"Oh yes."

"Then believe me when I say Ariel knows what she is doing. She is acting for a purpose—for me, although I cannot tell you why. Later, perhaps, I can."

"This is for you?" Etoile arched one slim eyebrow. "That I find most unbelievable; she has despised you for so long. And yet, was it really what it seemed, I wonder."

"I don't know," he replied truthfully. "I cannot answer for Ariel." He banished from his mind the images of her naked limbs wrapping themselves about him, of her mouth on his, her eyes half-closed with passion. Hardly the thoughts to have as he spoke to her mother.

Etoile wrung her hands. "I am so distressed. She loses her job, and everyone says such terrible things about her. She doesn't come to see me every day as she used to. But you, Kit," she said, turning her large eyes on him, "you reassure me that what she is doing is right."

It was right, but ultimately it would lead Ariel into danger, and he could not, would not, tell Etoile. He feared it would affect her delicate health.

"I ask that you be patient, Etoile, and in the end we will explain."

"Such dark happenings," she said, half to herself. "I cannot understand what is going on. It makes no sense."

Before he could reply, there was a knock on the door. Etoile brightened perceptibly.

"That will be Ariel now," she said to Drake. "Come in, *ma chérie.*"

It was Ariel. *"Maman."* She stopped, surprised to see Drake. "My lord."

Inwardly he sighed. She was being coolly polite once more,

though there seemed to be no anger. She, too, did not look well. She had dark circles under her eyes, and looked as though she had lost weight.

"My poor darling," Etoile said, holding her hands out to Ariel, "come here at once. You are so pale, my sweet. Do you feel all right?" she asked somewhat anxiously.

"Yes, I'm fine, *maman*," but as she said it she looked straight at Drake.

"I think you are lying to spare my feelings." Etoile said as she embraced the younger woman. "Sit by me, here." She patted the day couch.

"I'll sit here, *maman*, if you don't mind." Ariel dropped into a chair with little grace. Drake thought she acted almost defeated. That wasn't a good sign.

"How has your day been?" Etoile asked fretfully.

"Terrible. All my invitations have been withdrawn, and there haven't been any new ones." She gladly accepted the glass of wine that Drake handed to her. "My social life is almost nonexistent now. And I, who thought I once had numerous friends, have discovered they were never that. All of those I thought loyal have turned against me and will have nothing to do with me. I might as well be a leper." She did not look at Drake when she said this.

"I am so sorry, *ma chérie*." Etoile seemed on the verge of crying. "If you would only tell me, if you could confide."

Ariel shook her head. "I cannot, *maman*."

Etoile looked from Drake to Ariel, and then back at the man again. "All this secrecy, it makes me so very suspicious."

"Oh?" He smiled, a friendly expression. She might very well become suspicious, but she would never guess what her daughter was doing. No one would.

"Yes," Etoile said. "Very suspicious." She looked down at her thin hands clasped in her lap, then shrugged. "But I suppose you will tell me when you are ready, and not before."

"Quite correct, *maman*."

A silence fell between the three of them. Etoile was the first to break it.

"I sense that you two need to be alone to talk. Am I correct, Ariel?"

"Yes."

"Then run along, both of you," she said, her voice weary. "I have had enough of visitors today. I am tired and will rest, but do send in Lizzy."

"I'm already here, ma'm," the woman said, "come to look after you."

Ariel and Drake left the Rose Salon to go downstairs.

"Where would you like to go, Ariel?"

"Your home or mine," she said, shrugging, "it doesn't matter."

"My coach is outside. Come with me."

They ended up at his house, once more settled in the library. It had been some time since she had been there. He poured wine for them.

"Now, what do you wish to talk about, my dear?"

"This," she said, and pulled an object the size of a fist from her reticule. She tossed it to him, and he caught it deftly, then studied it.

A rock.

He raised an eyebrow. "Where—?"

"It was thrown through my window this morning. There was a note attached to it. I didn't bring that with me—it was too ugly, so I threw it away."

"I'm sorry, Ariel." He rose and stepped toward her to take her into his arms.

She held up a hand. "Don't."

Her tone stopped him.

"There have been those newspaper accounts here in London, as well," she continued.

Her eyes were bright with unshed tears, and he ached, wanting to help her and knowing she would not allow it. He remained standing, his arms at his sides, and watched her.

"I'm lonely. All my friends are gone. The only people who stand behind me are my mother and our servants." She gave a brittle laugh. "At least I know how loyal they are." She rose and paced through the room, distractedly running a hand through her hair. Her green eyes glowed with anger, and with something he couldn't identify. Pain? Hatred? Her voice became more and more agitated as she spoke. "My life, my career, everything I've worked for all these years is gone." She whirled to face him and raised an accusing finger. "Because of you. I was a fool—a fool!—to let you talk me into this. Not even paying my bills is worth the heartache I've had to go through, and you knew, you *knew* what it was going to be like, but you never thought to warn me, did you? Did you?'' She went back to the settee and took a hasty sip of wine, sloshing some of it onto the back of her hand.

"Ariel, I told you that everything will work out." He wanted the words to be reassuring but suspected they sounded insincere. "I know—and the prime minister knows—what you are doing and why. *You* know, and that is all that matters." He raised a hand before she could interrupt. "Yes, yes, I know your career has been sidetracked for a while, but I assure that it is not permanent. The prime minister and I will see to that. Besides, there is always the money."

Her voice trembled. "How dare you play upon my need—how dare you when you have done so much to me already? I have done this for you—and do not deny that I have—and lost everything, and still I haven't seen a penny of my money." She lifted her head defiantly. "I want my money. All of it, now. I don't want to wait any longer. If I'm to have the 'comfort' of the money, I want to see it; I don't want it delayed."

"Very well. I can arrange to have a bank account opened for you, and the amount will be deposited."

"When?"

"Tomorrow."

"No, that's too late. I want it done today. May I remind you that my bills are still unpaid, and though few people seem willing to visit me, my creditors have no compunction about showing up and demanding payment in full."

"Very well. I'll have it done today."

"Oh no, I want *you* to do it!"

"All right.'

"Good."

She picked up her reticule and walked to the door. "I suppose I'll be hearing from you again. Like it or not." And with that she left.

He sat down then, and realized his hands were trembling. He had sent many men—and not a few women—into the field, and he had been sorry to see them go, but always he had known it had to be done. But never had he used someone he loved, never had he been forced to hurt someone as much as he'd hurt Ariel. And yet it had to be done. There was no alternative. Perhaps in the end she would realize he was right, perhaps she wouldn't castigate him. But he suspected that time was a long way away.

Eighteen

❧❀❧

Ariel's life continued to deteriorate the first two weeks of June. The invitations withered away, fewer and fewer people spoke to her, and even those on the street turned to whisper as she passed. Those who were not so polite did more than whisper, and there were days when she feared to leave the house. But leave it she knew she must. She would not allow herself to become a prisoner of her own house.

Daily Coates brought her clippings from the various London journals and silently laid them before her. Silently she read these accounts of her "infamy" and "treachery."

Some were impassioned editorials claiming simple dismissal from the theatre was insufficient; they called for her imprisonment. She swallowed heavily as she read the word, and she reached for her cup of tea. It was the first time she'd seen that ugly word. On what basis could she be imprisoned? she wondered, then just as quickly dismissed the thought for she knew Pitt would never permit it.

She pushed aside the clippings to see a packet from Drake. She opened it and found more clippings from newspapers in France. She read through them and saw that as the dates progressed, her status as an outspoken heroine increased. She was commended for her brave stand. She was lauded for her honesty, for her righteousness, and these same journals decried her castigation by the English.

She smiled wryly. No matter how it affected her, she had to admit that Drake's plan was a success. She had become, after all, an Incident.

But now what? She knew she would soon leave for France, but she hadn't heard from Drake in weeks. True to his word, he'd opened a bank account for her, but since then there had been silence.

Should she send a note to him? Or wait? Sighing, she pushed away from the table and left the salon, where she had been reading what little mail she had received. She thought of riding, then quickly dismissed the idea with a shudder. It would be unpleasant in the park, for everyone would be watching her, and she would be unable to enjoy herself.

She returned to the salon to read. Late in the afternoon someone knocked at the front door. She wondered who it could be, for callers were rare these days. A few minutes later Coates brought in an official-looking packet. She broke the seal and drew out the letter. The signature at the bottom was Pitt's.

She scanned the lines, then reread them more slowly. The prime minister was asking her to leave the country because she was severely hampering the war effort by her vocal support of the French. He would give her two weeks—until the first of July—to put her things in order and depart. After that time, if she was still within the country, he would have no choice but to have her arrested and imprisoned.

Her hands trembled, and the paper drifted to the floor like a leaf borne on a breeze.

It was part of the glorious plan to discredit her with the English and win her a good reputation with the French. Yet it numbed her.

She sat in the room until the light faded. Sometime later there was a knock at the door. She said nothing, and the door opened.

"Ariel?"

It was Drake.

He repeated her name, but still she did not respond. He came over to her and knelt before her. She stared at him without blinking.

"Pitt told me today. I tried to get here before, but couldn't.

I'm afraid he's forced our hand.'' He smiled a little ruefully.

"Forced?" she said, her throat dry.

He nodded. "I must prepare you now when I thought we would have several more weeks.''

"Prepare?" she echoed.

He nodded. "Have you had anything to eat?" She shook her head. "First you should have dinner, then we'll talk."

Within half an hour she found herself in the dining room. There were roast beef and chicken, meat pies, and stewed vegetables to eat, but none of it appealed to her. Still, Drake insisted that she taste some of each. Mostly she pushed her food around with her fork and stared down at the plate. She had not yet recovered from the shock of her banishment.

Drake tried to talk to her, but she responded little, and only once asked if he would pour her more wine. When he was finished with his dinner, and when he thought she probably would not eat any more, he led her to the upstairs salon, where he sat her in a chair by the window.

"Now we must talk."

"Drake," she began, then stopped.

"What?"

"I . . . I am . . ." She couldn't go on. The words froze in her throat. Tears sprung to her eyes, blinding her. She felt his arms go around her.

"Go on. Cry. I know it's hard, despite having prepared yourself. It's all right," he said in a soothing tone. "Don't be afraid to cry."

The tears came, spilling down her cheeks, soaking her dress, and she clung to him and wept, and his hold tightened on her. Finally, the sobs subsided, and she hiccoughed once, then wiped her wet cheeks with one damp hand. She rested her head against his shoulder for a long time.

"Are you all right now, my love?" he asked.

Not trusting herself to speak, she nodded.

He brushed her hair away from her face and she raised her eyes to him. He kissed her, and she pressed herself against him. She needed his reassurance, his warmth, needed him tonight more than ever before.

Carefully, he took her into his arms and went into the bedroom.

She lay woodenly on the bed as he carefully undressed her, then threw off his own clothes. He crawled in beside her and pulled the coverlet over them. She was warm and comfortable and snuggled close to him, her eyes shut against the light of the single candle.

"Ariel," he said, stroking her hair. His fingertips tickled her cheeks, her chin, her forehead. His kisses were comforting. "Ariel, my love."

She turned so she could embrace him. Their breaths, ever so soft, mingled. In the faint light she saw the glint of his one eye, and she reached up to stroke his cheekbone. Her fingers trailed down his face, to the hair on his chest, lingered there, then continued their journey, going down until she reached his hardening manhood. He groaned as she stroked him, fondling him until he writhed with pleasure.

His hands were not idle. They roamed, tweaking her rosy nipples, caressing her sides, back, thighs, lingering over the dark gate to her pleasure. She arched her back, widened her legs, and gripped his forearms.

"Kit, please!" she urged, her whisper hoarse. "Come to me."

And he did. He rolled onto her gently, kissing and fondling, and the fiery passion built, burst, just as the anger had weeks before. They twisted on the bed, called to one another as the torrid liquid pleasure coursed through their veins. She felt her fingernails tear his skin, felt his teeth leave marks, and she didn't care. All she wanted was him in her and the two of them as one.

He entered her, and she cried with joy, and anger, and love, and fear, and they entwined, bursting into flame, locked in a never-ending embrace, fused, melded; they cried out, their voices one. Afterward, she felt him kiss her softly on the lips, and then she drifted away into sleep.

She awoke later and slipped out of bed for wine. By the time she returned, he was awake.

"Good evening," he said with a smile.

"Good evening." She handed him a glass of wine, and he kissed her hand.

She sat cross-legged on the bed and stared down at him. "Well, Kit?" She sipped her wine and ran the fingers of her left hand through the hair on his chest.

"Well what, my dear?"

"What is it you must tell me?"

"Ah, that." He stretched, careful not to spill his wine. "As Pitt's letter indicated, you must leave by July first. The passage across the Channel will be arranged, so you needn't worry. I imagine you'll go at once to Paris." She nodded. "Good. Once there, and once you are settled in, you should try to cultivate the acquaintance of one Philippe Baptiste Fouret, comte du Veilleur. A nobleman from the old regime, he managed to keep his head during the Revolution, and now under Bonaparte he is an important official; he is also an admirer of yours."

She looked surprised at this, and not a bit displeased that her reputation should have spread to another country. "How do you know?"

He smiled easily. "Ah, Ariel, there are ways, I assure you. Let us just say that I am quite familiar with the comte's tastes."

"Actresses?" she asked.

"Yes." He took another sip. "In earlier years he sometimes came across the Channel to attend plays here, particularly when the Paris theatres were closed. Does that surprise you, my dear? There has been more commerce between the two countries than is generally believed, though most of it is quite secret. While du Veilleur was here, I provided him with escorts, and thus learned much from him. Now he can no longer travel freely, but I don't wish to lose him as a contact. I think he will be of much help in the months to come."

"Very well." She paused. "Is he handsome, this du Veilleur?"

Drake frowned. "Yes, I suppose some women might think so." He seemed on the verge of saying something more, but did not, for which she was glad.

"Good." She smiled mysteriously and stretched her arms far over her head, so that her breasts thrust out. She picked up her glass once more. "Shall we drink a toast, Kit?"

He raised his glass. "To your success in the coming months, Ariel."

"To my success." And she smiled at him across the glass.

ACT THREE

July 1804

Nineteen

Ariel watched as the brown land mass that was the shore of France grew larger and closer. Now she could see some buildings and knew it wouldn't be very long before they reached port. White-capped waves slapped against the hull of the boat, the *Amsterdam*, rocking it vigorously. She gripped the railing tightly as the deck swayed and her footing became precarious on the wet wood. Soon, very soon, she would set foot on foreign soil.

No, it would be the soil of her native land. She had left that homeland many years before, fled it for the safety of England, and since then she had thought of herself as an English-woman. But now, at least for a while, she would be French again.

Closer and closer the Dutch ship sailed to the port of Calais, and she watched as some of the sailors clambered up the wooden spars and tossed down long lines to those below waiting to hold them. Several of the crew waited on the bowsprit with anchor in hand, all in preparation for the imminent docking.

Before she left England, she had written to a former associate of Etoile's from the long-ago theatre days in France. She said her mother insisted that she write, for she had a favor to ask of him. In the letter, she asked him if he would be will-

ing to locate an agent for her who would help with her travel
arrangements to Paris and lodgings in the city once she arrived. To her great surprise—and relief—she received a quick
response. Her mother's friend wrote that he would be delighted to help the daughter of his old flame.

And so arrangements had been made before she left London. Someone would be waiting for her once the ship docked
at Calais. Who, she did not know, but at least she would not
be expected to face France completely alone. She had brought
none of her servants with her, at least not yet. They would
follow with some of her belongings that she had packed and
that would be shipped later. She had been relieved to learn
from Drake that she could take the servants, for she had not
wanted to dismiss them after they had served her so faithfully
for so long. He had said it would be safer for her to have her
old servants than to hire French ones who could well turn out
to be spies.

Creaking alarmingly, the ship rocked hard to port, and she
nearly lost her balance. Her knuckles whitened on the railing
as she hung on. The deck was slippery with seawater, and a
fine mist of sea spray clung to her face and clothes. She had
never felt so damp in her life. Once the ship straightened, she
released one hand to smooth back her hair as it blew about in
the wind. She would be glad to reach an inn where she could
wash the salt from her skin and run a brush through her tangled locks.

The journey from London to Calais was not a long one,
which was a relief to her. She had stayed above deck away
from the cabins below that smelled of seawater and vomit and
tar. Those passengers who remained in their bunks from
seasickness only became more nauseated from the odors. During her journey she had walked along the deck, watching the
water and the crew as they did their work. And she had
thought.

She thought about the day she had said goodbye to her
mother. Etoile had cried and begged to come with her, but
Ariel had regretfully refused, knowing her mother could never
stand up to the trip. Too, she had to go to France alone. That
much Drake had made clear. She and her mother had dined

together, and the next afternoon Ariel had gone down to the docks to board the *Amsterdam*. She had been alone, seen off by no one, and when she had settled her things in her cabin, she had come out on deck and looked toward the pier. There she had seen the tall form of Drake. He had stared at her for a moment, half raised his hand in farewell, then turned and walked away.

She had felt very lonely as the ship sailed down the Thames toward the Channel.

During the trip she had thought much of what she was doing and was nearly overwhelmed by the enormity of her mission. To be sure, she had been trained by Chalmers and Drake, albeit for such a short time, but what did she really know of spying, of politics, of intrigue? She was, after all, as Drake had once said, only an actress.

She feared she was doomed to failure from the very first, doomed to some hideous fate, doomed never again to see England, or her mother, or Drake.

The ship shuddered as it neared the dock, and the sails drooped as the wind died. Several sailors threw ropes to other sailors on the dock. The ropes were tied, and the boat was dragged through the water, closer to the dock. As she watched, the gangplank was lowered.

She gathered up the few belongings she had carried with her—the rest had been packed in trunks stored in the cargo hold—and prepared to disembark. She had stored some of her things at her mother's, had packed some to be brought with her servants, but during the voyage she had resolved to purchase a completely new wardrobe when she reached France. The bills, she thought with a savage smile, she would save for Drake.

Once on solid ground again she looked around with interest. The dock bustled with activity. Passengers lugging baggage to and from ships were everywhere. Sailors from many different ships strolled along, some of them staring boldly at her. Over the noise of the docks she could hear the plaintive cries of beggars. She saw tradesmen who conducted their business more quietly and those who loudly hawked their wares. Everywhere it stank of sweat and tar, seawater and fish.

She felt a tap on her shoulder. She whirled around, fearing it was one of the Dutch sailors who'd been eyeing her during the journey.

She found not a flirtatious sailor standing behind her, but a brown-haired stranger dressed somberly in black pants and a black coat of good, though somewhat undistinguished, cloth. He was short of stature and in his middle years. He wore spectacles and a friendly expression on his oval face.

"Madame Greystone?" he asked in English.

"Yes?" she answered a little tentatively.

"I am Jules Senoille, the solicitor that Monsieur Gaine contacted for you." He spoke in a brisk tone that brooked no contradiction.

"Oh, how do you do, monsieur." They shook hands formally, and he took one of her valises from her.

"I have hired a coach to take us to Paris at once, Madame Greystone. Unless, of course, you find you are tired and wish to delay for a day while you rest." His words were solicitous, as was his tone, and she decided that she liked him. But just as quickly she reminded herself that she'd best not fall into the trap of trusting everyone she met here. After all, she was now a spy among them.

"Thank you, no, monsieur, I am a little tired, but I would rather keep traveling. I will rest once I am settled in Paris."

He escorted her off the dock to where a coach was waiting for them. As they approached it, a footman stepped forward to open the door. Senoille handed her up, then asked her to wait while he secured her luggage. He returned to the dock, and she leaned back and closed her eyes. She was used to the rocking motion of the boat, and it would be a few hours more before her body realized it was once more on solid ground.

She must have dozed, for the next thing she knew Monsieur Senoille had returned with her baggage. They were under way.

They faced a long journey, and it was well, she thought, that he seemed so amiable. As expected, conversation was about Napoleon and the theatre.

"I am afraid the emperor does not care for comedy," Senoille said. "Alas, he is a most somber man. But," he added hastily, "that is good for our nation. Do you not agree, madame?"

"Indeed. I have had roles in both comedies and dramas, and I think the dramas were far more interesting."

"Anyone may play the buffoon, but to capture the right nuance of heartbreak, to bring tears to the audience's eyes —ah, that is much harder, I think."

"Indeed," she murmured. Ever since he had stepped up to her, they had been speaking English. She shifted slightly, the material of her beige traveling dress rustling, and said, "I appreciate the courtesy, monsieur, but if English tires you, I would be most happy to converse with you in French."

"Ah," he said, resorting to this native tongue, "I would like that very much."

They lapsed into silence for some time, but later he pressed her—carefully, she thought—for details about her life, her profession, and the treatment she had received by the English.

"I have missed France for some time but with all the recent disturbances did not think I would be able to return." She allowed her voice to fill with disapproval. "And the English—fah! They have the hearts of cabbages," and she continued with stinging words to tell him precisely what she thought of the English who had forced her to leave the country.

Apparently that pleased Senoille, for he smiled at her after that.

"It is a great honor to serve you, madame," he said. "Indeed, Paris talks of no one but you."

"Surely you must be mistaken, monsieur," she said with a faint smile. "All of Paris cannot be talking about me when there are so many more important events happening."

"Ah, but they are, madame, for your plight has touched them. Too, you have many admirers in France, many admirers, yes, and they are so eager to meet you. I think you will not be lonely in your new house for long."

"About my house, Monsieur Senoille—"

"Forgive me, madame, but that has already been taken care of. I have rented for you a hôtel on the outskirts of Paris. You will find it easy to go into the city, but its location will also prove restful."

"Thank you for your thoughtfulness." She smiled at him and let him continue talking. She leaned back against the cushions and listened, hoping she might learn something of interest. She would not worry about the cost of the house, for all of her funds for this journey had been provided by Drake. If she needed more, he would provide for that as well.

Ariel and Monsieur Senoille stayed at a country inn each night of their journey, and it did seem as though her reputation had preceded her, for she met many in the inns who had heard of her and who welcomed her.

The journey proved tiring, and she was exceedingly glad when they finally arrived at her new home. The coach swept through tall black iron gates and up a winding gravel drive lined with willows, and there she saw the house for the first time.

Two stories high, it was constructed of red brick and had numerous windows. She was glad, for she hated gloomy rooms. The house appeared to have been built within recent times. Certainly it was not the ancestral home of a displaced aristocrat, for it looked no older than fifty or sixty years. She suspected it might have been the residence of a minor Parisian noble who had fled from—or perhaps lost his life in—the Revolution. Perhaps the house had been rebuilt, or perhaps during the chaos of the nineties there had been trouble here. She would ask Senoille later about its history. To the left she could see a wide terrace and the gardens, enclosed by a stone wall, and to the right were the stables. While it was much larger than her London town house, it was small for a mansion, and for that she was glad.

"Do you like it?" Senoille asked anxiously.

"Yes, very much, monsieur. It certainly looks more than adequate for my needs." Certainly it was the most gracious-looking house she had ever lived in.

The coach stopped, and once inside the house they were shown into a salon. Monsieur Senoille introduced her to her staff of servants: a butler, a housekeeper, one cook with two assistants, three maids, one of whom was her lady's maid, a groom, and a gardener.

"I did not know what you were doing with your other servants, so I went ahead and hired a staff."

"That's fine. I have several who are coming over later on."

A modest household, she thought, restraining a smile as Senoille took her on a rapid tour of the house's two floors. On the first floor she found a spacious kitchen and pantry, two beautifully decorated salons, a dining room, a small ballroom, and a book-lined library. On the second were four sizable bedrooms, the largest being hers, with its adjoining maid's quarters and bathing area. All the rooms were filled with old furniture that was now a little out of style. None of it was exceedingly valuable, she noted, but still it was pleasant and more than a little comfortable. While it might seem very modest for some, it was luxuriant for her and certainly not as shabby as her home in England.

They settled in the Gold Salon, where the gaunt butler brought them wine. They chatted for some time; then the Frenchman bowed and said he must now leave her alone.

"No doubt you wish to rest, madame, after such an arduous journey, and to talk, too, with your staff." He turned back at the door. "I hope that I may put to rest any fears you may have about the loneliness of your exile, madame. I do not think you will have to wait very long for the invitations."

She raised an eyebrow. "No?"

He smiled. "There is a tray in the front hall. I think you should examine it closely once I am gone. Now, I must go on to my office. Here is my card with my address, if you should need anything. If it is all right with you, I would wish to call upon you when you are settled. But only then, madame. It has been a distinct pleasure serving you." She thanked him for all that he had done, and then he bowed once more and left.

A tray in the front hall?

She left the salon in search of the front hall. There she found a long table of dark wood under a gilt mirror. On the table sat a tray.

She glanced at the numerous cards arrayed there. She had not been in Paris over three hours so far, and already her arrival was news. Quite a few people wished to see the scandalous actress sent into exile by the English. Most of the cards were invitations to parties, to come calling upon her.

She studied the names, recognizing some of the most important people in Paris. Had not Drake said she would find it easy to move into society? It looked as though he was right.

Near the bottom of the stack she found one of great interest. The comte du Veilleur had come calling and left his card,

The very man she needed to meet.

She smiled, thinking that her mission would not be as difficult as she had thought.

Twenty

But as it happened Ariel did not meet the comte for some time—in fact, not until a full week had elapsed.

After Monsieur Senoille had left, she became acquainted with her staff, telling them three of her servants would be coming later in the week. For the next few days she set about becoming accustomed to her new home and to the city just beyond it. Two days later an excited Hally, an unflappable Benjamin Coates, and a typically silent Wawles arrived with the bulk of her luggage. Once they settled in, she began sorting through the invitations, accepting as many of them as she could. She also knew she would have to begin searching for a new job, but that, she thought, she might be able to accomplish socially.

The first party she attended was a large one given by Monsieur Auguste Pierone, the manager of the soon-to-be-opened Théâtre d'Empire.

Pierone, a man whose wealth came from independent and, perhaps, suspicious sources, had been encouraged by Napoleon to start a theatre in Paris to replace those closed during the Revolution. Pierone had proved most eager to do so, but had waited until that summer to christen the theatre. When Napoleon was declared emperor, Pierone knew he had found a name for his fledgling project. At present he was searching for actors and actresses for his newly formed company, and

Ariel suspected the reason she was invited to his party was that he was considering her.

On one hand, she was highly flattered and would be relieved to have found a job so quickly and effortlessly; on the other hand, she knew her reputation had preceded her to France, and her name on a handbill would be a lurid attraction for crowds, something Pierone would have calculated.

No matter the reason, she would get what she desired—an entrance into the French theatrical world.

Hally helped her that afternoon as she prepared for that evening's party. She trusted Hally far more than the other maids, Sofie and Olympe, for she could not be sure they were not spies planted in her household. She had asked Hally when she first arrived to find out—discreetly, of course—if the other maids spoke English. If they did not, then she could speak English to Hally when they did not wish anyone else to know what they were discussing. Hally had soon come back to report that, to the best of her knowledge, the maids, both country girls, knew only French.

Ariel waited while Hally drew her bathwater, and when all was ready, she stepped into a tub redolent of lilacs. She leaned back, closing her eyes as she did so, and let the warm water caress her. Daily she had to remind herself she was in France. She must be ever vigilant lest she inadvertently reveal her secret. She knew there would be those who were suspicious of her; those she must win over. While the two maids did not speak or understand English, others in the household might, and she could not risk their accidentally overhearing something.

She had been so busy in the past week that she had had little time to think of Drake. She wondered when she would see him again. Would he come to visit? No; that would be too risky. He knew better than to do that.

She had had a few visitors this past week, one of the more frequent being Monsieur Senoille. Indeed, he had visited several times, always bringing with him papers on the house for her to look over or sign. She had begun wondering what he really wanted. Perhaps he was simply curious.

Or suspicious.

Ah, that could be, but she did not think so. Still, she must remember to regard everyone two ways—one more accepting, the other ever suspicious.

When the water began to cool, she picked up the bar of lavender soap and began lathering her body. She rinsed the suds off, stood, the water streaming from her oiled skin in tiny rivulets, and reached for a bath sheet. She dried herself, folded the sheet around herself, then stepped into the other room so that Hally could slip her dressing gown around her.

She sat at the vanity, and the girl began to towel-dry her hair in preparation for styling it. The fashion in France, too, was for shorter hair with tiny curls, but she still refused to cut hers.

"The other ones are jealous, I think, ma'am," the girl said as she ran the brush through Ariel's hair.

"Jealous?"

"Of me and my position, ma'am. You know they wanted it. Especially that Olympe. She's a sly one."

"Well, do keep an eye on her, Hally, won't you? I don't want her doing something that she'll regret."

"Oh, I will, ma'm," the maid declared loftily. "Mr. Coates keeps a firm eye on her, too, for he's said he's convinced that one of them Frenchies—beggin' your pardon, ma'm—will run off with the silver in the middle of the night or slit our throats while we're lyin' in our beds!"

Ariel smiled faintly, and secretly doubted that Benjamin Coates had ever said such a thing. Hally seemed to be voicing her own doubts about the French servants. The girl's father had been French, but she had been born in England and regarded herself as English, and the French were very foreign to her.

Humming softly to herself, Hally smoothly drew back her mistress's hair and deftly pinned it.

"*A la Chinoise,* madame," she announced proudly. "It's all the latest style."

Ariel studied herself in the oval mirror, turning her head this way and that. The simple hairstyle accentuated her high cheekbones and made her green eyes seem even larger and wider.

"I like it very much."

"Thank you, ma'm." The girl bobbed a curtsy as Ariel rose to go to her wardrobe. She must now choose with great care what she would wear, for she wanted to make a superb impression upon Monsieur Pierone.

Nearly an hour later Ariel finished dressing. She turned slowly in front of the large beveled mirror in her bedroom and admired herself.

She had decided upon a new gown of brocaded silver with long, tight sleeves. A short gauzy train fell from the belt of silver. The neckline was square and low-cut, and the bodice and hem were embroidered in an intricate pattern of silk and gray pearls, as was the belt, which was caught immediately under her bosom. A silk shawl in soft grays and pink was draped over one arm, and she wore a set of antique pearl earrings that matched the strand at her throat. She wore white gloves, and her slippers were without heels. Made of white kid, they were laced across the instep and tied around the ankle. In one hand she held a small fan, about six inches long, of fine silk and decorated with designs in silver thread. It was one of the gifts from her mother, and she treasured it. Her rather austere hairstyle, she noticed with approval, showed to good advantage her long white neck.

She arched a dark eyebrow and smiled at her image. Would Monsieur Pierone find her attractive? She would know all too shortly. And would the comte be there? That, too, she would know soon. More important, would the emperor be there, as well? No, she did not think so, and for that she was glad. She wanted to wait until she had been in Paris a little longer before meeting Napoleon: she wanted to wait until she felt more at home.

"Oh, madame." Hally, awed by her mistress's appearance, clasped her hands together and grinned. "You're the most beautiful woman I have ever seen. I know you'll outshine all the other women tonight. The men will have eyes only for you!"

"Nonsense, Hally," she said, though not unkindly, for she was pleased with her maid's praise. "But, thank you anyway."

"Oh no, I don't exaggerate."

There was a knock at the door, and Sofie entered. She took in a deep breath as she saw her mistress.

"Monsieur Wawles wished me to tell you the carriage

awaits, madame." She paused, then, turning in a deep red, said in her soft voice, "You are beautiful, madame, especially for an *Anglaise*."

"High praise indeed, Sofie," Ariel said, amused, "but you must remember that my mother is French." Hally looked a little jealous at the other maid's words, and Ariel hoped there would be no problems between them.

"Ah, that explains it," the French girl said, nodding her head knowingly.

Ariel refrained from smiling, drew her shawl up around her shoulders, and told them not to wait up for her. Downstairs, Wawles helped her into the newly purchased carriage, a stylish conveyance painted silver and forest green. Clasping her hands tightly in her lap so that she would not betray her excitement, she settled back for her first glimpse of Paris at night—and its first glimpse of her.

Twenty-One

❧❦❧

"Ah, Madame Greystone," said her host, lifting Ariel's hand to his lips in a gallant gesture. "I am so very pleased that you could come." His eyes raked across her face and down to her bosom, lingering there.

"I would not have missed this for the world," Ariel murmured truthfully. She smiled her most becoming smile and, as the seconds ticked by, wished he would release her hand.

In his late forties or possibly early fifties, Monsieur Auguste Pierone was a tall man, one of the tallest she had seen in France thus far. He was exceedingly heavyset, though it didn't seem to be fat, which surprised her. He had graying hair and eyebrows that she guessed had once been coal black, fleshy lips, and a prominent nose that looked as though it had once been broken. His voice rumbled across the room, and although obviously he was of good breeding, he possessed little physical grace.

Something about his body and face did not seem quite right to her, as though something did not fit, did not work properly, but she couldn't put her finger on it. It was almost as if he were misshapen. And he did not seem the type to appreciate the finer arts. Yet obviously he did, or he would not be opening a theatre.

His eyes lifted again to her face. "I am pleased to hear that, madame." He lowered her hand, though he still clasped it. His hand was hot and moist. She shifted her fingers, but he didn't notice. "When I heard that you were coming to France, I was so excited. I told Michel—my assistant—that I must see you as soon as you arrived in the city."

"I am at your command," she said with a faint smile.

"Indeed," he declared loftily, "and now that I have you before me, I see that what they have said pales beside the true object."

"And what do 'they' say?"

"They say you have the face of an angel, that you are the most ravishing creature upon this earth, and I see that they do not lie."

"You flatter me, sir," she said, amused.

"Not at all," he demurred. "Words are inadequate for your beauty, Madame Greystone."

She did not reply, for she feared she might begin to chuckle at his outrageous praise. She had arrived but a moment before, and had scarcely set foot in the large salon when Pierone had spotted her and lumbered across the room to greet her. She had not yet had a chance to look around her, although she could see that the salon was the size of her ballroom. Along one wall were windows, and along another were mirrors. Overhead thousands of candles burned in gilt chandeliers.

"How do you find Paris?" he asked.

"Beautiful from what little I have seen. I really haven't had much time to see the sights, for I've been so busy putting my household to rights."

"Ah, yes, there is much work there, I do not doubt. I do not envy you that chore, madame." He shook his head. "When your household is in order, what will you do?"

Ah, here it was at last, she realized, and she met his eyes directly. "I will search for work in the theatre."

"I hoped to hear you say that, for I feared—yes, I did!—that you would leave the theatre after what happened in London. Tragic, tragic! Others feel the same way, I assure you. I was not sure what you would do. But this news pleases me greatly. What is the Englishman's loss is the Frenchman's gain."

"Only," she pointed out, "if I find a job."

"I do not think you will find that difficult," he said, smiling. "As you might have heard, I have formed my new theatre company." She nodded to indicate she knew. "My Théâtre d'Empire will soon open to the public, and I wish it to have the most superb actors and actresses. That is why, Madame Greystone, I would be very honored if you would join my company."

She already knew what her answer would be, but didn't wish to appear to rush into the decision. "How kind you are, monsieur, but I—"

"It will pay very well," he added.

"Monsieur—," she began.

"And you will not have a strict schedule. That would allow a lovely lady such as yourself time to herself, and for other . . . things." His smile was nothing less than a leer. "Please, say yes to my offer, Madame Greystone. All of Paris awaits your reply!" He threw his arm out in a wide gesture, and she noticed that the murmur of conversation had now died down. It did look as though the roomful of people were waiting for her reply.

Slowly she lowered her eyelashes, aware that he watched her carefully. His eyes still strayed often to her bosom. It was a male proclivity she had grown accustomed to in the theatre.

"I would be most honored, sir," she replied in a throaty voice. Her reply was greeted with applause by those standing near her. "Although, of course, Monsieur Pierone, there are certain . . . monetary considerations which must now, I fear, be negotiated."

He threw back his head and laughed, a wild braying that made his guests stare in his direction. When they saw who it was, they smiled indulgently.

"That, I believe, we may leave until later. We will talk again whenever it is most convenient for you. But I promise you that I will be generous. Very generous."

She ignored the innuendo. "Thank you, monsieur."

"Now, I must not keep you entirely to myself or I'll have a house full of jealous guests!" He smiled at her, the expression closer to a leer again. "There are many others here to whom I wish to introduce you. Come, come, my little *Anglaise*, come with me."

Anglaise again, she thought with some humor. That was to

be expected, of course, but she wondered if it might not settle into some sort of nickname.

L'Anglaise Ariel, and she quickly hid a smile.

They approached a cluster of people who were talking intensely among themselves.

With a grand theatrical flourish Pierone announced: "My dear friends, I wish to introduce to you the famous *actrice* Madame Ariel Greystone, lately of London, now of Paris. She has been most gracious in accepting my offer and will henceforth be employed by the Théâtre d'Empire."

This time there was a hearty round of applause from the entire room, and she smiled and acknowledged it.

Pierone continued with the introductions. "This man who stands gawking at you, Madame Greystone, is my old friend Onfroi de Bonnot. You must watch out for him, for he is a sly fox." He chuckled at his own wit.

The man turned red with Pierone's words and bowed over her hand. He had regular features and a medium build, and there seemed nothing outstanding about him except that his smile looked genuinely friendly. He contrasted greatly with his "old friend" Auguste. Next to de Bonnot stood a distinguished-looking gentleman with a mass of silver hair. He was impeccably dressed and carried a walking stick and gave his name as Jean-Étienne Valazé. To his right was a married couple, Roland and Béatrice Hanriot, who appeared to be in their mid to late thirties, and next to them a small woman, simply attired and with the white hair of age, although her face was still unmarred by time. She stepped forward to greet Ariel.

"Welcome to our country, Madame Greystone," she said with a sincere smile. "I hope you will enjoy your stay. I am Eve Moreau."

Ariel had heard that name before. Surely it could not be the woman she was thinking of. "La Moreau?" Ariel asked, astonished.

The other woman gave a small laugh and looked genuinely pleased. "Yes, I fear I must own up to that."

"Ah, Mademoiselle Moreau, my mother has spoken highly of you to me. She admired you so very much in *The Maid of Orleans*."

"I am afraid," the actress said with a rueful smile, "that

Voltaire's heroine is a role I have not played for many years now, nor will I again. Those days are long over. But come, your mother must have been very young when she saw me."

"She was but fourteen, and said it had the most profound influence on her."

"I am pleased to hear that, but fear I feel quite old—your mother was but a child. Ah, well."

Ariel smiled at the older actress. "Will you be in Monsieur Pierone's company?" She hoped so, for Ariel wanted to become better acquainted with the small woman. There would be so much she could learn from this famous actress. Her mother would be ecstatic when she wrote her. But, she had to remind herself, as much as she wished to be a pupil of La Moreau's, acting was not her first priority here. Still, she would learn what she could from the woman.

"Oh yes, Auguste approached me some time ago." She cast a sly look in the manager's direction. "I think he feared that I would be snatched up by someone else." She laughed at the irony, and Ariel knew with some sadness that while the woman was famous throughout the Continent and England, there were few roles now for a woman her age. She little doubted that La Moreau would be retiring from the stage within the next few years.

"Tell me," said Madame Hanriot, turning to the two women and speaking for the first time, "how do you find France?"

"I lived here when I was a child, but in the southern provinces. I had never gone north at all. I confess that Paris is new to me. I am enjoying myself, although I have been quite busy with my household."

She waited for someone to ask her about her exile from England, but no one did. They were too polite for that, she decided. If they were inclined to discuss politics, it was not when strangers were present. She learned that Valazé was a writer, having penned a history of France published in eleven volumes, while Hanriot and de Bonnot were minor officials in the government. This she found of interest.

She arranged to have the Hanriots and Mademoiselle Moreau come to tea—an English custom she would not give up for anything—the next day, and Valazé, de Bonnot, and she would go riding the day after.

Finally, an increasingly impatient Pierone pulled Ariel away to take her on the full circuit of the large salon, introducing her to each of his guests. Many of them were from the theatrical world and were employed in Pierone's company, while others were politicians and government officials. She realized her acquisition of information would be that much simpler if she could freely mingle with those who were involved in the government. A smattering of old nobility were in attendance, too, ones who had managed to keep their heads. No doubt they had fled to other countries, only to return when Napoleon became leader.

Despite all the aristocrats she met, she was disappointed to realize the comte was not there, for she had been hoping to meet him.

A clock out in the hall struck the hour of midnight. She turned to her host, intending to plead a headache and exhaustion and return home. The headache was not far from the truth, and she realized she was tired as well.

"Monsieur Pierone—" she began.

He held up his hand in a showmanlike fashion. "Now," he said before she could continue, "there is something else I must beg of you, Madame Greystone."

"Something else?" She drew her eyebrows together.

"Ah, yes, I have a friend who is most *désireux* of meeting you." The leer had returned. Was this his own ploy to get her alone?

"I thought I had already met all of your friends tonight."

He chuckled and waggled a beefy finger at her. "I have many more friends than this, madame, let me assure you. But, still there is one more." He took her hand before she could protest and led her from the room. They walked down a dimly lit hall away from the salon, and the sounds of laughter and conversation grew fainter. Frowning, she wondered where he was taking her. She knew many managers viewed their actresses proprietarily, and that sometimes led to the bedroom. Something she could not contemplate with this man!

He stopped at the end of the hall, gave her a measured look from his sly eyes, and flung the door open. Beyond she could see there was another salon, although this one was much smaller.

"Madame Greystone!" he boomed out.

Across the room a man who had been sitting on a settee looked up. He stood and came toward them. Pierone turned to her and announced happily, "*Ma cherie*, may I introduce you to the Most Elevated Philippe Baptiste Fouret, comte du Veilleur!"

Twenty-Two

She took a long good look at the man she had wanted to meet. He stood a little over medium height and was quite slender, although his was a body that implied hidden strengths, not weakness. His golden hair was dressed in the latest style, its curls carefully tousled to look casual. His skin would have been the envy of any woman for it was a pale shade, almost a porcelain white, as though he was rarely exposed to the sun. How unlike Drake's, she thought, whose face had been darkened by the sun over many years.

The comte's face was slender, too, with the look of a fox in its long length. His brown eyes were fringed by thick dark lashes and looked very intelligent. His teeth were white and dazzling, perfectly formed, as was everything else about this man.

He was formally attired in a wine-colored velvet coat with claw-hammer tails, black satin breeches, and a gold silk waistcoat elaborately embroidered in greens and black. His shirt had frills at the waist, and white silk stockings and black pumps with gold buckles adorned his legs and feet. The starched points of his neckcloth rose so high that turning his head was almost an impossibility. She could not help but contrast his immaculate attire with the haphazard appearance of Drake.

If not for the shrewd expression on his face the comte might have looked like a dandy. No, not a dandy, she decided, but rather, a peacock. The thought amused her.

She held out her hand and smiled her most charming smile. "Good evening, monsieur."

He bowed over her hand, pressing it ardently to his lips. His breath was warm against her gloved hand, and sent a slight shiver down her back. When he straightened, he did not release her hand but held it tight while looking earnestly into her eyes.

"I am most delighted to meet you at last, Madame Greystone." His voice was moderately low and pleasing to the ear. "I must confess that I have long admired you but never thought that we would meet."

"You flatter me, sir," she murmured, lowering her eyes demurely.

"Not at all." Still he did not release her hand.

Pierone beamed at both of them. "Excellent, excellent!" he said. "I see that you two have hit it off. Well, I shan't delay any longer. I must return to my other guests. *Au revoir*," he said, bowed, and withdrew from the salon.

Once the door had closed and they were alone, the comte turned his dazzling smile once more upon her. "Wine, Madame Greystone? Or would you prefer champagne?"

"I would like champagne, please," she replied. He poured two glasses at an ebony sideboard, and once they were seated at either end of the settee, he handed her a glass.

The champagne was light and bubbly and tasted wonderful. Her mouth had grown quite dry in the past few minutes. As they sat in a comfortable silence she attempted to gather her thoughts. Now that she had met the comte and was alone with him, she was not sure how to proceed.

But you are an actress, she told herself. Act. He is already quite taken with you—that much would be obvious even if Drake had not already told you. The rest will be simple.

The rest of what?

Before she could speak, he did.

He leaned back in the settee and appraised her frankly. "I must confess that I was delighted to hear that Auguste was desirous of your joining his company. Believe me, he has talked of nothing else since learning you would be coming to

Paris, and he has been eagerly awaiting your arrival—as have all of your admirers. But now you must tell me, Madame Greystone," he said, leaning closer to her, "have you given him an answer?"

"Yes, just a short time ago."

He raised a thin eyebrow as an eager look came into his eyes. "And?"

"You will have to talk with Monsieur Pierone about that, I fear."

He laughed and stood up to pour himself more champagne. When he sat down again, it was a little closer to her than before. She tingled slightly, very aware of his presence and not at all immune to his charm. "I see that I must. But I trust you will not break my heart by informing me that I will not see you upon the stage while you sojourn in France."

She smiled as she raised the glass to her lips. She wanted to be as mysterious and alluring as possible. He was already interested in her and she wanted him absolutely riveted. So much so that . . . that what? she wondered. How far did this fascination need to go?

His face took on a suffering look. "I am wounded because you will not answer me!"

She laughed, delighted. "Ah, I see, I must relieve your burdened heart."

"Do." He took her hand. "Please." His brown eyes searched her face. "What is your answer?"

"I have accepted Monsieur Pierone's generous offer," she replied.

"Excellent! This calls for more champagne." He leaped to his feet and brought the bottle back.

She accepted another glass from him, and wondered how much wine and champagne she had had that day. Certainly not enough to make her sleepy. Who could sleep in the presence of this dazzling man?

Remember, one part of her urged, *you* are supposed to do the dazzling.

He pressed her for details about her new house, and she told him she was delighted with it and with the attention all had given her since her arrival a week before.

"It must be very difficult to be in exile from your country,

madame. I am sorry that you were forced to leave under such
circumstances, but it is our gain and England's loss." She was
aware that he was watching her carefully.

Her face contorted in a semblance of anger and disgust as
she looked away. "Yes, terrible circumstances, I fear, monsieur, for the English are most narrow-minded." She drank
the last of her champagne. "I should have left there years ago,
but I didn't because of my poor mother, whose health suffers
in such a miserable climate. She is absolutely besotted by the
English. How anyone could so like those cold people is quite
beyond me." She shook her head. "They have shown us very
little kindness, believe me, monsieur!"

"They are truly hypocritical, then."

"Priggish."

"Cold."

"Unfeeling."

"Brutal."

"They do not have the sentiment of the French, I confess,
and it has been wonderful for me to come home. France is,
after all, my home."

"More champagne?"

"Yes, please." After he filled her glass, she looked earnestly
into his face and asked, "May we change the subject? I have
had my fill of the English lately and have no further use for
them."

"Of course. I do not wish to distress you. I suggest a toast,
Madame Greystone!" He lifted his glass and smiled down at
her.

"Please, monsieur, you must not be so formal with me."
She laughed a little. "You must call me Ariel, as do all my
friends." He was so close now, only inches away, and heat
radiated from him, burned through the material covering her
thigh, and she wet her lower lip.

"Very well, Ariel." He seemed to like the sound of her
name on his tongue. "Ariel. I hope that I will be one of your
close friends. And you must call me Philippe. And now a
toast."

She stood, her dress rustling softly, and held her glass aloft,
as did he.

"To your new home," he said.

"To France," she said in a low tone. They took a sip of champagne, then she added, "To new friends, Philippe." Their eyes locked as they took another sip of the bubbly wine.

"Yes," he agreed, his eyes suggestively raking over her, "to new friends."

She smiled, and drank the last of her champagne. She felt a tremor of cold shake through her. This time she did not think it was the fault of the champagne.

Twenty-Three

"She has been there for a fortnight, and I have yet to receive a letter," Etoile said as she plucked at her coverlet. She stared anxiously at Drake sitting beside her bed.

"So she has, Etoile, but you mustn't fret unnecessarily." He took her hand in his and held it. It was so small and so cold, and lay in his palm as though she were no longer alive. No, he thought, pushing that image from his mind. He had come to her as soon as he had heard she was sick. With Ariel gone, he must look after Etoile, a task he did not regret for he was genuinely fond of the petite Frenchwoman. It saddened him to see how much she had shrunk in the intervening years since he had first met her. She seemed to be slipping away before his very eyes. He summoned his most confident tone. "I'm sure she's been very busy settling into her new home, as well as looking for a new job."

"You needn't coddle me," she said, her tone a little waspish and her accent becoming more pronounced, "as though I were a child, Kit. I know full well that she had things to do."

His look was sheepish. "I'm sorry, Etoile. I beg your forgiveness."

"I will forgive you only if you tell me the truth!" she announced.

He felt doubt shadow him. "The truth?"

"Yes, about Ariel."

"But Etoile—" he began.

She slipped her hand out of his and held a finger against his lips. "No, no, no. I do not wish to hear lies."

"Lies!"

"Perhaps that it is too strong a word." Her eyes twinkled with humor, and he was encouraged at the sign, for she seemed a little more lively now than when he had arrived half an hour earlier. She was watching him closely, and he hoped his face was shuttered, for she was very astute, this French-woman. "No, I do not know now if that word is too strong. Perhaps I can think of something even stronger." She shifted, trying to sit up straighter against her pillows, and he leaped to his feet to help her.

"You really are most unkind with me, Etoile. To accuse me of lying—or worse."

"Ah, but it is true, *mon cher*. You and my daughter have plotted for months against me."

"How so, Etoile?" he asked, regaining his seat.

Her dark eyes regarded him suspiciously. "I do not under-stand why, after all the years of silence and separation, you two are suddenly together again. Do not misunderstand, Kit. I am delighted with this unexpected development, for I have de-sired it most strongly for a long time, but frankly, I do not understand it." She wrinkled her nose. "It smells."

"Smells?" His look was genuinely amused."

"Yes, smells. It is most suspicious. Now, you must tell me what you are up to."

"I cannot, Etoile."

"Why?" she demanded.

"It is . . . a secret."

"A secret? There are none between mothers and daugh-ters."

"There is this time."

She reached out to take a sip of wine. There was a tray on the table beside the bed and on it sat a carafe of wine. Drake knew her doctor had prescribed three glasses of wine a day, and she was not drinking over one. Her hand trembled as she picked up the glass. Not a good sign, he thought.

"I know why she left." The look in her eyes was quite mis-chievous now.

He knew he would have to hear her out. "All right, Etoile, tell me why Ariel left."

She smiled slyly at him. "It's quite obvious, really. My daughter had to flee England because there was a Jack in the low cellar!"

"What!" Astonished, he could only stare at her. He was torn between laughter and shock that she knew such a phrase. "Etoile, really! Wherever can you have heard that outrageous phrase?"

She shrugged offhandedly. "I have had many admirers in my life, not all of them the most genteel, and I learned many things from them. Well?" she persisted. "Is that the truth?"

"No, it is not. Your daughter, as far as I know, is not in the family way."

"Oh."

He thought she sounded a little disappointed, and he tried hard not to smile. No doubt she had thought that if Ariel were pregnant, he would do the right thing by her and offer to marry her. And Etoile would have what she had wanted for so long. Of course, he had already proposed to Ariel many years ago, but where had that gotten both of them?

"You must tell me." She stared plaintively at him, almost as though she were willing him to speak.

"I must not do anything but let you rest now, Etoile. I don't wish to tire you." He started to rise, but she put a hand on his.

"Please, don't go, Kit. I am so lonely since she left."

Obediently he sat down and held her hand. She had closed her eyes, and he could tell she was very weary. No doubt she would fall asleep very soon, and then he would leave quietly. He waited, and after a few minutes she did not open her eyes, and her breathing became more regular. He slipped her hand under the coverlet, then brought the coverlet up to her chin so that she would be warm. He rose and moved quietly across the room. Just as he reached the door, she spoke.

"I am not asleep."

He turned, regarding her with wry amusement. "I see that."

"You were trying to slip away."

"I thought you slept."

"You *hoped* I slept!"

Resigned, he sighed and came back to sit by her bedside. "Is there anything that I can get you, Etoile, while I am still here?"

She considered it. "Perhaps something to eat, I think. I believe I have a slight hunger."

"Good." That was the best sign he'd seen since he'd come to visit her.

He rang for Lizzy, and when the servant came he instructed her to fetch a meal for her mistress. They did not have long to wait, for it would seem that the attentive Lizzy and Nooks had already prepared a meal for their mistress. Of course, he thought. They always managed to anticipate every detail.

She sipped delicately at the beef broth and offered him some, which he declined. For a long time she did not speak, but instead concentrated on her meal. When she was almost finished with the broth, she looked up and smiled at him.

"Do you have everything now, my dear?" he asked.

"Yes . . . except one thing."

"Name it, Etoile."

She gazed up at him. "I wish to know why my daughter is in France. I have that right, Kit, as her mother, and you know that very well."

"Yes, I know that. But I had thought to spare you," and even as the words were out of his mouth he regretted them.

"From what? What is she doing there? Is she in danger? You must tell me! I think it is so strange what has been happening. My daughter would never speak against the government. I don't understand. Why was she asked to leave? What has she done?" Her voice was rising, and her cheeks had flushed a dangerous red.

"Please, don't become agitated," he said, taking her hand. "I will tell you." He could no longer keep the truth from her, not unless he desired to see her become even more ill.

She settled back against the pillows and waited. Her color returned to normal.

"Ariel has gone to France for me."

"For you?" She drew her brows together in a puzzled look. "I do not understand. Why would she do that for you?"

He took a deep breath. This was very difficult for him, difficult because he didn't want to tell her. He knew she would worry, but he could no longer keep her in ignorance, either. He wondered briefly what Ariel would say if she knew that her mother had been told of her new occupation.

"Yes, Etoile, she is in France for me. I sent her there to—" He took another deep breath and the rest came out in a rush. "To spy on Napoleon."

There was silence. This wasn't the reaction he had expected.

"Etoile? Etoile!" He bent closer and stared at her, then drew away, appalled.

Etoile had fainted dead away.

Twenty-Four

Drake chafed her wrists and fanned her, and after a few minutes Etoile gradually came around. Her eyelids fluttered, then finally opened, and when she saw him standing over her, she mouthed a faint "Oh my" and closed them once more.

"I was afraid it would have this effect upon you," he said grimly. "That is why I didn't want to tell you. I regret that I did."

"No, no," she protested, struggling to sit up once more. He put an arm around her to help her. "You had to tell me, Kit. I had to know the truth," she said, her voice faltering, "even if it is so horrible." Her large eyes filled with tears. "I cannot believe what you have said. She went to France as a spy?" He nodded in confirmation. "How could she do something so dangerous? How could *you*, Kit, put her in danger? I thought you loved her!" Her dark eyes accused him.

He ignored her last statement with some difficulty. "I put her in danger because she was the only one who could do what has to be done, Etoile. And, besides, she wanted to help." This, of course, was not strictly true, indeed, was not even remotely true, but better he should say this than inform Etoile that he had coerced her daughter into helping him.

"I don't understand. Why couldn't some man have done your spying? Why use my Ariel?"

"There are many elements that led to my selecting her,

Etoile. One of which is that she is an actress, and Napoleon is fond of the theatre. It followed that she would have a much easier time obtaining an introduction to him."

She gave him a suspicious glance. "She won't have to seduce him, will she?"

His lips curved in a slight smile. "I trust not, my dear." He decided it was best not to say anything about the comte. Indeed, he did not like to think about Ariel and the comte together. The idea should not have bothered him, after all, but for some reason it did.

"But spying! What a terrible business!"

"Yes." There was no denying that.

"Will you not call her back?" she asked, her tone filled with hope. "Now that I know?"

He shook his head adamantly. "I cannot, Etoile, nor would Ariel want that. You know that she is a professional in all that she chooses to do. She has a job to do now and she will see it to the end."

"Even if the end is violent?" Etoile asked, her voice tremulous.

"Yes."

"I think, Kit," she said, closing her eyes and looking even more weary now than when he had arrived. She seemed to have aged rapidly in the past few minutes. "I think I do not like you very much right now. I wish you to leave."

He stood, bowed, and left, instructing Lizzy and Nooks to watch after their mistress for she appeared to have had a relapse. Their expressions clearly said they did not approve of his visits when their mistress was left feeling worse than before he had arrived.

It did not take him long to reach home, and once there, he settled at his desk in the library to do work he'd been postponing for the past few days.

He wrote letters for a while, then paused, his quill pen posed above the inkwell, and stared out the large window without really seeing. He wasn't happy with his visit. He had not reassured Etoile, but rather had alarmed her.

Yes, Ariel was put in some amount of danger by doing what she was doing, but he would do all he could to insure that she was not harmed. He would see to her safety even if he had to go there.

And he thought it odd, too, that Ariel had permitted two weeks to go by without writing her mother. She was a devoted daughter, and whenever she had been separated from her mother she had always written numerous letters to her. Her silence was not reassuring.

But, perhaps she was busy, busy with her new home, with her job.

He missed her, too.

A slight frown creasing his brow, and feeling less than relieved, he resumed writing.

Mademoiselle Moreau and Béatrice Hanriot came to tea, and the following day Ariel went riding with two men. A day later she dined with the Hanriots and Monsieur de Bonnot at the latter's house, and in the days following also managed to attend several parties, given by influential hostesses. Jules Senoille came to visit her several times, once bringing with him a bouquet of flowers. Genuinely pleased, she thanked him, but she wished that he would not be so serious with her. Even Auguste Pierone called upon her and declared her home a heavenly retreat for an actress.

To her amazement, she found she was enjoying the company of her newfound friends, and the ache of being away from her mother and home was easing somewhat.

Du Veilleur also called upon her. The night she met him they had talked until three in the morning, and then she had said she must leave. He had offered to escort her home, but she had demurred—she wanted to hold him off a little, just enough to tantalize him. He had bowed, and said he would be seeing her again. She had murmured that she hoped so.

So she had returned home, immensely pleased with herself and the evening and with the knowledge that du Veilleur was one of the very first men she'd met in Paris. Drake would no doubt be pleased.

She would have to let Drake know eventually that contact between herself and du Veilleur had been established almost immediately. But before she could do that, she would have to make the acquaintance of yet another man: Armand L'Croix.

This name had been given to her by Drake shortly before she left England. L'Croix, Drake had informed her, was a staunch royalist whose entire family had been killed in the Terror. He had escaped death by the guillotine and as an émigré had lived in Europe for some years, but he had returned to his homeland once Napoleon came to power. Although he worked with the then-Consul Bonaparte, L'Croix despised the man, deeming him nothing more than a usurper of the throne of the rightful kings, the Bourbons.

Thomas Hendricks, another of Drake's spies in France, had met L'Croix and begun talking with him, and once L'Croix made his views clear, Hendricks had approached him and L'Croix had agreed to pass along information.

Because of the close social circle of the elite in Paris, Ariel did not think she would have long to wait before she met L'Croix. Too, he had been alerted to her arrival and would no doubt soon seek her out. But until then, she would have to wait.

As for Hendricks, she doubted she would meet him during her sojourn, as du Veilleur termed it. Drake had said he preferred to keep his agents away from one another as much as possible while they were working. That way, if something went wrong and an agent were captured, he—or she—would not be able to name more than a few others, and the entire operation would not then be jeopardized.

An excellent idea, she reasoned, but it only served to make her job all the more lonely. She would have one single contact: L'Croix. Her only link to Drake.

Still, it was reassuring to know there was at least another English agent in Paris, for if she got into trouble he would probably be able to help her.

Every day was busy, and each morning Ariel found herself rising promptly at eight, an unheard-of hour for her. Yet there was so much to do each day that she could not linger in bed much beyond that hour—even if she had just fallen asleep some three or four hours before that.

When she had been in Paris a little over two weeks, she

realized with a pang of guilt that she had not written to her mother. Immediately she sat down and wrote a five-page letter, telling her of her new acting job, of the people she had met, particularly Monsieur Senoille and Mademoiselle Moreau, and of her new home. She could mention nothing else. She said she missed her mother and hoped that she was well.

She was still quite homesick and knew that would last for some time. There was nothing she could do for it except stay busy, which she was doing.

She glanced through her invitations, accepting some, begging off of others that conflicted. And once that was accomplished, she sat down with a hot cup of tea and, gazing out the window as the rain fell, began to think how she could come to know Philippe du Veilleur even better.

Twenty-Five

But Ariel did not have long to worry about how to better acquaint herself with the comte, for a few days later du Veilleur came calling. She was in the salon, just finishing another letter to her mother, when he was ushered in.

"Good afternoon, Ariel," the blond man said as he strode across the room to take her hand.

She rose to greet him. "I was just thinking of you, Philippe."

"Were you indeed? What a fortunate coincidence, for I was just out riding and was seized of a great desire to see you again. It has been so long!"

"Only a few days," she murmured. One of the servants came in, and she looked to du Veilleur. "You can stay to dinner, can't you?"

"Yes, I am quite free this evening."

They sat and chatted about the current fashions being set at court by Josephine. Ariel doubted mere chance had brought him to her house that day, but it was just a matter of waiting to find out his purpose.

"How is your new job?" he asked, draping one arm along the back of a hunter green settee.

"Very good. We are now rehearsing for the beginning of the season. I cannot believe it is less than two months away! There is so much to do yet!"

"Ah, but I know, Ariel, that you will be as excellent as ever."

"Thank you," she said, accepting the compliment, "but much of the credit must go to Monsieur Pierone, too, for he is a very capable manager."

"I am looking forward to seeing you upon a French stage," he said.

"You mean any stage," she amended with a laugh.

"No, I mean the French stage, for I have seen you in the English theatre."

"What?' She looked pleased. "But how could this be, Philippe?"

He glanced about the room, a slight smile playing at his lips. "I must confess that some years ago I went across the Channel to London. For the express purpose of seeing you perform."

She sat back, an amazed expression on her face. "No! Really?"

He nodded. "Yes, it is all true."

"But how could you—?"

He held up an admonishing finger. "Let me just say that there were ways, my dear. And that is how I came to be an admirer of yours, and why I am so pleased that you are now in France."

"I am most honored to be here, sir."

"And I am most delighted." He caught her hand and raised her fingers to his lips. His kiss sent a tingle through her. He was very handsome today in a velvet coat and pantaloons of Prussian blue decorated with gold braid and buttons. Very handsome, she decided.

"But that is not the only reason I came today, Ariel. I would like to know if you would come riding with me tomorrow—providing it is not raining."

"Of course! You have only to name the time."

"Not so late that it will interfere with your rehearsing, eh? Perhaps three or so?"

"Fine."

"And . . ."

She arched an eyebrow. "And what, Philippe?"

He chuckled. "You will think me a pest, I fear." She smiled to let him know she considered him anything but a pest. "I do not know if you are aware of it, but the emperor's birthday is next month. The fifteenth. There is to be a party held in his honor at court, and I would be honored if you would attend with me. Will you, Ariel?" He looked at her earnestly.

"Of course, Philippe." She smiled at him, and before she could say any more, dinner was announced.

As he escorted her into the dining room, Ariel could not help but smile. She had been invited to a party in honor of Napoleon. It would seem all was going very well indeed. She looked forward to the occasion.

The next day it did not rain, and she went riding with du Veilleur. The day after that she spent with Mademoiselle Moreau, and on the weekend she and du Veilleur attended an exclusive salon, a gathering of some of the more notable artists and patrons of Paris society.

She kept close to his side, laughing and smiling—and watching. Always she watched. She could see the envy in the eyes of many, men and women alike. Still, she was not there to make friends, but rather to find information, and du Veilleur, thus far, was her best source.

At one point du Veilleur went off to refill her punch glass, and Ariel watched the other couples dance and converse as she awaited du Veilleur's return. She was aware that a woman across the room was staring at her and had been doing so for many minutes now. Ariel frowned, thinking she recognized her, though she could not place her face.

The woman wore her heavy tresses looped in an outmoded style and had probably been attractive in her youth. She had a heart-shaped face and dark eyes, but the years had not been kind. Not even the careful application of makeup could disguise the creases around her mouth and the lines crinkling at the corners of her eyes, which were heavily outlined in black. Ariel suspected that her bright red hair had been tinted, for it was no shade she had ever seen. The woman was attired most spectacularly in a tightly cut ebony satin dress that brought emphasis to her ripe figure and full bosom, and diamonds glittered at her ears and throat and on her hands.

The woman stood with several men and would say something to them from time to time that drew their laughter.

Ariel suspected the wit was at her expense. She frowned, trying to place the woman's face, but was unable to identify her.

When du Veilleur returned, she thanked him for the punch.
He slipped his arm around her. It was the first time he had
taken such a step, and she did not want to discourage him, yet
she was ill at ease under the baleful scrutiny of the unknown
woman.

Finally, she could stay silent no longer. "Do you see that
red-haired woman over there, Philippe? The one in black?"

She thought his lips pressed together momentarily.

"Yes, I see her. What about her, my darling?"

"Who is she? She has been staring at us for minutes on
end."

He chuckled. "Give her no further thought, my dear. She is
of no consequence."

"She seems familiar, but I can't recall where I might have
seen her."

"Perhaps the theatre," he said. "She is—or claims to
be—an actress."

"The theatre!" she exclaimed. "That's it! I saw her for a
few minutes while Monsieur Pierone was interviewing for the
final positions. I remember it clearly now. One day she came
and gave a reading just as I was leaving, and Monsieur Pierone
called her back. I think that he is going to give her a job."

Du Veilleur shook his head. "I do not think that is good."

"Why?" She frowned slightly. "Do you know her,
Philippe?"

"Yes, I fear I do." He was looking across at the red-haired
woman now, who saw him and smiled coyly. "Yes, I know
her. She is a bad one, Ariel, and you would do well to leave
her alone. Take my advice, please."

"Very well. We haven't been introduced, so there should be
no problem."

"Of that I would not be so certain, *ma chère*."

He sipped his punch and talked with Ariel, but she could see
that his attention really wasn't on their conversation. From
time to time his eyes strayed to the other woman. Finally, he
spoke again. "I think, perhaps, that we should leave now, if
you do not mind."

"Of course not." She was a little surprised by his abrupt

decision to leave, but she didn't really mind. She gathered her shawl and took his arm, and they walked past the woman.

Ariel did not turn her head to look back. She had seen the woman watching with hate in her dark eyes, and she wondered why the woman felt this way.

Twenty-Six

Mademoiselle Madeleine La Châtelet watched the couple leave the room and fanned herself idly even though her teeth were clenched in anger.

She had been furious to see the *Anglaise* on the arm of Philippe, and then to see the hussy so brazenly stare at her while her precious Philippe was gone.

No wonder he had been acting so strangely this past week. Now she understood, and she cursed her stupidity. She should have suspected from the moment his attention began to lag that another woman was involved. Certainly it would not have been the first time that Philippe had strayed from her.

But to have strayed for that *Anglaise*, and another actress as well! That was the outside of enough! La Châtelet had seen the *Anglaise* act the day she had gone to get the job with the Théâtre d'Empire. She thought it had been a very wooden performance. The *Anglaise*'s expressions were scarcely above the level of grimaces. She looked as though she suffered from some pain all during the rehearsal. At least *she*, Madeleine La Châtelet, could act.

Yet her acting ability had not helped her to hold Philippe, and it was her age that had been her downfall. She was in her late thirties, although she said she was thirty.

Age. Bah! The other woman was not so young herself; that she could tell from clear across the room. The pretty little

Anglaise had best watch out, or she would soon be usurped by another woman much younger. That was how it always was with Philippe. He strayed, looking for younger game, but in the end he always came back to her.

Always.

She had not known who the woman was when she went to the Théâtre d'Empire, but tonight she recognized her.

Too, it was infuriating to find that the senile Pierone doted on the *Anglaise* and had promised her a part that earlier he had promised to La Châtelet. If only she had not traveled to the south of France for a month, if only she had stayed in the city, none of this would have happened.

Now something had to be done. She would see to it that Pierone did not continue doting on her rival. Nor would she allow Philippe to stay long with the *Anglaise*. She was, after all, only a shallow young woman, while La Châtelet was a woman of much experience—experience not only in life, but in teaching young women like that a lesson.

She smiled at Onfroi de Bonnot and Jean-Étienne Valazé, who had just joined her. They had noticed the direction of her eyes and were very quiet as they waited for her to say something. They well knew her temper and did not wish to ignite it.

"Who is that?" she inquired.

"She is the *Anglaise* that has been forced to leave her country," said de Bonnot. "Surely you must have heard of her."

"An *Anglaise*?" she asked, lifting one painted eyebrow. "Is this the fashion of the day, Onfroi? How novel, to be sure."

"I do not know if it is the fashion, Madeleine, but she seems to be very . . . likable," he said.

"Likeable? Come, come, Onfroi," she chided gently. "A dog is likable. A woman is lovable."

Valazé chuckled. "I think that Madeleine has once more bested you, Onfroi."

De Bonnot gave an exaggerated sigh. "Alas, you are right."

"Now, Madeleine, you must not worry that you will be supplanted by the *Anglaise*."

She flashed a brittle smile. "I do not worry about her. I worry about him."

"Philippe can take care of himself," de Bonnot said with a laugh.

"Perhaps, perhaps . . . but he was always a little naïve, I fear."

"Naïve?" asked Valazé with quickening interest. "What do you mean, my dear?"

"I mean," she said, turning her hands up in a gesture of impatience, "that dear Philippe is such an *enfant*. Truly! He is a man of the world in many ways; as for women, alas, he is not." She shook her head as though this news greatly depressed her.

"How so, as for women?" de Bonnot repeated.

"He is unlike you two."

"Eh, not like us, Jean?" He puffed his heavy chest out, and she thought he looked like a drab pigeon with his starched collar tips on either side of his face.

"True," the other man murmured, his brows drawn together in a frown. "He has many mistresses, it is true."

"And all of them have demanded much and taken from him all that they could," she said, an almost feline purr in her voice. "Is it any wonder that the poor man is nearly broke?" She paused to take a sip of the red wine and fingered the cut-crystal goblet. Men, she thought as she looked at the rapt faces of her two listeners. They were such *imbéciles*. Always so foolish to listen to women speak about other women.

"Then you think that the *Anglaise* is just using poor Philippe?" de Bonnot asked.

"I did not say that, precisely," she said.

He drew his brows together. "Hmm. That puts a different light on it, doesn't it, Jean?"

Valazé nodded, looking just as thoughtful as de Bonnot.

"I have seen countless others like her," La Châtelet said. "Poor and searching for some man with a fortune to support them." She sighed, as if this topic weighed heavily on her mind.

"Why was she forced to leave her own country?" de Bonnot asked.

"I heard," Valazé said, "it was because she made a great mistake there. Perhaps there was a scandal. She had to leave, and she came to France, and what better place to find a rich husband who will protect her, eh?"

"That is true," de Bonnot said, nodding sagely. He clasped his hands behind his back and shook his head. "Poor Philippe. Perhaps we should warn him."

"No," La Châtelet said rather quickly, "I will take care of that. After all, he might think that either one of you is attempting to take the *Anglaise* away from him, *n'est-ce pas*?"

"Ah, perhaps you have a point," de Bonnot said, elbowing his friend.

"Yes, yes." Valazé grinned at the woman.

"By the way, the *Anglaise* does have a name, doesn't she?" the woman asked.

"Ariel Greystone," de Bonnot supplied promptly. "But she was born here of the family de Juliers."

La Châtelet's eyes widened, for she had heard of the de Juliers family. Very interesting, she told herself.

There was a whisper of silken material, and the three friends looked up. Eve Moreau stood close by, and her features were set in a stern expression.

"I could not but overhear your conversation, Madeleine, and I would advise the three of you to leave the comte and Madame Greystone alone. I think your jealousy will accomplish nothing and it does not show you in a good light. Good evening." She nodded formally to them and walked away.

For a long moment Madeleine watched the other actress, then turned to look at the two startled men and smiled her sweetest smile.

"Bitch," she murmured, and the men chuckled.

"Thank you," Ariel whispered outside the front door of her house. They had arrived only a few minutes ago from the salon and du Veilleur had offered to escort her to the door.

"It was no trouble at all," he said. His arms slipped around her and held her close.

It was a warm July night with little breeze, and the air was fragrant with the perfume of blossoming flowers. Above them a glowing full moon sailed through dark cloudless skies.

His lips nuzzled her ear. " 'O thou art fairer than the evening air, Clad in the beauty of a thousand stars.' ''

"Marlowe!" she exclaimed. "You know him."

He grinned. "Are you surprised that I know the English poets?"

"Yes, very."

"Ah, but I am an educated man, my dear Ariel, as I know you to be an educated woman." His lips nibbled at her earlobe. "Do you know the rest of that quote?"

"No."

" 'Brighter art thou than flaming Jupiter, When he appeared to hapless Semele, More lovely than the monarch of the sky In wanton Arethusa's azured arms, and none but thou shalt be my paramour.' ''

She did not move. She scarcely breathed.

" 'And I will make thee beds of rose And a thousand fragrant posies.' ''

"Come inside, Philippe," she said.

He nodded and kissed her hard on the lips.

Twenty-Seven

On August 15, Ariel attended the party given in honor of Napoleon Bonaparte's thirty-fifth birthday.

Since the night of the salon, she and Philippe du Veilleur had been lovers.

He was thoughtful, and always kind and considerate to her, and yet their lovemaking lacked something. He seemed to enjoy himself thoroughly, but for her there was something missing. And while she had been impressed that he could quote Christopher Marlowe to her, it had only served to remind her of her own Christopher: Drake. Drake and this mission. Drake and her making love. Now du Veilleur and her making love.

She hoped Drake would never find out.

On the evening of the fifteenth, she waited nervously for du Veilleur to arrive. She had dressed early, then changed her clothing, and then had gone down to the salon to pace and wait for Philippe to show.

He was late; they would be late. She would not have a chance to meet either the emperor or the empress; everything would be ruined after she had been so looking forward to this night. She stopped her frantic pacing and checked the German clock on the mantel. It was not yet six. Philippe was not late, after all. She was just worrying about nothing. She had to calm herself, had to relax and breathe deeply, else she would have no strength left to carry her through the night. She suspected she would need all her reserves, for it would doubtless be a very long night indeed.

At that moment she heard the sound of a carriage outside and ran to the door of the salon. In a matter of moments du Veilleur was inside the house, with an arm around her, kissing her hands and face. He drew back to appraise her.

"You look simply ravishing tonight, Ariel, *ma chérie*. Absolutely beautiful."

She laughed, delighted with his compliments. She would never refuse one.

For her first meeting with Napoleon Bonaparte and his empress, she had selected a high-waisted gown of clinging gauzy white material that did little to conceal the figure beneath it. She was glad that it was warm these nights, although low temperatures rarely discouraged stylish women from wearing dresses made of the thin material—or from dampening it, even in the winter, so that the material clung to their bodies. She would not have to worry about that tonight, for she suspected she would be very warm. The sleeves were short and puffed: The rounded neckline was edged with gold ribbon on which diamonds had been sewn.

She wore topaz earrings and square-cut topazes set in a necklace of beaten gold. Quite striking, she thought wryly. Only she knew that the gems—both diamonds and topazes —were not real, but rather paste jewels skillfully cut to fool all but the truly expert eye. On her feet were new slippers of gold cloth. She picked up a white gauze shawl in case she should need it later.

Hally had dressed her hair in a chignon and curls and had carefully threaded a thin gold ribbon through the black tresses. She had set two diamond-and-pearl pins into the hair at the temples, and several curls caressed each cheek.

Du Veilleur kissed her again.

"I think you, too, are quite exquisite tonight, Philippe," she said as she admired what she saw before her. He was dressed in true court fashion in black velvet breeches and a violet satin frock coat with white satin lining. His brocade waistcoat was embroidered in silver and violet thread and had jeweled buttons. A jabot and cravat, with collar points, com-

pleted his neckgear, while at his cuffs were lace wrist frills. His
stockings were of the finest silk. Diamonds glittered on his
hands and on the buckles of his black pumps, and in one hand
he held a black felt hat with white velvet lining. A ceremonial
sword dangled from a ribbon at his side. His hair had been left
natural, without any powder, and it was tousled naturally. He
almost looked like a little boy.

She thought he looked quite dashing, and the black and
violet drew out his blond coloring quite well, making him very
handsome.

"Your valet is to be complimented for his excellent taste,"
she teased, and was quickly rewarded with an impish smile.

Pausing to pull on her elbow-length gloves, she glanced into
the hall mirror to once more check her attire. "I'm ready,"
she announced after a moment.

Du Veilleur helped her into his carriage, a sleek black vehi-
cle newly purchased, and they left promptly, rolling down the
wide carriage sweep.

The early-evening air was balmy, and off to the west the sky
was painted a brilliant crimson and salmon from the rays of
the setting sun. Only a few clouds drifted overhead. She enjoyed the short journey through the streets of Paris to the
royal palace of the Tuileries, and she wished that it could have
been longer.

He helped her out and put her hand through his arm as she
stared at the palace. The Tuileries, which stood on the right
bank of the Seine River, was begun in 1564 by Catherine de
Médicis but not finished until the 1600s. It was comprised of a
long, narrow band of buildings with high roofs and dormer
windows. At one end, du Veilleur explained, it was joined to
the Louvre Palace. Napoleon and his family and aides had
moved into the Tuileries in February of 1800.

The famous Tuileries gardens lay on the west side of the
palace grounds, where Maria de Médicis had them built on the
site of an old bricklaying yard. Their designer, Le Nôtre, who
had died in 1700, had borne the title "Supervisor of His Majesty's Gardens." He had also been responsible for the lake
and pathways that cut across the gardens.

"You cannot see much tonight," du Veilleur said, for most

of the light had already faded from the sky. "But perhaps later we could slip away and stroll through the gardens."

"I would like that," she said as a genuine thrill of excitement went through her. She envisioned a moonlit walk through the exquisite gardens, stopping and kissing, and yet the man in her vision had a patch across one eye.

Stop it, she told herself. Stop thinking about him. But try as hard as she could, the thoughts of Drake remained to taunt her.

Once inside, they found the palace ballroom awash with candlelight and resounding with laughter and conversation. In one corner a large orchestra played an aria from a recent Italian opera, and in the center of the ballroom numerous couples danced to the sprightly music. Tables along one entire wall were arranged with a tempting display of delicacies.

She drew out her fan, snapped it open, and gazed about the crowded ballroom. The elite of Paris and the court were represented here tonight. Much would be discussed, and perhaps she would overhear something. While she and du Veilleur were lovers, their relation was not a long-standing one, and so he had not yet come to trust her. Yet. That, she suspected, would soon change. Too, this would be an ideal place for Armand L'Croix to approach her and introduce himself. No one would suspect a chance meeting.

She glanced around, feeling a small knot of expectation in her stomach.

Du Veilleur displayed her proudly to all, as if she were a possession of his—a finely carved statue, perhaps, or a delicate piece of jewelry. She realized that, ironically, this Frenchman was doing precisely what she'd accused Drake of doing. Silently she apologized to Drake.

"Ah, one moment, my love," du Veilleur said after they had been there for an hour. "I see someone I must speak with briefly." He raised his hand slightly, and a balding man some feet away saw and nodded. They walked toward one another and stopped to talk. The music was loud, as was the conversation around her, but Ariel managed to push through the crowd a little in an effort to overhear what the two men were saying.

". . . the naval plan?" the balding man was saying.

"Yes, he's decided to discuss it after the coronation in December. I have the papers at home. Perhaps you can come by sometime and we'll discuss it."

"Very well."

She moved back to where she originally had been waiting for du Veilleur. The naval plan? What could that be? And who was the "he"? It sounded as though du Veilleur had meant Napoleon. Perhaps it meant nothing. But she did not believe so.

The two men did not speak much longer, and then her escort returned to her side.

"I hope you were not bored, Ariel," he said, and kissed her hand.

"Not at all."

"Would you care for something to eat?" She nodded, and he led the way across the immense room to the refreshment tables. There he loaded a plate for them to share and procured glasses of champagne.

She nibbled at the various cheeses and smoked meats while he identified various dignitaries. Finally, when she was finished with her small meal, and he had drunk another glass of champagne, they danced. There were many who watched the couple in envy.

Reluctantly, du Veilleur relinquished her to a tall gentleman, who was followed by a short man with clammy hands, who in turn was replaced by a dark-haired man with bright blue eyes. He was succeeded by an elderly man who informed her that he was a prince in his own right. After that the faces became a blur. Never before had she danced so much, and with so many different partners, and when du Veilleur finally claimed her at what seemed the end of the evening but wasn't, she was short of breath from the exertion but delighted by the attention. She knew all too well what had elicited it—she was a *cause célèbre* in Paris, and there were many who were anxious to learn firsthand about her exile.

She drank more glasses of the sparkling champagne and realized after a while that she was feeling a little giddy. She decided to eat more of the wonderful cheeses, and du Veilleur filled another plate with fresh strawberries and grapes. Playfully he fed the grapes to her one by one.

She found she was truly enjoying herself tonight, enjoying herself for the first time in many years. All her previous worries and concerns, as well as her mission, had faded from her mind. Tonight she would have fun, and no one could fault her for that.

When it was time again for more dancing, du Veilleur refused to surrender her, and with his eyes lingering admiringly on her face, and with the swell of the music rising around her, and the glittering lights blurring, she could almost have believed herself in another world. Everything seemed so far away, except for the lovely music and the look in this man's eyes.

All too soon the music slowed and stopped, and he bowed to her, and she curtsied, and they returned to the real world. But the excitement continued in her, growing to a fever pitch.

When it was close to midnight, du Veilleur put a hand on her arm and nodded to a crowd gathering at the other end of the ballroom.

"I believe we are about to witness the entrance of the emperor and empress," he murmured to her.

That news only stirred her even more, and she wondered what would come of the moment when she was at last face-to-face with Napoleon Bonaparte.

Twenty-Eight

❦

Napoleon Bonaparte was born in Ajaccio, Corsica, in 1769 and was the fourth of ten children. When he was only eight he went to a French military academy, which was to have a profound influence upon his life. There he eagerly studied mathematics, geography, and history, then went on to receive advanced instruction in Paris, and in 1785 he was assigned as a second lieutenant of artillery. His spare time was devoted to learning all he could about military history and theory.

In 1796, in the siege of Toulon, he was promoted from captain to general. Seven days later he married the beautiful Josephine, born Marie Josephine Rose Tascher de la Pagerie. The widow of the Vicomte Alexandre de Beauharnais, she was a Creole and had been born on the Caribbean island of Martinique. She had two children by her first marriage. She was also six years older than her twenty-seven-year-old husband.

Subsequently, Napoleon fought in Italy and Egypt against the English, brilliantly distinguishing himself in the campaigns and becoming increasingly popular with the French people. In 1799 he returned to France and was swept into power as one of three consuls. Not long idle, he maneuvered himself into the position of first consul and permitted the other two men to retire from office.

The Second Italian Campaign was fought in 1800, and in

1802 he signed the Peace of Amiens, bringing peace to France for the first time in over a decade. The grateful French people honored him by making him consul for life. From there it was a short step to making himself emperor, for he was that in all but name.

Ariel knew all this from what Drake had told her before she left England, but what he could not prepare her for was the sheer presence of Napoleon.

His chestnut hair had been cut short except for one lock dangling over his receding forehead. His hands attracted attention for the perfection of their skin and for their tapering fingers. He was short, only a few inches taller than Ariel. His lean face was sallow, while his head was large though well shaped: His shoulders were broad and his chest well developed. He was dressed simply—a gray coat over the uniform of a colonel of his guard, and plain knee breeches. He wore no jewelry, and his only decorations were the gold buckles on his shoes. His eyes were gray and gleamed with an intensity of ambition, pride, and relentless energy.

Those extraordinary eyes burned into her, searing, staring into the very depths of her soul. Ariel feared he would be able to read her mind and know why she was in Paris.

But that's absurd, she told herself, and yet she had to repress a shiver.

"Sire," said du Veilleur, bowing low, "may I present to you Mrs. Ariel Greystone, late of London."

"So," said Napoleon, continuing to stare intently at her, "you are the actress who criticized the English war effort."

Was there implicit criticism there? Did he feel she betrayed her country? She wanted him to like her from the outset.

Looking him directly in the eye, she replied, "Yes, I did, for while I am an Englishwoman by living there, I am a Frenchwoman by birth."

"Ah." What did that mean? she wondered. Abruptly, he turned. "This is my empress, Josephine."

Ariel curtsied to the slender dark-skinned woman standing beside Napoleon. The forty-two-year-old empress was still beautiful, with large dark blue eyes and a languorous expression. Diamonds, tiny pinpoints of a thousand fires, glittered on her elaborate gown of white velvet trimmed with delicate lace. The dress's demi-train was of a sheer gossamer, and the only color was the ladder of gold silk bows on her long sleeves. Diamonds shone in the woman's dark hair and at her earlobes, around her neck, and upon her hands.

It was obvious to Ariel that Napoleon indulged his wife her expensive whims. Obvious, too, was the affection the couple shared, for she saw it in the adoring look Josephine gave him, and heard it in his voice when he addressed her. Such affection surprised her.

The woman gave her a faint smile, and Ariel detected some hesitancy from the empress. Perhaps Josephine was not yet comfortable in her imperial role.

Napoleon, whose quick eyes had never left Ariel's face, now directed his attention to du Veilleur. "You may leave for the moment, Comte."

Earlier du Veilleur had warned her that the emperor was brusque and notably impatient at court and other social functions.

The comte smiled as he bowed. "Yes, Your Majesty." He walked away from the imperial couple and Ariel without looking back.

Ariel wished that du Veilleur could have stayed, for she wasn't sure she wanted to be interviewed by Napoleon alone. Still, she must face him alone sometime, and it might as well be now.

Napoleon focused his gaze on her as he reached for a snuff-box in his waistband. He flicked it open and paused. "Why did you leave England?"

"I was forced to leave because there were people in London who would not admit that you were doing the best for France. I maintained that you were." She wanted to strike the right note with him, neither outrageously flattering nor too bluntly honest.

"Ah, yes, I have told you, have I not, Josephine? The English have narrow minds, and because of that they hurt themselves." Josephine responded with a faint smile, but Ariel could tell she didn't understand what her husband meant. It was quite apparent now to Ariel that Josephine's intellect was not of the same caliber as Napoleon's. "Your job—do you like it?" He took his snuff and returned the box to his sash.

"Yes, Sire, very much, and Monsieur Pierone is an excellent manager. I am enjoying a different repertory than I was accustomed to."

"I want to hear about England."

"Whatever Your Majesty would like to discuss," Ariel replied graciously.

"The politics—tell me about that."

"The English are weary of war and blame their ills upon the government, for it has brought them burdensome taxes, among many other things." Napoleon nodded to himself. "As you know, Sire, when Mr. Addington was prime minister, he was quite interested in peace—despite the declaration of war upon France, which he was forced into by his own government," she hastened to add, seeing the darkening look in Napoleon's eyes. "But since Mr. Pitt has come into office, I fear he will want one thing only—the increasing strength of England. I think he means to match you in whatever you plan." That was certainly no revelation of a state secret. Anyone with common sense knew that Pitt would move against Napoleon.

His mouth quirked at the corner. "His plans?"

"I fear I do not know them, Your Majesty, for, alas, my expertise extends only as far as the theatre. I have, as others have pointed out, a weak head for politics."

"Many women do," he said, nodding.

She ignored the slur, for Drake had cautioned her that Napoleon possessed a low opinion of women. She planned to be an exception. If she could only be sure that she was impressing him and that he wasn't simply passing time with her.

But no, she told herself, he wouldn't do that. He was too busy for idle chatter.

All during their conversation Josephine had remained silent, nor had she seemed desirous of speaking, but rather she seemed content to allow her husband to do all the talking. How different, Ariel thought, it was with Drake and her, for even if they had married, she could not imagine herself being content to be silent while he did the talking.

"But now you are here to stay?" he asked.

"Yes, for I enjoy Paris. My family has lived only in the south, and I find life here much more diversified, Sire."

"Is the theatre different in Paris than in London?" Josephine finally ventured to ask.

"Yes," Ariel answered, "for here they are more willing to try new plays and methods. Here, there is a renaissance of the theatre." She could see this pleased the emperor. "The theatre in London is more established—less willing to change. As I discovered much to my chagrin. I had never realized how involved the theatre could be with politics."

"Strange bedfellows, eh?"

She smiled faintly at him. "Yes, Your Majesty. Very strange bedfellows indeed. I confess I was rather naïve about that sort of thing—as are many in the theatre. Politics is something best left to those running the government."

"An excellent idea." He looked to Josephine, who nodded as if by some prearranged signal. "Her Majesty and I agree that we wish you to attend our coronation in December. Will you attend?"

"Of course, Your Highnesses, I would truly be honored." She did not think many from the theatre would be there. Nor, she realized, would she have to be dependent upon du Veilleur.

"Good," said Napoleon, and the matter was settled. He beckoned to du Veilleur, who stood some distance away. The comte approached. "It was good seeing you tonight, du Veilleur. I will see you later—a meeting this morning at six."

"I will be there, Sire." Du Veilleur bowed.

"Good night, Madame Greystone," the emperor said, using her name for the first time since they had met. That was a good sign, she suspected.

Napoleon moved on, greeting aides and generals and those who sought an introduction, and Josephine, silent as ever, followed him.

When the imperial couple had left the ballroom, du Veilleur lifted a slim eyebrow and said, "That was an impressively long time he spoke with you, my dear. What did he say?"

"We chatted about England—he wanted to know why I left, as well as what Mr. Pitt plans. And"—here she paused

—"he invited me to the coronation."

Du Veilleur soundlessly whistled and gave her a speculative look. "Did he now? An invitation, is it? Very impressive."

She smiled a little triumphantly, suspecting that Drake would be pleased. The initial meeting with the Bonapartes had gone better than she could have hoped, she thought, and perhaps she would see the emperor again—and get more information.

"Are you tired, *ma chérie*?"

"A little, I think, after all the dancing and the excitement. You mustn't forget that you have an early meeting to attend."

"No, I shan't forget. Therefore, I think we should not stay too much longer." She nodded and he kissed her hand. "I will go now to call for the carriage. I will be back before long."

She watched as he wound his way through the crowd, which was beginning to thin out at this advanced hour of the morning. She was heading toward the refreshment table for another glass of champagne when someone cleared his throat.

Behind her stood a man in his forties. Gray streaked his black hair, and he wore a quiet smile on his pleasant face. He was attired formally in a black coat and breeches, and a gold stickpin secured his cravat.

"Madame Ariel Greystone?" he asked. His voice was also pleasant.

"Yes?"

"I am Baron L'Croix. I must confess that I saw you earlier and have wanted to meet you for some time, but, alas, I was preempted by the emperor." His eyes were brown and very open and direct.

"Ah, monsieur, I am most delighted to make your acquaintance." She must pretend that his name was completely new to her, for they were surrounded and could easily be overheard.

"I saw you with the comte du Veilleur," he said, "but he is not around now."

"He went to get the carriage," she murmured. "It is late and we are leaving."

"Ah yes, of course. Well, then certainly this is not the time to chat. Perhaps you would permit me to call upon you sometime at the theatre?"

"Yes, please do."

"Until then, madame." He bowed and left just as du
Veilleur was returning to her.

The comte's eyes narrowed. "Who was that man, *ma
chérie*?"

"The Baron L'Croix. He wanted to meet me earlier, but
was detained because of the emperor."

"What did he want?"

"Really, Philippe, all I know about the man is that he came
up to me to introduce himself." She smiled slightly. "Are you
jealous?"

"Jealous? Of course not!" He tucked her arm through his.
"The carriage should be waiting now, and I think we have
much to discuss this morning before I leave, *n'est-ce pas*?"

She smiled.

Twenty-Nine

◆❦◆

It was a week later before Armand L'Croix dropped by the theatre to see Ariel, and in that time she had been thinking over carefully what she would say to him. She remembered well what she'd overheard in the ballroom.

She had just finished a rehearsal and gone to her dressing room to change, when someone knocked on the door. It was L'Croix, and she greeted him as he entered. She pointed to the door, and, nodding his understanding, he locked it. They sat only inches apart so that they could speak in whispers just in case someone might be standing outside the door.

"You have been here almost two months," he said, "and I did not come any earlier because I knew you would not yet be settled."

"It's true it has taken me a while to settle, but I do have one or two pieces of information, I believe." Her voice became matter-of-fact. "First, you must tell Drake that the comte and I have become acquainted, and I think he grows to trust me more each day. Second, I have been personally invited by the emperor to attend the coronation in December."

"Quite an accomplishment, madame."

She looked pleased. "I couldn't have asked for anything more perfect, monsieur. Too, at the emperor's party the comte had a rather strange conversation with a stranger. He was balding, and had a lined face, as though he were very weary."

"Did he wear spectacles?"

"Yes. Do you know him?"

He nodded. "It's Bernard Desmoulins. One of Napoleon's most trusted aides." He leaned forward. "What were they saying?"

"I didn't hear all of it because they were some feet distant, but Desmoulins spoke about a naval plan, to which the comte replied by saying someone, I thought Napoleon, had decided to discuss it after the coronation. Then he said 'the papers' were at his home."

"Hmm, this is very interesting."

"But what does it mean?" She stopped. "Or perhaps I should not ask."

L'Croix shook his head. "We will leave interpretations to Monsieur Drake."

"How do you send this information?" She was curious to know what route it would take before it appeared as a letter on Drake's desk.

"I find someone who is going to London—generally an English citizen—and request that they take a personal letter to a 'friend.' That friend is not Drake, nor any one else in the government, but rather someone who works with him. The friend receives the letters—for there are two: one is personal; the other contains what I wish to pass along—and takes them both to Drake."

A loud knock on the door startled both of them. The doorknob was rattled, and L'Croix stood up.

"I must go, for I have stayed overlong," he said softly. Swiftly he bent over her hand, then said loudly so that he could be overheard by whoever was on the other side of the door, "It has been a delight, Madame Greystone. I am very glad I could meet you. I look forward to your first Paris performance in September." He crossed the room, unlocked the door, and opened it. August Pierone stood in the hall, a perplexed expression on his face.

"The door was locked," he said.

Ariel forced an embarrassed blush to come to her face, then

looked away. She peeked in the mirror to see the manager's expression.

His face turned sly as he realized he had interrupted what he thought was a tryst. "Ah, I am sorry, madame. Perhaps I should come back later—"

"No, please, Monsieur—Pierone, is it? I must leave now," L'Croix said. "Please come in." He pressed past the manager, then glanced back at Ariel and smiled as he bowed low.

She waved to him, then indicated for Pierone to come in. She kept her eyes demurely lowered, but she knew that Pierone's expression had turned to a leer. Good, let him think that she was conducting an affair with this man. That would simply allow L'Croix easier access to her at the theatre. No one would be suspicious then.

"You are such a sly one," Pierone said with an oily chuckle. He reached out to pinch her cheek.

Her tone innocent, she asked, "What was it you wished to see me about, monsieur?"

He shook an admonitory finger at her. "Ah, you conquer the hearts, Ariel." He heaved a great sigh. "I can well imagine what it will be like on our opening night. They will adore you! The broken hearts will lie strewn at your feet, and you will have your pick of the men of Paris. How cruel they will consider you when you finally decide." She began blushing. "Such a fox among the hounds, eh? Ah, if I were only younger, even ten years. There are some women, though, who like a man much older. . . ." When she did not answer, he sighed and seemed to collect himself. "Yes, yes, why I came to see you. There is someone I wish you to meet; she is the newest member of our little company. You two will be working together, and she is one of the finest actresses in all of France." He lumbered to the door. "Mademoiselle."

A moment later a woman appeared in the doorway, and Ariel stared.

It was the red-haired woman Ariel had seen at the soirée, the one who had stared at her with such hatred. A faint smile now curved her lips. She wore a salmon-colored dress that did not go well with her hair.

"This is Madame Ariel Greystone," Pierone announced

with an elaborate gesture, "the *Anglaise* actress you have
heard so much about, my dear, and this is Madeleine La
Châtelet. A very old friend of mine." He smiled at the
Frenchwoman.

Ariel thought the woman had stiffened at his use of "old,"
and she refrained from smiling. Rising gracefully, she extended her hand. The Frenchwoman did not deign to take it.

"Welcome to the company, mademoiselle."

"Thank you," said the woman. Her voice was throaty, her
dark eyes smoldering. "I have no doubt that we shall work
well together."

And with that Ariel began to sense a great foreboding that
only increased when the other woman smiled at her, for it was
a smile filled with hatred, a hatred she could not understand.

Thirty

"Ma chérie, ma chérie," a sleeping Auguste Pierone mumbled as he rolled over heavily, then began snoring raucously.

Disgusted, Madeleine La Châtelet slid out of the rumpled bed and walked to the open window to stare out at the night-washed street. A cool breeze sifted across her naked body, and she breathed deeply. The fresh air felt so cooling, and she tossed her heavy hair back over her shoulders.

Pierone was such a pig, snuffling and wheezing all the while he made love, slobbering on her with his garlic breath. His hands were hot and clammy, his embraces awkward and unrewarding. Her full bottom lip curled. He thought he was an expert lover. Ha! She had had better from a crude shepherd. Pierone's stage managing was on the same level as his lovemaking. There were many better managers to be found in Paris now that the theatres were being reopened, but this man, for some reason she could not fathom, had the ear of Napoleon, and she knew that could only do her good.

She was filled with ambition. She had known a hard life, being one of fifteen children born to an ignorant maid who did not understand that when the master of the house used her, a child would be born nine months later. Her mother had died in the throes of childbirth, when Madeleine was twelve, and to this day she could still remember the blood and the screams of her dying parent.

She had vowed that that life was not for her. She emulated the daughter of the household, had stolen old clothes and brushes and soap so that she could take care of herself. She caught the attention of the master when she was thirteen and had begun to blossom into ripe womanhood. He had come to her late one night, and had taken her maidenhood—but on her terms. She would not be a brood cow like her mother. He dressed her like a lady and educated her in the ways of the world. She was his mistress for five years until his death, whereupon the wife and daughter threw her from the house.

She went to Paris and soon found a new protector who kept her in luxurious quarters and provided her with whatever she wanted. But it was not enough, for she feared what would happen to her if he should die. She needed more security, and thus decided to become an actress. She did possess some acting ability, though she was hardly the greatest actress of France as Pierone so stupidly proclaimed. She was capable but not inspired. She was beautiful, too, and displayed her full figure to its advantage. That and her red hair drew men to her like moths to a flame.

She had been rewarded for her affection, showered with expensive gifts—jewels, furs, and horses. As the years passed, she went from man to man, demanding more.

She had loved many men, though only in body, never in spirit.

Until she found Philippe.

Du Veilleur she loved with all her heart, and it tore her heart every time he found another woman and strayed from her. If only she and Philippe had found each other when she was younger, more attractive. But that reasoning would drive her to the grave if she thought too long on it. There could be no "if only" for her.

Now she had lost Philippe to the *Anglaise*, the woman all of Paris was talking about. Her name was on the lips of men and women alike. They sang her praises, talked incessantly of her charm and magnificent acting ability, of her fresh beauty and ready wit.

The woman was young, too, far younger than she, and beautiful in a way she never had been.

Madeleine laughed softly. She recognized another whore when she saw one.

That was all the *Anglaise* was, but she was a subtle, clever one and had fooled them all, even poor dear Philippe.

Worse, too, the *Anglaise* really could act, and now Paris treated her as though she were the only actress to be found. Madeleine could not forgive her any of her talents. The combination of them all was particularly deadly.

But she was not about to give up Philippe without a fierce fight. She had been with him too long, loved him too much.

No, she would strike back at the *Anglaise*, would undermine the smug bitch. A few remarks here and there to those in the company; a stray comment to Pierone, and it would all begin to add up after a while. She would keeping hunting for the *something* that would prove the *Anglaise*'s downfall, because she knew the woman did not possess an unblemished past.

Something she hoped would be fatal.

La Châtelet smiled broadly and licked her lips. They gleamed wetly in the moonlight. She leaned forward, resting her arms on the sill of the window, and saw a horseman in the street below pause to stare up at her. She stood so that he could see her nude form, pirouetted slowly and provocatively, and laughed when he made a crude gesture.

A fatal flaw. She rather liked the notion. One would be found: Of that she was quite, quite certain. And then Philippe would come back to her. Again.

Bernard Desmoulins shook his head. "I don't know, Philippe. I don't think it's practical. I know what *he* says, of course, but—"

"I disagree," du Veilleur said as he reached for a glass of wine. He and the emperor's aide had met several times since the party at the Tuileries over a week earlier, and still they turned one matter over and over. Now, they were once more at du Veilleur's home, discussing the same issue. "It *is* practical, Bernard," he said, his voice growing eager. "Think of it—we would win this damned war at last. At last! It has been a long, weary one, one that strains our economy. Further, England blockades our ports, suppresses our trade. We cannot afford *not* to invade, for they mean to ruin France.''

Desmoulins rubbed a hand over his broad face and straightened his spectacles so that he could peer at the other man. ''I don't know. The earlier plan . . . we gave that up.'' He finished the last of his wine, and du Veilleur poured more.

''Which is why the English will not be expecting the invasion, I tell you,'' du Veilleur said earnestly. ''Believe me, they will not look for it, for they know that the emperor had dismissed the idea before. Why should he look to it again?''

''The enormity of the project—'' Desmoulins glanced at the scrawl on a page before him. ''Project of England. My God, the troops to be moved!''

''Over one hundred thousand,'' du Veilleur said crisply. ''To be massed along the English coast for such time as we can invade—and we can. England rules the seas at present! Do you not see that if we, a nation considered so much weaker than England, should invade and defeat it, our allies in Europe will be heartened? Those of England will be disheartened, and we will survive.''

''I don't know, Philippe.'' Desmoulins shook his head. ''If we didn't conquer them—''

''How could we not conquer them? Our army is far superior to theirs. Look at the figures! We outnumber them in every way.'' He patted a sheaf of papers. ''Look at these.''

''I've seen them before,'' the other man said wearily. ''I have written some of those reports myself. Still, unexpected turns of events can happen, you know. England has not been invaded since the eleventh century. There is so much to consider.'' He stood up and paced around the library. He took his spectacles off and finally stopped before the fireplace to wipe them clean on a linen handkerchief. He stuck them back on his nose and peered at du Veilleur, whose obstinate expression remained the same. He sighed and threw up his hands. ''Very well, very well, I'll listen to this plan. I'll study your damned papers, only please let me do it in peace.''

Du Veilleur laughed and stood to clap the other man on the shoulder. ''I thought you would change your mind, Bernard.''

''If you should lead the invasion force, then we most certainly will win—through sheer intimidation.'' Desmoulins's head came up sharply. ''What was that noise?'' He looked around the room. Only they were present.

Du Veilleur shook his head, and in three strides he reached the door and flung it open. He looked up and down the corridor, but he saw no one. Desmoulins had gone to the French windows to peer outside.

"No one on the terrace."

"A mouse, perhaps, or some animal outside," du Veilleur said. "I would not worry about it, but rather would concern myself with this." He tapped the papers.

Sighing, Desmoulins sat down at the desk to review the plan he thought folly.

Ariel crept soundlessly up the stairs as quickly as she could and jumped into bed, pulling the covers up to her chin even though it was too hot in the room.

She had overheard all of the conversation downstairs in the library because she had been kneeling outside the door, her ear pressed against the wood. It had been risky, extremely so, for a servant could have come along at any moment and discovered her, but she had known she had to chance it, had to find out more about the plan the two men had discussed at the Tuileries.

Project of England, Desmoulins had called it. An invasion of England. They were actually considering such a thing.

She hadn't believed they were serious, but the more they talked, the more she realized Philippe was very intent on that invasion. She had to convey this information to Drake, had to inform him of the plans. But she needed those papers that du Veilleur had referred to. If only she hadn't made that noise, then she could have heard more about the Project of England, could have learned perhaps what the men planned to do with the papers.

She needed to find them, needed to copy the important information and send it along to Drake without any delay. Which meant she had to notify L'Croix. Unfortunately, that would prove difficult. She didn't know where he lived, for he had never told her. He preferred to come to the theatre to visit her, to "pay court," as Pierone and the others suspected. So, she would have to wait for him to visit. She would not have to wait too long for he generally came three times a week.

Once she had told him the information, he would write out the letters for his courier to take to England, and in a matter of days Drake would receive the news.

She smiled to herself, pleased and proud.

Drake.

She sighed in the darkness of the room and kicked off the smothering covers. Drake. She wanted him very badly tonight.

She heard the sound of a board creaking outside the room, and she knew du Veilleur had come.

Quickly she rolled over onto her side and closed her eyes, evening her breath to feign sleep. The door opened and he came softly across to her. He touched her cheek gently.

"Sleep well, my little one."

She did not respond.

She heard him undress and then crawl into bed. He put an arm around her, and she lay silent and unmoving. She could not sleep for her mind was filled with her important find.

Thirty-One

❧❦❧

"Opening night only a week away, eh?" L'Croix asked, smiling at Ariel.

"Yes, and I'm nervous, of course. It's the first time I've ever been on the French stage." She sighed and ran her fingers through her hair. "Well, we shall see in seven days' time. I wish it were tomorrow, though."

"Well, I will see you again. And thank you."

His hand touched his coat. Earlier she had talked with him and told him what she had learned. Now, with the door of her dressing room open, they could only speak in general pleasantries.

"Good night, Ariel."

"Good night, Armand."

She went back to her dressing table and, smiling to herself, began running a brush through her hair. Soon, very soon, Drake would know what the French planned to do.

Outside in the hallway L'Croix paused to watch some of the actors try on various costumes for the play. A hand lightly touched his arm, startling him. He whirled around to see a red-haired woman. He frowned, trying to remember her name. It came to him gradually. Madeleine La Châtelet. She was the second female lead to Ariel's first.

"Good evening," he said politely.

"Good evening, monsieur," she said. Her hand still

lingered on the sleeve of his rust-colored coat. He looked pointedly at it. She did not remove it.

"Madame La Châtelet, is it?"

"Mademoiselle," she informed him sweetly.

"Ah." There was an awkward pause. "Madam—that is, mademoiselle, I must go, or I shall be late. I beg that you—" Her smiled deepened. Her lips were very red, very wet, and he could not keep from staring at them, fascinated by their fullness.

"I have seen you often at the theatre," she said in a throaty tone.

"Yes," he said, nodding, and feeling foolish.

"Do you enjoy Molière?"

"Very much. I look forward to opening night. I am sure that you will be splendid." He smiled at her, and she leaned toward him, and he could see the shadowed valley between her plump breasts. He licked his lips. "What part do you play, mademoiselle?"

"Please, do not be so formal with me. My name is Madeleine. Call me that."

"Madeleine." It rolled easily across his tongue. "Madeleine. A lovely name . . . for a beautiful woman." Her long black lashes swept down over the dark eyes, and he thought she was remarkably striking.

"If you have time, perhaps we could discuss it over a glass of wine in my dressing room. It's just down the hall." She pointed to the end of the corridor. "Oh, but yes, you said you would be late."

There was a musky scent about her that captivated him, and a sheen of perspiration shone on the skin above her bosom. She was warm, oh so warm, radiating heat, and he could scarcely stand it. Her hand was burning through the material of his coat, burning into his skin, branding him. He raised tortured eyes to her and licked his dry lips.

"I would enjoy that, Madeleine. Very much."

"Then come." She smiled, showing a dimple, and led L'Croix to her dressing room.

A week passed all too quickly in Ariel's estimation, and before she even knew it, it was time for the play to open.

Just before she went onstage, Pierone whispered to her that the emperor was in the audience tonight, and that did much to shake her. She nodded to indicate she understood, and then swept out of the wings.

She concentrated on each cue, each line. She wanted her performance to be perfect—not only because it was her first play in Paris, but because she wished to impress Napoleon. And she wished to show up Madeleine, who had been missing cues and forgetting lines during rehearsals.

She looked to the imperial box and saw Napoleon and Josephine. The emperor smiled and inclined his head slightly.

The play moved swiftly, and it seemed that in no time at all the members of the company were taking their bows.

It was a thunderous success, judging from the reaction of the audience, who were on their feet, clapping wildly and cheering and stamping. Even Napoleon stood and applauded.

Backstage, Auguste Pierone hurried up to Ariel and clasped her hands to his chest.

"Marvelous, marvelous, Ariel!" he said, his tone enthusiastic. "I knew I had made the right choice in you. Indeed, I did!"

Yes, her performance had not only been one of the best in her long career, it had been spectacular. And she was flushed with success.

Pierone grinned inanely. "My dear, dear Ariel, I did not realize that you had the eye of Napoleon! How very fortunate for you!"

"I don't," she said as she continued on her way to her dressing room. Pierone hurried after her.

"Ah," he said slyly, "but you do. I can tell. He is most certainly not immune to a pretty face. After all, he is a man, and you are a woman."

"How very astute," she responded tartly.

He was not daunted by her sarcasm. "Yes, and I must say that it would not do the theatre any harm if some of . . . his favor . . . were to come our way."

She faced the manager, her brows drawn together. "Monsieur, what are you suggesting?"

"Suggesting? I am only saying—"

"Saying, I think, that I should try to seduce him." His look confirmed that. "No, thank you, monsieur. He is a married man—as well as being the emperor. Quite beyond my league. I must change, for I am very tired and want to go home. Good evening." She slipped into the dressing room, closing the door quickly so that he could not follow her. She heard Pierone's voice now from the other side of the hall, and listened as it faded. Good, he was leaving.

She crossed to the dressing table, dropped wearily onto the bench, and shook her head. All she needed was to become Napoleon's mistress as Pierone was intimating. She admired the emperor, but become his mistress? No, for he saw too much. Too, she was not attracted to him that way.

The door flew open as Ariel was unclasping her necklace. She looked up, completely taken aback.

It was Madeleine La Châtelet. Her hair was disheveled, her face flushed. Her hands were clenched into fists at her sides.

"You damned harlot," she said.

"I beg your pardon?" Ariel set the necklace down and turned around to look at La Châtelet.

"I called you a harlot."

"I heard the first time," Ariel said quietly. The Frenchwoman looked as though she had been drinking. Her part in the play had been pared smaller and smaller by Pierone because she seemed unable to learn her role completely. All during the performance she had tried to upstage Ariel.

"Perhaps you should lie down for a while," Ariel suggested.

"I'm not the one who's doing the lying down, *Madame* Greystone." She stepped inside the room, her movements unsteady, and she lurched slightly and grabbed on to the edge of the door for support.

Ariel half rose. "You are unwell."

"I am drunk, but quite well, *Anglaise*, quite well indeed, and will be even better when you leave."

"But I'm not leaving."

"You should, *Anglaise*." Her voice was getting louder and louder, and a crowd of curious onlookers was gathering out in the hall.

"Madeleine," Ariel began.

"Do not presume with me," the Frenchwoman replied

haughtily. "You are a cold English bitch, and not a very good actress, either, though you've fooled many people. But not me. No, *Anglaise*, not me. I saw through you from the beginning. Philippe didn't really believe me, but that doesn't matter because he will, just as others will know what you really are. Pgh!" Eyeing Ariel with distaste, she spat at her. Ariel leaped back. "I don't know what Philippe or the emperor see in you." She shrugged. "What do they care what you're like once you've spread your legs—"

"That is enough, mademoiselle," commanded a stern voice.

Ariel stared.

It was Napoleon.

"Your Majesty—" Ariel stopped at a gesture from him.

"Mademoiselle La Châtelet," he said.

The Frenchwoman turned bleary eyes to him.

"You are a disgrace to your womanhood, and to your nation. You are to leave this theatre at once. You will not attend our coronation, and it would be most fortunate for you if you'd not appear at court." His tone was cold, the anger barely controlled.

"I—" began the Frenchwoman.

"She didn't—" Ariel started.

"Thank you, thank you," Pierone said, hurrying up at that moment to take the older actress by the arm. He shook her, but she didn't seem to notice. "Thank you, Your Majesty. I am sure that Madeleine didn't mean—that is, she has not been feeling— Come along, mademoiselle." He almost jerked her from the room.

Napoleon turned to Ariel. "I am sorry, Madame Greystone, that you had to face such unpleasantness."

She shook her head. "I fear that being in the theatre, Your Majesty, has accustomed me to such outbursts—from actors as well as admirers."

"Well," he said, his tone clipped, "I do not think she will bother you again."

She thanked him for his intervention but could not dismiss the chill that traced its cold finger down her spine. She wished she could really believe Madeleine would not bother her again.

*   *   *

Pierone shoved La Châtelet into her dressing room. Weeping, she fell to the floor.

"You disgusting creature," he said scornfully. "Get up, get up at once."

"That's enough," said a quiet voice behind him.

Pierone turned. It was Armand L'Croix.

"This is theatre business—" Pierone began.

"Don't worry. I'm taking her home." He bent, and gathered her into his arms. Pierone said nothing, but merely stood by and watched as the other man carried the weeping woman out of the room.

Outside the theatre, L'Croix helped her carefully into his coach, then settled beside her. The coach lurched forward, but she didn't notice. She had stopped weeping and was completely silent.

Once they returned to his house, he escorted her into a salon and there rang for wine. A servant brought a bottle and L'Croix held out a filled goblet to her.

"I shouldn't have any more," she said after a moment's hesitation. She had curled up in a wingback chair, her feet drawn up under her, her knees under her chin. The black around her eyes had smudged, and her nose was red from weeping. Although he suspected her real age, he thought she looked very young at the moment. Almost like a lost waif. His lost waif.

"Have a little to steady you," he said, kneeling by her and taking her hand. "You don't have to go back out tonight, Madeleine. Only I will see you."

She raised her head, and her dark eyes, wet with unshed tears, stared at him. What she read there on his face seemed to sober her. "Armand?" she whispered. She shifted forward, slipping her arms around his neck, and lay her head on his shoulder.

He held the cup to her lips and she swallowed some wine, choking just a little, then shook her head to indicate she didn't want any more. He finished the wine, then set the goblet down. There was silence in the room. She moved her head and placed her lips on his neck.

A tremor seized him, and he turned his face so that he could kiss her. Her warm mouth was open and waiting for him as his tongue plunged into it. She moaned, her fingers tightening on his shoulders, and he brought his hand up to her bodice and could feel her firm nipples poking against the thin material of her dress. He tweaked one, and she bit his ear. Excitement pulsed through him, hardening his manhood, and she put one hand down to his breeches and squeezed. Tears of pain and pleasure sprang to his eyes.

"Armand," she whispered, "Armand," and she brushed her fingers across his cheek.

They embraced and kissed, and he could scarcely breathe for what she was doing to him. Suddenly she was out of his arms and standing before him as he still knelt.

"What?" He blinked.

In one fluid motion she pulled her gown over her head and let it fall to the floor. Beneath it she had been wearing nothing.

Fascinated, he stared at her nakedness and wet his lips with his tongue. Her ripe breasts sagged only a little, while the cinnabar nipples, large and moist, thrust up at an angle. Her waist was small, her hips round and womanly, and at the juncture of her white thighs the tuft of silky hair was as red as that on her head. Resting her hands on her hips, she thrust her pelvis forward, just inches from his face.

With a groan, he pushed her down onto the floor none too gently, and kissed and lapped at her, beginning at the coppery triangle and inching up slowly until his lips fastened onto hers. They sucked at each other's breaths, the fire spreading through his veins. He pulled off his clothes with unsteady hands. She had him in hand, and he was already hard, and it hurt so much, and he was so ready for her, so ready, and she was spreading her legs, opening her warmth to him, gripping him so tightly, so tightly, that—

He burst across her hand and stomach. Appalled, he stared at her.

"Madeleine, I—"

"Don't worry." She laughed throatily and rubbed her hand across the stickiness, then touched her fingers to her lips. She pulled him down on top of her. "There is plenty of time, plenty of time for love, Armand." And she bit his lip, drawing blood.

Armand L'Croix nodded, lost in her spell.

Thirty-Two

The late-October evening was crisp, and she'd had an exhausting performance that night. There had been the usual number of admirers, as well as an impromptu party afterward, but she had come home early to be by herself. There had been so much entertaining recently, on her part as well as by others, that she was getting very little sleep. Du Veilleur was out of Paris at present, and it was a perfect time to spend alone.

She went straight upstairs to bathe in a tub filled with hot scented water, and she stayed there until the water cooled. Hally brought her mulled wine, and after dismissing the maid for the rest of the night, she settled into a large chair by the fire. It was just cool enough outside for a fire to feel comfortable. She had a book of French poetry to read, and she wanted just to relax.

She yawned, and closed her eyes momentarily. Part of her exhaustion came from searching ceaselessly for the papers in du Veilleur's home. L'Croix had assured her that he had already sent his message to Drake, but he needed the papers now to pass along. She knew that, and she was determined to find them but still hadn't. She wondered if Philippe carried them at all times, but that seemed absurd. He must have locked them somewhere. But where?

They had to be there someplace. She had gone to his home once while he was away, and she had searched one room but had found nothing. She would just have to keep trying.

Opening the old volume, she began reading until the black print swam before her eyes. She must have dozed for a moment, for suddenly her head lolled forward. She brought it up with a jerk and paused. Had she heard something? Or was it her imagination? She glanced around the dark room. The twisting shadows of the flames fluttered across the expanse of wall and stretched up onto the ceiling, but she could see nothing out of the ordinary, nor did she hear the noise again.

Perhaps she'd been dreaming.

She picked up the poetry book from the floor where it had slipped while she dozed, and she thumbed through the pages until she found her place again. As she reached for the mulled wine, she paused, again. She *had* heard a noise. Frowning slightly, she set the book down and stood.

It came from a definite direction now. The window. She started toward it, then stopped. She didn't know what was making the sound, after all.

Something tapped softly at the window covered by the closed brocade drapes. Her mouth was dry as she considered the possibilities. A small ledge ran just below the level of her second-story bedroom window and wrapped around the house completely. The noise came from the ledge. What—or who— could it be? Her room was at the back of the house, the window looking out over a small walled garden. It would be relatively easy for someone to scale the wall, to creep up to the house. There were no neighbors for some distance, and in the black of night no one would see or hear a thing. She licked her lips.

Ariel heard a slight grating sound, as though some object pushed against the window. Perhaps a body, a hand, a shoulder. She heard the window scraping as it slowly eased inward. She stood frozen, unable to move, waiting to see.

She watched in horror as the curtains were thrust aside and a dark shape stepped down from the window into the room.

As her eyes adjusted, she could see it was a man wearing a low-brimmed hat. His clothes were black and shapeless, giving no clue to his identity. He took a step forward, and she fought against the scream rising in her throat. Suddenly she was no longer frozen in one spot, but leaped across the room to pull open a drawer and grab the knife Drake had given her.

She whirled, brandishing the blade. "Who are you? What do you want?" she demanded. "Speak now, before I cut you up."

A dry chuckle escaped the specter; then in a muffled tone it asked: "Are you alone?"

She frowned, thinking she recognized that voice. It was . . . No, it couldn't be.

In three strides she was across the room. She grabbed the man's hat and sent it sailing. The face was revealed in the light from the fire.

"You!" she said, and lowered the knife.

"The very same, ma'm," Christopher Drake responded with a mocking bow. He glanced around the room. "Are you alone?" he repeated.

"Of course I am, Drake." Emotions tumbled within her as, still shocked to see who it was, she gazed at her nocturnal visitor. Certainly she was glad to see him, yet she was shaken—particularly by his unorthodox entrance. She was worried as well for she knew it was dangerous for him. And she was angry that he had presumed to enter this way when he knew she would be frightened. And yet she was so glad, so very glad he was here.

She didn't want him to read these sentiments in her face or eyes, so she turned and went back to the chair by the fire. She dropped the blade onto the hearth.

"So it's Drake now, it is?"

"Kit, then."

"You don't sound very pleased to see me." He stepped away from the window, removing his black coat as he did so. He drew up another chair before the fire and sat opposite her.

"I am, of course."

"Of course."

"Let's not fight, please, Kit," she pleaded, aware that her hands were very cold.

"I'm not." The harsh firelight glinted off the planes of his face, and the ache in her chest that she had ignored for so long pulsed harder.

There was silence between them for a few moments; then she drew her brows together in a frown. "What are you doing here?'' she demanded. "Why did you come when you know it's foolhardy—you might be recognized. God knows, you are certainly distinguishable."

His fingers slipped to the patch across his left eye as he smiled ruefully. " 'Tis true I can't readily disguise myself, Ariel."

The sound of her name on his lips stirred her, forced roiling emotions up out of the depths of her soul, and she looked into the flames and fought against the rising heat in her body.

"You must leave at once before someone sees you, Kit," she murmured, her eyes still averted. "One of the servants might come in."

"It's late, and they're probably asleep. I know it's dangerous, but I had information for you that only I could pass along."

"Information? I have to talk to you, too."

"Good."

She couldn't keep from looking at him, and saw he was smiling. Unable to restrain herself any longer, she flung herself into his arms, and kissed him soundly on the lips.

"I missed you," she said huskily.

His arms wrapped tightly around her. "And I you, my sweet."

Their lips met again, and it was a very long time before they spoke. She sat on his lap, her head resting against his shoulder, and sighed, contented. At that very moment she could ask for nothing more, nothing except him. All thoughts of what she had to tell him had flown from her mind. That would keep until later, much later.

Drake brushed his fingers against her lips, and she kissed them one by one. His hand slipped down to her chin, then to her neck, where it lingered, and slowly he caressed the smooth skin above her breast.

"I want you, Kit."

"Ariel." His voice was hoarse with passion, and she felt his fingers trembling against her. She moved her head, kissed his palm.

He rose easily, cradling her in his arms. Her head rolled back against his arm, and she stared up at him as he started for the bed.

"Not there," she whispered. "Let's stay before the fire."

"As you so desire, madame."

"I so desire," and she reached up to kiss him.

He carefully placed her on the carpet before the fireplace and lay alongside her. They kissed. His tongue gently probed her lips, and then he became more insistent, and she opened to him. He explored the soft depths of her mouth, their tongues pressing together, and she felt faint at the fire that ran through her veins, inflaming her with passions she had not experienced since she left England. Yet this time it was different, even better with him than before. The fire burned through her, and her skin smoldered, and she thought if she lifted her hand she would see sparks flying from it. She had never felt this way before, and as she reached out to grip him by the arms, she knew she was being swept along in a current she could not control. Nor did she want to.

He moaned, a low animal sound that quickened her pulse. No man had made her body come alive as he did. Not even Philippe, who was a good, experienced lover. No one but Kit. Their breaths were warm, mingling, one, and for a magic moment they were joined, and she was him, and he was her, and she was nothing more, nothing less. She dived through his body, twisted and arched, swam and slid and searched, exploring each cavity, each crevice, each wonderful part that was him, that was her, and she knew him as she had never known him before. Knew then that she loved him with all her heart, that she would never stop loving him. She knew that he, too, felt the same; that he, too, explored and sensed her as she did him. She wept that they shared so much.

They pulled away from their embrace and stared at one another, visibly shaken by the experience. He started to speak, but she pressed her fingers against his lips and shook her head. To speak now would diminish the moment, and she wanted to savor it in silence.

The firelight painted his eyes bloodred, and it seemed to burn into her as he gazed at her. She reached out to him, felt him become her again, and they held on to each other as they were swept along that strange path.

He knelt alongside her as his hands slowly trailed down her body to the belt of her robe and loosened it. He pushed the robe away, then pulled the nightgown off so that she lay naked before him. He smiled, and bent to kiss the smoothness of her stomach. His lips were feather-soft, warm, and sent a shiver of desire down her back, up her legs, to her womanly spot.

She stretched her arms high above her head, her breasts thrusting out with the motion.

He chuckled. "Wanton," he whispered, and she smiled up at him.

"Only with you, my lord."

"As I should hope, my lady."

"Am I the only one permitted to lie here shivering, or do you mean to undress sometime this night?"

"Sometime," he said, grinning.

She reached up and with quick fingers unknotted his cravat and tossed it away. She unbuttoned his shirt and pushed it off his shoulders, undid his trousers and watched as he stood to step out of them. When he was undressed, she studied his wide shoulders, narrow hips, long legs. How manly, how strong his body was, even with the scars. He knelt again beside her, and she traced the scars and kissed them. Old wounds that did not diminish his desirability in the least.

Drake watched, his lips curved into an amused smile, as Ariel explored the traces of old wounds on his body. Perhaps if she kissed them enough, they would mend completely and fade, and he would have only the memories of his pain, and not these terrible reminders.

He lay down beside her with his head propped up on one hand.

"I think there is something special about tonight," Drake said.

"I know. I've felt it, and knew that you felt it as well. But I don't understand."

"I don't think we're meant to. Or perhaps later on we'll know what it means. But until then, my love, until then . . . ," and he leaned over to kiss her. Her lips opened under his, and their tongues touched, darting into each other's mouths, caressing.

A tickling sensation began in the pit of her stomach and crept through her arms and down her legs and up again to settle at the juncture of her thighs, where it burned and throbbed.

She shifted, but the feeling did not go away. Indeed, it increased, and she moaned, the tickling becoming a maddening itch that needed relief.

He kissed her lips, the tip of her patrician nose, her eyelids and forehead. His fingers touched the curves of her cheeks, and she sighed with happiness. She reached out to him and stroked his chest, playfully tugging at his dark hair.

His lips crept downward, down past the shadowy hollow of her neck, kissing and nipping gently until they reached her small firm breasts. There he covered her breasts with kisses and his lips touched one of her pink buds. It blossomed under his ministrations, and she arched her back and pulled him closer to her. His tongue played across the nipple, flicking it, rolling it. He cupped her breasts with his hands and brushed their tips with his thumbs. The sensation sent a shock of excitement through her.

"Rogue!" she cried. "How dare you!"

"I dare much," he murmured, and resumed his attention to her.

His hands traveled across the hard plain of her stomach, to the softness of her ivory thighs, then back up to her waist, which he could span with his two hands, and then once more up to the firmness of her breasts. She in turn reached out to find the tumescent length of his manhood. She stroked, and rubbed, caressed and trailed her fingertips along its long shaft, wakening it until it grew more and more rigid with desire.

"I want you. My God, how I want you, Ariel," he growled. "Now," and he flung himself onto her, but she was too quick for him and rolled over so that she was straddling him. "What's this?" He breathed heavily.

"Wait," she said with a slight smile. "Wait for a while."

"Minx."

"Oh yes, that I am."

"I'll see if I wait," he said with a smile.

"I think you will," she replied lightly.

She kissed his lips, licked at them with maddening slowness, then moved her mouth to his chin, down his throat to his chest, where she rained dozens of kisses on the warm skin. His arms reached for her, and she forced them back behind his head.

"What?"

"You'll have to wait and see," she said softly. "I have a surprise for you."

His lips twitched slightly. "I don't know if I like the tone of that."

"You will. That I can promise."

She had inched down his body so that she now sat upon his legs. She smiled at him.

"What are you—"

She held up one slim, tapering hand. "I told you, you have to wait, and so you will, my dear." She smiled impishly. "I think you've waited long enough, Kit." She twisted her fingers in the dark curling hair on his groin and tugged slightly.

"Ouch!"

"My poor darling," she said with a very unsympathetic smile. He mock-growled at her, and she laughed. He closed his eye and slipped his hands behind his head. She clasped his hardened manhood with both hands, fondling it with her fingertips, stroking the length with an ever increasing rhythm. Then abruptly she bent down, her hair swinging across his stomach, and brushed her lips against the glistening head.

"My God," he whispered, his eye flying open to stare at her. His chest heaved as he strove to breathe.

Delighted with the effect, she laughed, but said nothing and bent to kiss him once more. Her tongue flicked out and tasted the drop of saltiness there. She kissed him again, spread her warm breath against him, lapped and sucked, ran her tongue across him, and he groaned and twisted under her attentions. He throbbed against her, so hot, so very hot, and little by little she withdrew her mouth. She licked her lips and smiled lazily at him.

"You are wanton," he said, but there was not censure in his tone, only approval. "Where did you learn that, or do I dare ask?"

"I learned it in my dreams of you," she replied huskily. She tossed her head, her hair haloing around her; then she flung herself down on his chest.

He pressed his mouth against hers, and they sucked greedily at one another's breaths, as if each could suck the very soul out of the other. He rolled over so that he was on top of her.

Her black hair fanned out against the carpet, and he

wrapped his hands in it as he kissed her face. His lips lingered on her eyelids, and the fluttering of her lashes tickled and excited him. He stroked her body in long circular motions, and the fingers of one hand trailed down her body, down past her stomach, down to her creamy thighs and their junction. They sought her warmth, and she opened her legs to let him enter. She groaned with pleasure as he found that center of her passion, and she licked her dry lips.

He covered her face, neck, breasts, legs with kisses that seared. She knew that if she looked she would see the burns, for surely they had left a mark. She twisted her fingers in his hair, and he reached down to kiss her warmth. She groaned aloud and arched her back as he sought to delve into her with his tongue.

Once more he kissed her lips, her eyelids, her cheeks. His legs were between hers, and she felt the pulsing throbbing length that was his manhood, felt it pushing insistently, impatiently against her. She wrapped her legs around him, drawing him closer, and he pushed even harder against her. He reached down to meet her hand, stroked it, and together they guided his manhood. He thrust, and she cried out a wild call. He thrust again and again, and she opened under him, opened wider and wider, and he slid in, and he murmured deep in his throat as she panted with pleasure. He was inside her, thrusting, delving deeper and deeper into that womanly core. But still she wanted him deeper, and thought her body would split in two. Their bodies were slick with sweat now as she gripped him by the buttocks and pressed her fingers into his skin, knowing too late that her nails left marks. But in her passion, it did not matter; nothing mattered but their pleasure.

They rocked together. She felt a burning sensation all through her body, as though she were being consumed by that seductive fire. Flames lapped along their bodies. She cried out and kissed him, feeling their breaths mingle. Ripples of delight shuddered through her, and she arched higher, rising until she reached up with one hand to touch the sun, and then for a glorious moment she and he and the sun were one fiery being. They burned together, and blazed and *lived,* and then a wind drew them into its fast current, and they were pulled away, and went tumbling downward, away from the heat and the fire, away, away, and she heard him call out her name, and saw him beyond the ring of flames, and reached for him, and was him, and she sobbed in her fulfillment, crying out to him. He answered, and then gradually the rocking steadied, and the passion ebbed, and their wet bodies stilled, and they were left, clasped in each other's arms, breathless.

They could not speak and remained locked in their tight embrace, still one, his head cradled on her breast. She let her eyes drift shut, and in the darkness she remembered the fire. Hot tears pricked at her eyelids.

"What's this?" he asked gently as he raised his head and touched the wetness on her cheeks. "Why are you crying? Are you unhappy?"

"No. It's with joy," she said, and she sobbed, clinging to him. He held her close, and they rocked together as though she were a child to be comforted and soothed. He let her cry, and he murmured to her, and they held each other until her sobbing stopped with a hiccough. She buried her face against his chest and said something that was muffled.

"What, my dear? I couldn't hear you," he said, stroking her damp hair.

She raised her tear stained face to him. "I said, Kit, that I love you."

He stared down at her, and traced her lips and cheeks with his fingers. "I love you, too, Ariel. Oh God, how I do, and how I've missed you."

In a burst of happiness she knew then that her life was complete, and that never again would she need anything more than his love.

Thirty-Three

❧❀❧

They made love again, this time much slower. It was sweeter, complete as they already were in themselves, but they wanted to share their love again and again, and afterward, lazy and replete, they fell asleep in each other's arms.

Ariel awoke first and blinked a little sleepily in the near darkness, then gazed with love at him as he dozed before the fire. The firelight outlined his profile, and she could see each scar, the silver in his hair, the patch, all the imperfections, and she did not love him any less for them.

He had said he loved her. He had said that before, but this time it was different. She knew that. And yet now there was no time for their love. She had work to do first.

There might be no future, none at all for her. Her life could end here in France. She shuddered. Did she really believe that? Yes; this was no game she played, and yet surely she would not die, surely she would be able to return to England and see her mother again, and be with Drake.

Stirring in his sleep, he reached out for her. She put her head on his shoulder and wished she could fall asleep again. She closed her eyes and listened to the crackling and sputtering of the fire. She'd best get up and throw another log onto the flames. In a minute or so, she thought, and shortly after that he opened his eyes.

He smiled, sat, and stretched, his arms high over his head.

"Good evening, my love, or perhaps I should say good morning." He kissed her.

"Good evening yourself." She sat up and belted her robe around her. He stood and pulled her to him, and slipped his hands into her robe to rest lightly on her hips. The touch sent shivers through her even then. "Would you like some wine, Kit?"

"Yes, I'd like that very much." His lips brushed the top of her head.

"I have to go downstairs for it, but I'll be back shortly. Then we can discuss our business—or have you forgotten about that?"

"Hardly," he said with a faint twitch of his thin lips. "Business is rarely off my mind—except when I am with a beautiful woman like you."

"If someone knocks at the door, for God's sake jump into bed so you won't be seen."

"Aye, aye, madame." He kissed her again.

At the door she paused to check for servants, but none were in the corridor. No doubt he was right; they were probably in bed. She slipped out of the room, closing the door behind her.

Left on his own, Drake dressed hurriedly, then began to make a circuit of the room, examining the furnishings, all of them mahogany and quite finely finished. He admired the single tapestry and the numerous large oil portraits. He whistled softly under his breath, then remembered where he was and stopped with a rueful grin to himself. He walked over to the window and pushed the drape aside slightly. There was not yet a glimmer of light in the sky, so it was still early.

He felt good, very good, and had not felt this way in . . . how long had it been? Too long to recall, and he was glad he had come, even though he knew he was taking a risk.

He returned to the room, found the half-filled cup of mulled wine, and drank that with one swallow. He picked up the dagger, returned it to the drawer, then stopped when he came to her secretary. It was built of satinwood, with a drop front, a Sèvres plaque, and a marble top. He ran his hand along the cool marble and thought the desk was a very fine piece of furniture.

On the desk was a brass candlestick with the stub of a white candle in it, an ornate key, a green ribbon that no doubt was for her hair, several jeweled pins, and a quill that hadn't been trimmed yet.

There were also several stacks of papers scattered across the desk. Just as he was moving away, an expensive-looking paper caught his attention, and without any hesitation he picked it up.

His gaze raked over the graceful words written on the sheet. *"Ma chérie,"* the letter began. He skipped to the bottom to see the signature. Phillippe Fouret. He pressed his lips together into a hard line and stared at the paper in his hand, reading the words of love there and hating each one.

At that moment he heard a noise at the door, and Ariel entered carrying a silver tray on which were two wine glasses and a bottle of wine. Just as she closed the door and began to cross to the chairs in front of the fireplace, he whirled, with the letter in hand, and demanded, "What is this?"

"Going through my correspondence?" she asked as she put the tray down on the table.

"It caught my eye."

"Let me see." She reached for the sheet, scanned it, then blushed a little. "It's obvious what it is, Kit. That much you should know."

"A love letter." The contempt was underlined in his voice.

"Yes." She began to pour the wine.

"You have a lover," he accused.

"Yes, I do," she said, slamming down one of the wine goblets. "Is that so very surprising? Am I so homely, so meek, that I could not attract one? Why are you so disapproving? You have only yourself to blame, for you're the one who pushed me into du Veilleur's arms. Tell me, Kit, isn't this what you wanted?"

For a moment Drake, silent, stared into the flames. Several emotions seemed at war within him, and once he was on the verge of speaking, but he didn't.

"Well?" she demanded. "I'm waiting for your answer." She went to the fireplace and tossed a small log on the flames. Sparks flew upward.

When he spoke he was businesslike, and it was as though they hadn't made love a short time ago.

"We must discuss why I came, Ariel."

She took her wineglass and sat before the fire. She left his on the table.

"Go ahead, Drake."

He frowned slightly at her use of his last name. "One of the English agents at the French court hasn't reported to me for some time, and Pitt and I are concerned about his silence." He finally sat and took a long swallow of wine. He spoke almost absently, as if his mind were not entirely on what he had to say. "The man's name is Thomas Hendricks. I believe I mentioned him to you before you left. There have been times before when he did not report in for a long time, but this is different. I know something is wrong, and I fear he's been discovered and captured."

"And?"

"And if he has been, then you must find him and let me know, and I'll organize a rescue."

"I see." She considered his words. "You'll have to get me a description of him and the name he was using here. I assume he was using an alias."

"Yes. Tom's been here for some time, and while the French haven't always been hostile to the English, he thought it best not to tip his hand. As for appearance, he's only a few inches taller than you, and rather stocky and muscular in build. Long blond hair and pale green eyes. A rather remarkable appearance here, so he claimed to be a Dutch merchant named Pieter van Cleve. He also has a scar on the right side of his neck. I think that's all. Is that of any help?"

"I think it will be." She sipped her wine. "I have something to ask you, Drake."

"Go ahead."

"You did receive my message about the planned invasion, didn't you?"

"Project of England. Yes, I did, and that's one of the reasons I came, too." He frowned slightly and rubbed at the cheekbone below the patch. "Have you found any papers confirming it?"

"No, though I've been searching. Du Veilleur is away right now, and I went to his house. I managed to search only one room before a servant came in. I don't know if the man suspected something was wrong, or what. He has to have those papers somewhere, and I don't believe he took them with him. Will you be here for a while, or do you go back immediately?"

"I'll stay a week or so, in case you learn something more of Project of England. The more recent the information I take back to Pitt, the better." He paused. "Du Veilleur," he said with distaste. He rolled the stem of the glass between his fingers. "Ariel, about the letter I found—"

"Leave the letter alone," she responded briskly. "It's none of your business."

"I'm not so sure," he said coldly.

She arched an eyebrow. "Really? And how is it your business? You have no claim on me, not after all these years, may I remind you."

"You needn't remind me of anything," he said, standing. "Perhaps you should remind yourself that it was *you*, not I, who broke our engagement." With that he picked up his coat, slipped it on, put on his hat, and marched toward the window. When he had reached it, he turned back. "I will be in contact with you again, Mrs. Greystone." He disappeared behind the drapes and then she heard the window close.

Mrs. Greystone. He hadn't called her that for a long time. He was angry—but so was she.

She should have known, really, she should have. He was so irritating, so interfering—meddling in her affairs again! She was glad to see him leave! And yet he was jealous—that much was apparent. So he must still love her.

He had said so.

Or was that an act?

She took the glass back to the kitchen without incident, and when she heard someone stirring about, she hurried back upstairs, where she drank more wine, then stretched and told herself sternly she had to go to bed. She had been tired when she came home hours ago, and doubtless it was close to dawn by now. She'd have to sleep late to make up for this night so she would be refreshed for the next performance.

She looked out the window once, then crawled into her spacious bed, suddenly aware of how empty it was, and pulled the covers up to her chin. She closed her eyes, and yet she could not sleep immediately, for in her mind's eye she saw

Drake again, as vividly as if he were in the room with her again.

She could feel his hands warm upon her body, his lips pressing hers, and she ached down deep again. She wished he were there to hold her, to love her, and all her anger evaporated. The tears welled up in her eyes, but she wouldn't let them fall. She would *not* cry over him, she told herself. She would not. But she knew it was a losing battle.

There had been—there still was—so much anger between them. No matter how well the evening started, how much love they had and how wonderful it was, they always fought.

Perhaps sometime they might learn not to, but she didn't see how.

When the first light of dawn began to streak the sky, she told herself she must go to sleep. She tried, but sleep did not come till much later.

Thirty-Four

"My God, Madeleine," L'Croix whispered. He was drained, an empty husk. He rose up on one wobbly arm and stared down at the nude woman lying next to him. "You're beautiful, do you know that?"

Her kiss-inflamed lips parted into a seductive smile, and she reached up and slipped an arm around his neck to pull him down on top of her. He touched her hair, and she nuzzled against his fingers.

"Again, *mon chéri*?" She wiggled provocatively against him.

"There's nothing left, Madeleine. Nothing at all. You've taken it all." Licking his lips, L'Croix shook his head. "Everything."

"There's more, Armand," she said, trailing her fingers along his now-limp manhood. To his astonishment, his body responded, though somewhat weakly. Delighted, she laughed and kissed him on the lips. "You see! You are not drained—at least not yet, *mon chéri*." She put her hands on his shoulders and wrapped her legs around his, bringing him closer to her.

He shut his eyes, feeling the heat of her body beneath his.

"I'm tired, Madeleine. I don't know—"

"We shall proceed slowly," she said in a teasing tone. She raked her nails down his back, paused at the rise of his buttocks, and stroked in a long circular motion.

L'Croix drew in a sharp breath. His body was growing warm, liquid again, hardening quickly, and he could feel the desire building inside, the desire he had given her for the past three hours. He gripped her full breasts with his hands and squeezed hard, crushed them together, burying his face in them. She moaned and undulated, her groin grinding into his. Ruthlessly he kneaded the soft flesh, pinching and tweaking, and she licked her lips and stared at him through half-shut eyes.

"Armand," she cooed. Her experienced fingers sought the tumescent organ, teased it so that it hardened even more.

He shifted his head, brought his mouth down greedily to her full breast, and sucked at the dark aureole and the hard nubbin there. His tongue lapped at the nipple, felt it stiffen, and he grinned.

"You are such a clever man," she said as she drew her nails along his rigid manhood.

He gasped and brought his head up. She was smiling at him, that temptress smile that filled him with lust. He swallowed, knowing he would have to take her soon. Very soon.

"You're so beautiful," he said. He pushed her legs apart, slid between them.

She gave his penis a sharp jerk, and he threw his head back and cried out in pain and pleasure. She rolled it back and forth between her hands, pinching and caressing, and he knew he had no time left.

She raised her hips up as he rammed into her. She moaned, her fingers wrapped in his lank wet hair. He pushed his way past the already moistened gate, slid effortlessly into the well of her, and thrust hard. She cried out, and he grinned. She ground her hips, thrust, withdrew, and all the while he was driving deeper into her. They rocked, and bucked, and he forced her legs wider and wider. He hammered at her, beating at her, plunging into the very core of her, and then in a sudden rush of white heat he bit his lip, threw back his head, and cried out in a strangled voice. She still undulated beneath him, sucking him dry as she had done before, and finally, spent, he collapsed on top of her, his head resting on her shoulder.

"My darling," she said, massaging his sweaty shoulders. She was staring at a point beyond the bed, a faint smile on her lips.

"Hmm?" he murmured sleepily.

"I am so glad we found each other."

"So 'm I."

"So very glad, because you know that whatever you want, Armand, I will do for you. You have only to ask, and you know I will willingly do it. As you did earlier tonight. Remember, *mon chéri*? Such a naughty boy!" She playfully thumped his arm.

He smiled at the memory. "It was good, wasn't it? I hadn't done that before."

"There'll be other times, if you so desire."

"Good." He kissed her arm. "And you know, Madeleine, that I'll do whatever you want. It's only fair, after all."

"Really, Armand?" Her smile had become cold, her eyes calculating.

"Of course. Anything. Anything at all."

"You are so generous, *mon chéri*. What am I to do with you, eh?"

"I don't know," he said, his eyes closed. He was close to drifting off to sleep. It had been an exceedingly vigorous evening. He couldn't remember the last time he had been loved so well. Madeleine certainly knew what she was doing.

"My wonderful darling," she said. Her hands had moved down his back and were stroking lightly across his skin, sending shivers through his body.

"Is there something you want, my pet?" He stifled a yawn. "You have but to tell me."

"Are you sure, *mon chéri*? I do not want to impose on you."

"It's no imposition, Madeleine. None at all. You have but to name it."

The smile grew icy. "There is one thing I must ask of you, Armand."

"Yes."

"It concerns Ariel Greystone."

And with that he raised his head to stare into the dark eyes filled with hate.

*   *   *

The coronation was a month away, Ariel realized, and she was still no closer to finding the information for Drake than she had been a few days ago, when he had paid his surprise visit to her.

Du Veilleur had returned, and she would be seeing him soon. Perhaps then she could search for the papers. Too, her job had become twofold, with Drake asking her to find out all she could about Hendricks.

Her best plan was to notify L'Croix. He might well know the Englishman, and he could make inquiries more safely than she.

Surely, she reasoned, du Veilleur could not be involved in this matter. She suspected that Hendricks's disappearance was due to natural causes. Perhaps he'd met with an accident out in the country or fallen prey to bandits. Well, with luck and L'Croix's help, she would soon know.

Then she could tell Drake.

If she saw him again.

She would; she knew that. He wouldn't be able to stay away.

Nor did she want him to.

Drake left his rented room in the small inn and made his way down the street. He needed a meal and wanted to buy some cheese, meat, bread, and wine to take back with him. The less he was seen outside, the less chance that he would be recognized.

He found a market and made his purchases, and was on his way back to the inn when he realized he was being followed. Or at least it seemed that way. He paused by an apothecary shop and stared into the window, hoping to get a glance at his follower. But the man had seen him and paused likewise, his face averted.

Interesting, Drake thought as he continued on his way. Who could it be? Perhaps it had nothing to do with his job. Perhaps it was someone out to rob him, a common enough occurrence in Paris.

He came to the inn and looked back, but he did not see the shadowy figure, and as he went upstairs to his room, he thought he'd best say something to Ariel the next time he saw her.

"Good evening, Philippe."

In the semidarkness of the room, he glanced at the woman on the bed and frowned. She had pulled the covers to her chin. "What are you doing here?" he asked.

"Not a very warm greeting," she pouted.

"I'm not feeling particularly warm tonight. How did you get upstairs?"

"They let me, *mon chéri*; after all, I have been here before."

He started unbuttoning his cerulean coat. She slid out of the bed to help him off with it. She wore nothing. He turned to give her a frank appraisal.

"You're looking well, very well. As always. Wine?" He crossed to a table.

"Yes, please." She followed him and draped her arms around him as he poured the wine into two glasses.

"What do you want, Madeleine?"

"You needn't sound so suspicious, Philippe."

"Needn't I?"

"No." She accepted the glass from him and marched across the room to lie on the bed. He sat in a chair some feet away. She cast a languorous glance his way, but he ignored it.

"Well?"

"I'll be direct, Philippe." La Châtelet smiled. "I want an invitation to the coronation."

"That's impossible, and you know it. Particularly after what happened at the theatre. Napoleon won't forget that, I can assure you."

"I thought I might be able to change that."

"How?"

She smiled and took a sip of the wine. "A good vintage, as always, Philippe. You stock such excellent wines. Does your new mistress appreciate them as much as I did?"

"Did you come to talk about Ariel, or what? I don't have much time, Madeleine."

"You know, you aren't the only one to have found someone new."

"No?" His shrug was offhanded. He sighed to himself. He should have gone to the study first, and perhaps after a while she would have gone away. She was so very tiresome. "I'm glad you are not alone, then."

"Me?" Her laugh was chilling. "I don't mean me, Philippe."

"Whom do you mean?" He had found there was no way to hurry the woman. She would tell her story when she was ready.

"I mean the *Anglaise*, of course."

He drew his brows together. "She's found someone? How do you know that?"

"Because I saw him one night. Oh yes, you needn't look so astonished, *mon chéri*. I have been suspicious of her, you know—she acts so very pious. And now I find she is just as tarnished as the rest of us." She laughed. "I followed him to his lodgings to catch a glimpse of him. He was a very remarkable man, too, *mon chéri*. Very tall, and quite handsome, though serious, and with a patch over one eye."

"What?" He sat up and stared intently at her. "A patch? Which eye, Madeleine?"

"The left one," she replied with some surprise. Obviously, she hadn't expected him to respond in this manner.

"The left," he repeated. He drummed his fingertips on the arm of the chair. "Tell me what happened that night. Everything, Madeleine."

"I followed her home. She had left the theatre early, and I thought that was odd, although you were not in Paris. She had been home for about an hour or two when I saw a man sneaking through the garden. He climbed up to the second story and entered through a window."

"It was not a thief?"

"He did not come out with anything, *mon chéri*, and I would have noticed that. No, he was there for a more . . . personal reason. When I knew he was inside, I crept up to the house."

"Did you hear anything?"

She smiled and ran a finger around the rim of the glass, then licked her finger. "At times their voices were very clear, very loud, and I heard much, although I don't know much English, *mon chéri*, so I cannot tell you what they were saying precisely. But there were many times when they were not, shall we say, talking?''

His face flushed. "And?"

"And I waited a very long time. Finally, I heard their voices raised, as though in a lovers' quarrel, for your name was brought up, and then I heard footsteps approaching the window. I quickly hid myself behind a nearby tree, and then he left. I followed."

A man, who spoke English, visiting Ariel in the middle of the night. A man who had a patch across his eye. His left eye.

"Leave now, Madeleine."

"What?" She dropped her wineglass. "I brought you this—"

"I know, I know, and I . . . appreciate it," he said with a curl of his lip. "But I must think. Leave, and I'll talk to you tomorrow." He found her clothes and tossed them at her and waited while she dressed. Then he gave her a brief kiss. "Where is this inn?"

She smiled. "I already have someone watching him, *mon chéri*. A friend of mine. You see, I have thought of everything."

"So you have. Come tomorrow afternoon, and we will talk more of this matter, Madeleine. Let me know if the man visits Ariel again. Indeed, report all his movements to me."

"I will, Philippe." She crossed to the door, then paused to look back. "About the invitation to the coronation . . ."

His mind was already elsewhere. "What? The coronation? Don't worry, Madeleine. I think that you will be attending after all."

She smiled triumphantly and blew a kiss at him as she left. He took a swallow of wine and frowned. It would have to be checked out, of course, for he could never trust Madeleine completely, particularly when she was jealous. And yet, how could she have invented this story?

An Englishman with a patch over the left eye. It had to be Lord Drake. But what was he doing here? Seeing Ariel. And why? Simply to see her perform, as he had years before? He did not think so.

It had to be due to Thomas Hendricks's disappearance

earlier in the month. Drake's sudden appearance was too much of a coincidence at this point, particularly as his visit had been furtive. Why had Drake come to see Ariel? Because he missed her? It had to be something important, something crucial, that had brought him across the Channel. A government matter, perhaps. The actress he had admired for so long—his mistress—was an English spy. All too clearly now he saw how he had been duped. They had arranged her "exile" from England; they had had her meet him, an admirer of hers, which Drake well knew. As for the rest . . . ah, well, we shall see about that, he thought. Still, he had to concede it was a clever plan. No doubt Drake's.

He frowned suddenly. Had he said anything to her that could be used by the English? He didn't think so; but then, she had had many opportunities to eavesdrop, as well as to go through his study while he was out of the room. Not that she would find anything there. After he had found Hendricks rifling through the papers, he had made copies. Ones that contained the wrong information. They would be of no use to anyone.

Certainly the English were intent on discovering more about this plan. Three agents: Hendricks, Drake and Ariel. He would have Drake taken, but he would wait with Ariel. Napoleon liked her and would not be pleased to discover her duplicity. Too, if he delayed in having her arrested, he might be able to use her as a lure for more English agents.

He smiled. He would send for Desmoulins, and they would talk. Then they would see Madeleine. After that, he would take care of things.

Thirty-Five

❧◦❧

Desmoulins stared at du Veilleur incredulously as he finished the story. It was late morning of the following day, and du Veilleur had had all of the night to think over what he had learned from the red-haired actress. He was quite warm toward Desmoulins when he arrived, sat him down with a stiff drink, and then proceeded to fill him in on everything.

"Why didn't you say something earlier, Phillipe? My God!"

Philippe shrugged. "I had Hendricks safely under lock, and so I thought there was no sense in saying anything yet. I did not know about the others."

"English agents here. Incredible!"

"Oh, come, Bernard, they know we have our own spies in London. The surprise here comes in learning who they are." He tapped a forefinger against the polished top of the table. "Ariel Greystone a spy."

"An actress—who would have thought?"

"Yes, well, certainly we were expected to be duped. And would have continued to be had it not been for the jealousy of one woman."

"Mademoiselle La Châtelet?"

"Yes, certainly a bitch, but she has her uses. As we have

learned. She's coming here later. I am going to permit her to help us in this matter."

"Good." Desmoulins frowned. "Is it wise, though, Philippe, to let her know too much? Too much knowledge in the hands of . . ." He left the statement unfinished, merely spreading his hands wide.

"Whom would she tell? She's known to be a spiteful bitch. Besides, it's in her interest to keep quiet. She wants to attend the coronation."

"Ah, I see."

Du Veilleur smiled. "I sent a note around earlier to her, and she'll be here shortly. Her 'friend' is still watching Drake, and will until we say otherwise." He smiled. "I think that tonight would be an excellent time for the man to disappear."

"Disappear?" Desmoulins was clearly nervous. He was, du Veilleur thought sadly, only a bureaucrat and had no courage nor imagination when it came to important matters.

"Yes, we'll round him up—not murder him."

"Ah." Desmoulins relaxed.

"At least not now."

The other man stiffened again. "Philippe—"

"Drake is a spy, may I remind you. As are Hendricks and the woman, and as such, they stand to be executed."

"But—"

"But not before the coronation. I don't want anyone to know about this, not even the emperor. He has told us that he wants nothing to go wrong—*nothing*, Bernard—and I do not think this would please him. After all, the woman fooled him, as well. That won't sit well with his pride. We'll wait until after the coronation—when he has been affirmed in his power. Then I'll tell him."

"I don't know if you should wait that long," Desmoulins said. "It's still two weeks away."

"Nothing else will happen. Paris is in a frenzy right now, and even if Ariel finds the papers—and now I realize why she wanted to visit me so often—they're not the real ones."

"But won't she try to pass them along? And won't that alert someone back in England if the papers, even the fake ones, reach there?"

"We simply won't permit her to pass them along," du Veilleur said. "We'll intercept them. No one will know. And then one day three English agents will disappear." He laughed.

There was a knock on the door of the study, and his butler, Joncher, entered. On his heels followed La Châtelet, who swept in with a wide smile for the two men. Both stood and bowed.

"How good to see you again, Philippe," she said, offering her cheek to be kissed.

He smiled. She was acting already. "This is Madeleine La Châtelet, Bernard, and this is Monsieur Desmoulins, a good friend of mine."

"Charmed," she said.

"The pleasure is mine," Desmoulins murmured, "for I have often admired you upon the stage."

"Indeed?" Her expression brightened. "You must tell me which plays you have seen—"

"Not now, Madeleine," Philippe said impatiently. "I want to talk to you about your friend." She smiled. "I assume he's still watching the Englishman?"

"Yes, and will stay there until I tell him otherwise. He's quite devoted to me."

"Would he bring the man to me?"

She laughed. "Why, of course. I have only to ask it, *mon chéri.*"

"Good, because I want the Englishman brought here tonight—unhurt, if possible. I will send Joncher with you, Madeleine."

"Armand hardly needs a servant to help him!" she responded indignantly.

"I don't want anyone hurt," Philippe replied quietly. "And it might take two men to subdue Drake."

"What then?" she asked.

"What then, Madeleine? Why, we wait, of course. Now, don't pout, or you won't get your invitation. Yes, that's much better." He smiled. "Much better indeed."

Drake left his room and passed through the common room of the inn. Outside the night air was cold, and all day the leaden sky had seemed to promise snow. He paused to look around, then headed toward the stable where he had rented a horse. He was on his way to see Ariel and find out if she'd learned anything more. He had stayed away for well over two weeks. Stayed away to give her time to look for those papers and to learn what she could about Hendricks. And to give himself time to cool down.

Du Veilleur. The thought of the Frenchman brought a dangerous dark flush to his face and caused his hands to tighten convulsively into fists. He would kill the bastard the next time he saw him. He would take his neck— No, he would do nothing of the sort. The man was a valuable source of information. They needed him. For the time being.

Drake smiled grimly as he entered the small stable. It was almost as dark inside as out in the night air, although several lanterns had been lit. As he passed the tack room he flipped a coin to the stableboy, who nodded in sleepy recognition. He walked between the stalls. Old straw covered the dirt floor and muffled his footsteps. He breathed deeply, taking in the odors of manure, sweat, and new hay. Earlier he'd arranged to have the horse saddled by this hour so there would be no delay.

The horse he'd rented was in the last stall, and when he reached the box, the bay mare tossed her head and walked toward him. His hand went to the latch, but it paused as he heard a noise. He cocked his head to listen better. There were the usual rustlings of horses moving about in the stalls, the sound of them munching on hay, whickering softly to one another. The other sound had stopped. No doubt a rat somewhere in the stable.

He turned back to open the stall door. The next moment something heavy struck against the back of his head, and he blacked out.

When he awoke, he was in a brightly lit room, and it took a few seconds for his eyes to adjust. His skull ached. His hands were tied behind his back. He blinked and looked around.

A man sat behind a desk, smiling. Drake frowned as he recognized him.

"Welcome, Lord Drake. What a pleasure—and a surprise —it is to have you here."

Drake didn't respond. His mind raced through the possibilities. Somehow du Veilleur had discovered he was in Paris. The man who had been following him on the street. The sound he'd heard in the stable. They made sense now. Much too late, they made sense.

But how had he been discovered? Certainly Ariel wouldn't have said anything to anyone, much less to du Veilleur. And no one else knew he was here. So how? Could he have been followed the night he visited her? He had known it was folly, but he couldn't stay away. That had to be it.

But it still didn't make sense. First Hendricks, and now him. Well, thank God Ariel was still safe.

"Come," said du Veilleur amiably, "I know you are a man of few words, but you are much too quiet. Say what is on your mind, Drake."

"How did you know about me?"

"Someone saw you when you left Madame Greystone's house, and you've been followed ever since. I commend you on your cleverness, Drake. I really do." The Frenchman's smile did not quite reach his eyes. "But, I'm afraid it won't help any of you—not you, nor Hendricks. Nor Madame Greystone."

She wasn't safe as he'd hoped. And he had placed her in this danger.

Du Veilleur smiled. "Don't worry, Drake, you'll be seeing her in a few days. We have something else to do first."

Drake frowned, not liking the sound of that, but there was little he could do now. Du Veilleur snapped his fingers, and two men Drake had not seen before grabbed him by the arms and dragged him from the room.

After making his way through Italy and France, Pope Pius VII arrived November 25 at Fontainebleau, where he was met by Napoleon. An escort of soldiers and priests then led the pontiff to the Tuileries, where he was established in a special apartment in the Pavillion de Flore.

All of Paris was seized with an agitation bordering on madness, and in the days following the pontiff's arrival there was dancing in the streets, singing, and loud shouting day and night. Ariel, leaning out the window, listened to the cries and wild laughter. It brought back memories from her childhood, memories of a Paris that did not rejoice in an impending coronation of an imperial couple, but instead ruthlessly hunted down the aristocracy as though they were diseased rats and then exterminated them.

Shivering, she drew back inside and closed the window. She returned to the fire and rubbed her arms. She was chilled from the cold air and from the memory. Perhaps her mulled wine would help. But not even that could dispel the chill.

The chill was from fear. Though she had felt fear before, this was a fear that went beyond concern for her own personal safety. For what, she didn't know.

She had not seen Drake since their evening together. She had waited for him, but she didn't have any more to report than before, so perhaps it was best that he didn't visit again. She hadn't seen much of L'Croix, either. Suddenly she felt deserted. She had been frustrated, too, in her attempt to find anything more about the plan or about Hendricks. Time was running out. She had to do something.

She hadn't seen much of Philippe lately, either. Some days ago, after her last performance before the coronation, he'd sent flowers and a note saying that he would be working late hours for a while but would like to see her in a few days. They planned to attend the coronation together, and that was only a few days away.

Perhaps she would pay a call upon him.

She smiled, thinking how surprised he would be to see her.

Thirty-Six

Several carriages sat outside du Veilleur's house when Ariel arrived, and the windows were well lit. This might be the best time to do some searching, with all these people around to hold his attention.

The door opened and Joncher admitted her, though he informed her the comte was with friends.

"I'll wait," she said. She went to the large oval mirror hanging on the wall and patted her curls.

A few minutes later a door down he hallway was thrown open, and Philippe came striding out.

"Ariel, *ma chérie*, how perfectly delightful to see you." He took her hands and kissed her lingeringly. "I have been expecting you, but you must have forgotten—I am working tonight."

"I didn't forget, Philippe," she said softly. "I couldn't wait. It's been so long since I've seen you. Perhaps later, *mon chéri*. I could wait somewhere for you. Yes?"

He smiled, and there seemed to be something else in it she had never seen before. "But, of course, Ariel. There is the upstairs drawing room."

"Oh, Philippe, there's nothing to do there. Perhaps downstairs in the library, if you're not using it for your work."

"I'm sorry, but we are. There are many of us here tonight, and we need someplace large."

"The study, then?"

"Fine. I'll have Joncher bring some wine. Are you hungry?"

"Famished," she replied throatily.

He chuckled, kissed her again, his tongue running along her lips, and then escorted her to the study. He opened the door and pinched her as she passed him. She made a lighthearted swipe at him, and they both laughed.

"Joncher will be back in a moment to see what you want," he said.

"I want . . . only you."

"Ah, you will have me. But much later, I fear." He started out the door.

"Philippe?"

"Yes?"

"How much later?"

She had thrown off her pelisse, and looked up to see that his smile had faded.

"Long enough."

"What?"

"For you to have a dinner, if you wish." He smiled urbanely. "Perhaps an hour or two. Perhaps three, but I will try to hurry them. You must understand, politicians are long-winded."

She slipped her arms around his necks, then pressed herself against him. "*All* your work at night is important, Philippe."

"Impudent witch."

"Of course."

They kissed, and he closed the door, and she was left to amuse herself.

Philippe and the other men were in the next room. She had wanted to stay in the study because it was close, and she hoped she might overhear something important; then too, his papers were in the study. Obviously he had no need of them tonight.

She had no sooner sat in a chair by the fireplace than Joncher entered. He set a tray before her.

"The comte said you wished to dine, madame." It was obvious from his voice that he did not approve of her visit. She knew he did not like her. She was, after all, an *actress*.

She ordered a roast chicken—something that would take

time to prepare—and as soon as he left, she tiptoed to the door. She heard the low murmur of voices from the room next door, but heard no one moving outside. Good. She selected a book from one of the shelves by the desk, set it open on her chair, and then went to du Veilleur's desk and began sorting through his papers.

They were mostly government papers. Salaries and reprimands. Nothing of interest. He wouldn't keep important papers on top of the desk, she reminded herself. Yet he'd hardly think it necessary to hide them in this own home. He wouldn't expect his guests to look through the drawers.

She opened the top left drawer. She saw a sheaf of papers bound together, and on the first sheet was a list of names. Her eyes ran down the list. Ships' names. Opposite was another column. Berths?

She located fresh paper, pen, and ink and quickly copied the information. When the ink was dry, she folded the paper and set it on the desk, then thumbed through the remaining pages. She found nothing of interest. The same went for the drawer below, and the bottom one as well.

The other side of the desk proved of more interest, however, for in the middle right-hand drawer she found a paper from Napoleon to his staff, reaffirming a proposed invasion of England, set for sometime in '06. She quickly summarized its contents on a fresh sheet of paper. She replaced the originals, and was reaching for a third drawer when she heard a noise in the corridor. She grabbed her notes and raced across the room. Reaching her chair, she thrust her notes into her reticule and picked up her book just as the door opened.

It was Joncher. "Your meal, Madame Greystone." He stood beside her.

"Please put it here, Joncher." He set the tray down and waited for further orders. "That will be all. Thank you."

He bowed and left, and she leaned back in her chair and breathed a sigh of relief. That had been close. Too close.

She downed a glass of wine, then savagely sliced through the breast of the chicken and ate it as quickly as possible. It was delicious, redolent with tarragon, and she discovered she was genuinely hungry. She finished the chicken, then went on to the stewed carrots and the plum tart, finishing her meal in record time. When she was finished, she wiped her fingers on her napkin. It would never do to get greasemarks on the papers she was examining, she thought with a smile.

She poured another glass of wine, took a sip, and returned to the desk. The third drawer on the right was locked. Frowning, she stared at it. Where was the key? If Philippe kept it, then she could do no more. But she did not recall his ever carrying any keys.

The key must be here. She opened a leather box on top of the desk and found an old pen nib, a sou, and a polished stone. Nothing more. She looked through all the drawers, then sat down and stared at the desk.

He wouldn't keep it in a different room, she thought; he'd want it close at hand, in case he had to open or close the drawer suddenly.

At hand.

She smiled and reached up under the middle drawer, her fingers tracing the wood. About a foot into the desk's knee well, she found what she wanted. An irregularity. She pushed hard, and something slid back. A key dropped out into her hand. She brandished it with a smile and inserted it in the lock.

A perfect fit.

Inside were more papers. She began reading, careful to keep them in the order in which she found them. There was a note from Philippe to an unknown man about Hendricks. He was being "detained" on du Veilleur's country estate. At least he was still alive, or had been a week before when the note was dated. There were figures, too, for the armaments of the ships, the number in the fleet. She began scribbling the figures down. This was very important for Drake to see.

She heard a burst of laughter outside the study and dropped the pen, splattering one of the papers with ink. Quickly she blotted it. She had been so engrossed that she hadn't bothered to listen for the men. It sounded as though they stood right outside the door. Any moment they could walk in and—

She thrust the papers inside the drawer and locked it. She was panting as though she had been running. She reached under the desk and inserted the key in its slot, then tried to push the hidden spring door back in place. It wouldn't move.

The voices were louder.

". . . next time, Bernard," she heard du Veilleur say. There was a loud laugh.

She pushed at the spring lock. The key fell. She got down on the floor, retrieved the key, thrust it back inside the hidden panel, and had just managed to close it and leap back in the chair, fold her notes, and slip them into her dress, when the door opened.

Close, too close, she thought, as du Veilleur entered the room alone. She smiled at him and was aware that she was perspiring lightly.

He smiled. "How pretty you look behind my desk, *ma chérie*."

"Thank you, Philippe. I was looking for paper and ink to write you a note."

"A note?" He came across to her. "Whatever for? Was I gone that long?"

"Yes!" she declared. "I've been locked away for hours by myself—"

"Not hours, my pet. I trust you kept busy, though."

She waved a vague hand at the book. "I was reading, after my wonderful meal."

"Good, good."

"I thought you had forgotten me."

"Never."

He helped her up and put his arms around her waist. He nuzzled her. She closed her eyes and leaned against him, thanking God that du Veilleur had not entered the room any sooner. Now, she just had to get the papers to Drake.

"Well, I wondered. . . ."

"No," he said softly, kissing the skin just above her right breast. She shivered, but not from desire. "Perhaps you are a little tired and need to rest?"

"Yes, I've had a long day."

"I know. I , too, have been busy. I think you would be quite surprised just how much. Perhaps we should both retire."

They kissed and left the study.

She did not smile as they went up the darkened stairs. She didn't want to stay now, but she had to. For now, her notes would have to wait.

Thirty-Seven

◆◎◆

As soon as Ariel arrived home the following morning, she wrote a note to L'Croix. The last time he visited her, she had asked for his address, and now she didn't have to wait for him to come to her. She asked him to visit her that afternoon. In the meantime she bathed and dressed, and she had eaten a light lunch by the time he was ushered into the salon.

"Ah, monsieur, I am so glad you could come."

"How could I refuse a beautiful woman?" he said with a gallant bow. He looked tired, and not a little strained.

"Are you all right?"

"Yes, quite. Your note said it was urgent that you see me."

"Yes. I have important information."

"Important? He leaned forward. "What is it?"

"I was at Philippe's last night and searched his study. In a locked drawer I found some papers that obviously have to do with the invasion. I made notes on the names of the ships, and the numbers, and where they are located. In fact, everything that looked important I wrote down."

"Good."

"There's more. I found out where Hendricks is being held."

"Where?"

"At du Veilleur's country estate. Do you know where that is?"

243

"Yes, I've been out there before. I'll find some excuse to visit." There was a faint shine of sweat on his face, and he licked his lips. She thought he looked a little nervous. She could understand. This was dangerous business.

"If only we could reach Drake." Why hadn't he visited again? Had he been detained somehow?

"Don't worry. I'll take care of everything. I'll try to be back this evening with a report. Do you want me to take the papers? N-No? Very well." He stood and started to leave, then turned back. "Good news, eh, Ariel?" he said in a hearty tone, then left.

She did little after that, for she had begun to worry. This was the part of her job that she had not permitted herself to think about, the part that could involve danger, perhaps even death.

How she wanted Drake here, with his arms around her. She knew they'd probably start arguing about something —anything—but even that would be preferable to sitting alone in her house and waiting.

Waiting for what, she did not know.

"Excellent. Very well done," du Veilleur said, leaning back in his chair.

Armand L'Croix and Madeleine La Châtelet were sitting opposite him in his study. L'Croix had come straight back to du Veilleur's house after meeting with Ariel.

When du Veilleur had first met L'Croix, he had not suspected the latter's duplicity, but as the months went on, L'Croix's conscience had begun to nag him. After a while, du Veilleur had sensed that something was wrong, but it was not until tonight, when Madeleine brought him along, that du Veilleur began to realize what was going on. He had pressed L'Croix for details, and the man had given in. Too easily, du Veilleur thought, and for a moment he had suspected a trap. He dismissed that after he saw how L'Croix stared hungrily at Madeleine.

Confessing was the sensible thing for L'Croix to do, du Veilleur thought, but it wouldn't save him. Not now. He would take care of L'Croix, along with the others, just as soon as the coronation was over, and this very ugly matter would be finished once and for all. But first he had other uses for the man.

"It is fortunate that Madame Greystone trusts you," he said dryly.

L'Croix paled and licked his lips but did not speak. He glanced once at Madeleine, who smiled reassuringly.

The stupid bastard, du Veilleur thought. He had risked his neck by betraying Drake and Ariel, all to have Madeleine in bed. The irony was that she would no doubt tire of him soon. He was surprised her interest had lasted this long. The man must be spectacular in bed.

"I told you he was good," Madeleine said with a wicked smile.

Du Veilleur smiled at her double meaning. L'Croix stared at the floor. The man had a conscience, despite all the spying he'd done on his own people. Obviously, he was worried about something and would bear close watching during this time. Du Veilleur didn't want him trying to help Ariel in the end.

"What do I say to her?" L'Croix asked. His voice was almost a whisper.

"Say that you've found out I'm giving the servants the night off because of the coronation and therefore the house will be empty. And tell her she can't delay, because Hendricks is scheduled to be executed the morning after the coronation, and so you both must act quickly."

"On the day of the coronation," L'Croix said slowly. His eyes met those of the man behind the desk.

"Yes, on the day of the coronation." Du Veilleur smiled with his lips only.

L'Croix didn't return that evening, and Ariel worried about his absence. Had something happened? Or perhaps he simply had been delayed. No doubt he was finding it difficult to leave the estate. After all, she did want him to be careful.

She went to bed and slept peacefully and rose feeling refreshed.

The next morning, one day prior to the coronation, L'Croix called upon her. She was on her way to the breakfast parlor when L'Croix was announced.

"Good morning, monsieur," she called cheerfully. "You're just in time to join me for breakfast."

"I'm afraid I cannot, madame."

There was something wrong with his tone. Her smile faltered. "What is it?"

He looked about, saw none of the servants lingering nearby, but pulled her into the parlor nonetheless. "I went out to the estate and found that Hendricks is still there. I also discovered that he's to be executed the day after tomorrow."

"Oh my God. What are we to do?"

"Do?" L'Croix laughed hollowly. "There is only one thing we can do. You and I must rescue him before he's murdered."

She stared, almost uncomprehending. *You and I.* Go out to du Veilleur's estate to rescue an English agent scheduled to die. She, a woman, and this man. The two of them against God knew who. She could have laughed, but didn't.

"Du Veilleur is giving his servants the day off because of the coronation, so that will help us." She didn't speak. "Are you all right?" he asked a little more sharply than was necessary.

"I'm fine."

"Will you do it?"

"I have to," she said slowly. "I have no choice, do I? We must rescue Hendricks." Drake—wherever he was—would be depending upon her. She wished she could tell him about all of this, let him think of a solution and take care of everything. Coward! she told herself abruptly. She hadn't been raised to be one, and her mother would have been ashamed.

No, her mother would have wanted her home, safe and alive.

She wouldn't be hurt, she told herself. Drake and Chalmers had trained her in preparation for just such an event as this.

She would be all right.

She wished she could have smiled with confidence, but at the moment she was feeling far less than sure of her abilities.

ACT FOUR

December 1804

Thirty-Eight

The day of the coronation, December 2, 1804, dawned cloudy, cold, and snowy.

A few days earlier Ariel had arranged to await Philippe at her house, from which they would go to the coronation together. The preceding night she had gone to bed early, listening to the salvos of artillery that were fired every hour from six in the evening until midnight. The following morning she rose reluctantly at four, bathed and dressed slowly. She was nervous, thinking of what was to come after the coronation. To take her mind off those thoughts, she listened to the prattle of Hally as the girl dressed her hair.

When Ariel was finally finished with her toilette, she turned in front of the mirror and tried to ignore the knot of fear and excitement in the pit of her stomach.

Her gown was new, just received from her harried dressmaker, and was of white satin, trimmed with gold lace, and worn over a sheer chemise. The long sleeves were marmeluke, ones divided into several puffs by gold ribbons. The neckline was cut low and threaded with a green ribbon, and the gown was belted just below her bosom with a petit point strip of embroidery done in delicate greens and golds. Hally had styled her hair in soft curls, so very becoming to her face, and it gave her a coquettish look. Around her throat she clasped a strand of smoky topazes—a recent gift from Philippe. She knew that it would please him to see her wearing them. Matching topaz earrings glimmered at her earlobes, and she had set diamond pins in her hair so that whenever she moved, the diamonds caught the light and sparkled. White satin slippers and long white gloves completed her coronation outfit.

She picked up her fan, then tapped her foot as she continued to examine herself.

"Do you think the comte will approve?" she asked the maid. She really didn't care if du Veilleur approved or not. The time had passed when she cared, but she needed to say something.

"I'm quite sure he will, madame," the girl replied in a reproving voice. Hally did not like the comte and had never hidden her dislike. "You're so beautiful today, ma'm. It's a shame that—" Abruptly she stopped and turned red faced.

"A shame that what?" Ariel probed.

"It's a terrible shame that Lord Drake can't be here to see you, ma'm!" the girl burst out, then lapsed into embarrassed silence.

A shame, yes, and not for the first time she wondered what had become of Drake. He had only visited her that one time. Was he still angry? Was he waiting until after the coronation to see her again? If only she knew, for that knowledge might give her more confidence in what she and L'Croix must do.

She smiled at the maid to show her she wasn't angry at the mention of Drake's name. "Now run along, Hally, and get dressed. I won't need you further."

"Thank you, ma'm!" The girl grinned, bobbed a curtsy, and rushed from the room.

Ariel had given her servants the day off because of the special occasion. Too, it would be best if they were not around the house and thus did not see her leave later in the day. She wanted no witnesses for that, not even her trusted English servants.

She prepared to wait for du Veilleur. After the coronation was over she would return home and change and get her pistols, and when L'Croix arrived they would leave Paris for the estate.

And then . . . she could not bear to think of it. She had slept little the night before for all the plans of rescue that had tumbled through her mind. One after another she had concocted them, found something wrong with them, and dismissed them as folly, until finally she had risen, feeling drawn and very tired, and not at all sure of a plan. She was sure L'Croix would have one.

She rang to have a cup of tea, and she had just finished it when du Veilleur arrived, as promptly as usual. He was very handsome in his formal attire of black breeches and coat, and she told him so. His eyes glittered with more than usual excitement. She knew that he was looking forward to receiving an additional title from the emperor, but something more than that expectation was exciting him today. What, she did not know.

"You are looking stunning, *ma chérie*," he said after he had kissed her.

"Thank you, Philippe. I'm so nervous," she confided.

"Nervous? I would not doubt that in the least." His voice was ironic, and she frowned, puzzled. When she looked at him, he was smiling.

She pulled on her new pelisse, and he escorted her outside to his waiting carriage. The streets, sprinkled with sand to prevent the processional horses from slipping, were already crowded, and his coach made its way slowly.

While the sun had been up for well over an hour, the air was cold and the sky a dirty gray. Large snowflakes drifted downward from time to time. She shivered, huddling down inside her pelisse.

"You know, Philippe, I have never seen anything like this," she said. "I don't know what to do. But I find it so exciting."

"There is little you can do," he said. "Other than simply observe, as we all will do." He leaned across and caressed her knee. "Don't worry, my love. Everything will be all right."

"I certainly hope so," she said, but at the moment she wasn't thinking about the ceremony. She forced herself to concentrate on listening to what he had to say. That was the only way she would not think of the rescue.

Du Veilleur reported that a full dozen processions had already begun to make their way to the Notre Dame Cathedral in Paris, and that he had seen them wending their way as he'd come to her house.

"Deputations from the cities, as well as from the army and navy, the legislative assemblies, the judiciary, and the administrative corps will be there, and of course the Legion of Honor will be represented as well." He tapped his fingers impatiently against the cushion. In the faint light in the carriage, she could see he was frowning. "I hope there is no delay."

"When we reach the Tuileries, what are we to do?" she asked.

"Waiting will be carriages for the leading officers of the government, of which I am one, and for their ladies, which you most certainly are." He reached out and kissed her gloved hand. "And then we should all leave, though God knows how long it will take with all the carriages."

Their carriage stopped from time to time, and du Veilleur was becoming more and more impatient at the delay. Lost in their own thoughts, they spoke little until they reached the Tuileries, where they found a scene of organized chaos. She was amazed that anything was being accomplished at all. Du Veilleur excused himself and left her in the carriage. He returned shortly to report that he had found the carriage to which they were assigned.

He led her to one drawn by six horses, and once they were settled inside he said, "There are reports that the cathedral is already nearly filled with civilians." She shook her head. "The procession is not to leave here until nine."

"It's just seven-thirty now," she said with some dismay.

"I know. We will simply have to wait, *ma chérie*. I am sorry."

She merely nodded and leaned back, closing her eyes. She would rest a little; it was going to be a long day, after all. She must have fallen asleep, because when she opened her eyes, she found her head resting against a cushion, and her neck was stiff. She blinked sleepily at him.

"Did you have a good rest?" he asked.

"Very." She yawned behind a gloved hand and looked out the window, not surprised to find they hadn't moved. All the coaches in the procession were gaily decorated, displaying elaborate arms and designs, and the horses, either white or black, were exceedingly beautiful. Although well trained, none of them appeared quiet today, for the hecticness of the Tuileries had infected them.

Shortly before nine they heard the sounds of remote cheering and applause. Du Veilleur asked a young man passing by what that meant.

"The Holy Father has just stepped out of the Pavillion de Flore, my lord," the boy answered politely. "He has just climbed into his coach."

"Ah, then it will not be long," du Veilleur said, settling back.

The affable Pius VII was followed into the carriage by his servitors, the cardinals, and the grand officers of the Curia, and then the papal procession began. In front rode a bishop on a mule, holding aloft the papal crucifix.

A few minutes after the ninth hours, the imperial cavalcade began to move away from the Tuileries, much to Ariel's relief. The hours of waiting had not helped her nerves any. Du Veilleur pointed out the various dignitaries as their coaches passed.

"There is Marshal Murat," he said.

Murat was governor of Paris as well as being married to Caroline Bonaparte, one of the emperor's sisters. With him was his staff. Twenty squadrons of cavalry followed.

Du Veilleur's carriage rolled forward at that moment, and they exchanged smiles.

"At last," du Veilleur said. "I could not have lasted much longer."

Nor could she. She was impatient to get on with the day.

Now she could see the royal coach emblazoned with an *N*. Drawn by eight pure white horses, it carried the emperor and empress. On its roof four eagles with outstretched wings held aloft a golden crown. The coach's sides were of glass so that the crowds could view the couple.

Napoleon wore a crimson velvet jacket lined with white velvet and over it a short crimson cloak lined with white satin. His expression was stern. Beside him sat Josephine, robed in a silver-fringed satin dress embroidered with golden bees. Her shoulders were bare, and the tight sleeves were embroidered in gold with the upper part adorned with diamonds. A lace ruff rose halfway up behind her head. She also wore a diadem of four rows of pearls, as well as diamond bracelets, necklaces, and earrings. She was so exquisitely made up that day that, with the blush of excitement on her face, Ariel thought she looked far younger than her true age. From time to time Josephine looked at her husband with an expression of pride and love.

Eighteen carriages, each drawn by six horses, followed the royal coach, and these carried the ladies and officers of the imperial court.

Ariel marveled at the extent of the procession, its precision, and the fact that they had started out right on time. That must have been due in part to Napoleon, who disliked tardiness. She marveled, too, that she was included in the procession. She refused to think of anything more.

They passed cheering and applauding citizens along the streets of Paris, and Ariel peered out, wondering if she would see Hally or any of her other servants. Everyone's face seemed to blur, and she blinked quickly, then leaned back against the soft cushions.

It took a full hour for the procession to reach the Notre Dame Cathedral on the Île de la Cité, an island in the Seine River.

Work on the cathedral had begun in 1163, its cornerstone laid by Pope Alexander III, and about 150 years later it was completed. Here Napoleon was to be crowned.

In an earlier century Mary, Queen of Scots, had been married to the dauphin of France at the cathedral, and it was there, too, in 1431, that Henry VI of England had been crowned king of France. Ariel knew that Napoleon was not unaware of the historical significance of the magnificent church, and it was no accident that he had selected this site.

The pope and his delegation had arrived and were walking into the great Gothic cathedral through lanes of soldiers. All the dignitaries were being carefully guarded, she knew, because several years ago there had been an assassination attempt against Napoleon's life, and no one wished a repeat of that nightmare on this glorious day.

When their coach stopped, du Veilleur and Ariel had a few minutes' wait before it was their turn to walk into the cathedral. When they did so, Ariel stared in amazement. It was the first time she had seen the interior of the famous church, and she was awestruck by its immensity and beauty. The play of colored light from the rose windows created a mood of mystery. She peered at the rose window on the north side. Du Veilleur whispered to her that it had remained intact since it was made in 1250. Predominantly blue and red, it depicted no fewer than eighty-four tableaux of the kings of the Old Testament, the patriarchs, and the prophets.

Above the three portals was a gallery of some twenty-eight statues portraying the kings of Judah. Above them was the huge rose window, and finally above that a gallery connecting the two towers. The main doorway depicted the Last Judgment, with the sculpted souls of the elect guided by angels on their way to salvation, or to hell and damnation.

Though it was cold and snowing outside, and normally would have been icy as well inside the cathedral, Ariel found she was really quite comfortable. Excitement because of the coronation and what was to follow, in addition to the large number of people around her, kept her warm. It was hushed inside, as though those waiting feared to talk, and there was an air of urgency and expectancy.

Her hand resting on du Veilleur's arm, Ariel stood on her toes to see beyond those in front of her. In the great nave a throne had been placed at the altar's left, and there the pope stood. He was wearing white robes trimmed in gold.

"Where are the emperor and empress?" she asked du Veilleur. She had lost sight of them once they'd arrived.

"They're changing into coronation robes and should be here shortly."

She gazed around, wondering if she would recognize anyone, and to her immense surprise she did. Some she had seen at various court functions, and others had come up to her after performances to congratulate her. She always made an effort to remember those who praised her work.

Some rows back she thought she saw a woman she recognized. She peered, trying to focus more clearly in the gloom to identify the woman. Madeleine La Châtelet? But surely that could not be. Ariel remembered all too well the scene at the theatre with La Châtelet and Napoleon. The woman would not have enough nerve to attend. Or would she?

Ariel had just turned back and was about to ask du Veilleur to take a look at the woman, when a door opened and the imperial party entered.

First came ushers, heralds, pages, and aides, and finally Napoleon and Josephine. They were both resplendent. In a tight-fitting coronation gown of white satin with gold-embroidered seams, he looked, Ariel thought, much like a Roman emperor must have so many centuries ago. A crimson velvet mantle trimmed in ermine was draped across his shoulders. It was adorned with golden bees, a border of olive branches, and laurel and oak leaves in circles enclosing the letter N. The cape weighed eighty pounds and was held by four men. Napoleon wore a diamond necklace of the Legion of Honor around his neck; a sword in a blue enamel scabbard hung on his left. Josephine's dress of white satin was long sleeved, and she wore a cloak of red velvet trimmed with ermine, the train of which was supported by two of Napoleon's sisters.

The archbishop of Paris led the couple to the thrones in the choir. The pope rose and came down from his chair. The litany was chanted, and then the imperial couple knelt on a blue velvet cushion on the first steps of the altar to be anointed. They returned to their chairs while the pope sang the mass. Then the emperor and empress stepped down to where General François-Étienne Kellermann stood with two crowns, blessed by the pope, on a tray.

Ariel watched, and her breath caught as Napoleon took the crown in his hands and looked out toward the great nave of the cathedral. This was the moment when he would give the crown to the pope so that the Holy Father could place it upon the new emperor's head.

Instead Napoleon placed the crown upon his own head, and his gaze across the church was bold, as if he dared anyone to challenge him. There was a rustling murmur at this unorthodoxy, for it had never been done before. Proud Napoleon, she suspected, had never knelt before another man, nor would he begin now.

Josephine moved gracefully to kneel on a step below the level of her husband, and he placed the crown of diamonds

upon her jeweled hair. There was a moment of hushed silence
as the imperial couple bowed their heads in prayer.

Pius, who did not seem at all upset by this usurpation of his
authority, kissed Napoleon upon the cheek, then proclaimed
loudly the official formula, *"Vivat Imperator in aeternum."*

Finally, the pontiff's assistants brought a book of the
Gospels to him, and Napoleon stepped up to him and placed
his hand on the book, reciting an oath. His voice was loud and
strong as he spoke, and the sound of it, ringing through the
centuries-old cathedral, brought a chill to Ariel.

"I swear to maintain the territory of the Republic in its in-
tegrity; to respect and enforce the laws of the Concordat and
the Freedom of Worship; to respect and enforce Equality
before the Law, political and civil liberty, and the irreversi-
bility of the sales of national property; to lay on no duty, to
impose no tax, except according to law; to maintain the in-
stitution of the Legion of Honor; and to govern only in ac-
cordance with the interests, the happiness, and the glory of the
French people."

"What is this?" Ariel asked du Veilleur in an undertone.

"It affirms that Napoleon is still a son of the Revolution,"
he replied, but there was a cynical twist to his lips.

"May the emperor live forever!" the pope called after he
had again kissed Napoleon's cheek, and those in the great
cathedral took up the refrain. It was now three o'clock, and
the great bell of Notre Dame, weighing some fifteen tons,
began to ring in the South Tower. The peals tolled the beginning of a new empire, and hundreds of voices rose in cheer
after cheer for the imperial couple. The salvos of artillery
mingled with the applause of the crowd. From outside could
be heard the hoarse cheering of thousands of Parisians.

Napoleon and Josephine raised their hands in tribute,
smiled out at those in the church, and then, with the pope,
left. Slowly the cathedral began to empty, and Ariel and du
Veilleur waited while the others around them passed. There
was no sense in rushing out to the coach when they wouldn't
be able to leave right away. Too, it was no doubt warmer in
here than outside.

Ariel sighed, and waveringly she put a hand out to steady
herself. Du Veilleur caught her before she toppled to the floor.

"What is wrong?"

"I . . . I don't seem to feel very well," she said. She knew she would need a good excuse for leaving his company, and illness was the only one she could think of. "Perhaps I should go home and rest."

"Yes," he said, and his tone was dry. She glanced surreptitiously at him, and once again his look was ironic. "No doubt the ceremony has proved too exciting for you, *ma chérie*."

"No doubt," she murmured. "What will happen now? Where will everyone go?"

"Some are to dine privately with Napoleon's family now, and much later in the evening there will be a ball at the palace. It is a shame you will miss that, but perhaps, if you are feeling better, you will attend. What do you say, *ma chérie*?"

"Yes, I would like that. Should I send a note around to you if I feel better?"

"An excellent suggestion."

They were finally able to leave the cathedral, and outside they found the streets even more clogged than earlier. Carriages and riders on horseback and people on foot mingled in the streets. Many had begun drinking already.

Paris would not soon end its celebration of its new empire, Ariel suspected.

The trip back to her home took well over an hour, and Ariel was becoming more and more nervous. It was close to five now. Five in the afternoon, and she had so much to do yet. Du Veilleur lingered for a while and seemed disinclined to leave. Finally, she was able to persuade him that she must go to bed—alone.

He kissed her, said he would no doubt see her again later in the evening, and left. She closed the door behind him, leaned against it for a moment, and then thought of what she had to do. Her stomach rumbled, and she pressed her hands against it.

Already it was time, and she prayed she would have the courage to see it through.

Thirty-Nine

When she had heard du Veilleur's carriage rumble off into the distance, Ariel went straight upstairs to change. She selected an old yet serviceable riding habit to wear. She had briefly considered changing into men's attire, but she dismissed the idea because she was unaccustomed to wearing it and feared her discomfort might be noticeable.

The servants were all gone, and she went downstairs to the library and locked herself in. There she loaded both pistols given to her by Drake when she was in England. She slipped her dagger into her boot as he had shown her and breathed deeply. She had been trained, she told herself; she had spent many weeks in training.

Ariel left the library to wander through the house. She paced about the salon, clenching and unclenching her hands, stopping occasionally to gaze out the window. The flakes of snow had grown smaller and wetter and were sticking to everything. Darkness had fallen early across the cloudy sky, and a wind had come up. It would not be a pleasant ride tonight.

She went back to her bedroom and took out all the money she had and wrapped it in a handkerchief, then stuffed it in a leather pouch. She slipped the packet inside her coat. She might have to flee after tonight, and she would need what money she had.

She lifted down her jewelry box and stared at the array of

contents. Most of them weren't real, but they had some sentimental value for her. A handful were genuine—the topazes she had worn earlier, a strand of pearls given her by her mother, some others—and she might need those as well as the money. Carefully she wrapped them in a second handkerchief and put it in her coat. She realized that most of her real jewels had been given to her by Philippe.

She licked her lips and rang for wine before she remembered she was alone. She went back downstairs, poured herself a glass of wine, and drained it quickly for she was thirsty, but it felt sour in the pit of her stomach, and made her feel ill. She decided she should eat a little, too, for she didn't know when she would have time to do so again. She went to the kitchen and nibbled on some sausage, bread, cold chicken, and apples.

She wanted to leave a note for her English servants, to let them know what to do in case she did not return. She went back upstairs and sat at her writing desk and penned a brief note to Hally and Coates and Wawles, explaining that, should she disappear, she wished them to return at once to England, but not to worry about bringing back all her belongings. She dusted the note, then stared at it, and felt tears forming in her eyes. It could well be that she would never see them again. She sniffed, folded and sealed the letter, and placed it on the mantel so that Hally would find it when she came to lay a fire.

She headed back to the first floor and began pacing again. Fear and nervousness tugged at her, and she wished Drake were there, wished he could be present to reassure her.

Someone knocked on the front door. She glanced at the clock. Six o'clock. It must be L'Croix. She prayed that it was. If it was someone else—no, she thought, it won't be.

"Good evening, Ariel," L'Croix said once she let him in. "I trust you are alone?" His eyes flicked down the hall, as though he expected to see someone waiting in the shadows.

"Yes, come in."

He nodded and followed.

Once they had seated themselves, he asked, "Are you ready?" He seemed unusually tense to her and did not meet her eyes.

She nodded. "More than ready, I think."

She offered him a glass of wine and noticed his hand shook

when he took the glass from her. He was nervous, too, she thought, and it made her feel a little better to know that she was not the only one.

He quickly drank the wine and asked for a refill. She poured more into the glass, and wondered if he should drink so much before they left. That small amount, she decided, wouldn't hurt. Particularly if it steadied his nerves. The wine she had drunk seemed to have calmed her.

"Do you have any weapons?" he asked.

"Yes, two pistols." She said nothing about the knife, forgetting that it was even in her boot.

"Excellent. I have several, too, although if all goes well, I don't think we'll have to use them."

"I hope not," she said fervently. "What is the plan?" she asked. "I want to know ahead of time what we'll be doing."

The wine goblet was clasped in his hand and he rolled the stem back and forth between his fingers. It was a nervous gesture, and it made her a little uneasy.

"It will take some time for us to ride there. We should leave in a few minutes." His eyes were focused on the carpet, his voice low, and she sensed that he was even more disturbed than when he'd first arrived. "As I said before, the servants will be gone, thus providing us easier access. Once we have Hendricks free, we'll split up. You will return home, and I'll ride with Hendricks to the coast and see that he gets on a boat heading to England."

She wasn't sure why he needed her to go along. Surely he could have handled Hendricks by himself—or could he? Still, there seemed little for her to do.

"I don't think I should come home. How could I just sit around, knowing what I know? How will I be able to meet with du Veilleur, or any of the others? And what if they suspect me?"

"I don't think they will."

"But it won't be you sitting here waiting," she pressed.

"That is true. Still, I think you should wait to hear from Drake. After all, he's the one who sent you here, and no doubt he has plans."

"I still don't like it. I don't like having to come back to the house. I want to ride with you."

"It will be dangerous."

She laughed. "Everything we're about to do is dangerous, Armand. Come now, be reasonable."

He shook his head. "You are a stubborn woman."

"So I've been told." She waited for the span of a heartbeat. "Well? May I go with you?"

"Yes, you may." He threw up his hands in defeat. "Still, if Drake—"

"Drake would understand, I believe." She frowned slightly. "You don't think anything has gone wrong, do you?"

"Wrong? No, no, not at all," he said heartily, although she thought the tone seemed forced. "Come, we must go now."

She nodded, feeling even more the need for Drake's arms around her, then jumped to her feet and followed him outside. There they paused. Where she lived it was relatively quiet, but occasionally they could hear gusts of laughter blown on the wind. In the distance lights twinkled.

"There's a lot of celebration tonight," she said, recalling that there was a ball going on. She could imagine how magnificent it was, with all the exquisitely dressed couples, the strains of lively music, the warmth and cheeriness of the ballroom. She shook herself. That dream was not for her.

"Yes, all for the emperor."

There was no trace of his usual bitterness when he spoke of Napoleon. She shrugged in the darkness. Both of them worried and of course would be acting a little odd.

They walked around the house to the stables, neither hurrying nor taking their time. They saddled the horses they would ride, and when she went to get tack for a third, he stopped her.

"We'll just take two, Ariel. A third will slow us down. Hendricks will ride with me after we leave the du Veilleur estate."

"Very well."

"Ariel."

She stopped, her reins in hand, and looked up at him inquiringly. The yellow light cast from the lantern washed across his face, giving it a strange, gaunt appearance, and tonight there was a haunted look in his eyes. "Yes, Armand?"

He opened his mouth to speak, but didn't.

They mounted and left, riding slowly away from her house.

She turned once in the saddle to stare at the few windows that were warm with light from within, then turned around again.

Snow had continued to fall until they left the house, but now only a few flakes occasionally drifted downward. Above, the sky was gradually clearing of the heavy, somber clouds that had been there all day. How different the landscape looked tonight with its new blanket of white, she thought. So unfamiliar. They rode past skeletal trees with black twisted limbs that reached out toward them, past darkened houses wearing the ragged trim of icicles. From time to time ice slid off the trees and bushes and shattered, startling them. In the distance a cat howled, its cry thin and piercing, making her feel even more uneasy.

Once, something dark and small darted between her horse's legs, startling the creature, who reared up and whinnied with fright. Ariel spoke in a low soothing tone to the mare and stroked the horse's neck, and after a few minutes the animal stopped trembling and they were able to ride on.

"Must have been a dog," L'Croix said, and she nodded, then realized that was foolish because in the darkness he couldn't haven't seen what it was.

The moon now shone down on them, and she stared up at its cold and remote face. Not at all reassuring tonight, she thought with a shiver.

The du Veilleur estate lay some miles south of Paris, and they rode for well over an hour. In that time they saw no one except one man who ran across the road to a farmhouse. The door had opened and he had slipped in. That had been many miles back, though. Eventually L'Croix indicated for them to slow to a trot, then raised his hand for them to stop. He paused and listened.

Nothing could be heard except the snorting of their horses.

"The house lies some distance back from the road," L'Croix said. "If someone should pass by—and that I doubt —they won't see anything."

"What about our horses?" she asked nervously. "Won't someone see or hear them?"

"No, there's a copse of trees near the house where we'll tie the horses. It's close enough that we can reach them in minutes."

She licked her lips and blew on her gloved hands, though that brought no real warmth.

They began riding again, and not long after that she saw a large house looming up in the moonlight. Only a few windows were lit, and she thought it did look deserted, which heartened her. Still, her stomach twisted and churned, and her mouth was dry.

"What if there are guards with Hendricks?" she asked, her voice soft.

"Then we take care of them."

To the right of the house was the copse, and they headed straight for it. Once they were under the cover of the trees, they dismounted, tied their horses, and walked toward the house.

"Won't someone see us?" she asked, looking about in the moonlight. She worried that against the moonlit landscape they would be quite visible.

"*If* someone were there, they might see us. But I doubt it. Remember, they'd be looking from a well-lit room and would see little."

They reached the outer wall of the house, and she followed him as he turned to the right, heading around to the back. There, they paused. She could see a terrace, and beyond it a formal garden. A door led from the terrace into the house. Perhaps that was the library. None of the windows in the back were lit. L'Croix touched her shoulder and pointed to a door some feet away. To reach it they would have to go down a few steps. She suspected it led to a root cellar.

"This is how I entered the other day," he whispered, pointing to the recessed door. "Beyond is an unused cellar, and the door seems never to be locked. Careless man, this du Veilleur."

She nodded. He quietly went down the four steps and pushed open the door, which resisted slightly. "Should I close the door?" she whispered.

"Leave it open, in case we need to leave quickly by this route."

She swallowed heavily as she lit a candle to guide them through the cellar. As L'Croix had said, it was unused, although she could see that crates and baskets were stored there. A thick layer of dust covered everything. As they walked, the dust rose up in choking billows, threatening to make her sneeze, and she held her gloved hand against her nose until the tickle subsided.

Once, L'Croix hit a crate, and a basket balanced precariously on the box fell to the floor. Something inside it shattered. The sound echoed through the cellar, and they waited breathlessly for someone to come downstairs. When no one did they continued on their way. Finally, they reached another set of steps, much longer than the ones into the cellar. At the top, a door opened into a large kitchen.

It was deserted. He beckoned her to follow as they slipped through the room.

"Where is he?" she asked in a low tone as they entered a corridor just outside the kitchen. Now that they were in the house itself she was exceedingly nervous. Every slight noise made her jump.

"I don't know," he admitted. "I couldn't find him when I was here, but I know he's still in the house."

But was he? she wondered. What if, in the past day or so, du Veilleur had moved his prisoner? What if they had made all these plans and had come out here to find nothing? She could have laughed, only it was far too serious.

"Maybe we should split up to search," he said.

"What if we need each other's help?" she pointed out. "It would be too risky to call out. I think we should stay together."

He agreed, and they proceeded to search the lower floor. They looked into two dining rooms, a ballroom in which the furniture was draped with covers, a library that she saw did lead out onto the terrace, and several salons. All empty.

They retraced their steps to the grand staircase, close to the front door. A lush red carpet muffled their footsteps as they ascended the stairs. She slipped her hand into one pocket and fingered the pistol there, its touch reassuring her. Upstairs they found a corridor stretching to the left and right.

He pointed to the left, and she nodded. They paused at each door, listened, heard nothing, peeked in, and when they found nothing, proceeded to the next one. By now Ariel had pulled the pistol from her pocket. They rounded a corner and still

L'Croix kept on. Again and again there was nothing. They reached the last door on the right. He pressed his ear to it.

"I don't hear anything. I think it's safe." He opened the door and she again readied her pistol. They walked into the room and gazed around. It was a large sitting room, with a roaring fire in the marble fireplace—the first fire they'd seen in any of the rooms. Several candles had been lit, casting a warm glow on the antique furniture. But the room was empty. On their left was still another door.

She could scarcely breathe, for the expectation of discovery was high, and she was growing more and more uneasy by the minute.

"Bedroom," he mouthed, and she nodded.

Suddenly that door opened, and a man and woman stepped out.

It was du Veilleur and La Châtelet; du Veilleur was smiling.

Ariel blinked in surprise for only a second, then raised her pistol and trained it on du Veilleur's chest.

"Do not move, sir," she said. "We have them, Armand. We've found them now."

She glanced back over her shoulder when he did not respond. In L'Croix's hands were two pistols. Both cocked. And aimed. At her.

"I am afraid, Madame Greystone, that I cannot be of any service to you."

With growing dismay, she realized he was part of a very clever trap into which she had so blithely, so stupidly, walked.

Forty

Unsmiling, Armand L'Croix walked slowly around her and nodded to her pistol.

"Put it down on the floor, Ariel. And take the other one out very carefully—and slowly."

Her mind raced, trying to think of something. She bent slowly to put the pistol she held on the floor. She reached into her pocket with the other hand and grasped the pistol, and in that moment she stood up swiftly and fired it through the pocket of her coat just as du Veilleur shouted a warning.

L'Croix reacted too slowly, and the shot caught him in the arm, spun him around, and his pistols flew from his hands. He grasped his wounded arm, the blood seeping through his fingers. He stared at her with new respect in his eyes.

Ariel picked up the pistol she'd dropped. She aimed it directly at La Châtelet's heart.

"Don't move, Philippe, or I'll kill her."

"I doubt that," he said, although his smile was a little forced now.

"I shot Armand—and I like him."

"Don't let her kill me, Philippe," the red-haired woman screeched. She grabbed du Veilleur's arm and shook it, her nails digging into the cloth. "Don't let her, for God's sake, I beg you!"

"Shut up, Madeleine!" the comte said irritably. "No one is

going to kill anyone—for now."

"That's quite correct," Ariel said quietly. Her mind refused to think of this trap she had been led into. She had other matters to attend to first. "Now, if you will kindly tell me where I may find Hendricks, I shall release him and we'll be on our way without further bother to anyone here."

She had begun backing slowly toward the door leading to the hallway. She didn't know if she could lock it from the outside, but she could slam it shut, throw something in front of it to slow them down, and at least get a few minutes' lead on them. She could then free Hendricks, and the two of them could hold off the others—especially since L'Croix was wounded. Now, if she could just get those other two pistols, she'd pocket them as well.

"Armand," she said not unkindly. She hadn't liked shooting him. "Please shove those pistols away very carefully with your foot."

His face was pale, and he moved to obey.

"I don't think you'll be going anywhere," du Veilleur said.

"What?" And then she knew.

Too late, she whirled, firing the pistol. The shot went wild, missing by inches the man who was hurtling into the room from the hall. Full force he struck her, knocking her off her feet and onto the floor. Her head slammed against the floor, and her vision dimmed and blurred. A heavy weight crushed her chest and pinned her arms.

She could hardly breathe, couldn't think for the searing pain in her skull. She struggled weakly against the man on top of her who was smothering her, but she struggled in vain. Finally, through a fog, she could make out someone talking.

"Let her up."

Miraculously the crushing weight eased, and she felt herself being pulled up by her wrists. She was jerked to her feet, and she stood there wobbling as though she might fall at any moment. Gradually her vision cleared. She could see who had hit her. It was Joncher, du Veilleur's burly servant, who had thrown her to the ground.

He gripped her by her wrists and wouldn't let go no matter how much she twisted her arms. She turned her head to stare at du Veilleur.

His smiled broadened. "That wasn't very wise of you, *ma chérie*." He held one of L'Croix's pistols. The other one was on a table far out of her reach.

It was obvious to her now what had happened. Joncher had been somewhere in the house—no doubt down the hallway they hadn't yet explored—and when he heard the shot had come running. How stupid she had been to turn her back.

A moan escaped L'Croix's lips at that moment, and they all looked at him. He was even paler than before.

"Madeleine, please take L'Croix into the next room," du Veilleur said. "At least bandage him, so he won't bleed all over my fine carpet."

La Châtelet glared at du Veilleur, then rushed over to L'Croix, crooning words of comfort. L'Croix leaned heavily on her arm.

"Now," said the comte, a sneer on his face as he watched the couple leave the sitting room, "isn't that the very ideal of true love? Or should I say true lust? A very unexpected development, too."

She tried to pull her wrists away from Joncher. His grip tightened, and it felt as though her bones were being crushed beneath his immense fingers.

"Let me go," she said shortly. "I won't try to run away."

The comte laughed. "On your honor?" Before she could respond he nodded to the servant, who released her abruptly.

She stumbled backward a little and rubbed her sore wrists. Dark bruises were already forming there. A curl straggled into her eyes, and she pushed it away impatiently, then bit back a cry as pain ripped through her arms. She glared at the brute, who merely grinned back.

"You're looking very well tonight, *ma chérie*, as beautiful as you did before your illness. Could we call this a miraculous recovery? It's no wonder you didn't wish my company this afternoon, when you had such an important task at hand."

She said nothing.

"I think you should search her now, Joncher, before we proceed further. And do be careful—she seems to be full of tricks tonight."

The man nodded and stepped toward her. She stepped back. He ran his hands across her body, and she closed her eyes as his fingers lingered on her thighs. He forced her to sit down and take off her boots. Joncher held up the concealed dagger.

Du Veilleur raised an eyebrow, then gazed at her. "Nasty, Ariel. Very nasty, and quite unexpected for an Englishwoman. But then, I forget that you have the hot blood of the French in you as well as the reserve of the English. Ah, yes, one might say that you and Madeleine are sisters under the skin."

Ariel didn't say a word. She wasn't sure that she could, feeling the way she did. The pain in her wrists had subsided a little, but she was aware now that she hurt all over her body.

"We will go downstairs and visit another cellar—one that you did not see when you entered so quietly earlier in the evening."

Madeleine came out of the bedroom at that moment, and she glared at Ariel.

"How is your Armand?" du Veilleur asked, sarcasm in his voice.

"He's doing better," La Châtelet said shortly, "no thanks to that bitch."

"Come, Madeleine," the comte said reprovingly, "your language is not befitting a lady."

The French actress said nothing. Her eyes were filled with hate as she looked at Ariel.

"I want you and L'Croix to stay upstairs for a while. Will you?"

La Châtelet shrugged. "I suppose so." She returned to the other room, slamming the door behind her. Ariel winced at the sound.

"Come along, *ma chérie*. I have something important to show you."

How long had L'Croix been working with the comte? Ariel asked herself. How had these two come to work together? That was certainly puzzling. Had any of her information reached Drake at all? It must have, or surely he would have said something when he came to visit her in late October. How stupid she had been, she thought dully as they began heading downstairs.

Where was Drake? she wondered. He might even be on his way to England by now. And if so, how long would it be before he returned to France? Before he missed her? Before he knew that something was wrong? Too late for her rescue.

They reached the kitchen, and du Veilleur pointed to a door she hadn't noticed before. "A second cellar, *ma chérie*. Go on."

Joncher lit a five-branch candelabrum and held it aloft as they descended a rough set of stairs. They were narrow and treacherous, for some of the boards were loose, and dust rose around them in clouds, momentarily blinding them. Each step down seemed to seal her fate even more. They would reach the cellar, and he would kill her, and that would be the end of that.

She would never see Drake again, would never be able to erase the angry words with which they had parted. His final memory of her would not be kind, and that she sorely regretted.

They reached the bottom of the stairs and took a sharp turn to the left. Joncher set the candlestick down beyond a tall stack of crates, and the flickering flames threw elongated shadows across everything, giving the cellar an even spookier atmosphere. Ariel heard a low drawn-out sound from somewhere ahead of her. She took a few steps forward, then stopped. To her horror, she saw two men chained to the cellar wall.

One was Drake, and the other she suspected was Hendricks.

Du Veilleur nodded to the two prisoners. "We have had Hendricks as our guest for quite some time, but Lord Drake has only been here since a few weeks after his visit to you in October."

"Then he's been here for almost a month," she whispered.

"Yes."

"How—" She could not go on.

"How did I know of his spying?" He waved a hand airily and smiled an evil smile. "I owe it all to Madeleine, you see."

"Madeleine?"

"Yes, she hated you, *ma chérie*, was intensely jealous of you. She followed you, she watched you, and one night she saw a man leaving your house quite late. She knew I was not in Paris, and she was, of course, intrigued by the secrecy. She followed him, and was able to see his face and thus provide me with a good description. Instantly I realized it was Lord

Drake. And poor L'Croix upstairs is so besotted with Madeleine that he would do anything for her. She sent him to watch Drake, and in mid-November I had L'Croix and Joncher bring him here. But, I do not think he has suffered his detainment well.''

Horrified, she turned around to study Drake, and she bit back a cry. His head was slumped on his breast, and so far he had not talked nor given any sign that he even knew she was there. Dried blood stained his torn clothing; bruises on his pale skin showed a vivid yellow and purple; dirt and straw matted his hair, clung to his clothing. He was very gaunt, as though he had been starved.

If du Veilleur thought she would beg for Drake's release, he was quite mistaken.

A great hate and anger boiled up in Ariel, searing her brain, clouding her eyes, and she whirled, baring her teeth at du Veilleur. Before he could even respond, she flung herself across the few feet separating them, her hands closing into strong fists that pummeled his face and chest. He dropped back, flinging his arms over his head as her hands sought to hurt him as he had hurt Drake.

The next moment she was lifted off the ground and flung away from du Veilleur. She slammed into the wall with a force that knocked the breath out of her. She slid down to lie in a heap on the floor. Joncher, she told herself. Her eyes teared from pain, and she wiped them, then blinked to clear her vision. Feebly she moved her arms and legs, fearing something had been broken. But everything worked properly, if somewhat slowly. She drew in a ragged breath and pushed herself up to a sitting position.

A few feet away, Hendricks stared at her. He winked, then closed his eyes. It had been so quick that she wondered if it had really happened.

''Now, I think, Madame Greystone needs to learn not to be so impetuous.'' Du Veilleur pulled her to her feet and held on to her.

Nodding, Joncher picked up a black bullwhip she had not seen before.

''No!'' she shrieked. ''Let me go!'' She tried to twist out of his grasp, but his fingers tightened, digging into her already bruised flesh. "Don't, Philippe, my God, don't!"

Du Veilleur nodded to the servant, who placed himself a few feet in front of Drake. Joncher hefted the sinuous whip, stroked its black length, then raised it as he drew back his arm. He whipped it forward, and the lash caught Drake across the chest, making another tear in his shirt. Drake groaned, but did not otherwise stir. Ariel stared in horror as Joncher thrashed Drake, drawing more blood. Still, he made no sound.

More crimson rivulets ran down Drake's legs, his chest, and once the lash caught his cheek, cutting it wide open. Blood trickled down to his chin. She put one hand to her mouth, refusing to cry out.

Finally, when the Englishman's shirt was soaked red, du Veilleur ordered Joncher to stop. The servant stepped back and wiped the whip clean, then coiled it carefully.

"You've made your point, Philippe," she said wearily. She ached from her own bruises, and inside she ached to see Drake hurt so severely. She closed her eyes momentarily, vowing that the Frenchman would pay for what he had done to Drake.

"Some time later, *ma chérie*, you will see how a spy is treated. You will be permitted to watch as Lord Drake's remaining eye is put out with a red-hot poker. I assure you that Joncher looks forward to that."

She swallowed quickly but said nothing. She wouldn't give him the satisfaction of pleading again.

They returned upstairs to the sitting room. Du Veilleur sat while La Châtelet poured wine. L'Croix, his arm bandaged, had settled by the fire and spoke little. Ariel sat at the other end of the fireplace. Outside the door, Joncher waited.

"I will go to Paris tonight to tell Napoleon," du Veilleur said after he had drained his glass. "I think the emperor will be very displeased when he learns you were a spy, *ma chérie*. Shall I remind you of the punishment for spying? The fate you will share with the Englishmen? No, I thought not. However, you will not lose your pretty eyes, so do not worry about that." He laughed.

"Napoleon may be disappointed by my so-called betrayal," Ariel responded fiercely, "but I suggest that you worry a little yourself, Comte. No doubt he'll be just as displeased with your unmasking of me, for that will make him look the fool as well."

Du Veilleur flushed. He recognized the truth of her words.

"Don't listen to her, Philippe," the Frenchwoman warned, glaring at Ariel. "She's just trying to save her neck. Kill her right now, and be done with it before she proves even more troublesome. The others you can deal with later." The redhead's smile in the candlelight was not pleasant.

"No, Madeleine, I'm not ready for that, particularly if Napoleon wishes to see her." He shook his head and called for Joncher. When the man was inside the room, du Veilleur said, "Lock her in the storeroom downstairs."

The burly servant marched her downstairs to the same cellar, but instead of going left, they turned right. He shoved her into a storeroom, then locked the door. Alone, she paced, counting the storeroom's length and width. It was about twenty feet long, five wide, and very dark. She saw a faint glimmer high up on one wall and groped through the darkness until she reached it. Crates had been stacked to cover a window. She carefully pulled them away and stared at the window. It let in some moonlight, allowing her to see better, but the window was too narrow for her to escape through.

She found a dusty crate to sit on and rested her head in her hands. She was weary, sore, and already hungry again. And she didn't want to stay down here alone in the dark. Especially if du Veilleur was leaving shortly for Paris. She trusted neither Joncher nor La Châtelet, and she wasn't sure what they would do in the comte's absence. Yet, even if she found a way to get out of the storeroom, she still had to help the two men chained to the wall, for they were in no shape to escape on their own. If she tried to bring back help first—she could rely only on her servants—Drake and Hendricks would no doubt be relocated by that time. Or dead.

All of which meant she should do something tonight—and very soon.

She went to the door. "Kit," she called, not sure how far they were from her. "Kit, can you hear me?"

"He's unconscious," Hendricks called. "Has been since they whipped him."

That didn't bode well, especially if they managed to escape. Would he be able to sit a horse? She knew she couldn't leave him.

Outside, the sound of hooves echoed hollowly, and she climbed atop a crate to look out the window. A horseman rode away from the house. Du Veilleur. It would take a while for him to reach Paris and the Tuileries, locate Napoleon and tell him what had happened, and then wait for the emperor to send someone. More than an hour each way, she quickly calculated. Two and a half hours at the most. That was all the time they had left to find a way to escape from the storeroom, the chains, the cellar.

She began searching through the storeroom for something she could use to get her out of her prison. She found some tools, none of which would help her. If she tried to break down the door or hammer off the lock the others would hear upstairs.

She found a long jagged piece of metal to use as a weapon, but nothing else. Despair began to fill her, until she remembered the handkerchiefs filled with coins and jewelry in her coat. Joncher had left those on her. Fingers trembling, she untied the one with the gems in it and sifted through them until she found what she wanted. A jeweled hair clasp. She unlatched it and felt along the small metal shaft on the back. It might be long enough and thin enough. She wrapped up the others, returned them to her coat, and went to the door. She found the lock, stuck the back of the pin in, and worked at it, twisting and reinserting the pin until finally there was a click. Hardly able to breathe, she pushed the door open, picked up her makeshift dagger, and rushed over to the men.

"My God," Hendricks said. They could see each other just faintly, thanks to the moonlight in the storeroom, but he had heard the click of the lock. "How did you get out?"

"Hairpin," she said shortly. She began working on his shackled wrists. "We have to get going. I don't have the papers I copied about the invasion—"

"They're fakes," Hendricks said. "I found the real ones and hid them. The ones you saw were falsified by du Veilleur."

"Where are the real ones?" She had the right shackle off

now and was working on the left.

"They are in the ruins of a Norman abbey just outside Chartres. A dried well is in the courtyard. I put them down there, under a loose stone."

"Outside Chartres," she repeated. "There! That's done."

His arms released, he raised them to rub the chafed wrists. "Hurry."

"I am!" She was working fast, holding her breath, fearing that someone would come down.

Her head was bent over the shackles around his ankles when she heard the sound. She froze, then rose, turning slowly.

At the top of the stairs stood Madeleine La Châtelet, a candle in her hand.

Forty-One

"Here!" Ariel thrust the pin into Hendricks's hand and rushed toward the stairs. La Châtelet couldn't be allowed to alert the others.

La Châtelet set the candle on the steps and ran downstairs, not back to the door. The feeble light flickered as she launched herself at Ariel. In her hand was a dagger with a long thin blade. Ariel sidestepped her, but not before the knife grazed her side. She bit down on her lip against the searing pain, then leaped to the left as the Frenchwoman brought the dagger up in an arc that would have stabbed through her ribs. Ariel thrust her own crude knife at her opponent, and La Châtelet cried out as it pierced her wrist.

The only sound now was their harsh breathing as the two women circled warily, each eyeing the other. Ariel prayed that she would incapacitate the other woman before she herself was too badly hurt. Without warning, La Châtelet sprang at her, bringing the dagger up. Ariel twisted out of the way, then rounded once more on her and thrust with her own weapon.

"Watch out!" Hendricks called at that moment. "Behind you!"

She whirled. L'Croix had entered the cellar, coming down the stairs so quietly that they had not heard him. In that moment he was able to grab her knife and knock her away. She was sent sprawling next to Hendricks.

"Madeleine, put the knife down. Don't hurt her." He stared at the Frenchwoman, who shook her head vehemently. She was breathing hard and there was a strange glint in her eyes. Blood trickled down her arm from the cut on the wrist.

"No, I want the bitch," the actress said. Stealthily she approached Ariel.

Ariel knew she had to act now. She leaped to her feet, grabbed La Châtelet by the arm, and flung her against L'Croix, hoping that would knock both of them down long enough for her to overpower them.

La Châtelet screamed, then slowly backed away from L'Croix. The knife he had been holding had pierced her stomach. She stared dully at the blood dripping down her skirt. She tried to speak and could not. She looked to L'Croix, then collapsed.

L'Croix gave a strangled cry and cradled the dying woman in his arms. That gave Ariel the edge she needed. She grabbed La Châtelet's knife, which had fallen on the floor. L'Croix looked up and, snarling, sprang to his feet and grappled with her. Suddenly Hendricks was there, pulling L'Croix away from Ariel. L'Croix twisted and turned, trying to free himself from the Englishman's grip, and jabbed his elbow into Hendricks's stomach. He broke away and charged toward Ariel. She brought her dagger up, and it caught him in the throat. He stopped and gave her a puzzled look as blood spurted from the jagged wound in his neck. He clasped it with both hands, then pitched forward, falling only inches away from Madeleine La Châtelet.

Ariel stared numbly at the two bodies. Both L'Croix and La Châtelet were dead. She had killed them. She looked at the knife gripped in her hand and dropped it. Slowly she backed away until she felt the solidity of a wall behind her. Breathing deeply, she shuddered as she gazed at the blood and death around her. She touched the dark stains on her riding habit. Blood came away on her fingers, and she wiped it off against the wall.

She heard a slight noise from the right and glanced over. Hendricks had just unlocked the chains on Drake's arms. Drake sagged weakly into Hendricks's arms, and Hendricks lowered him into a sitting position against the wall.

"We have to go now," she said urgently. "We can't delay any longer. Du Veilleur will be back soon with imperial soldiers."

"I know. Just a moment. Drake seems to be coming around."

Drake didn't seem surprised to see her there. "You're hurt, Ariel." His voice was rough, as if he hadn't used it for a while.

She glanced at the rent in the side of her habit and shrugged. "It's only a scratch, Kit." Strangely, now she felt no pain.

He just nodded, and they helped him upstairs. In the kitchen Ariel found some bread and cheese to give to Drake, which he wolfed down. Then both Hendricks and she wrapped some food in packets.

"Weapons," Hendricks said. "We need some pistols. I'll go look for them."

"Wait—there's a servant upstairs. Joncher. A big burly man."

He nodded. "I'll take care of him."

Ariel found wine and poured it into mugs for them. Drake downed his as if he hadn't had anything to drink for days. Perhaps, she thought with sudden fury, he hadn't. Finally, when there was little left but crumbs, and only a drop of wine left, he rested his elbows on the table, his head in his hands.

"Are you feeling better?"

"Yes, a little. Thank you, Ariel." He smiled at her, raised his hand to stroke her cheek, and winced a little at the pain.

"Don't move when you don't have to," she said. "I want you to conserve your strength."

She packed more wine bottles with their food packets and started looking through all the cupboards in case she had missed something they might be able to use. God only knew when they would be able to find food again. Suddenly she heard a shot from upstairs. They looked at each other, then to the door of the kitchen.

"I'll go," he said, struggling to his feet.

"No." She rested her hand on his shoulder. "I've got to get the daggers." She ran down the stairs, paused when she saw the two bodies, then steeled herself and grabbed the two daggers. She rubbed them clean on a discarded cloth, then returned to the kitchen just in time to see Hendricks come in with several pistols and swords. He also carried several blankets.

"Drake has told me," he said, handing a pistol to her, "that you're very proficient with weapons. I didn't believe that until tonight. Thank you for getting me out."

She nodded, but shuddered as she recalled the bloody scene below.

Drake, now standing, buckled a sword on, then gripped a pistol. "I'm feeling better. Are we ready?"

They nodded. As they were leaving the kitchen, a wisp of smoke curled out from under the door to the cellar. She looked at the two men.

"The candle that Madeleine brought down. I must have knocked it over when I went to get the daggers."

"To the stables," Drake said. "Quickly!"

By the time they reached the stables they could see the flames flickering through the windows of the first floor. They quickly saddled three horses and were swinging up onto them when they heard the faint thunder of approaching hooves. Du Veilleur and the soldiers were arriving from Paris.

As they galloped away from the house, they heard a hideous cracking, as though dozens of panes of glass were breaking. They saw flames shoot out of the windows on the first and second floors. In the hellish light they could see the soldiers pulling up at the house. Some of them jumped off to contend with the fire, while a handful continued to pursue Ariel, Drake, and Hendricks.

The cold wind whipped at them, bringing with it the acrid smell of smoke, as Ariel bent low over her horse. Hendricks rode last. Drake was in front. From time to time she glanced at Drake, fearing he would fall out of the saddle. But somewhere deep inside he'd found a reserve of strength and he managed to cling to his horse. They heard several sharp cracks: The soldiers were firing on them. The night was black, the clouds covering the moon's face now. Also in their favor was the freshness of their mounts. The soldiers' horses would be tiring after their hour's ride.

There was no fighting back now. They simply had to try to outrun their pursuers. She heard a crack, a cut-off cry, and glanced back in time to see Hendricks, some twenty feet back, topple from his horse. She started to pull up, but the first of the soldiers reached him and he was trampled underneath.

"Come on," Drake called over his shoulder, "he's dead, Ariel."

She nodded, and kicked her horse to go faster. The chestnut shot ahead until it was shoulder to shoulder with Drake's mount.

They swerved into a dense forest, hoping to lose the soldiers, but they followed unerringly. She began to think they would never be rid of their pursuers, but as time blurred for her and minutes lengthened, she knew the soldiers were dropping back, one by one. Finally, when she and Drake were well out of the woods again, they could see no one following them. They left the main road then and headed across country, hoping that might throw off anyone in pursuit. They slowed their winded mounts to an easy trot.

Ariel glanced at Drake. His head was slumped on his chest once more, and she knew he wouldn't be able to ride much longer. Yet they had to stay ahead, had to get away from the soldiers. Surely the troops would make camp for the night and begin searching for them in the morning.

Which meant that she and Drake should travel far tonight. She reached across and grabbed the other horse's reins to bring it to a walk. Its sides heaving, the horse blew noisily through its nostrils. Drake did not even stir.

She kept the horses at a walk, letting them cool off, as she looked around. They had entered still another forest, this one even denser than the first. She didn't know where they were except that they had been heading in a generally southern direction. To reach Chartres they had to head southwest. All in good time, she told herself. Their first concern was to make sure they weren't being pursued. When they reached a stream and she was sure the horses had cooled sufficiently, she let them drink. She didn't want one of them foundering now.

They rode on. Drake hadn't spoken in hours, had barely moved, and she wondered if he had been shot. She reached over and touched him, and he murmured in his sleep. He was exhausted. As she was. She yawned, rubbed her weary eyes with a gloved hand, and looked around. She could see more clearly now, which meant dawn must be approaching.

Overhead, through the skeletal branches, she could see the first faint traces of gray light streaking the sky.

They had to find a place to rest. As it grew lighter, she could see that Drake's face was flushed. But she didn't dare stop now, for she feared the soldiers were just behind. Occasionally she dozed in the saddle, only to jerk awake, thinking she heard pounding hooves behind her.

Finally, when the sky changed from gray to a faint yellow, she saw a ridge ahead that jutted out of the forest. When they reached it, she saw that along one side there was a cave with a well-concealed entrance.

The roof of the cave was just high enough for the horses and riders to enter, and once they were inside and well back from the entrance, she dismounted, her knees nearly buckling as she landed on the soft sand. She turned to pull Drake off, and she staggered under his weight. She pulled him to the ground, trying not to hurt him too much, and laid him down gently. She covered him with one of the blankets they'd packed.

She found an outcropping of rock and tethered the horses, then took down a second blanket and went back to where Drake slept and lay down beside him. She touched his face. Burning with fever. Later, she would bathe his face with snow. Later she would worry about eating. Later she would . . .

She fell into an exhausted sleep.

Forty-Two

❦

Ariel awoke later in the day, cold and hungry, sore and stiff. At once she checked on Drake. His face was still flushed, and now he was trembling. She had to find some place warmer. He would die if they continued to stay in the cave. She stretched, then winced from the wound in her side. She had almost forgotten about that.

Now to feed the horses. She paused at the mouth of the cave as her eyes adjusted to the sunlight. Snow had fallen again after they'd entered the cave, and it was much deeper now. She searched through the woods, brushing aside snow, and brought back grass for the hungry horses. It took several trips to get enough for just one horse, and on her way back to the cave with an armload of grass, she heard an animal whicker. It wasn't one of theirs. Scarcely breathing, her heart hammering, she slipped behind the wide trunk of a tree.

"Seen any sign?" a man called.

A second man answered, but the wind blew his answer away so she couldn't hear. She licked her lips. They had to be soldiers looking for them, and here she stood scarcely ten feet away. She listened as the horsemen crashed through the woods, calling to one another. She had a dagger in her boot, but the pistols were in the cave. What if they discovered her? What if they took her away? Drake would lie there burning with fever and die from the cold.

She closed her eyes and waited, expecting discovery at any moment, but they moved away, their shouts growing fainter. She waited longer, then returned to the cave, where she found the horses had gotten loose. They stood by the entrance, grazing on some grass they had managed to uncover. She gave them what she had, patted them on their flanks, and silently promised them more.

Drake was still flushed, still asleep. She unwound his soiled cravat and filled it with clean snow. She pressed it against his face. He stirred and moved his cracked lips as though about to speak. At one point his eyes opened and he seemed to recognize her, but then he fell back into an uneasy slumber. She trickled wine into his mouth, alternating with snow, and continued this for several hours. When it was close to sunset, she managed to get him on his horse, then swung up on hers, grabbed the reins of the second horse, and set out to find better shelter. Another night in that freezing cave would kill him.

It was long after sunset before she found the farmhouse. She watched it from the woods for some time. When she saw no one stirring, and when no lights appeared inside, she knew it was deserted and safe to approach. The house was old and small, but it was set well away from the road in the midst of tangled underbrush, and would not be easily seen. It would be warmer than the cave.

She tied their horses to a post, then pulled Drake inside. She found a few pieces of furniture, an unswept floor littered with dried leaves and twigs, and a bird's nest. There was a rudely made cot in one corner, and she laid Drake there. She found dry firewood in another corner and set about making a fire. She had taken flint and tinder from the kitchen of the du Veilleur mansion. Before long she had a fire going.

She dragged the cot closer to the fire so that he could keep warm, then went outside and found a shed in the back for the two horses. She took off their tack, rubbed them down with an old blanket she found there, gave them some grass and water, and went back inside.

Already the room was warmer, and his face was less flushed than it had been earlier. She knew sleep and warmth would be best for him, and she sat on the floor and prepared to bathe his face with snow again.

They stayed several days before she grew nervous and

wanted to move on. Drake was feeling better. His fever was down, and he was managing to eat a little. Most of the wine was gone now, as were the bread and cheese. She'd shot a rabbit, but still their food supply was dangerously low.

On the fourth day they left the farmhouse. Drake's eyes remained open while they rode, although he didn't speak. She wondered how long the soldiers would continue searching for them, how long they would have to keep running. She had to start heading toward Chartres soon so that she could find those papers.

De Veilleur still lived, and he would want them stopped at all costs.

At midmorning she stopped to get her bearings and began heading toward the southwest. In the afternoon snow started falling, and by dusk they could barely see in front of them. She found another deserted farmhouse. Drake's fever had returned, and once more she bathed his face and body with snow. Sometime before dawn his fever left. She fell asleep. When she woke later and heard the howling wind and saw the blowing snow, she knew they wouldn't be traveling that day.

Snow fell heavily the next day, and she sat by a window and stared out. There was a sound behind her, and she turned to see Drake sitting up on his own for the first time since they'd left the estate.

"Where are we?" He tried to stand up but couldn't, and he fell back on a makeshift cot.

"In a farmhouse, somewhere south of Paris," she said. "I don't know where precisely."

He ran a hand across his face. "What happened? Where's Hendricks?"

"He was killed right after we left the estate. The soldiers pursued us, but we finally lost them. We've been traveling for six days. The first night we slept in a cave, but then it was too cold, and I found a farmhouse. We moved on and ended up here. This is our second day here—it's storming outside, and I think we'd get lost if we left."

He managed to stand, although a little unsteadily, and wobbled across to look out at the whiteness.

"Winter," he murmured. "I remember being hot and hearing voices."

"Mine, no doubt, and you've been running a fever for a

long time. I broke it with snow. Now," she said, watching his legs begin to buckle, "I think you ought to lie down again."

She helped him back to bed, and there he held her hand. "Thank you, Ariel." He didn't release her hand, nor did she want him to. A great gust of wind that rattled the small cottage reminded her she needed to see about getting food.

"What have we been eating?"

"Bread, cheese, and wine from the estate; only one small chunk of cheese is left. We also had fresh rabbit one day."

"What? Did you—"

"Yes," she said with an ironic smile, "I did. I've done many things in the past few days that I didn't think myself capable of." At the memory of the two dead people in the cellar, she frowned. "Well, I should get going before it gets dark."

"How will you find your way back through the snow?"

She held up a rope. "I'll tie one end around my waist, the other to the tree out front."

"Clever."

When she was ready, she looked at him, and her expression softened. "Promise me you'll stay down while I'm gone. Please, Drake."

"I will if . . ."

"If what?"

"If you'll call me Kit again."

"Of course, Kit." She kissed him on the lips, then went outside.

She didn't find a rabbit this time, but instead had to settle for a small bird. She brushed aside some snow, pulled up some greens, and returned to the cottage to make a simple stew.

"Delicious," he said when they sat down later to eat.

"You're saying that because you're starved," she replied.

"No I'm not."

They ate the remaining cheese, and most of the stew, and then cuddled on the cot close to the fire. She had broken up some of the old furniture in the cottage to use as firewood, and that afternoon she had gathered wood from outside and brought it in to dry.

"Tell me what I've missed," he said.

She related in detail what had happened since she saw him in

October. She also mentioned that Hendricks had told her he'd hidden the papers at the ruins of the abbey.

"So," she concluded, "we are heading, I hope, in the direction of Chartres, and if the snow lets up we should be there in a few days." She sighed and brushed back the hair that had straggled into her eyes. It was filthy; she was filthy; what she would give for a bath. And a comfortable bed. And a decent meal. She sighed.

"With luck." He closed his eyes. "I was so certain of L'Croix. I trusted him—I never suspected he'd turn on us like that."

"You couldn't know he'd fall in love with Madeleine. That changed everything." They listened to the scream of the wind and the crackling of the fire. "If we can find a village," she said, "we can buy food. I brought money and jewels from home that we can use."

"Clever you," he said.

"For once," she said dryly.

"You've always been clever."

She turned her head, unable to look at him. The memory of their last night remained fresh in her mind: the love; the anger and arguing that had followed.

"Ariel," he said softly, "I have to thank you."

"For what?"

"Saving my life."

She didn't know what to say. Finally, she said, "I'm just glad I could be there."

"So am I." She closed her eyes and within a short time was sound asleep.

For a while longer Drake watched her, aware that his love for her was growing. Finally, he too put his head down to sleep.

The snow stopped the next day, and Drake declared he was strong enough to ride on. She didn't argue for she knew they were running out of time. In late afternoon they reached a village where they bought food and clothing and asked for directions. They were told they were heading toward Chartres.

Four days later they arrived. They passed through the town, alert to the danger of soldiers. But no one paid them any attention. Few people were out for it was a cold, blustery day and most of the town's citizens stayed inside to enjoy a warm fire and a warm meal.

The road out of the town led south, and only a few miles outside of Chartres they saw the ruins of the abbey, dating from Norman times. When they entered the courtyard, Drake looked around.

"Hendricks said it was in the well." She nodded. "Why couldn't he have put it up here somewhere?" he grumbled. "Well, no matter. Now to find the damned thing."

Only a few walls and part of the bell tower remained of the original structure. Gnarled vines coiled around the stones, pushing through the mortar and creeping across the uneven courtyard. Trees and bushes had grown wild and thick around the ruins. She wanted to hurry and find the papers and be gone; the place made her uneasy. She felt as though she were being watched by hidden eyes. She looked around, saw nothing, licked her lips, and hurried across to Drake. They explored the snow-covered courtyard and finally found the remains of the crumbling well. They gazed down into it. Snow lay on the bottom.

"I'll go down," he said.

"And how will I bring you up?"

"By tying the rope around me and the other end to a horse, and having it back up slowly."

"Clever you," she said mockingly, and kissed him.

They tied one end of the rope around his middle and the other to the horse's saddle, and gradually she walked the horse forward, lowering Drake deeper into the well. When he reached the bottom he called to her. She peered down into it.

"What do you see?"

"Snow," came the reply.

"Besides that!"

"Leaves and mud, a dead bird, and—ah, wait a minute." He stooped, and she heard a scraping sound, as though something heavy were being pushed aside. "I have it!" He waved something at her. "Let me up!"

She urged the horse to back up, and finally she could see Drake's head appear, then his body, and then he was out. She rushed over to him and hugged him tightly.

"What's this?"

"I want to leave now," she said, glancing around, expecting to see something.

"All right." He stroked her hair briefly, then untied the rope.

They mounted, and when they were some distance away, she looked back at the ruined abbey. Their luck had been too good, she told herself; it was bound to run out. She shivered and wished that their ordeal could be over.

Forty-Three

❧❀❧

L'Croix and La Châtelet circled her, around and around, calling, beckoning with the gleaming blades in their hands. Shadows lay across their faces, but she knew who they were because she could smell the stench of decay, of death. They whispered her name, and she cried out that they were dead, that she had killed them. They laughed and whispered, and crept closer and laughed. They raised their knives and laughed, and she couldn't move, she was rooted to the spot, and they laughed, and—

"Ariel, Ariel!"

Someone was calling, shaking her, *laughing*. No, the laughter was part of the dream. *"Ariel."* Again and again her name was called, and she tried to push the voice away but couldn't. Finally, she fought her way out of the web of sleep and opened her eyes.

Drake was there, his face concerned. "You had a bad dream," he said.

She sat up and looked around her. She was safe, lying before the hearth of an abandoned shed. "I know. L'Croix and La Châtelet were alive and held knives and were coming after me." Tears welled up in her green eyes. "Kit, I killed them!" For the first time since that terrible night, she let herself react to what she had done, to what she had seen. Warm tears rolled down her cheeks, and her shoulders shook.

"I know, my love, I know. But you had to. Otherwise they would have killed you, just as they had planned to kill me and Hendricks."

She nodded against his shoulder, but the sobs wouldn't stop. His arms were warm and safe, and she escaped into the haven of his embrace, losing herself in darkness. Finally, when her tears subsided, he tipped her chin with his finger and kissed the tears away. Their lips sought each other's hungrily, and there before the fire on that wintry night they made love. Tender and slow, gentle and all-encompassing, it healed the poisoned wounds of her mind and soul. He held her tightly, caressed and stroked her, murmured words of love, and she clung to him as never before.

Afterward, content and comfortable, they slept in each other's arms, and when morning came they rose and left.

They trotted along the road, seeing no one else out that day.

At least the wind has stopped, Ariel thought. The sun had come out to shine and glint on the snow, giving it the appearance of a million tiny diamonds strewn across the fields and rolling hills. She sat up in the saddle and stretched, and smiled across at Drake. She felt so much better, so much more optimistic.

A few hours later they came to a village and purchased more food. They were traveling almost due west now, heading toward the coast. Drake wanted to avoid the northern coastal towns where he suspected soldiers would be waiting for them.

Twice they heard soldiers in the woods and managed to hide until the patrols had gone by. These near encounters only made them push harder to reach the coast.

On a clear, crisp day, the first of the new year 1805, they saw ahead the small fishing town of Saint-Giles in Poitou. The province was directly beneath Brittany, which thrust out into the Channel. They would have to hire a boat and swing around Brittany to get to Plymouth, England, which lay almost opposite in a straight line north. They were, he reminded her, still a long way from home.

As they rode into Saint-Giles they looked for signs of soldiers but saw none.

"Hire or steal, we need a boat," Drake said as they approached the docks. "And at once." She nodded. The strain of the past weeks was catching up with her, and she was finding it more and more difficult to keep up.

They dismounted and led their horses as they surveyed the various boats tied to the docks. Most of them were under repair or did not look seaworthy. At one end of the pier they came upon a grizzled individual who, while mending a net, had been watching them.

"Good day, monsieur," Ariel said pleasantly. "We wish to hire a boat to take us to England, and in exchange we will trade our horses, which as you can see are very fine beasts." Very fine indeed, she thought wryly; the poor animals had been run ragged.

The fisherman eyed them speculatively, and she realized how odd she and Drake looked. Neither had bathed for a long time, and their clothes were soiled. She tried not to let him see the desperation in her eyes.

"Plus a gold piece, mademoiselle," he said.

"That's impossible!" she replied.

"A gold piece and the two horses." He turned back to his net.

"Oh, very well. A gold piece it is, and the two horses."

"Good, good." He grinned, showing a gap where his front teeth would have been. "Come this way."

He introduced himself as Emile and led them down the dock to where a boat no longer than twenty feet was moored. It was badly in need of a painting. Its sails looked to have been mended and remended. Overall the boat appeared ancient, but as long as it was seaworthy and got them safely to England, neither cared what it looked like.

"This is my boat," Emile said proudly. "We go tonight."

"We go now," said Drake. "We cannot wait any longer, Monsieur Emile."

"Why?" the man asked, peering at them suspiciously. For the past few minutes he had been looking at Drake's eye patch, then at her.

"Here's your money," Ariel said, thrusting the coin in his hands, "and you have your horses. You needn't ask any questions."

He bit the coin, slipped it into a pocket, and was about to turn back to the boat when there were several sharp cracking sounds, and wood splintered nearby. They were being shot at! Both Drake and Ariel looked back toward the village. Horsemen rode toward the dock.

Soldiers.

More shots followed, and Ariel and Drake jumped down into the boat. Emile untied the mooring rope and flung it to Drake and then was shot. He spun around and collapsed on the dock. More shots followed, and Ariel cried out as one caught her shoulder.

"Get down!" Drake yelled, pushing her flat on the deck. He unfurled the sails and pushed the boat from the pier with a long pole he found. He threw himself down as more shots rang out. The boat rocked, floating free for a few seconds, and then the wind caught the sails. They turned into the draft, and the boat drew farther away just as the soldiers reached the dock's edge. More shots followed, but they were too far away.

When the dock was fading into the distance, Drake sat up. He helped Ariel up and took a look at her wound.

"I think it's just a flesh wound," he said after a moment.

"Is the bullet there?"

"Gone through. I'll try to keep it clean, though, with seawater. Still, it's serious enough." She nodded, fear in her eyes. "The seawater should help. I don't think there'll be any blood poisoning."

She didn't feel very confident, especially now that she was in pain. She sat while he looked below deck for food. He came up a few minutes later, his arms loaded with several bread loaves, a round of cheese, and some wine.

"A now-familiar staple for us, I think," he said with a slight chuckle, and she smiled.

They sailed for the remainder of the day, the wind proving good, and that night put in at a small cove some miles up the coast. They went ashore to shoot some small game and came back to the boat to sleep.

As she lay in the single narrow bunk below deck, she relaxed, letting the gentle rhythm of the waves lull her. Much of her soreness was fading, except for the wound in her shoulder, and with Drake's diligent care of it, the injury was already a little healed.

The blankets they'd found on board were soiled and stank

of fish and brine. But they had taken their packs from the horses, and so they had blankets and at least were warm and moderately comfortable. More so than they had been in those rude cottages.

She listened to Drake's soft breathing as he slept on the floor, only a few feet away. So much had happened in the past months. They had shared so much. She closed her eyes and told herself to sleep, but not even the rocking of the boat could induce her to lose consciousness. She was too restless. Pushing the blankets off, she sat up.

"What's wrong?" he asked. In the darkness she could not see him.

"I can't sleep."

"Is the shoulder bothering you?"

"A little, but that's not it."

"What is it, then?" His voice was closer. She reached out and met his hands, and drew him to her on the bunk.

"Will you hold me, please?"

"Always."

He lay alongside her and wrapped his arms around her, taking care not to touch her wounded shoulder. She sighed, feeling the nearness of him. He brushed the top of her head with his lips.

Later, after they had slept a little, they made languorous, delicious love, the soothing rocking of the boat guiding them in the time-old art. They kissed, and caressed, and held one another so tightly that they could hear each other's heartbeats.

In the morning he showed her how to steer the boat. She held on to the rudder and threw back her hair and breathed deeply of the fresh air.

The days drifted by as they sailed steadily toward England. The boat was not fast, and the winds were sometimes poor and the sea stormy. Yet Drake was a good sailor and she had confidence in him. He tried to keep the boat close to the coastline, although not too close, for they wanted to avoid being fired upon should anyone see them. Too, if he kept the coastline in sight, he could guide them more easily. At night he studied the stars for their position.

Their sea journey was idyllic for all of its hardships of uninteresting food and a hard bed, and she wasn't sure she wanted it to end. When they arrived in England, everything would change: Politics would intrude again, and perhaps they would no longer be as close, something she did not wish to consider.

"How long until we reach England?" she asked the third day out.

"A week, if we're lucky," he said. He glanced up at the sky. Gray clouds streaked it, and behind them glowed a yellow light. Above the boat, sea gulls circled, shrieking into the wind. Occasionally one swooped down to catch a fish in its talons.

A week longer. If they were lucky. She sighed and leaned back against a mast and gazed out at the water. In the days they had been asail, they had not seen another vessel, and she sometimes wondered if they were the last man and woman on earth.

"We should be off the coast of Brittany by now," he said. "Across there," and he pointed due north, "is Plymouth. At least, I hope it is. I think my readings have been accurate enough so that we may be no more than a few miles off." He smiled at her. "We're going to anchor off the shore and spend the night there."

"Is that safe?"

He shrugged. "I don't know, but we need more food. Maybe I can find a village and buy us something."

"We could build a fire," she said, "and bake clams that we dig."

"Yes." He took her hands in his and kissed them. "Yes, we could do that," and she knew that he remembered that first dinner they'd had together.

For the rest of the day she helped him whenever she could, and finally, when the sun was setting in the west, painting the ocean and sky a salmon color, he rowed them to shore. Once on land again, she collapsed on the white sand, and he sat down beside her. Some hundred feet away boulders lay tumbled, and beyond that a sparse forest rose up a hill.

"Tired?"

She nodded, still watching the colors shift in the sky and on the ocean. "I'll be glad to get home." She sighed, thinking of all that she had left behind in her house outside Paris. She wondered if her servants had left; she hoped so.

"There's so much to do when we return," he said softly, and traced the line of her face with his fingers. "But I'm glad we've had this time together, Ariel. It's made things . . . more quiet between us."

"I'm glad we've had it, too." She sighed. "And if you mean we haven't fought for a long time, you're right, Kit," she said, smiling.

"I like that."

"So do I."

"Certainly it's a novel experience."

"Yes."

They were quiet for a few minutes, and then she glanced at him. "Shouldn't we start looking for food and firewood?" she asked.

"Later, I think. There's no hurry right now."

"Good."

He shifted closer to her, and she leaned back so that she could put her head into his lap. He stroked her forehead and they both watched the light fade from the sky. They had brought blankets to keep warm. They were tired, very tired, and it was so pleasant just to sit quietly on the small beach.

Drake smiled down at her, and she breathed in deeply, expectantly. He bent to kiss her. Their lips had just met, when they heard a scuffling noise behind them. He leaped to his feet, and she rose more slowly; then as one they both turned to face the unknown.

A man was coming toward them from the direction of the boulders, and they could see he was holding a pistol in each hand.

As he came closer, his features grew more recognizable in the twilight. When he was only a few feet away, he stopped and smiled.

It was Philippe du Veilleur.

Forty-Four

"Good evening," du Veilleur said pleasantly, nodding to the couple.

Ariel stared in disbelief and was tempted to rub her eyes as if that would prove this was just a terrible dream. It couldn't be the comte. How had he found them? How, when they were so close to being home? Despair filled her as she realized they had not eluded him after all.

He wore clean clothes, but his face had grown leaner, and there were circles under his eyes. At least this ordeal had proved exhausting to him as well, she thought with some pleasure.

Drake had not said a word, had not even acknowledged du Veilleur. She wondered what he was thinking. Was he planning something? Or was he wrapped in his own despair?

She could stand it no longer. "How did you find us?" she demanded.

He smiled. "That, *ma cherie*, was a relatively easy task. When I saw you take the boat, I thought I'd lost you. But after a moment's reflection I realized what Lord Drake would have to do to guide the boat toward England, and so I followed you, day and night, on horseback. When you anchored, I made camp. When you set sail, I began riding. You kept most considerately to the coastline, so that you were almost always within my range of vision. Several times I was nearby when you camped.''

"Yet you didn't take us then," she said, puzzled by his admission. She had clasped her hands together to keep them from trembling. She still could not fully believe that he had actually found them. Her shoulder throbbed more intensely than it had for days. He would take them back to Paris, and they would stand trial before the emperor, who would not be pleased to see her, and they would be sentenced, and then—

Death.

She would not escape the guillotine after all.

"The time was not yet right, *ma chérie*, to draw close to the pursued.''

"But now it is?'' Drake asked, speaking for the first time.

"I have wearied of the hunt, although I enjoyed it for some time,'' du Veilleur said. "I want to bring the stag and doe down, carve off the heads, and take my bloody trophies back to Paris.''

The strong wind blew cold across her back, chilling her to the bone. She wished she could wrap up in one of the blankets to keep warm, but she didn't think the comte would let her. She didn't think they would be on the beach much longer.

"You know that I cannot allow you to take us back, du Veilleur,'' Drake said evenly. "There's too much at stake—on both our sides.''

The other man shrugged elegantly. "Come, Drake, admit it. You have lost the game. You played well—although certainly not by the rules. I will say that you gave me a good run, but you failed. Checkmate, eh? Although, too, I must commend you on your selection of agents. Far more attractive than the late Monsieur Hendricks.'' He bowed slightly in her direction. "You did very well, Madame Greystone—for an amateur. And I would never have known had it not been for poor Madeleine's jealousy.''

She did not respond. Her teeth were chattering now, though whether from cold or nerves she could not decide. She edged closer to Drake, seeking his warmth.

"And now the papers, if you please.''

"Papers?'' Drake asked.

"Yes, the papers. I know that you are playing the ignorant

one, but really you should leave the acting to Madame Greystone. She is a consummate artist. The papers that Monsieur Hendricks stole, and that later I made falsified copies of. Surely he must have told you about them while you were in the cellar.''

"I don't recall that he did," Drake replied evenly, and she held her breath, wondering if du Veilleur would believe him.

The comte chuckled. "Then what can have proved so fascinating at the bottom of the well in the ruined abbey?''

Ariel stared. He had been following them even then. She remembered how uneasy she had been, how she had felt they were being watched. How long had he had been shadowing their every step?

"I should commend you, du Veilleur," Drake said, "on your tracking ability. Most men would not have been able to follow us.''

"I knew, you see, how you would think. That was your downfall.''

She pressed her fingers to her temple and tried to still her racing thoughts, tried to be logical so that she could think of *something*. There had to be something they could do. But what?

"What will you do now that you've found us?" she asked "Will you take us back to Paris to stand trial?" To stand trial and be executed. Her mouth grew dry, and her wound throbbed.

"First, I will take care of the papers. But as to returning to Paris, no, I am afraid not, although I admit that would be my preference. The problem is this: I am not the one in charge. You have proved a great embarrassment to the emperor, who trusted and liked you so well. He prefers never to see you again. Alive. Nor does Napoleon wish anyone in this country to know what has happened.''

A chill, not from the sea wind, ran down her spine. The comte was going to kill them. Here. On this deserted beach, so far from home, yet so close.

"I have money," she said boldly, stepping forward. "There is a lot of gold in my handkerchief, Philippe. You could let us escape, and keep the gold for yourself. And no one would ever know that you had not killed us.''

He laughed. "You know, *ma chérie*, that I have no need of that gold, although I must admit I could use it to rebuild my country home." He shook his head. "I was not very pleased to see it burning."

Again, Drake did not speak. She looked from one man to the other, barely able to discern their features in the dimness. The light was fading fast, and soon it would be dark. Then what? she wondered.

"Come," said du Veilleur, "do not make this any harder for me."

Suddenly Drake brought his hand up, flinging sand into the other man's eyes. Du Veilleur dropped the pistols and wiped frantically at his eyes. In the instant du Veilleur was blinded, Drake launched forward, tackling him. They grappled and fell to the beach, locked in a silent struggle. Ariel ran forward, grabbed one of the pistols, and cocked it. She aimed, but they had switched positions, and Drake was on top now. She had to be very careful; she couldn't afford to miss the Frenchman and accidentally hit Drake. She breathed heavily, and her hand trembled ever so slightly. It was getting darker, almost too dark to see clearly. She took a few tentative steps forward, then stopped to wipe her sweaty palms on her riding outfit. She watched as they slugged at each other, occasionally hearing a groan. Their fists slammed each into each other's bodies and arms while boots found vulnerable spots. They rolled farther down the beach, almost to the water's edge.

Du Veilleur had pinned Drake down, and the Englishman was taking the worst of it. He couldn't last long, not after his long imprisonment, not after the fever he'd run. He was growing weaker, and du Veilleur seemed intent on killing him with his bare fists.

She circled the two men. "Stand up, du Veilleur," she ordered calmly.

He saw the pistol in her hands but didn't obey. Instead he grinned, and with a flick of his hand there appeared a nasty-looking knife. He laid it across Drake's throat.

"If you come any closer, Madame Greystone, I'll slit his throat. Now, just set the pistol down and back away very slowly."

"Don't listen to him," Drake gritted.

She stared at him and at the knife, now a strange silvery color in the last light of the day. Du Veilleur was grinning savagely. He knew he had her, knew he'd won. She didn't want Drake's throat slit, but even if she obeyed, du Veilleur might still kill him. Time passed with agonizing slowness as she debated what to do.

She looked to Drake, then du Veilleur, and holding her breath, pulled the trigger. The pistol jerked back in her hand, wrenching her shoulder as orange sparks blossomed in the night. She heard a deep thud, almost a wet sound, as the bullet impacted. The grin on du Veilleur's face vanished, to be replaced by an expression of surprise as he stared down at the gaping, smoking hole that had been his chest. He tried to rise, found he couldn't, and in slow motion he toppled backward off Drake.

For a long moment she stood there, stunned by what she had done; then she dropped the pistol and ran to Drake. "Are you all right?" she asked, helping him to sit.

"Yes." He passed a hand through his hair and felt cuts and bruises where de Veilleur's blows had landed. There was a thin pink line on his throat where the knife had pricked him. "At least, I think so. What about you?"

She nodded, unable to speak. She couldn't look at the corpse, couldn't acknowledge that she had killed another man.

Drake put his arms around her and held her close. She wanted to cry, but no tears would come. The two sat on the sand a while longer, and then she pulled away slightly.

"Let's go home," she pleaded.

He nodded. "We will, soon, but . . ." He looked at the body. "I have to bury him first."

"I'll help."

With their hands they dug a hole in the sand deep enough to drop du Veilleur's body in, and then piled rocks on it to keep marauding animals from disturbing it. And as the full moon edged up over the eastern horizon, they returned to the boat.

They slept little that night, and when the sun was first painting the sky a pale pink gray, Drake pulled up the anchor and they set sail.

Ariel spoke little. She was exhausted. Drake, who could

have provided some comfort, seemed aloof, and she wondered what she had done. Was it because her work for him was finished? Or because she had killed du Veilleur? It didn't make sense. Nothing did now. Only that she was going home.

In two days' time he called her up on deck and pointed to a shoreline only a few hundred feet away.

"Plymouth," he said.

Soon, very soon, they would be home.

ACT FIVE

February 1805

Forty-Five

Ariel awoke in her mother's town house. She lay in her bed, savoring the sunshine streaming in through the window and the warmth of the comforters on top of her. She stretched, then closed her eyes and pretended to be asleep when the door opened quietly.

"I know you are awake," Etoile said.

"Come in, *maman*," she said, smiling.

Etoile sat by the bed. "How are you feeling now, *ma chérie*?"

"Better today." She touched the bandage on her right shoulder. "It hardly hurts at all."

"Time heals all," Etoile said, and Ariel knew she meant more than the flesh wound.

It had been nearly two weeks since she and Drake had landed at Plymouth. With her remaining money they had purchased horses and ridden across the country to London. Once arrived, he'd taken her to her mother's and left without providing an explanation for Ariel's terrible condition.

Appalled at her daughter's wounds, Etoile had called for Dr. Liggott at once. Luckily, both proved clean, with little sign of infection. He washed the areas, bandaged them, and instructed her to rest in bed as long as possible. He left, and Etoile came in with soup for her daughter, and a demand to know what had happened.

Between sips of the broth, Ariel related the story, and as the tale unfolded, Etoile gasped and grew paler. But when Ariel came to the fight on the beach, she could go no further. Etoile put her arms around her daughter and held her close as she cried.

Since then they hadn't talked about what had happened. Nor had Drake visited.

By the first of February, Ariel was strong enough to move about on her own, and she spent most of the day with her mother in the parlor, or alone, sitting by a window and staring out at the snowy streets. She dared not venture outside, for she was still despised in London.

"I am so worried about you," Etoile said.

"Don't be."

"But I am. You are drooping. You are so in love with him."

"I said you needn't worry!" Ariel snapped.

Etoile sighed. "I know you are feeling much better—your temper has returned."

"I'm sorry. I didn't mean to bite off your head." She sighed and ran her hands through her hair. It was wonderful to be clean again. Since coming home, she took long baths twice a day, savoring the hot water and soap and the feeling of being clean. She never would have thought she'd be free again from the brine and fish odors that had clung to her.

"Are you going to come down for luncheon?"

"Yes, I'll be done in a moment. You go first and rest yourself, *maman*."

Etoile reluctantly agreed, and after she left, Ariel rose. She washed her face and hands and selected a simple white muslin dress to wear. She'd left behind many of her belongings in France, but some had been rescued by her servants, who, upon finding her note, had packed as much as they could and then promptly left for England. She ran a brush through her hair and stared at herself in the mirror. Reddened eyes, and a pallor yet. She did not look well, although physically she felt much better.

Downstairs, she ate with little appetite, then retired to the parlor.

The days continued in the same manner, and each one was leaden for her.

Drake hadn't contacted her. He had deserted her. She would never see him again.

He had just wanted her aid. That was all, she thought dully, and that brought more pain to her.

One day she could no longer tolerate staying inside and she called for her mother's coach for a country drive. That relieved some of the tedium, but she realized she was eager to return to work. She remembered how the theatre had treated her. She couldn't work for any theatre in London. Not after what had happened.

On her way home she saw Drake riding down the street. He saw her at the same instant and drew alongside. She was pleased to see him, but would not admit it. She demanded to know why he hadn't contacted her after dumping her at her mother's door.

"I had important business to attend to," Drake replied gruffly.

"Ah, yes, your business. I have always finished a poor second. I should have known nothing would change. Ride on!" she called to the coachman.

"Ariel," Drake called as the coach pulled away. "Ariel, don't leave."

She refused to heed him, and when she returned home she found her mother waiting for her.

"Kit was here today," Etoile said a little nervously. She glanced sidelong at her daughter.

"It was very kind of him to come see you."

"No, no, *ma chérie*, he came to see you."

"Ha!"

"Ariel, he did! He really did! He has been very busy and couldn't come any sooner—"

"Mother, please," Ariel said wearily, "don't make excuses for him. He never came because he didn't wish to, and that's the end of it."

"But Ariel, he loves you. He told me so himself."

"He probably wants me for some other damned mission."

"Ariel!" said her mother, shocked.

"He always brings out the worst in me."

"I counseled patience, but he isn't a patient man."

Ariel shook her head and left the room, not wishing to hear any more.

The following day Drake was ushered into the salon where

Etoile was working on her needlepoint. Ariel was reading by the window. Both women looked up, startled to see him.

"Good afternoon, ladies," he said, sweeping a low bow. "Etoile, I would like to speak with Ariel."

"Oh yes, of course." She scrambled to her feet, clutching her needlepoint to her chest, and as she went out the door, she winked at him. He gave no indication that he saw.

"Mother, don't desert me!"

Etoile turned to face her daughter. "Oh, I must lie down, Ariel. I have become suddenly fatigued," she said, and continued on her way.

Ariel glared after her.

"Well, will you offer me a seat," Drake demanded, "or must I stand during this session?"

"Please sit," she said stiffly.

He brought a straight-backed chair to the window where she was and sat. She tried to move away a little, but couldn't.

"I have something for you," he said after a long moment.

"Oh?" She raised an eyebrow. "Another mission? What country do you plan to have me thrown out of now?"

"None, Ariel." He looked earnest, and she could almost believe he was sincere. Almost. Hadn't he seemed sincere a year ago when he'd approached her? "We have something else to discuss."

"Ah, what is this? Do you want your money back?" she asked sweetly.

"No!" His thunderous reply startled her into silence. "Will you kindly be quiet and listen to me?" She nodded. "I have this for you." He reached into his coat pocket and pulled out a parcel. With it was a letter. She stared at the seal.

"This is the royal seal," she said, puzzled.

"I know. Read it."

She broke the seal, unfolded the letter, and began reading. By the end of it, she was frowning. She reread the letter, then looked up.

"His Majesty says I am to be decorated."

"And so you are, along with me."

"For my valor, he says."

"For service to your country."

"I don't understand."

"I told Pitt the story and he suggested the decoration. The king was most agreeable."

"What's in the package?"

"Open it."

She pulled at the twine and paper and saw a small silver box. She opened the lid. Nestled on black velvet was a gold broach set with dozens of tiny diamonds. She blinked at Drake, then at the broach.

"It's lovely."

"It's from the king," he said.

"The king," she repeated, as she touched the sparkling jewelry.

"As part of his thanks for your job."

She continued to stare at the pin. "Did the papers help? Will England be able to fend off the French?"

"I think so. I've talked with Nelson in our meetings, and we won't be caught off guard. Already there are reports of the French fleet moving out of port. We returned just in time."

She said nothing, would not meet his eyes.

"Do you know what today is?" he asked.

"The tenth of February. One year ago today you came to ask for my aid."

In silence they both recalled that day.

"What are your plans now?" he asked after a while.

She shrugged. "I don't know. I have nothing left, thanks to you, and I thought I would go away, perhaps to America, to start afresh. I'm sure they can use actresses there."

"I have a better idea," he said.

"Oh? What? Another mission?"

He flushed a little. "No. I want you to read this." He drew out another envelope. It, too, had the royal seal on it.

She read the second letter quickly. Signed by the king, the paper exonerated her, restoring her citizenship and good name. Accounts of what she had done for her country would be given to the newspapers and publicly spread. Further, she was to have her job back at Drury Lane. Speechless, she stared at Drake. She could hardly think for the thoughts tumbling and roiling through her mind.

"I have one further request," Drake said softly.

She gained her speech at that moment, and said in a

suspicious tone, "I say no to your request. I don't care what it is, I'm not agreeing to it, and I don't want to hear it. I just know it's going to prove distressing to me, and I have taken a vow, Drake, a vow that I'll never work with you again!"

He was smiling now. "I wasn't thinking of asking you to work with me."

"What then?" She was clearly puzzled. Why had he come back to plague her? She almost smiled at how she'd thought a year ago that he was plaguing her. She hadn't known the half of it then.

"Ariel, I love you," he said simply. "I always have. I want to marry you. *This* time, though, there will be no backing out. What do you say?"

She swallowed and stared at him, her eyes wide. "You love me?"

"Yes, damnit."

"You want to marry me?" She could not believe she had heard him correctly. "Is that what you're asking?"

"Of course. But no backing out. We *will* make it to the altar this time."

"Oh, Drake!" Then she remembered what he had said before. She half turned away. "I can't marry you."

"Why not?" he demanded.

"Because . . . because . . ."

"Because of what happened six years ago?"

Mute, she nodded.

"Please, Ariel, *you* tell me what happened."

"I saw you," she said, her voice small, "I saw you with Claire."

"Yes?"

She stared at him. He didn't know what she meant. "I saw you coming out of the summerhouse—we were at the Parkins' party—and I saw the two of you coming out. Her face was flushed, and you were arm in arm. And—" She choked. She could say no more.

"Good God, Ariel, you don't think that Claire and I—" He stopped. "But you do think that, don't you?" She nodded. "And you have thought that for six years. My darling." He stood and pulled her into his arms. She remained stiff. "We were engaged in something much more innocent, my dear.

Claire was planning a surprise for our wedding—more specifically a present for you—and we wanted to go where you would not overhear. I never thought that you would misunderstand."

"But you acted so strangely the week before," she said, frowning.

"Would you not have behaved oddly if you were a young naval officer about to get married and then discovered you would soon be fighting in a war?"

"Oh." There was silence for a moment. "Then you didn't . . . that is, you and Claire never . . ."

"Never," he said firmly. "Claire and I were only friends."

"Then why didn't you say so!" she exclaimed, pulling away to stare indignantly up into his face.

"Why didn't I?" he asked, arching a brow. "May I remind you that I never had a chance?"

"You should have knocked the door down to see me!"

"Don't you think I tried? Ariel, I tried everything to see you. I sent flowers and notes, visited day after day, reasoned with your mother—although God knows she's the only one in the family with any sense at all—and it was all to no avail. You simply didn't want to see me. What was I supposed to do? Wear my heart on my sleeve all these years?"

"Yes," she replied after a moment's reflection.

He stared at her, not knowing whether to swear or laugh. "You are just as exasperating as ever."

"Me!"

"Yes, you."

He glared at her; she glared at him.

"Just what are you saying?"

"It would be so much easier if you would simply think before you jump to conclusions," Drake said. "Had you thought about it for a single moment, you would have known that I had no liking for women such as Claire. Too mild tempered and sweet by half. I much prefer black-haired vixens."

"Vixens! How dare—"

"I dare much," he said, grinning rakishly at her. "As you well know, my dear. And may I ask something?"

"What?" she replied somewhat woodenly.

"Are we about to have another argument?" he asked, lifting one dark brow. There was an amused glint in his eye.

She opened her mouth, shut it, then smiled slowly. "Yes, I believe we are."

"Then for God's sake, Ariel, before we do, will you please answer the question?"

"The question?" she asked innocently.

"Regarding our marriage!" he thundered.

"Oh, *that* question," she responded airily. "Why, yes," she said, wrapping her arms around him, "I think I will marry you. I do love you, Kit, with all my heart. I've loved you all these years, but I was such a fool. Can you ever forgive me for what I did? I know I should have listened and asked and thought, but I never did—"

"Shh," he said, touching his lips to hers. "I've already forgiven you. God knows you saved my life often enough in France."

Embracing, they kissed deeply. The heaviness that had been with her since coming home lifted. Now she could heal in mind and spirit as well as body.

When they finally drew apart, they regarded one another a little breathlessly.

"What about the date for our wedding, my dear?" he asked.

"Next month," she replied promptly.

"Ariel, I can't wait that long."

"There's simply too much to be done first, Kit," she said, "and so many people to contact—do you think the prime minister will attend?—and we have to—"

"I want you now."

"I want you, too, my love, but we can't—"

"My darling, are we bickering again?"

"I believe so," she said with a smile.

"Good."

And he kissed her again.

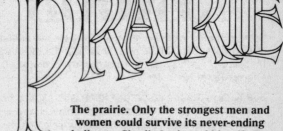